A LADY'S LESSON IN SCANDAL

DARCY MCGUIRE

Boldwood

First published in Great Britain in 2024 by Boldwood Books Ltd.

Cover Design by Head Design Ltd

Cover Photography: Shutterstock and iStock

A CIP catalogue record for this book is available from the British Library.

Paperback ISBN 978-1-83603-542-8

Large Print ISBN 978-1-83603-541-1

Hardback ISBN 978-1-83603-540-4

Ebook ISBN 978-1-83603-543-5

Kindle ISBN 978-1-83603-544-2

Audio CD ISBN 978-1-83603-535-0

MP3 CD ISBN 978-1-83603-536-7

Digital audio download ISBN 978-1-83603-538-1

Boldwood Books Ltd
23 Bowerdean Street
London SW6 3TN
www.boldwoodbooks.com

To Mari and Barry (aka mom and dad), for teaching me to love stories, and empowering me to create my own. And to Derek, my forever.

1

Millicent Whittenburg was in quite a pickle.

First, the potted palm she hid behind was far too short and woefully bereft of foliage.

Second, Viscount Tread, a man smelling of mouldy paper and dusty mothballs – and only two years younger than her father – doddered ever closer to her inadequate hiding spot. His watery blue eyes wildly searched the crush of lords and ladies for his betrothed.

Third and most troubling, Millie was his betrothed.

Tonight's ball was in their honour, officially announcing an engagement arranged by her horrid stepmother.

'Shall I make some kind of scene?' Millie's best friend, Ivy Cavendale, leaned close. 'You can slip out the back. I'll meet you in the gardens.' Her light floral scent reminded Millie of wildflowers after a spring rain. Ivy shifted in her icy-blue satin gown, trying to shield Millie further from view with her body. Which was laughable. Millie towered over her friend and was about three times Ivy in width.

'It's no use. He'd smell me out like one of Father's pointers. And the last thing you need is more scandal.' Millie smiled at her oldest friend. Poor Ivy had experienced her share of gossip when her father and brother died a few months prior under highly suspicious circumstances. Ivy became a social pariah overnight. Not that either of them enjoyed warming the walls of London's finest ballrooms, but it was still nice to receive invitations. Ivy didn't get those any more.

Ivy had become a recluse. Millie worried her friend might never recover from the double blow of grief and shame caused by her father's and brother's deaths. Ivy only agreed to attend the ball tonight because she knew Millie needed her support.

Just the thought of lying beneath Viscount Tread as he wheezed and sweated was enough to make any girl gather her friends near and run to the closest nunnery. Millie swallowed down the rising bile.

Things couldn't get any worse.

'Oh, there you are, Daughter.'

Hellfire. Things just got worse.

As a matter of course, when her stepmother, Patricia Whittenburg, became involved, things *always* got worse.

'I've been looking for you, dear. Poor Viscount Tread has been almost frantic with worry thinking you might have slipped away.' Patricia's stretched vowels made Millie cringe as the woman's perfectly painted eyebrows raised like a guillotine.

Perhaps Millie could run. Patricia had no chance of catching her in the ridiculously heeled slippers she wore.

Hope died swiftly as her stepmother wrapped bony fingers around Millie's arm. Sadly, the only thing escaping was Millie's chances to be free.

Her stepmother wore a lime-green monstrosity cut so low, Millie could almost see the woman's nipples. Patricia's waist was cinched tight enough to crack a rib. It was a wonder she could breathe at all, let alone brandish the commanding tone she directed at Millie.

'Come out from behind that plant, you silly girl.' Patricia's mouth crimped in disdain as her nails dug into Millie's skin. 'And you.' She narrowed her eyes at

Ivy. 'I distinctly remember *not* inviting you. The last thing we need at this ball is the stench of scandal.'

Ivy took a half step back. Her thin shoulders drooped like a flower bereft of rain.

Millie hated the defeat she saw in her friend. 'She came as a guest of the Duchess of Dorsett.' Not precisely true, but Patricia wouldn't dare question the duchess. Lady Philippa Winterbourne, Duchess of Dorsett, was widely known to have the ear and favour of Queen Victoria herself. One didn't disagree with the duchess. Ever.

Despite her stepmother's talons digging ever deeper, Millie stifled a smug smile. This round went to Millie.

'How the two of you won her approval, I'll never know.' Patricia's grip hardened, making Millie wince. She could pull free, but that would only draw attention to them, and Viscount Tread bumbled ever closer.

Patricia eyed Ivy like a worm in her apple. 'You may have snuck into this party on the arm of the duchess, but she isn't here now. Get away from us, child. I have things to discuss with my daughter.'

Millie almost laughed aloud. Patricia was barely six months older than Millie and two months older than Ivy. They'd all come out in the same season, for cripes sake. Hearing her stepmother refer to Millie as her daughter or Ivy as a child was almost as ridiculous as being engaged to a man within squinting distance of seventy. So, not ridiculous at all, according to Patricia.

Ivy's gaze bounced back and forth from Millie to Patricia. Millie knew Ivy would never abandon her. But if she stayed, Patricia would become even more cruel.

'I'll be fine, Ivy. Why don't you get some food.' Ivy wasn't eating nearly enough. She had always been slight, but after the loss of her brother and father, she was painfully thin.

'I shall be just over there if you need me.' Ivy pointed to the refreshments table.

Millie smiled. 'All will be well. Trust me.'

Ivy nodded, but she didn't look convinced.

Smart woman. I'm not convinced either.

As Ivy wove through the crowd, her dress winking like a jewel caught in moonlight, Patricia made a clicking sound in the back of her throat. 'How dare the duchess bring that disgusting girl to my house? All the rumours say the child's father murdered her brother. The whole family is sick with madness. I'm sure of it. Once you're married to Viscount Tread, you won't be permitted to socialise with people like that, mark my words, Millicent.'

Patricia wrenched Millie around and assessed her from the top of her wild, red curls struggling to escape their pins, down her cream evening gown failing to contain her generous curves, to her flat slippers taking nothing away from her lamentable height.

Sighing dramatically, Patricia shook her head, her grip loosening enough for Millie to shake off the offending hand. 'For the first and likely last time, you are the belle of this ball. Everyone has come tonight to celebrate you and your betrothal. To a viscount, nonetheless. You should be thrilled. And tripping over your huge feet with gratitude to *me* for arranging this match. Ungrateful wretch.'

Millie opened her mouth to protest, but Patricia kept talking.

'Finding a man willing to marry a ginger-haired girl who is too tall and too fat to ever be fashionable was no easy feat.'

Ouch.

Even from her horrid stepmother, the words cut. Millie clenched her teeth and straightened her shoulders.

I don't care what you think. Your words can't hurt me.

But they did. And Patricia knew it.

The pernicious woman tilted her head, candle-light sparkling in the amethysts threaded throughout her perfect, blonde ringlets. Millie couldn't begin to fathom how Patricia thought the purple jewels would complement her hideous gown. 'Imagine where you would be without my help. An awkward, chubby spinster doomed to a life of solitude.'

'I prefer solitude, especially when the present company is so tedious.' Millie stuck out her chin and pressed her lips together. She knew Patricia would have slapped her for talking back – or at least tried – if they weren't in a crowded ballroom. But Millie savoured the safety of the crush tonight.

Patricia stretched her lips into an ugly smile. 'Viscount Tread is old, smelly, and rumoured to suffer from gout. He'll be perfect for you, dear daughter.'

'Why are you so cruel, Patricia? Do you think it makes you powerful? Because it doesn't. It only highlights your weakness.'

Patricia grabbed Millie's arm again, tugging viciously, almost causing Millie to stumble.

Remember your training.

Widen your stance.

Centre your weight on the balls of your feet.

Punch Patricia in the face.

No. Don't punch Patricia in her pointy little rat nose. She will bleed all over the carpet.

Patricia spoke through clenched teeth. 'Come out of there this instant. Proper young ladies don't loiter behind the foliage.'

Millie did many things proper young ladies never dared. She blamed it on being raised at her father's side. A tomboy through and through. Millie rode horses astride. She threw knives with surprising accuracy. And recently, she had been secretly training with the duchess to become a private investigator. Lady Philippa Winterbourne was more than a filthy-rich widow. She was fierce. Formidable. Fashion-forward. Femme fatale. And lots of other fabulous 'F' words. Everything Millie one day hoped to become.

Under the duchess' demanding tutelage, Millie was learning the tricks and trade of becoming a private investigator. A career offering her freedom. Not that her stepmother knew any of those things. The very idea would cause Patricia to swoon upon the chalked ballroom floor in a heap of sickly-green silk.

Millie twisted free of her stepmother's grip, surprising the woman with how easily she escaped. 'I am not loitering. And I already told you, I will not marry Viscount Treadful.'

It was a nickname she and Ivy devised. She was

quite proud of it. When she shared the moniker with Lady Philippa during her weekly visits for tea – which were actually training sessions – she could have sworn the duchess almost cracked a smile. At the very least, the left corner of her lip *had* curled and her eyes *had* sparkled. Millie was chuffed. It was quite a feat to get the indomitable duchess to show any emotion at all.

Patricia's lips hardened and her eyes narrowed. 'You will do as you're told. Or your father will ship you off to care for his aging sister. Would you prefer that dismal future?'

'I would prefer any future free from Viscount Treadful. He's almost as old as Father. Not all of us are willing to go to the lengths you did to ensnare a wealthy man. There's a word for women like you, Patricia, and it certainly isn't "Mother".' Millie threw back her shoulders and relished a rare moment where her five-foot-eleven frame and fuller-than-fashionable figure put her at an advantage. She towered over her stepmother's delicate physique.

But Patricia Whittenburg was as intelligent as she was mercenary. She could exert her power over Millie with no more physical strength than crooking a finger.

Patricia had to tip her head back to meet her 'daughter's' gaze. She batted her charcoal-darkened lashes. Everything about the woman was fake. Her beauty, her smile, her calculated kindness. She was a cruel, heartless monster wrapped in a package of perfect, blonde ringlets, a tiny waist, a pert nose, and the Devil's soul.

'There's a word for women like you as well, dear. Women who refuse to marry. Women who prefer the company of other ladies to a man. It's unnatural.'

A thrill of alarm skated up Millie's spine. 'I've no idea what you mean.' Surely Patricia wouldn't be so bold as to accuse her of sexual deviance.

'Sometimes, I wonder exactly what you and the Duchess of Dorsett do every week at your so-called salons.' Patricia's green eyes sparked with an unholy fire. She had used the belladonna drops advertised in Mrs S. D. Powers' *The Ugly Girl Papers*, and her pupils were so dilated, the black almost encompassed her irises. 'She certainly can't find your conversational skills that entertaining.'

Millie's heart thumped painfully at her stepmother's threat. While she was not a sapphic, she wasn't confident about Lady Philippa's proclivities. Not that it should matter. But Patricia could wreak havoc in the beau monde by merely hinting at homosexuality. Even someone as powerful as the duchess might be brought low by such scandalous accusations.

Millie owed Lady Philippa a great debt. Philippa

wasn't just acquainted with Queen Victoria. She was the Queen's right-hand lady, hired to uncover villainy amongst the titled gentlemen long protected by their brethren in the House of Lords. And she believed Millie would make an excellent addition to their team.

Millie could still hardly believe it. Too tall, too chubby, too outspoken. But Philippa found her athletic, intelligent, and resourceful. She thought she was perfect for the job. She believed in Millie.

Philippa had also promised to help Millie escape her betrothal to the ancient Viscount Treadful. A feat they intended to accomplish this very evening.

Unless Patricia ruined everything with her devastating threats.

She won't. I will not allow it.

When faced with conflict, attack was preferable to defence.

'I hardly think you are stupid enough to offend someone as grand and powerful as the Duchess of Dorsett. Especially with such preposterous accusations.' Millie raised her brows in a haughty expression she'd been practising in her mirror.

'Let's see what the House of Lords thinks. Homosexuality is illegal last time I checked.'

Millie shook her head. 'What a ridiculous law. It shouldn't matter who someone is attracted to. Love is love regardless of the body parts involved.' Millie should have left the last part unsaid, but it was true. And she always spoke the truth, even when it made her life more difficult. It was a character flaw she tried and failed to correct.

'Spoken like a true invert.' Patricia's lips twisted in disgust. 'If you refuse to marry the viscount, I will have no recourse but to confess your perverseness to your father. A wicked woman engaged in immoral activity. With the Duchess of Dorsett, no less.'

'And you would turn your own "daughter" into the authorities?'

Patricia snorted. 'I won't have to. If *The Star of Venus* catches wind of the scandal, and I can assure you, it will, the bobbies will come to us.'

Patricia was addicted to scandal sheets, gasping at the latest juicy piece of gossip while she sipped her morning cup of tea. *The Star of Venus* was by far the most appalling of the lot. They wouldn't hesitate to print such licentious tripe regardless of how baseless the accusation. Publications like *The Star* rarely troubled themselves with details like facts or truth. Though Scotland Yard certainly should.

Still, the prattle of small-minded people created untold horror. News of a duchess engaged in sexual perversion would spread through the beau monde like wildfire. Even if no legal ramifications occurred, Lady Philippa's reputation would be decimated.

'You are despicable.' Millie narrowed her gaze and wished she could throw her ever-improving right hook at Patricia's powdered cheekbone.

Patricia tsked, shaking her head. 'Really, dear, your skin turns such an unsightly shade of red when you're in high temper. Calm yourself.'

Millie was ready to calm herself with a rousing game of 'crush Patricia's windpipe and watch her turn puce'.

Adjusting one of the curls bouncing near her chin, Patricia sighed. 'You know your father won't question me. You've already displayed your sexual depravity with Lord Franklin St George. Now this? Does your immorality know no bounds?'

The blood drained from Millie's face. How did her horrid stepmother find out about Franklin St George? That had been over ten years ago. She was barely seven and ten when St George courted her. Her father wouldn't have betrayed her trust so grievously.

Patricia widened her carmine-stained lips, flashing a perfect row of blunt, little teeth. 'Your father keeps no secrets from me, dear. He told me all about it and the money it cost him to keep St George quiet about your indiscretion. How do you suppose it will go over when I tell your dear, devoted father about this new twist?'

'He would never believe you.' And once, that would have been true. But now, the words tasted bitter in Millie's mouth.

'Test me, dear. I dare you.' Patricia's green eyes flashed triumphantly. 'At the very least, we'll need to commit you to an asylum. Don't worry. You'll have your devoted duchess to keep you company in your filthy cell.'

Millie's stomach twisted painfully. While accustomed to Patricia's spite, she could not allow the duchess to be harmed.

I won't be frightened. I have a plan. It will work. It must *work.*

She and the Duchess of Dorsett had put their heads together weeks ago and created a solution to escape her stepmother's maniacal grip. It wasn't ideal, but it might be her best chance for freedom. Millie only needed to be bold enough to carry it out.

Tonight.

Before she lost her nerve.

'Not even you would be so vicious, Patricia.' Another lie. Her stepmother was cruelty in curls.

Patricia's bell-like laughter rang out, mocking Millie. 'Silly girl. Of course I would.'

'Why are you so hateful? Truly?'

Patricia's pretty mask slipped, and Millie glimpsed the terrifying creature beneath. 'You've been the light in your father's eye for far too long. I am his wife. His loyalty belongs to me. As does his title and his money. With you married off, when your father comes to his end, nothing will stand in my way. He has no heirs, no distant relatives waiting to inherit. I'll be taking a page out of your dear duchess' notebook. Everything that was his will come to me. His poor, devoted widow.'

With Patricia's master plan laid out, Millie felt ill. Since the beastly woman married Lord Whittenburg, she had patiently and meticulously thrust a wedge between father and daughter. Insidious little lies, manipulations of truth, contrived scenes designed to place Millie in an unflattering light.

And her father wasn't innocent in the horrid affair. He'd never been the same after her error with St George, but since Patricia came into their house, things had gotten significantly worse. At every turn, he chose his young, nubile wife over his devoted daughter. The divide was now so deep, Millie's relationship with her father had fractured completely.

Game, set, match, Patricia.

'Mark my words, Millicent. A madhouse is your future unless you marry the viscount. I don't care how disgusting he is. I don't care how old. I don't care how perverted his proclivities. Given your own behaviours, you might actually enjoy it.' Patricia's pointed little nose tilted toward the ceiling as she laughed again, a delicate, tinkling melody juxtaposing her venomous words. 'He's probably the only man here who won't care that you are no longer intact. No need to thank me. I just want what's best for my sweet girl.'

Anger roused Millie from the pain of betrayal. 'You will pay for this, Patricia.' But it was an empty threat, and they both knew it.

Before Patricia could respond, their gazes were drawn to the striking figure of Lady Philippa Winterbourne, the Duchess of Dorsett, as she strode across the ballroom floor. A wave of relief washed over Millie.

Reinforcements.

Lady Winterbourne cut through dancing couples, sharp as a blade and without a hint of hesitation. She wore a blackberry gown dripping with crystals that caught the candlelight as she swept through the crush of people. Philippa was a dark star shining in a bright sky. Lords and ladies scrambled to get out of her way.

The duchess intercepted Viscount Tread as he turned slow circles, still scanning the crowd for Millie. His ruddy complexion darkened close to scarlet when he saw Philippa. He almost tripped over himself attempting a gallant bow. She gestured with her fan in the opposite direction of where Millie hid in the shadows. His bushy, grey brows furrowed as he squinted at a young lady in the far corner whose only resemblance to Millie was the cream colour of her dress. Relief washed over his face as he smiled wide at the poor girl and blundered off. Lady Winterbourne continued her graceful journey toward Millie and her stepmother.

Patricia's lips hardened, and she lowered her voice to a harsh whisper. 'Viscount Tread is your future, Millicent. No one, not even the Duchess of Dorsett, can save you from your fate. Accept it, or I will make sure you suffer beyond your worst imaginings.'

I'd rather accept a knife in my belly.

Millie refused to be a pawn in Patricia's game. She would carve out her own future. One free of her malicious stepmother's stratagems.

Tonight. It must happen tonight.

As quickly as wiping clean a chalkboard, Patricia adopted a cheerful expression and turned toward the duchess. Her voice was too loud, her smile too wide.

Why had her father made such a horrific choice? Were men so blind? Their logic and loyalty turned by a pretty face, a small waist, a nice pair of... eyes? It was horrific! A father should always fight for his children.

But Lord Whittenburg deferred to Patricia at every turn. Millie grieved his loss as though he were dead. Because the man she knew from childhood was gone.

Men are inconstant, fickle fools.

One more reason why she wanted nothing to do with them.

Except tonight, a man will save me from the hell Patricia has planned.

'Lady Winterbourne! You honour us with your presence.' Patricia's shrill voice cut through the musicians playing a lively waltz.

Millie looked over her stepmother's head at the Duchess of Dorsett and reminded herself she was far more powerful than Patricia would ever know. Even if her stepmother seemed to hold Millie's future in her sharpened claws.

Lady Philippa Winterbourne's beauty was fierce rather than delicate. A jaw almost too square, lips stained only a few shades lighter than the deep purple of her gown, hair blacker than sin and just as luscious, boldly streaked with silver and piled high in an intricate coiffure. She was a visual force and everything Patricia Whittenburg would never be in both poise and power. Millie watched her stepmother's eyes narrow with envy.

Lady Philippa lifted a perfectly arched brow. 'It's

lucky you are so pretty, Lady Whittenburg, as your personality leaves much to be desired. At least your face will recommend you for a few more years, though I would limit your consumption of wine. It dulls the wits and complexion, two things you can't afford to lose any more of, wouldn't you agree?'

Patricia's mouth fell open. Air rushed out in a strangled squeak. 'Pardon?' She hastily deposited the empty wine glass she was holding into the potted palm.

'Pay attention, please. I do not repeat myself. I came to speak with Miss Millicent. Excuse us.' She nodded at Millie and turned to walk away, her command impossible to refuse.

Before Millie could follow in the duchess' impressive wake, Patricia once more grabbed her arm, pulling her close.

The cloying scent of lilies invaded Millie's nostrils. She fought not to gag as Patricia hissed in her ear. 'The viscount is expecting to dance with you before the announcement of your engagement. You will not disappoint him.'

Millie took a measured step away from Patricia. 'The viscount should accustom himself to disappointment, madame. As should you.' Her stepmother was sure to make Millie pay for this later. But the moment was too delicious not to enjoy.

'Remember this, Millicent. The moment you sealed your fate.'

Millie smiled, though she worried her skin might crack from the effort. 'I'm counting on it.' She turned and walked away, her legs only shaking a little.

2

Major General Beaufort Drake, Earl of Tetly, scarred war hero, private investigator for the prime minister, fearsome warrior, loyal friend to few, and deadly foe to many, had suffered more than most men. Tortured at the hands of Afghanistan's cruellest warriors, his body bore the evidence of grievous wounds. A wicked scar carved him from forehead to chin in a diagonal slash of roped tissue, turning once rugged features into a gruesome mask. A beautifully fitted suit hid even more brutal evidence of the pain he'd endured.

His soul was steeped in sin, and his heart had fossilised years ago. But Drake would gladly relive every nightmare that created him into a cruel, cold, deadly weapon if it granted him freedom from his current circumstances.

Trussed up in his best suit.

Sipping watered-down ratafia.

Avoiding the curious and horrified gazes of the beau monde's bluest of bloods.

Cursing the ache in his leg currently reaching a crescendo of pulsing agony.

Cooling his heels at the edge of the Devil's most dastardly affair.

A ball.

He repressed a shudder.

Give him fire-heated blades, rusty daggers, the rack. Anything but a soiree of England's most pampered, pompous lords and ladies. But the prime minister needed his best man for a mission, and Drake always answered the call, regardless of how treacherous the terrain.

This glittering battlefield was diabolical in the extreme.

If one more mercenary mama thrust her clearly horrified daughter in his face, hoping for a match with the Earl of Tetly, he might be sick in the potted palms framing the ballroom. It was unthinkable how easily a matron could sell her child to the highest title or largest bank account in the room. Even if the man behind the money and title was a heartless dragon. A monster his friend Killian often likened to Drake.

Drake wouldn't wish himself upon any of these delicate virginal sacrifices, nor would he ever choose to suffer their company. He was not here to dance. Or flirt. Or seek out a wife.

He was here to find a killer.

'Don't look now, but another young miss is heading this way, led by none other than the Duchess of Dorsett.' The man next to him whistled low. 'I may have been in France for the last two years, but even across the Channel, Lady Winterbourne's reputation is renowned.' General Reynard Renquist once fought under Drake's leadership. His older brother, Major General William Renquist, Marquess of Stoneway, was a fellow commander in the Anglo-Afghan war. They had all been taken prisoner together with their lead commander, Lieutenant General Robert Killian. Months of hideous torture nearly destroyed them. But it also forged friendships extending beyond the bonds of brotherhood. Theirs was a kinship created in the fires of hell, amalgamating the four men like tempered steel.

Drake had been working with Lieutenant General Killian on their current mission, tracking a murderous group of men operating a sex ring. In Killian's absence,

Drake was glad for Reynard's return from France and his assistance on this mission.

The unfortunate Lieutenant General Killian had fallen prey to a terrible tragedy. Marriage. To the infuriating Miss Hannah Simmons. Drake would never forgive Killian for succumbing to the deadliest of all ailments. Love.

Horse shit!

Love was a lie.

Drake huffed out a disgusted sigh. He supposed for a man like Killian, chasing a beautiful woman across Europe on an extended honeymoon tour might be preferable to ferreting out a killer amongst England's most elite. The opposite was true for Drake. Not that he wished ill upon his friend, but Drake secretly hoped Killian ate some bad meat or perhaps developed sea sickness. Nothing lethal, just painful enough to ruin his disgustingly romantic holiday. After all, Killian had abandoned Drake to muddle through this mess of an assignment alone. All for the sake of a woman.

He shuddered at the thought of willingly strapping on the shackles of matrimony. Though Prime Minister Russell was making veiled threats about Drake finally submitting to the inevitable. Apparently, Killian started quite the trend. A married lord was far less suspicious than a single one. The prime minister believed a wife would make it easier for Drake to continue his clandestine investigations into the gentry's worst crimes.

Russell can bugger off!

Drake drained his cup, forgetting for a moment what filled it. He winced at the disgustingly sweet drink. The naïve ideal of love and marriage had tempted him once, and the resulting betrayal almost destroyed him. He would not willingly enter into a contract with any creature as mercurial as a woman. Instead, he would prove Prime Minister Russell's theory wrong by using speed and efficiency to capture his prey, not hiding behind the skirts of some duplicitous female.

I dare any married blighter to be a more effective executor of the law.

'I'm glad you are here, Reynard. It's certainly nice to have someone with me I can trust since Killian stuck his neck in the Parson's noose.' Drake continued to scan the crowd, refusing to let his gaze linger on Miss Whittenburg, her bright hair a beacon in the crowded ballroom.

Reynard chuckled. 'God save us from such a horrific fate, eh old friend?'

'I may be thirteen years your senior, Reynard. But

I'm not in my dotage yet. Let's leave off the old.'
Though despite his six and thirty years, he felt ancient. Drake stretched his neck, sighing when the ver-
tebrae popped. It was insufferably warm in the
Whittenburg's ballroom, and the overpowering stench
of pomade, perfume, and sweat did not improve the
atmosphere. 'But yes, I would happily saw off my own
arm to avoid being trapped by any of these misses. Especially that one.' He nodded toward the statuesque
Miss Whittenburg, gliding behind the Duchess of
Dorsett as proud as a goddess perched on the prow of
a warship.

While many would consider Miss Whittenburg too
old, too tall, too bold in her colouring with such a riot
of red hair piled high, red lips glistening, red cheeks
glowing, Drake found her annoyingly captivating. A
man could overfill his hands with breasts so generous.

Where the Devil did that thought come from?

His cock strained against his breeches in an eloquent response.

Absolutely not.

Drake crushed the attraction stirring his long-dead
libido with an iron will. He hadn't felt such interest in
a woman since Nora, though Miss Millicent Whittenburg couldn't be more different from his ex-fiancée.
Where Miss Millicent was luscious curves and pow-

erful limbs, Nora's waif-like figure and angelic colouring made her a true English rose.

Complete with sharp and deadly thorns.

No part of him wished to think about his first – and only – love or how that disaster ended.

Still, he learned well the lesson Nora taught him about the dangers of being vulnerable. The last thing he needed was to become entangled with a woman destined to destroy his carefully constructed calm. The redheaded Valkyrie making a beeline toward him was just such a creature. Drake would do well to turn and run. But he ran from nothing.

Clad in cream silk nearly matching the tone of her skin, it was all too easy to picture her without the dress. His cock heartily agreed with his imaginings.

Dear God, I am not some cad lead around by my prick!

If Miss Millicent knew his thoughts, she would run screaming in the opposite direction. The woman distracted him when nothing ever destroyed his focus. Instead of scanning the crowd for a killer, Drake contemplated the exact texture of her lips. Would they be soft or firm? Sweet or tart? And for that alone, he should keep his distance. He couldn't afford to lose sight of this mission.

As if to further prove his point, his inner calm evaporated, along with any hope of control, as the women approached. Miss Millicent Whittenburg was wild and unpredictable. Everything he despised in the fairer sex. Everything that made him ache in places long forgotten.

'Ah, Major General Drake. I distinctly remember you abhorring social events. What possibly induced you to attend this soiree?' Lady Philippa raised an eyebrow in an expression designed to quell a lesser man. He resisted the urge to step backward in retreat.

'Your Grace, always an honour.' Bowing his head at the duchess, he noticed Miss Millicent's skirt had caught, revealing an inch of surprisingly slim ankle. Heat suffused his neck, and he clenched his jaw before she shifted and the buttery silk fell smoothly back into place.

'And who is your new friend?' Lady Philippa thrust her chin toward Reynard.

'Allow me to introduce General Reynard Renquist. We fought together in the war.' Drake stepped back so Reynard could bow.

'Ah. Well.' Lady Winterbourne thwacked a jewel-encrusted fan against her hand. 'Renquist. Hmm. I know your brother. Though we haven't seen much of him since he returned from the war.'

'An honour, Your Grace. Yes, William prefers his own company these days.' Reynard's mouth twitched before he turned his mischievous dark gaze on Miss Millicent. 'I don't believe I've had the pleasure, Miss...?'

Women fell to Reynard's charm like autumn leaves in a brisk wind. He was everything Drake would never be. He looked like a naughty cherub who'd turned into a man, complete with golden, curly locks. Reynard even had dimples, which women were known to swoon over. After years of watching the dashing reprobate use his gilded tongue to talk women out of their lacy underthings, Drake more than expected it. He welcomed Reynard's skills. It took all the attention away from Drake. No lady would choose a scarred old man over a dashing young rake. But for some reason, the idea of Millicent Whittenburg blushing in flustered appreciation at Reynard's practised flirtations filled Drake with a black rage.

He recognised this feeling. He experienced the same rush of impotent anger when he returned from the war to see Nora on the arm of his brother, her ring finger glinting with a diamond wedding band. Jealousy. But it made no sense for him to suffer the emotion now. Certainly not for the bold redhead.

'Miss Millicent Whittenburg, sir.' Millicent didn't blush. She didn't bat her eyelashes or raise her fan to hide a coquettish smile. Instead, she narrowed her coffee-brown gaze. Sharp intelligence flashed in her eyes. 'How odd. This ball is being held in my honour, but I don't remember seeing either of your names on the guest list.'

'Most peculiar, as we both received invitations.' Drake straightened his shoulders and leaned into the lie.

The Marquess Henry Whittenburg and his Marchioness may not have summoned them, but Prime Minister Russell made sure Reynard and Drake were equipped with expertly forged invitations. Besides, no one paid attention to the guest list at a ball this crowded. Except for Miss Millicent Whittenburg. Maddening woman.

Facing a lady so close to him in height disconcerted Drake. At six foot three inches, he towered over most people. But Miss Millicent almost reached his chin and held his gaze with the fortitude of a commander.

Did she inwardly recoil at the devastation of his scars? This close, in the blazing light of a thousand candles from the chandelier above, she would see the gruesome stretch of roped tissue as it pulled against healthy skin. The white scar cut across his brow, bisecting his left eyebrow, slashing across the bridge of his nose, and slicing through his right cheek to end at his jaw. There were no surgeons in the Afghanistan prison, but a young bootmaker-turned-soldier had done his best in the dank cell they shared. Drake knew his visage was grotesque, but Millicent's eyes – darker than cocoa beans and just as rich – didn't stray from his own icy glare.

Just as she opened her indecently plump lips to no doubt deliver a blistering retort, the orchestra swelled to a crescendo, signalling the end of the set.

'I believe they are readying for the next dance.' Lady Philippa drew his gaze away from Miss Whittenburg.

Dear God, surely the duchess doesn't expect me to dance with her.

Drake cleared his throat, unsure of how to respond. He hadn't seen Lady Winterbourne since Everly Manor. Her ward was the same Hannah Simmons who married his friend right after the courageous young woman saved Lieutenant General Robert Killian from a killer.

Perhaps Killian wasn't quite as foolish in marrying the girl as Drake thought.

Hardly. Even courageous women are dangerous. More so, sometimes.

'Thank you, Your Grace. Though I am certainly no

fit partner for someone as dignified as yourself.' His rusty social skills were on full display.

The duchess snorted. 'I know. I have no interest in dancing with you. But you should suffice for Miss Whittenburg.'

'I beg your pardon?'

'Dance, Major General Drake. With Miss Whittenburg. Now.' Lady Philippa blinked at him, and the effect was similar to a firing squad sending its first volley into the fray.

If the Queen's military were run by the Duchess of Dorsett, we would rule the world in under a sennight.

He couldn't refuse such a blatant command. It would be an unpardonable offence to the duchess and a grave insult to Miss Whittenburg.

Bloody fucking hell.

Just the idea of holding Miss Millicent within the circle of his arms, her soft curves pressed against his hard planes, her dark eyes melting like hot chocolate over flames, her scent – an intriguing blend of citrus and crisp cotton – infiltrating his senses was enough to make him forget his whole reason for attending this blasted ball.

Laundry and lemons shouldn't cause a wave of lust to wash through him like lava, but it did. Not a good sign.

Miss Millicent's reaction to Lady Winterbourne's command was even more confounding. The beautiful disaster of a woman swallowed hard and tucked her hands behind her back.

His suspicious nature sparked to life. She was usually bold and brazen. He watched her ride a horse with the skill of a seasoned infantry soldier, trade insults while wielding her wit like a sword, and defend her friends with reckless courage both inspiring and intriguing. She was a harridan of the highest order, but her audacity also impressed him.

Yet, standing close enough for him to see the dusting of freckles across her nose, it was clear Miss Millicent was flummoxed. Her expressive skin flushed as she ducked her head in a rare display of nerves or embarrassment.

The woman was less inclined to dance with him than he was to ask for the privilege.

How interesting. I wonder how often she is asked to dance.

'This is a mistake,' she murmured.

He almost missed her words in the cacophony of conversation surrounding them. But Millicent's husky voice was like a siren song, calling to him. She expected him to refuse the duchess' command. So, he did the opposite.

'Miss Millicent, would you do me the honour?'
Drake extended his gloved hand.

* * *

Millie wanted to gasp for air as she drowned in regret.
The plan seemed so brilliant when the duchess first
discussed it with her weeks ago. An excellent way to
avoid Viscount Treadful, spurn her stepmother, and
gain the one thing she wanted most: freedom.

Lady Philippa made it seem so simple. Seduce the
one man who would never offer for her. Major General Drake fit the bill perfectly. He was many things.
Cold. Deadly. Unfeeling. And most importantly, he
despised the fairer sex.

Millie had sat in Philippa's sitting room, sipping
whiskey-laced tea, her attention completely focused
on the duchess as Philippa recounted the vicious
gossip surrounding Major General Drake and his fiancée, Miss Elnora Fitzwilliam. One of the beau
monde's jammiest bits of jam, desperately in love with
the dashing Earl of Tetly, until Elnora abandoned
Major General Drake when news of his capture in the
Afghan desert reached England. Believing him as
good as dead, Elnora married his younger brother.
Quite the scandal.

When Major General Drake returned from the An-glo-Afghan war, scarred, damaged, hardened by the atrocities he'd endured but still very much alive, it was to the news his fiancée was married to his brother. Major General Drake never attempted to court an-other lady. All signs pointed to the man remaining single forever.

Incredibly tragic for Major General Drake. But perfect for their plan. His hatred of women would eclipse his honour once Millie tricked him into ru-ining her. Or, more accurately, re-ruining her. But this time, there was an important difference. This time, her ruination would be public.

Count Treadful would be forced to rescind his offer of marriage. Drake would never ask for her hand – or any other part of her for that matter. Millie's fa-ther and stepmother would be more than happy to hand her over to Lady Philippa Winterbourne, and the duchess would secret her away in the country where her sinful nature could do no more harm.

Except Millie wouldn't be languishing away picking roses and dodging bumblebees.

There was a diabolical ring of men kidnapping country girls and forcing them into the flesh trade. Lady Philippa needed someone to pose as a maid. Bait for the secret society of lords orchestrating this sex-trafficking ring. Millie was going to be that bait. Not something she could accomplish as the dutiful wife of Lord Tread.

Major General Drake was her way out. All she had to sacrifice was something she'd already destroyed years ago. Her virtue.

Simple as a Sunday tea party. Just seduce the Earl of Tetly.

A man who thus far had shown nothing but an acute dislike of Millie.

He doesn't have to like me to ruin me. St George certainly didn't care a whit about me, but that didn't stop him from throwing up my skirts.

But that is where she and Philippa mis-stepped. While the idea of seducing Major General Drake seemed easy to achieve, the reality was quite different. Looking into Major General Drake's glacial gaze created a most unwelcome heat in embarrassing places. The back of her neck. The hollow of her knee. The apex of her thighs. Her whole body was enflamed, her skin stretching too tightly. She was unaccountably sensitive to the brush of satin against her legs.

Bloody hell!

Millie was no innocent, but she had never reacted so strongly to a man as she did to the major general's frigid stare. Highly annoying and very inappropriate.

She certainly never felt such ardent heat with her one-time lover, Franklin St George, and at the time, his gaze had held nothing but impassioned affection, not the cold disdain sharpening Major General Drake's glacial glare.

What if Patricia is right? What if I'm a wanton?

This was nothing like the mild tingles she'd felt with Franklin. He had been her childhood obsession. Their country estates abutted one another, and they grew up playing together on the grounds of their neighbouring properties. Millie's ability to run faster, punch harder, ride better, and shoot more accurately than St George created some friction, but generally, they got along famously. Both families assumed Millie and Franklin would marry one day, joining the two ancient titles in property and bloodlines. It wasn't surprising when Franklin St George asked to court Millie during her first season out.

It *was* surprising how easily she succumbed to seduction. Some might say Millie leapt forward when others would have hastened a retreat.

While she never thought herself a lustful woman, Franklin's clumsy attempts at kissing quickly evolved into much more. Millie found she ached for an elusive *something* shimmering on the horizon as his hands became bolder and her skirts were shoved around her ears in a frenzy during one sunny afternoon picnic. Unfortunately, the entire event was rather disappointing for Millie and far messier than she guessed. In a sticky, painful, frantic moment, her virtue was gone, and soon after that, so was her betrothal to Franklin St George.

Foolish Millie, believing the pretty lies St George fed her during their doomed romance. After their disappointing picnic, Franklin met with her father and confessed their crimes, though she was the only one thought to be guilty. In the meeting, he insinuated Millie's virginal state to be in question prior to their dalliance. While he had been swept away by affection for Millie and succumbed to her seductive skills, once certain truths came to light – namely, her lack of virtue – St George no longer wished to pursue a spoiled maid.

Which was ridiculous. Given the fact *he* spoiled her, and his only argument proving she wasn't a virgin involved compromising her himself as evidence of her wanton nature.

Men are such illogical creatures!

It was embarrassingly obvious Millie's virtue had been intact prior to their fateful picnic. However, no one asked her to confirm or refute St George's accusations. Her guilt was established the moment St George spread her thighs. Her father's heart was broken by his sinful daughter. And Millie's shame was complete.

St George agreed to quietly end the betrothal and never reveal her sexual immorality in exchange for a tidy sum bestowed upon him by Millie's father. Which was Franklin's purpose from the beginning.

Mortifying to know his sole interest in Millie centred on the money he gained by *not* marrying her. Especially considering the tendre she had long carried for the bastard.

She pulled herself back to the present.

No more of that nonsense!

It was insufferable. A man could swive about London carousing with prostitutes, mistresses, and merry widows to his heart's content. Reformed rakes were in high demand on the husband market. But women received no such chances for redemption. A lady caught with her skirts above her knees was immediately and irrevocably invalid. The unfairness of it lit a fire in Millie.

So, she would use this inequity to bring her carefully laid plan to fruition.

Major General Drake would compromise her tonight, even if Millie had to force the man with brute strength. But this time, her ruination wouldn't be swept under the rug like unwanted dirt. The entire beau monde would be privy to Millie's indiscretion, and her chances of ever marrying would be destroyed.

Thank God!

Millie took a deep breath and threw back her shoulders. Even though it felt manipulative and wrong, even though an oily coating of shame made her stomach twist uncomfortably, she had committed to this course. There were no other options. Major General Drake could bugger off if he didn't like it. She didn't much like it either, but it was her only hope for freedom. And besides, her reputation would suffer far more greatly than his.

She reached out to grasp the major general's gloved hand and, in lieu of a smile, ducked her head in an abbreviated curtsey.

In a few moments, my entire life will be changed.

Major General Drake had very shiny boots. Millie wanted to scuff them. Instead, she let him tuck her hand in the crook of his arm and lead her smoothly to the dance floor. A hint of leather and spice tickled her nose. Cloves, if she wasn't mistaken. The man smelled of saddles and sweet buns.

I do love sweet buns. And saddles, for that matter.

Still, the combination shouldn't cause her tummy to erupt into a million bubbles. Millie's mouth watered as her nipples constricted. Odd, considering the ballroom was insufferably warm. And why couldn't she breathe? Franklin St George had certainly never caused her lungs to seize.

A murmur rippled throughout the assembly as a hundred gazes burned into her back. Fresh fodder for the gossips tonight.

You haven't seen anything yet, ladies. Prepare yourselves for a truly scandalous evening!

If she was going to be painted as a wicked wanton, she might as well enjoy herself. Not only had she avoided dancing with her intended for the expected display of affection required at such events, but she had also managed to convince one of the most reclusive and intimidating bachelors of the season to squire her onto the dance floor.

Nothing to it, ladies. Just employ the Duchess of Dorsett as matchmaker, and almost any ungainly spinster can bag an earl.

She should stitch the instructions onto handkerchiefs and hand them out at balls. Millie almost smiled. But then she remembered the task at hand.

This was serious business. It wasn't fair. It wasn't kind. But she was tired of being kind and fair at the expense of her own happiness. She wished the circumstances were different. But wishes were as useless as tea in a typhoon. No one would save Millie from her fate except Millie herself. With some assistance from the duchess, of course.

The major general swept her onto the floor, his right palm pressed against her left. His left hand resting on the generous swell of her hip. She had noticed Major General Drake walked with a slight limp, but it didn't hinder his graceful movements on the chalked floor. She lifted her right hand and placed it on his shoulder. A shoulder made of granite.

Good heavens!

The man must have replaced his musculature with something impenetrable and unyielding. Millie fleetingly wondered how one achieved such a medical miracle. But then the violins began to sing, the cello resonated through the crowd, and like the wind in the rowan trees or the sea swelling on the sand, they began to move.

Never before did her feet float above the floor. Never did she feel delicate and fragile in a man's arms. Never had her heart beat so loudly, she feared the whole assembly might hear it. Perhaps it was because the major general was so tall. And powerful. And terrifying.

And desirable.

Poppycock!

Millie didn't *desire* Major General Drake.

Ridiculous notion.

From her first meeting with him four months prior at Lord Geoffrey Bradford's dinner party, he had continually been rude and dismissive toward her.

If she was bold enough to bring her scheme to fruition, his disdain would only intensify.

But what choice do I have? Pernicious Patricia and her ridiculous plans!

No. She couldn't blame her stepmother for what she was going to do to Major General Drake. This decision was hers, and she must shoulder the consequences alone.

Besides, adding 'rake' to his reputation will only increase Major General Drake's appeal with young ladies who like dangerous, mysterious men with dashing scars. Which I do not. She viciously reminded herself.

But honestly! Did he have to look like some romanticised Viking warrior with the most startingly blue eyes she'd ever seen? So light, they reminded Millie of a description she'd read about icebergs written by the courageous Captain John Biscoe in the *Journal of the Royal Geographical Society of London.* It was incredibly unfair.

No wonder Lord Drake's gaze could freeze her like

a blast of arctic chill. Chips of frigid water trapped in a face both fearsome and striking. Though his gaze didn't seem cold tonight.

Can glaciers smoulder?

If only Millie's conundrum could be solved with a solid round of sparring instead of a waltz. She was getting quite good at physical combat. Philippa said her height and general athletic prowess made her a dangerous pugilist. It would be so much easier to grapple with Major General Drake than glide across the dance floor in his strong arms.

But not nearly as pleasant.

Millie's thoughts were becoming muddled. An unfortunate habit she developed around Major General Drake.

'I should offer you my felicitations on your upcoming wedding.' The major general's gravelled voice created vibrations along her spine, spiralling over nerve endings, zinging through her veins like a primal pulse.

Mingling with his leather and clove scent was something dark and smoky. Perhaps it was the cheroots she'd seen him smoking. She wanted to lean closer and inhale him.

'Do you ever tire of doing things you should instead of what you want?' Millie pressed her lips together. *Where had that come from?* She risked glancing up.

He pulled her infinitesimally closer.

'Yes.'

One syllable and her core turned liquid.

Candlelight glinted on the blond stubble covering his chin. His shadow beard matched the shade of his hair. What little hair he had. He kept it shorn so close to his head, he almost seemed bald. A shocking fashion choice, but who was she to judge?

He had a remarkably symmetrical head. What would it feel like to rub her hand over the bristled edges of his hair? She shivered.

'Are you cold, Miss Millicent?' He leaned close, his words tickling her ear.

'Actually, I find myself overly warm. Perhaps we could step onto the veranda for a bit of air?' She held her breath. This was the moment. If he refused or escorted her back to the wall where she belonged, her plan would be sunk.

He stiffened against her. 'I don't think—'

'Just for a moment. I might swoon.' She tried for 'breathy desperation' but feared her tone was closer to 'forceful command'.

Major General Drake leaned back, narrowing his gaze on her face. 'You do look flushed.'

'Of course I'm flushed. Patricia invited so many people to this ridiculous ball, we're packed in here like pickled herrings.' It wasn't a delicate simile. But Millie wasn't a delicate woman.

Without missing a beat, the major general swooped her in a spin that made her dizzy. It was the flex of his bicep beneath her fingers. The heat from his body seeping past her silk, stays, and chemise. The pressure of his hand on her hip. Her bones melted to jelly.

Jumping junipers!

She needed to get out of his arms and off the dance floor. Immediately. Or she would completely lose the plot. Which was unacceptable. She was seducing the man against his will, not mooning over him like some milksop, for heaven's sake!

Taking advantage of their position near the French doors, Millie broke free of his dance frame and escaped onto the stone veranda. Hopefully, he followed her.

Or, hopefully, he does not. And then I can abandon this entirely horrendous idea. I shall tell the duchess we must create a new plan. I could always sail to Australia.

The idea of absconding to an island populated by

criminals shouldn't seem safer than seducing the Earl of Tetly. But there it was.

Millie leaned against the balustrade and took a healthy breath of wintry air as she gazed across the grounds. The oak trees were naked of leaves. Their limbs reached into the moonlight like skeletal fingers coated in a light dusting of snow. Frost sparkled over the frozen landscape; a thousand trapped raindrops scattered like diamonds over the manicured lawns. Christmas was still a month away, but a cold snap embraced London reminding Millie that Patricia had promised she would see her married by Yuletide.

Not bloody likely.

Major General Drake approached from behind. For such a large man, he moved with the stealth of a jungle cat. But her senses were attuned to him. She felt his heat warming her back, and she couldn't bear the vulnerability.

Turning to face him, she leaned against the cold stone. 'I imagine you will regret this moment for the rest of your life, sir.'

Major General Drake's light eyebrows drew together, forming a vertical crease above his scarred nose. He took a step closer. 'What do you mean? Are you quite all right, Miss Millicent?'

Millie's gaze dipped to his lips. For such a hard

man, his mouth was unabashedly sensual, his bottom lip obscenely full. She wondered if he would taste of cloves and smoke.

'I'm not doing this because I want to. I'm doing this because I must.' Millie's voice hummed low and husky in the quiet night. She almost believed herself, if not for the delicious flutter low in her belly calling her a liar. She *wanted* to kiss him.

His sense for danger must have engaged because Major General Drake's entire person hardened.

Fascinating.

A Viking warrior caught in silver moonlight. His aristocratic features bordered on beautiful, save for the savage scar transforming him into something far more dangerous.

If Millie wasn't committed to her task, she would have turned and fled. She couldn't possibly seduce such a lethal man. But fear wasn't causing the tremors throughout her body. Something far more treacherous rushed through her blood, sparking nerve endings long dormant in the tips of her breasts, the apex of her thighs, the soft skin just behind her ear.

'Miss Millicent, I believe we should return to the ballroom.'

It was now or never. She couldn't lose her chance at freedom, all for the cost of a kiss.

Millie leapt forward. Gripping Major General Drake around his thick neck, she pulled his head down. It was lucky she was so tall and strong or he would have had time to resist her before she crushed her mouth against his.

3

Someone had drugged his ratafia. He was hallucinating. That was the only explanation for why Millicent Whittenburg was pressing her lush body into his, smashing her lips against his mouth in the world's most clumsy kiss.

Drake prepared to extricate himself from the woman's surprisingly warm embrace, but something happened. She softened against him. Her mouth trembled beneath his lips. Her fingers rubbed rhythmically along the knotted cords of his neck. A powerful woman turned devastatingly vulnerable in the space of a heartbeat.

Millicent's rawness broke him. Need washed

through Drake like a rogue wave, sweeping logic from his mind and replacing it with vicious longing. It was an ache so deep, he felt it echo in his bones. He wrapped his arms around her, pulling her chest flush against his and revelling in her abundant curves. She was like a feast to his senses after years of starvation. Her soft moan breathed new life into his desire.

He cupped her face, angling her head so he could take control. Instead of plunging deep, he grazed his lips over hers, tasting, testing, savouring the madness and magic.

When he would have pulled back, she gripped his jacket, bringing him even closer. She licked the seam of his mouth. He opened, letting her tongue play a tantalising game of discovery with his own.

Bold and brave, even in this.

Drake hadn't been with a woman since Nora, but he recognised the skill of experience. Millicent may not have kissed many men, but Drake definitely wasn't her first. The knowledge granted him an unexpected freedom. He wasn't debauching a complete innocent. It also filled him with determination to eclipse whoever had gone before him.

Stepping forward, he backed her against the stone railing. It was delightful to embrace a woman so tall and strong. With Nora, he had always worried his brutish power would dominate and crush her. But Millicent was altogether different. He didn't have to bend to reach her. When he thrust his thick thigh between her legs, she squeezed him tight between lithe limbs.

Fucking hell.

Her ability as a horsewoman was apparent and inspired illicit images racing through Drake's feverish mind. How would it feel to have her long legs wrapped around his waist as he unleashed the full power of his passion? To let her ride him like a wild creature until they both shattered and reformed into completely new beings?

He growled low, biting her bottom lip hard enough to blend pleasure with pain. It only seemed to enflame her growing ardour. She scraped her nails over his scalp, and his hand delved lower, filling his palm with the flare of her firm bottom. They were two equally matched warriors engaged in a fierce battle for dominance. She gave him no quarter, and he plunged deeper into the fray.

I'm in trouble. Big trouble.

He needed to pull back, regain control of his body, restore some semblance of order. Soon. Any moment. Maybe never.

An audible gasp behind him doused the flames of his passion.

Miss Millicent pulled away, her hand pressed against a flushed cheek, eyes wide with shock. Or was it regret?

'You wilful, wanton, awful girl.' A familiar, shrill voice rose into the cold night like a banshee's shriek.

Drake didn't have to turn around to know Patricia Whittenburg stood behind him. And while he was the rake responsible for Millicent's ruin, it came as no shock that her poisonous stepmother would lay all the blame at Millicent's slippers.

Dread filled Drake as the reality of their situation crystalised like raindrops in a blizzard.

Fucking hell.

One moment of weakness and his world shifted on its axis. The very last thing he expected to find at this ball was a bride. The very last thing he *wanted* to find at this ball was a bride. But Drake was a gentleman despite the brutality embracing his soul. He would face the repercussions of his actions with his head held high and his shoulders squared.

He turned, shifting so Millicent was hidden behind his back, providing her whatever protection he could from the voracious glare of half the beau monde. His gesture was futile. Of course. The damage had been done. The consequences inescapable. For both of them. And while most of him recoiled violently at the thought of what he must do, a small, hidden piece of his fractured soul exhaled in a whisper of relief.

No. That isn't right. I'm certainly not relieved to be marrying Millicent Whittenburg.

But the whisper got louder.

Drake shook his head. He didn't have time to ruminate on the inner workings of his clearly broken psyche. He was in the middle of a complete mess. Thanks to his lack of control. Which was clearly Miss Millicent's fault.

Lord and Lady Whittenburg, Viscount Tread, the Duchess of Dorsett, and Reynard all stood in a shocked huddle just outside the French doors. Behind them, half the assembly strained to see what was happening in the silvery moonlight on the veranda.

Lady Whittenburg screeched loudly, fanning herself with her bejewelled hand.

Lord Whittenburg blinked like an owl, his lips crimping at the corners, creating a stern parenthesis.

Viscount Tread's mouth opened and closed like a carp out of water. His face was mottled red. Drake worried the man might suffer an apoplectic fit.

Reynard sipped whiskey from a crystal glass in an

effort to hide what Drake could only guess was a wicked smile.

The Duchess of Dorsett thwacked her fan against her hip. While her mouth was set in a firm line, her cobalt eyes twinkled with mischief.

His suspicions increased. Something was terribly amiss.

Drake turned his gaze to Millicent, and the worst happened. Her coffee eyes filled with tears.

'I'm so very sorry,' she whispered.

The heat burning through Drake's veins and clouding his thoughts dissipated like vapour. Cold comprehension dawned.

She planned this whole thing.

The deceitful damsel had duped Drake.

Sometimes, rage ran hotter than molten iron. Sometimes, it was colder than a tempered blade in winter and just as sharp. The whisper in his chest went silent as ice filled his veins. He watched Millicent's face crumple. She had doomed them both. Intentionally. But why?

I suppose she prefers a scarred dragon to a red-faced, wheezing elephant three days older than dirt.

Without a word to her, he turned and strode toward Lord Whittenburg and Lord Tread.

'Gentlemen, I think it best we retire to Lord Whittenburg's study.' His gaze flicked over to Millicent. 'You shall join us.'

Lady Patricia – who was leaning heavily on Reynard and furiously fanning herself – perked up at Drake's command. 'Yes, as will I.'

She directed her words to Lord Whittenburg, but Drake responded. 'No. You will stay here. Reynard, please see to Lady Whittenburg.' The last thing he needed was more females complicating an already disastrous situation.

'Major General.' Millicent rushed to him, gripping his arm. 'There's no need. I mean, please, let me explain.'

Using all the skills honed in combat, Drake turned to her, his face a mask of pure marble, any emotion hidden deep in the blackness of his core. 'Explain exactly what, madame? That you are deceitful? Devious? Diabolical? Those terms are redundant, as you are a woman. No different from any other creature of your sex. You lie. Cheat. Scheme and destroy. I know this as well as I know my own ruined reflection in the mirror. I am only disappointed in myself for letting down my guard. I promise you it shan't happen again.'

Millicent opened her mouth, no doubt to refute his claims, but he wouldn't listen to further farce. The truth was painfully clear. In an effort to evade an old, lecherous man, Miss Millicent Whittenburg had forced a trade. If he wasn't so disgusted with the entire affair, he would admire her enterprise.

Turning back to her father, Drake shook his head. Millicent didn't understand yet, but her circumstances were exponentially worse. While Lord Tread was a miserable, decrepit man, Drake was a monster. If she was intent on cornering him into a forced marriage, he would make sure she paid her part of the bargain. Even dragons were allowed to savour their spoils.

* * *

Millie followed the men into her father's study, refusing to show any nerves.

Major General Drake took control of the meeting as soon as they entered the room. 'Lord Tread, obviously you have been grievously mistreated. For my part in this mess, I apologise.' Drake sent Millie a scathing glare.

If Major General Drake was expecting her to follow his example, he was destined for disappointment. She would apologise to no one.

Moving to the leather couch, she sat, inhaling the comforting scent of sandalwood. This room was once her favourite place. Her mother died bringing Millie into the world, and her father developed a fear of losing Millie as well. So, he kept her close by his side, always. She was his shadow, following him everywhere. He taught her to ride, shoot, climb trees, and capture frogs. They spent hours together in this room, Millie drawing horses or planning epic adventures while her father worked on business.

Until she let St George seduce her. She broke her father's heart that day. Then Patricia arrived. She won his affections and weaselled her way into his broken heart, ensuring Millie's complete rejection.

Patricia banned her from disturbing her father while he worked. They no longer read together by the fireplace in the evenings, sharing their favourite passages. Patricia preferred to play cards. Always Piquet or Quinze, games involving two players with no room for Millie to join. Slowly but surely, Patricia pushed Millie out of every corner of Lord Whittenburg's life.

There was a time Millie would have given anything to be invited back into her father's sanctum. In all her wild imaginings, she never expected to return under such dire circumstances.

Well, that cat is well and truly out of the bag. No putting it back.

Crossing her arms over her chest, she stuck out her chin. Millie might be here under duress, but she'd be damned if she let any man shame her for fighting to claim her freedom. She would never ask for Viscount Tread's forgiveness. No matter how viciously Major General Drake glared at her, silently demanding she do just that. Viscount Treadful hadn't even courted her, deeming the effort worthless as Patricia had already promised Millie's agreement to his suit. He had given nothing to Millie and now, he would get nothing from her. He deserved nothing.

'Henry, I must say, I can't believe your daughter is such a wilful, obstinate child. I'm only glad I found out before being leg-shackled to a harlot.' The viscount's watery gaze turned to Millie, filled with hatred.

Her face heated as Drake growled an oath, taking a menacing step closer to Viscount Tread.

Why he cared about the viscount's insults, Millie couldn't guess. Only moments before, Major General Drake called her devious and deceitful. Surely harlot wasn't any more offensive, although it felt worse.

Her father stepped between the men. 'I am sorry, Bartholomew. There is no excuse for Millicent's behaviour. You are obviously released from our agreement. I only hope we can remain friends.'

Dear God. Bartholomew? I was almost married to a man named Bartholomew Tread?

Nothing about this situation was funny, but manic

bubbles of mirth frothed up Millie's throat. She turned the laughter into a cough.

'She should be locked in an asylum. Or thrown out on the streets to earn a living in one of St Giles' whore houses.'

'Enough, sir.' Major General Drake spoke softly, but the small hairs on Millie's neck rose to attention, sensing violence. 'The events of this evening are regrettable. But Miss Millicent is no longer your concern. I recommend you leave. Now.' Major General Drake's gravelled voice created a buzz along Millie's skin.

Viscount Tread's face darkened from red to crimson. He must have sensed the threat emanating from Major General Drake like an arctic blast of chilled air. Without another word, Viscount Treadful turned, leaning heavily on his cane as he shuffled to the door. 'I shan't forget this, Henry. Never in all my days have I been treated so rudely.'

'Bartholomew, please.' Lord Whittenburg followed his friend into the hall, leaving Millie alone with Drake.

This was her chance. Before her father returned and took her control away... again. Major General Drake obviously did not wish to marry her. She just needed to make it clear she held no such expectations of him.

Standing, she threw back her shoulders and walked around the couch to face him.

I will not show fear in the face of a tall, muscular, dashing, very angry man. Philippa has trained me better than that.

'My lord, please understand, I have no intentions of trapping you in marriage. I release you from any expectations.' There. Clear, concise, assertive. All he needed to do was thank her and be on his way.

Major General Drake's eyebrow rose like a bird of prey taking flight.

What a wonderful trick. Quite intimidating. I wonder if he'd teach me how to do that.

'You release me?'

Millie nodded, taking a step back as he strode closer. 'Yes. I was trying to explain myself earlier. I don't want to marry you.' She just needed to be ruined. So she could be free.

Major General Drake's lips pressed together in a tight line. 'Really? You didn't seem so repulsed by me on the veranda.'

Her brow drew down. 'Repulsed?' He misunderstood. 'This has nothing to do with attraction or repulsion.' She was freeing him of his duty to marry her. It was so simple, but he seemed determined to complicate matters. 'I know you don't want to marry me, Major General Drake. And luckily, there's no need.' She kept her voice cheerful. 'After all, it was just a kiss.'

He took another step, his wide chest encompassing her entire frame of vision. 'Just a kiss?'

'Yes.' The air must have thickened because it was almost impossible to breathe. 'A kiss isn't worth sacrificing your life over, is it?'

Even a wonderous kiss that still sparked through her veins like firecrackers.

Major General Drake drew closer, forcing Millie against the back of the couch. She gripped the leather sofa to steady herself. His heat washed over her like a gloriously tropical wave.

'I think that depends entirely on the kiss.' The muscle in his jaw jumped as he inhaled her.

Cheese and crust!

She had to tilt her head back to meet his icy-blue gaze. Millie forced herself to focus on the scar cutting through his eyebrow, nearly catching the lid of his left eye. 'Exactly. Err, I mean, that isn't what I was trying... You're muddling my words. I'm trying to tell you, you're free to leave, Major General. Before Father comes back. I shall tell him you refused to marry a... what did Viscount Tread say? A h-harlot, I believe.' She hated her wobbling voice. Her cheeks were flaming. To be called such a thing by an old, smelly man was embarrassing, but to own the title herself in front of Major General Drake was even worse.

Sacrificing a bit of dignity is worth the price of freedom.

She couldn't maintain eye contact, so instead, she examined his neatly tied cravat. Severe. Controlled. Efficient. Much like the man himself.

He leaned forward, putting both hands on either side of Millicent's hips, trapping her. His chest almost brushed against hers as cloves, leather, and smoke embraced her like a lover.

'One kiss doesn't make you a whore, Millicent. And neither of us are free. Not any more. You made a bargain with the Devil tonight, damning us both.'

Bollocking bloody shit shovelling fuck.

They were all the bad words Millie knew, though she wasn't sure she'd used them correctly. Still, she wanted to scream every one of them at his stupid, smug, devastatingly attractive face. His mouth was only a breath away from hers. She licked her lips, suddenly unable to look away.

'B-but why?' She couldn't fathom his reasoning. He hated women, her in particular. Why wasn't he running for the door?

He opened his mouth to answer, but Millie's father returned.

'I say, what's all this?' Henry Whittenburg's gaze skipped over Major General Drake to land like an anvil on Millie.

Drake straightened, taking a measured step away from her. He faced her father. 'Lord Whittenburg, I would like to marry your daughter. I think a quick engagement would be best, don't you?'

4

He had done the inconceivable. Offered marriage. To Millicent. And her father had agreed. Major General Drake planned to get a special licence the very next morning.

Of all the asinine, godawful outcomes. He really was the most stubborn man.

Millie struggled to sleep that night and woke from heated dreams, her sheets tangled around her legs. She could imagine Major General Drake striding up to the Archbishop of Canterbury, demanding a special licence while she sat in her bedroom, sipping tea and crunching on burnt toast. It was madness.

She was determined to visit Philippa as soon as she could get dressed. Together, they'd sort out this horrific mess. But when she rushed down the steps, ready to take her father's carriage to Lady Winterbourne's Belgrave Square mansion, Patricia met her at the bottom of the stairs.

'You aren't going anywhere, you wicked girl.'

Millie continued walking, ready to push past the woman.

'You cannot stop me from seeing Lady Philippa. She is my friend.'

'Davies!' Patricia screeched.

Their butler arrived. Davies had worked for the Whittenburg's since before Millie was born. He was a stickler for propriety but could never refuse Millie. He used to sneak her lemon drops from his pockets when she was a child.

'Yes, my lady?'

'Secure Miss Millicent in her room. Lock the door. We don't need her escaping, do we?'

Two red slashes painted his wrinkled cheeks as he looked from Millie to Patricia. He would never use force on Millie. Already, she could see the flash of shame in his eyes at Patricia's command.

Patricia knew his loyalty to Millie. She knew her orders put him in an untenable situation where he couldn't obey, but nor could he refuse. She was punishing Davies just as much as she was trying to control

Millie.

'Miss Millicent, please.' He extended his arm toward the stairs, his stoic face trembling, his brown eyes pleading with her to comply.

Millie huffed out a frustrated breath. She relented, more to save poor Davies' feelings than to appease her stepmother.

'Of course, Davies. I know the way.'

Returning to her room, she heard the lock click behind her.

'If Patricia thinks she can contain me with a measly lock, she's an even bigger idiot than I imagined,' Millie muttered to herself.

She sat on her bed and plotted her next move.

Day turned to evening with not even her maid being allowed to bring her a tray for lunch or dinner. As the sun descended and darkness fell, Millie waited for the house to grow silent. Her coat – still draped over the bedframe from her thwarted excursion – was a dark grey. Perfect for keeping her hidden in the shadows. She put it on and approached the door, pressing her ear against the wood to listen.

Silence greeted her. Everyone was abed.

Philippa had taught her to pick all different kinds of locks with a ring of skeleton keys in varying lengths and sizes. She kept them tied to her petticoat. It took several tries, but after three minutes of whispered curses, the lock turned.

Huzzah! I'm a lock-picking genius!

Millie carefully opened the door and poked her head out, looking down the hall to her father's and Patricia's suite of rooms. Their doors were closed and no light shone from the cracks. Glancing the other direction toward the stairs, the hall was empty. She slipped out, carefully shutting the door behind her.

As she crept down the stairs – making sure to avoid the creaking third step – her heart pounded in her ears, and a thrill of excitement coursed through her veins.

Here I come. Femme fatale. Brilliant secret spy for the Queen of bloody England!

A door creaked.

Millie nearly screamed.

Ah. Well. Perhaps not exactly femme fatale.

Davies emerged from the darkness. Millie opened her mouth, desperately seeking a viable lie. Aaannd... nothing.

'I'm just...'

Davies shook his head, his finger pressing against his lips. He motioned her to a door cleverly hidden in the wooden panelling. When they were inside the dimly lit servants' corridor, he spoke. 'Lady Whittenburg drank enough wine to keep her sleeping till noon tomorrow, but your father's always been a light sleeper. Take this to the kitchens and use the servants' entrance. I'll make sure the door stays unlocked. Be careful, Miss Whittenburg. The streets are not safe for a lady.'

Millie felt tears burn her eyes. She wished she could hug the dear man but knew he would hate such a show of familiarity. Instead, she winked.

'Thank you, Davies.'

The stern butler ducked his head like a bashful schoolboy. 'Off with you, Miss Millicent.' In addition to the lantern, he handed her a wrapped sandwich and a lemon drop. 'In case you might be hungry.' Millie couldn't stop the wobble in her chin, but Davies pretended not to notice her emotional display. 'Be back before sunrise, or your father will be taking his breakfast and might see you.'

'You are wonderful, Davies. I hope you know how lucky we are to have you.' Even in the dim light of the lantern, she could see the man's cheeks turn red. Not wishing to cause him further embarrassment, Millie slipped past him and rushed down the servants' hall toward the kitchen.

* * *

Lady Winterbourne lived in Belgrave Square, a mere ten-minute carriage ride from Millie's house. But in the middle of the night, on foot, the journey seemed daunting.

'Pull yourself together, Millie.' Refusing to let her imagination run wild, she put her long legs to use, striding through the London night as if it belonged to her. The sandwich and lemon drop helped immensely. Thirty minutes later, she climbed the stone stairs of Lady Winterbourne's house.

She knocked twice, and the huge door opened. A tall, dour man stared at her. He stood as straight as a ruler and blinked at Millie. His thin lips tightened into a pale line.

'Hello, Stokes. Please tell Her Grace I must see her.'

The butler pulled a gold watch from his waistcoat pocket and took his time flicking it open. 'Her Grace is not accepting callers at half past midnight.' His voice was as cold and hard as his gaze.

'Stokes, who is at the door?' Philippa's familiar voice filled Millie with relief.

Stokes refused to turn around, but Millie didn't miss how his shoulders jerked like he'd been hit with a bullet.

The door opened wider and Philippa shoved Stokes out of the way. 'Millicent. What's happened?

Come in. Stokes, don't just stand there like some decaying statue. Take Millicent's coat.' When Stokes only blinked at Philippa, she scowled. 'Can you hear me?' She repeated the command, almost yelling in the man's ear. 'Take Millicent's coat!'

Stokes' face remained impressively blank. Without a word, he took Millie's jacket, turning to walk slowly down the hall.

'Horrid man.' Philippa's gaze followed him before she turned, her blue eyes assessing Millie. 'Are you well?'

Emphatically not.

Millie shook her head. 'No.' She followed Philippa into her front sitting room, spilling out the entire awful affair.

By the time Philippa had heard everything, Millie had a tumbler of whiskey in her hand and felt marginally better. The duchess would know what to do.

'I must say, Millicent. I'm not sure what to do.'

Bollocks!

'Can't I just run away?' Though the thought of never seeing Major General Drake again filled her with a surprisingly hollow ache.

Philippa waved her hand, dismissing Millie's question like a fly buzzing around a cream cake. 'We don't run away, Millicent. We run toward. We are the

Queen's trusted few. No. I think the best course of action is to convince Major General Drake to break the engagement.'

'I tried that. He is a stubborn, stupid,' *delicious*, 'pompous ass.'

'Of course he is. He's a man.'

Millie snorted.

Philippa rubbed her index finger against her thumb. 'Fine. If you can't convince him to beg off, then our plans to set you up as a maid are dashed.' She took a healthy sip of her own glass. 'We can still make this work. I have a meeting with the Queen tomorrow. She has a certain lord of interest she wishes us to focus on in our investigation. Once I have his name, we can take advantage of your wedding to create a trap.'

Millie shook her head. 'I don't understand.'

'Your stepmother's sure to invite the entire beau monde to watch your humiliation. We can use that to our advantage. I shall write to Patricia and encourage a week-long celebration at Major General Drake's country house. In the wilds of Bedfordshire, as I recall. Once I know who the Queen wishes for us to target, I can ensure your stepmother sends him an invitation.'

'And then what?'

'Then we trap a killer, Millicent.' Philippa's red lips curled in a vicious smile. 'The Queen will be duly impressed by your skills, and a married woman has much more freedom in the beau monde. Especially when her husband prefers a distant marriage, as Major General Drake is sure to do. This could work splendidly. By the by, I have an early wedding gift for you.'

Millie almost fumbled her cup. 'Dear Lord. A wedding gift.' It all suddenly felt very real.

Philippa stood and walked to the bell pull, ringing for Stokes. Several minutes later, he appeared.

'Shall I call for a doctor, madame? I've heard insomnia is an early sign of your mental faculties failing.'

Philippa arched her brow. 'I'm quite well, thank you, Stokes. If you feel my hours are too exhausting for you, I'm more than prepared to pension you off to a nice cottage in the country where you can eat your supper at noon and retire to bed before the sun descends.'

'On the contrary, madame. I'm invigorated by your complete disregard of social rules.'

'Wonderful. Why don't you use that vigour to fetch the package on my dresser.'

Twenty minutes later, Stokes returned, a leather pouch in his hands.

'Finally. I thought you'd succumbed to your excessive age and expired on your way back here.' Philippa took the gift from Stokes, dismissing him with a wave of her hand.

The butler's stiff posture tightened further as he turned and exited.

Millie stood and approached Philippa. The duchess handed her the soft pouch dyed the colour of fresh fern leaves in spring.

'It's beautiful.' Millie brushed her fingers over the supple leather.

Philippa's lips twitched. 'You haven't opened it yet. The real gift is inside. Go on.'

'Your Grace, you really shouldn't have.'

'Stop with the "Your Grace" nonsense and open the damn gift. You might not even like it.'

Millie ducked her head to hide her smile. She carefully unbound the leather ties and flipped open the soft case to reveal a set of five dangerously sharp throwing knives. Mother of pearl was inlaid into each hilt. They must have cost a small fortune. Millie gasped as she carefully removed one from where it was secured in the leather case.

'Phillipa. They're gorgeous! And far too dear to give me as a gift.'

'I'm the Duchess of Dorsett. I'm lousy with money and can do whatever the hell I please.' Philippa lifted her chin and sniffed. She pointed to the case. 'There are straps and sheaths for each of them in the pocket there. You can strap them on your thighs or wrists. But be careful. I have no desire to see you cut yourself to ribbons.'

Millie nodded, her eyes still on the knives as she put the blade back and looked in the pocket.

'Your skill at throwing blades is impressive. You should have weapons worthy of your abilities.'

Millie's throat ached, and she swallowed hard. It was such a thoughtful gift. But the real prize was Philippa thinking her worthy of such beautiful weapons.

'Hannah trained with me for ten years before I felt comfortable letting her take on men as dangerous and deadly as the bastards we are inviting to your wedding. Their secret society is powerful, Millie. They wouldn't hesitate to kill anyone who stands in their way. And if we aim to expose them – as we do – we pose an even greater threat. You are talented, but you are also new to this. I won't have you racing into a dangerous situation unarmed and unprepared.'

Fear tightened Millie's chest. In the weeks of training with Phillipa, she appreciated her skills improving, her body becoming stronger, and her confidence growing. However, she had always viewed the actual task of investigating as somewhat of a lark. But Philippa was correct. This wasn't a game. Real girls were being sold, some of them killed. The men responsible stood to lose everything if they were discovered. She mustn't let her newfound confidence lead her into a situation where she might be out of her depth.

'I'll be careful, Phillipa.'

'We have some time. We must practise even harder to prepare.'

Millie took an unsteady breath. 'Patricia won't let me come. I'm sure of it. She's so angry with me for thwarting her plans with Viscount Tread. I had to pick the lock to my door to come here tonight.'

Philippa hissed out a breath. 'Fine. Then you must train on your own until we reunite at the wedding.'

'I will. I promise. I should go before anyone notices I'm gone.'

'You'll take my carriage.' Philippa walked back to the bell pull. 'Stokes will have to rouse the stable boys. A task I'm sure he'll love.' Her wicked smile told a different tale.

* * *

Millie's trip home was much faster and more comfortable than her journey to Philippa's.

She carefully opened the door to the servants' entrance. Davies was as good as his word, making sure it was unlocked. He had even put a candle stub on the kitchen counter.

Such a sweet man!

Millicent lit a wisp with a coal from the banked fire, then lit the candle. She blinked in the sudden light.

'My, my. What exactly were you up to, Daughter?'

Blast!

Patricia sat at the kitchen table in a nightgown of frills and lace. A silk wrapper was tied tightly around her waist. Her lips twisted into a predatory smile. 'I have you now, Millicent.'

* * *

Millie learned much of suffering and humiliation in the two weeks following her evening at Philippa's. When she looked at her reflection in the glass, she almost didn't recognise the woman staring back.

Patricia's treatment of Millie had shifted from mild bullying to unbridled abuse the moment Millie snuck back into the kitchen. She hadn't realised her father's efforts to protect her against Patricia's punishments until Marquess Whittenburg ceased shielding his daughter from his wife's retribution. And Patricia took to the task of disciplining Millie with relish.

Stretching carefully, Millie's broken skin pulled as fresh blood welled in the deep wounds covering her back.

She had never been whipped before, but Patricia made sure to remedy that lack in her education the morning after she caught her sneaking back into the kitchen. For a delicate woman, Patricia wielded the whip with devastating accuracy, not stopping until Millie had passed out from the pain. But even the beckoning blackness would never erase the sensation of warm blood dripping down her side and growing cool or the fiery brand of the whip as it cracked through the air.

What was worse than the lightning strikes on her back was knowing she couldn't fight back. For now, Patricia held all the cards. Her threat of exposing Millie and Philippa to the censure and punishment of the beau monde was a blade pressed against Millie's throat. Despite her skills, despite knowing she could easily best her stepmother, Millie had to endure Patricia's wrath or face even greater retribution. It added a unique layer of humiliation to her punishment. So, she rebelled the only way she could. Refusing to cry out. Her stubbornness increased her stepmother's rage, causing the woman to break a sweat from her exertions. Just the scent of Patricia's overpowering lily perfume was enough to make Millie gag.

Millie spent several days after the first whipping on her belly as her back scabbed over. Patricia only allowed her water, broth, and a few crusts of bread. She claimed the diet was restorative and would also aid Millie in attaining a more pleasing figure prior to the wedding.

As soon as Millie was able to stand without her vision spotting, she renewed her training, letting her futile anger fuel her. Obviously, she couldn't grapple alone in her room, but she could continue with the exercises Philippa assigned to strengthen her already athletic body. She focused on slowing her movements, concentrating on the fighting forms Philippa had taught her, ignoring the burn of her wounds as she shifted and twisted her body.

She set up the grate of her fireplace as a practice throwing range for her knives, using pillows and a few books as her target. Her accuracy improved daily. She could hit a fly from the distance of one side of her room to the other, and the satisfaction she felt dulled the pain of her stepmother's punishments.

Lack of proper food made it difficult, but Millie refused to stop. Her poor maid tried to sneak Millie a plate from dinner on the fourth day, but one of the servants loyal to Patricia caught her. Patricia threatened to sack the girl with no references if she ever disobeyed her again. And Millie received another whipping for coercing her maid into such devious acts. The second session was even more horrific than the first as barely healed wounds broke open anew. She would likely carry scars.

'Something you'll have in common with your new husband.' Patricia sneered as the whip whistled through the air, cracking against Millie's back.

What bothered Millie most about the brutal second whipping was the interruption her new lashes caused for her training sessions. Three more days lost while she waited for her wounds to close.

She would survive this ordeal. She would heal. And grow stronger. And destroy her stepmother. She just needed to endure long enough to stand at the altar.

Two weeks passed while Millie spent her days alone in her room training and her nights collapsing into exhausted sleep. Her father didn't visit her once. She only saw Patricia on the two occasions her step-mother administered her discipline.

Now, the wedding was only five days away, and they were scheduled to depart for Major General Drake's expansive estate in Bedfordshire directly after breakfast, though Millie was only allowed burnt toast and weak tea.

It would be impossible for Patricia to continue with her diabolical behaviour once they were settled at Alder House. The only benefit Millie could see in marrying Major General Drake was freedom from her stepmother forever. She was also unlikely to see her father. That hurt more than she could describe. Although his love for Millie had been lost, she still missed him fiercely.

Millie bit her lip, refusing to let the tears slip free. She was desperate for comfort and comradery. She had been denied access to Lady Philippa and Ivy over the past two weeks and longed for their support. The only thing keeping her hopes from shrivelling to dust were her daily training sessions.

* * *

Patricia swept into her room at half past seven. She glanced around, a smile playing over her lips at the various cases packed and ready to be loaded onto carriages.

'You best make sure everything is ready before we leave. You are no longer welcome here and won't be returning to this house ever again, dear Daughter.'

Millie never thought she would be relieved to escape her family home. The house where she learned to walk. Where her father taught her to ride. Where she spun tales with her best friend about the fantastic futures they would share. Futures full of adventure, freedom, and maybe love. But her home had turned into a prison. Her father was a stranger to her now, and her stepmother achieved her goal of ousting Millie and claiming her place as ruler of the Whittenburg legacy.

Patricia could fall from the heights of her aspirations and splat onto the dirt for all Millie cared. But she mourned the loss of her father's affections. If love so easily turned a trusted parent from his beloved daughter, then Millie was grateful she need never concern herself with the emotion. Patricia's punishments had hollowed out anything soft or weak within Millie. Major General Drake certainly wouldn't show her anything close to affection. Which was perfectly fine.

She only hoped his hatred of her would ensure a distant marriage where she could live her life free of anyone's demands but her own – and the Queen's, of course. She had spent much of her dreadful confinement contemplating how to continue working with Philippa while being married to the Earl of Tetly. If she couldn't convince him to beg off the marriage, at least a distant union would provide her with much-needed privacy to continue her important work.

Drake would want nothing to do with her, so it would be easy to recommend they live separately. The plan would suit him down to his stupid shiny shoes. Once this wedding was complete, she would live in his London residence and return to her training with Lady Philippa. Millie was determined to hone herself into a weapon of cold steel. Something that couldn't be broken with a whip. Something that didn't long for affection. Or kindness. Or affirmation. Because she would find nothing gentle in her new husband. A man who despised her. A man who would forever be a stranger.

A man whose kisses make me melt.

Madness. A moment never to be repeated. Millie had learned her lesson well with Franklin St George. Where her body led, her heart soon followed. And allowing her heart to become involved with the cold, cruel, dangerous Earl of Tetly was foolishness of the highest order. Millie was no man's fool. Certainly not Major General Beaufort Drake's.

5

Major General Beaufort Drake was England's biggest fool.

He stood on the gravelled entrance leading from his drive to the massive stone steps of his country estate and watched the carriage carrying his fiancée trundle ever closer down the alder-lined drive. The frigid wind whistled through the courtyard, embracing him with cold fingers.

'Well, on the bright side of things, this wedding celebration is an excellent reason to invite our biggest suspect into your home.' Reynard elbowed Drake in the side as he stood with him, waiting for Millicent to arrive.

Drake rolled his eyes and pressed his lips together.

Not only had he allowed a fiery-haired witch of a woman to trick him into a marriage, but he then let Prime Minister Russell convince him to turn the whole sordid affair into a trap for a killer. It was madness. And it just might work.

'I had no idea a "small wedding" meant inviting every duke, earl, viscount, and baron within throwing distance of London to descend upon us.' Drake rocked back on his heels, willing his anger to dissipate. It wasn't Millicent's fault her sadistic stepmother wanted a huge affair. 'Thank God Killian is still on his honeymoon.' Seeing his smug face would be too much to bear. This entire farce of a wedding guaranteed to fray Drake's nerves and test his very short fuse without any help from his snarky friend.

'Of us all, you were the last I expected to fall.' Reynard clapped Drake on the back. 'Even the best of us get caught out sometimes, eh?'

'Especially when a scheming minx has you in her sights,' Drake grumbled.

'Quite a coincidence that our next suspect is a childhood friend of your betrothed.' Reynard squinted up at the winter sky before returning his gaze to the carriage rolling closer along the winding drive.

'Lord Franklin St George.' Drake felt his face pull into a grimace. Prime Minister Russell's orders were explicit. Focus on St George and determine what role he played in this diabolical game. 'I spent some time with him a few months back at Bradford's house party. Even if he's innocent of this, the man is despicable.' Loathing for St George added another layer of bitterness fuelling Drake.

St George was a slimy toad who hurled insults at women, couldn't ride to save his soul, and had a history with Drake's future wife. The specifics of that history lay shrouded in shadow, but not for long. It was one mystery Drake was intent on discovering. And the key to that particular lock was fast approaching.

'Do you think he's capable of luring young country girls to interview for maid positions, drugging them, nailing them into coffins, and then shipping them across the English Channel to France?' Reynard's cheek ticked in disgust.

Drake couldn't imagine Franklin holding a hammer to nail anything, but the rest was possible. 'I think he's capable of trying, though I doubt he has the intelligence or power to orchestrate anything alone. This secret society of men calls themselves The Devil's Sons. I believe St George is a member. If we catch him red-handed, he can lead us to those who are powerful enough to keep this sex trade running. That is our aim.'

The girls who survived the journey across the Channel had no money, no family, no protection. They were forced into prostitution, and the money they earned lined the pockets of snivelling peers of the realm like fucking Franklin St George. But not for long.

'We'll keep a close eye on the bastard. See who he talks to. If he reveals anything. One way or another, we'll catch him.' Reynard nodded, always confident.

All evidence pointed to St George's participation in procuring these women. Which meant he knew who was in charge. Drake was going to enjoy making him spill his secrets. He was almost as desperate to catch the fucker red-handed as he was to see his fiancée again. Which troubled Drake in the extreme.

Two weeks had never felt so long. Not even in the stinking Afghanistan pit of a prison he called home for two years. Completely confounding. He didn't like Millicent Whittenburg. She had trapped him in an unwanted marriage. She was too tall. Too bold. Too fierce.

Too bloody tempting.

His mind kept wandering back to their kiss on the veranda. His body hardened as he imagined all her curves pressed against him, only in his mind, she was naked, and they weren't interrupted by the entire sodding beau monde.

His cock thickened at the memory of their brief interlude.

Fucking hell!

Drake prided himself on control. His body was a weapon, something he wielded with the same fierce detachment as a sword or pistol. But somehow, just the thought of Millicent created a rebellion within him. He yearned for her.

Major General Drake Beaufort yearns for no one.

Yet, still. He ached.

The anger boiling beneath his skin had a new target. His conniving wife-to-be. A woman who dared to make him feel again. Such an affront to his autonomy was not to be borne. She would pay for her gamble. Whatever she hoped to reap from this marriage, a felicitous union was not forthcoming. He would double down on his efforts to keep her at a distance.

'Ah. Here they are. Your betrothed and her lovely parents. I must say, having Patricia Whittenburg for a mother-in-law would send most men running for the hills. Myself included.' Reynard watched the coach with a wary eye. 'She's a horror.'

'On a good day,' Drake agreed.

A footman rushed to set the step, and Drake strode

forward, ready to greet his betrothed with all the hospitality of a wounded dragon. Reynard wisely stayed back to watch from a distance.

Lord Whittenburg emerged first, his coat wrinkled from the journey. He assisted his wife, a woman significantly younger and exponentially crueller than her husband. Lord Whittenburg's weakness highlighted his wife's determination. Drake was not a fan of Millicent's pretty, spiteful, grasping stepmother. His opinion of the woman grew even more severe when Millicent appeared, blinking at the bright day.

It had only been two weeks since their last meeting, but Millicent's appearance was drastically altered. She had lost weight, her face pale and gaunt. It was also blatantly apparent she was in some kind of discomfort. Although her movements were still fluid and graceful, belying an athleticism most young ladies of the beau monde would be embarrassed to display, she winced as she stepped down from the carriage. But then, ladies were supposed to be delicate, fragile flowers in need of protection. Perhaps his perception of her being different from all the gentle ladies of the beau monde was faulty.

Hogwash!

Millicent was about as delicate as a rapier sword. Which piqued Drake's suspicion. Why would a young miss carry herself with such self-assurance? When she glanced at him, her steady gaze held the confidence of an equal. He'd only seen that kind of power in three women. The Queen. The Duchess of Dorsett. And Hannah Simmons when she looked at his friend, Killian. Drake shuddered at the thought.

The bloody cliffs of Dover will fall into the sea before I end up as love-drunk as my idiot friend, Killian.

Watching his betrothed as she threw back her shoulders and sent her stepmother a withering glare, Drake's mouth watered. Even in her suffering, she was defiant. He'd never wanted anyone with such desperation. But it was just another appetite, and he could control his hunger. He *would* control it with the same ruthless discipline he applied to all areas of his life.

Patricia walked over to her stepdaughter in an overture of motherly affection, but Drake saw the vicious pinch she delivered to Millicent's arm before gracing him with one of her calculated smiles.

Whatever changes he perceived in his betrothed, the orchestrator was obvious. Patricia Whittenburg had been punishing her stepdaughter. Most grievously.

'My lord, what a stunning home you have so far in the country.' Patricia pulled Millicent with her as they approached.

Millicent wrenched free of her stepmother and glanced at the stone entrance to his home. 'It is quite impressive, sir.' Her husky voice stroked along his senses like the pleasant scratch of nails digging into his back. Rough and delicious.

'I'm sure you can come up with something better than that, dear.' Patricia's tinkling laughter rang across the gravel drive. 'A home like this is deserving of a much grander compliment than merely "impressive". And a much grander mistress, but I suppose the *Earl of Tetly* will make do.'

Drake didn't miss her emphasis on his title. The woman was single-minded in her focus to climb the social ladder at any cost. While she lost a viscount thanks to Millicent's awkward – surprisingly arousing – attempt at seduction, she gained an earl. Not a bad trade while still ensuring Millicent remained below her stepmother in the hierarchy of the beau monde.

'On the contrary, madame, I find that Miss Millicent is uniquely suited to become a countess.' Drake defended his betrothed before he could think better of it.

Patricia's smile turned brittle. Millicent's eyes widened to stare at Drake. He could only guess she was as surprised at his defence of her as he was.

Strangely, the idea made him feel uncomfortable. Had he been such a beast that she expected no kindness?

Probably. I am a dragon, after all.

'A countess bringing shame onto all of us. But perhaps you can train her better than we were able.' A bright winter sun highlighted Patricia's sharp features, emphasising her cold beauty. Gold ringlets swung gracefully against a cheek both smooth and pink like a petal. Full lips painted the same delicate shade of rose pursed in a practised smile. But her beauty hid an ugly woman beneath. She was a conniving, heartless bitch, and no abundance of delicate features or carefully applied cosmetics would ever change that.

Lord Whittenburg joined them from where he had been directing the unloading of their luggage.

'Lord Whittenburg.' Drake nodded curtly, then turned his gaze to Millicent, dismissing both of her parents rudely. 'Miss Millicent, welcome to Alder House.'

Millicent's gaze captured him like a siren's song. Sunlight brought out amber hues in Millicent's rich-brown eyes. Her thick lashes, a few shades darker than her blazing hair, perfectly framed her brilliant gaze. Where her stepmother's complexion and features mirrored a porcelain doll, Millicent was powerful, bold, absolutely stunning. Or she would be once she ate a decent meal and regained some of the colour in her cheeks.

His anger deepened. A usually comfortable emotion. But this amalgamation of rage and desire, this need to protect Millicent and ensure she was healthy and well while simultaneously destroying anyone who threatened her, was new and alarming. He did not like it. Not one bit. Distance and decorum. That is what this relationship required. Demands he intended to lay out immediately.

'Allow me to introduce you to your staff, then you can settle into your rooms and refresh yourself before we meet in my study.'

Millicent's gaze swept to his. 'Meet in your study? For what purpose?'

'There are things we must discuss.' He spared a withering glance at her parents. 'Alone.'

'But surely that's not proper.' Patricia had overheard his comment and inserted herself into the conversation, gliding across the gravel drive to land next to Millicent. Drake kept a sharp gaze on her hand. If she reached over to pinch Millicent again, he might well hit her. A first for him, as he did not condone violence toward women. Patricia Whittenburg would be a well-deserving exception to his rule.

'Even engaged couples can't be cloistered together,

unchaperoned.' Her eyebrows rose toward her blonde hairline, creating unsightly wrinkles that would horrify her if she knew.

'I think you'll find I can do whatever I damn well please in my own house with my soon-to-be wife, madame. Lord Whittenburg, please remind your wife of her manners, or I will ask both of you to leave.'

Patricia gasped, her hand fluttering over a barely contained bosom. Her dress – a garish orange – was cut so scandalously low, Drake feared she might fall out of it and embarrass them all. The foolish woman had opted not to wear a cape, though the temperatures were frigid. It was likely there would be snow soon. She was the last person to be handing out advice on propriety.

'How dare you!' she sputtered.

'Quite easily, madame. I have welcomed you to stay here, allowed you to invite God-knows-who to my estate for a wedding celebration thrust upon me after being entrapped by an enterprising young miss.' Millicent stiffened against him, and he felt a moment of remorse at his harsh words.

Well, what does she expect? That I might be overjoyed in a forced marriage?

While his insult had been directed at Patricia, he wouldn't feel guilty about pointing out Millicent's devious behaviour. He hardened his stare. 'Tread carefully, Lady Whittenburg. You'll find I'm not nearly so accommodating as your husband.'

Lord Whittenburg's cheeks flushed at the implied slight.

In mere moments, Drake had insulted his betrothed, offended his new in-laws, and established his brutish nature.

Well, better they know now than find out later.

'I assure you, sir, we are grateful for your generous offer after my daughter's disastrous behaviour. My wife is only concerned with salvaging Millicent's already damaged reputation. An endeavour equally benefitting you.' Henry Whittenburg didn't even spare his daughter a glance.

Millicent dropped her head, a blush staining her neck crimson.

Drake rankled at Lord Whittenburg's words, though they were no less insulting than his own had been toward his betrothed. 'Her reputation is none of your concern any more.'

'I'm right here.' Millicent spoke quietly. She raised her chin, and Drake didn't miss the tremble in her full lips. He wanted to lick the seam of her mouth. Taste her again. Bite her bottom lip until the only tremble through her body was one of desire.

Control yourself, man!

'Yes, of course you're here, silly girl. Where else would you be?' Patricia hissed.

'You don't need to speak about me as if I'm a naughty child or some kind of hideous vase you can't decide whether to hide in the attic or throw out with the rubbish.' Anger brought a flush to her cheeks, and her eyes flashed. Drake almost nodded in encouragement. Watching Millicent fight back was a damn sight better than the defeated woman who had slumped next to him moments before.

'Perhaps we should set you on the mantel, Miss Millicent. You can stand quietly while we all admire your...' His gaze was drawn to the luscious curve of her breasts, hidden beneath a sensible coat. 'Numerous assets.' The dry words slipped out before he could stop himself.

Millicent narrowed her gaze, pulling her arm free of his grip. 'I have a better idea, my Lord. Let's abandon this farce of a wedding. I can retire to the country in shame, another ruined woman disappearing into the heather. You will be free of an unwanted wife. Lord and Lady Whittenburg can distance themselves from their wayward daughter. A task they shall apply themselves to with vigour, I'd wager.' She spared her father a glance that had the man looking quickly away. 'I will happily spend my days wandering the woods and riding across the moors, and the rest of you will never see me again. A desirable outcome for all involved.'

Everything in him recoiled at the thought of breaking their engagement, which was bewildering. He had only offered for Millicent out of honour.

And that kiss.

Drake blinked, refusing to revisit the incendiary moment. His rogue desires had nothing to do with this wedding. But the thought of never seeing Millicent again filled him with a strange hollowness.

Bollocks to that! I am not some shell of a man waiting to be filled up by the next beautiful woman who kisses me on a veranda. But neither am I a libertine.

Regardless of his feelings about marriage, he would not be responsible for ruining a young woman, even if it meant doing the unthinkable and willingly sacrificing his quiet, calm solitude for matrimonial agony. The prime minister's encouragement to find a wife didn't hurt. While not Drake's choice, having a bride foisted upon him was awfully convenient.

Still, he should jump at her offer to rescind the proposal. He could hardly be considered a feckless profligate if *she* was rejecting *him*.

Something kicked in the vicinity of his chest. A strange pounding.

Mine.

The word rang through his head in rhythm with the beating, like war drums decrying an impending battle. Giving Millicent up to live as a tainted woman on the edges of society was unthinkable.

'Mad Millicent of the Moors. Yes, that would be a fitting future for you. Shameless girl! You would happily soak in your scandal while destroying all our reputations with your wanton ways,' Patricia hissed, bony fingers reaching for Millicent's arm.

Drake stepped between Patricia and Millicent. Lady Whittenburg's fingers smashed into his back before she quickly retreated. Drake took immense pleasure in the strangled sound she made at being thwarted.

He forgot how tall Millicent was. He barely needed to lean down to whisper in her ear, his lips almost grazing the sensitive lobe. 'We will marry, my lady. Reconcile yourself to the fact.' Lemons and fresh laundry engulfed him in a scent unique to Millicent.

He reached out and carefully gripped Millicent's arm, forcing her to walk with him up the stone staircase leading to the grand entrance of his estate. Drake cared not if Millicent's parents followed them into the house or got back in the carriage and left. Reynard – always displaying exemplary manners – swept in and introduced himself to Lord and Lady Whittenburg, glossing over Drake's rude dismissal.

'You cannot manhandle me, sir,' Millicent whispered furiously.

The household staff created an orderly line, waiting to meet their new mistress.

'Then stop fighting me, my lady.'

She hissed in pain as she twisted away from him. Drake gentled his grip, murmuring quietly, 'Are you quite well, Millicent?'

For a moment, she froze. Perhaps it was his use of her first name. Or his question. Or the fact she was clearly injured and trying to hide her discomfort.

'I'm perfectly fine.' Her words were barely discernible as her voice caught.

Bollocks to that!

This was not the time to discover her secrets. Drake would leave it. For now. But he would find out what Patricia had done to her stepdaughter. And the woman would pay for every injury Millicent was forced to suffer.

'Then come and meet your staff. After which, you may get settled in your rooms.'

Drake had appointed her a lady's maid. A new girl

his housekeeper had hired. He would expect a report from the woman on exactly what pained his be-trothed. 'I expect you in my study in an hour. You have that long to prepare yourself.' It was time to discuss the terms of their marriage. Which was problematic. As the terms Drake thought he wanted a few moments ago seemed less clear.

A marriage of convenience was the only acceptable way forward for Drake. They would be joined in name only. He had no interest in producing an heir. His brother would inherit the title upon Drake's death. But as it was the one thing Drake's ex-fiancée – now sister-in-law – wanted most, Drake intended to live a long, long time. With any luck, his brother and sister-in-law would die first, and the bloody title could go to a dis-tant cousin.

Millicent would make no demands on his time. In return, he would allow her to live as she pleased. There would be a handful of events requiring her presence but their individual lives need not change. She would live separately from him. He had several properties from which to choose. They could pursue their individual interests, and this alarming attraction would dissipate.

I will not be swept into madness.

This was a simple business arrangement allowing

him more freedom in his investigations for the prime minister. Nothing more. He would explain the boundaries of their relationship to Millicent with cold efficiency. An emotion she should learn to expect from him, as it was all he would give.

So why did the thought of a convenient marriage feel so suddenly and unaccountably *inconvenient*?

* * *

Millie wanted a bath. But after meeting the staff – including a mischievous lad of nine who introduced himself as Master Bright and winked at her before disappearing back to the kitchens – investigating her expansive suite of rooms, and organising the unpacking of her trunks, Millie barely had time to wash her face and change her clothes before her meeting with Major General Drake.

Her husband-to-be might not rank as highly as her father and stepmother in the beau monde, but based on his estate, his bank account seemed far healthier than Lord Whittenburg's quickly diminishing finances.

It doesn't help that Patricia spends money like a wildfire blazing through dry wood.

Before Patricia met her father, Lord Whittenburg

let Millie join him in his meetings with his man of business. It was unheard of for a woman to take any interest in running an estate, but Millie was good with numbers, and her father had grown to depend on her frugal habits. Then Patricia joined their family, and their finances plummeted as drastically as Patricia's necklines.

My father's affairs don't concern me now.

But she still worried for him, for all the good it did. That was her past. It was time to start focusing on her future. For now, that meant getting ready for her meeting with Drake.

Her lady's maid, Penny, was a sturdy young thing. Millicent would guess her to be in her mid-twenties, though she carried herself with the confidence of a much older woman. Her keen gaze took in the bandages poking out of Millie's corset as she helped her to change from her traveling clothes into a deep-green day dress with black, lace trimming.

'I don't wish to overstep, miss, but I have a poultice for... injuries. If you like, I can bring it to you. We can apply it before bed.' Penny kept her gaze on her hands as she fastened the tiny, obsidian buttons along the back of Millie's dress. 'We wouldn't want infection to take root. I was always getting into scrapes as a child. My mother learned the best potions to keep a body healthy. She still sends me this and that when she can, so I have plenty. It would be no trouble.'

Millie bit her lip against a sudden need to burst into tears at her maid's small act of kindness. She hadn't cried once since the fated kiss. She didn't dare show such weakness. But Penny's no-nonsense tone, her offer of comfort without pity, nearly burst the damn. Digging her nails into her palm, she focused on that pain instead of the much larger ache in her soul. She would not turn into a watering pot. Not now. Maybe later.

What would the duchess think of Millie if she dissolved into a puddle on the floor? Philippa believed Millie to be strong and resilient. And so, she would pretend to be exactly that until her moment of weakness passed. She would get through this week, marry the earl, and get back to training. There was important work to be done. Millie was determined to make something useful of her life by stopping people even more twisted than her stepmother. Murderers who were exploiting innocent girls. Those young women needed courageous, powerful champions to keep them safe. That is exactly what Millie would become.

She cleared her throat of any pesky emotions. 'A very thoughtful offer, Penny. Please do bring it to me this evening. Thank you.'

Penny looked up from her task and smiled at Millie in the mirror. Her hazel eyes sparkled in the late-afternoon sunlight streaming through a large window to Millie's left.

'I'm glad Major General Drake chose you to assist me, Penny. I think we shall get along famously.'

Penny ducked her head as a mahogany strand of hair escaped her cap. 'Thank you, miss.'

'These rooms really are quite splendid.' Millie spoke brightly, attempting to dispel the sudden awkwardness as she looked around at her new home. How odd to think she lived here now. Soon to be the wife of a man she barely knew. A contradictory, mysterious, confusing man.

Her bedroom was adorned in shades of lavender and sage. Windows looked onto the back of the property where manicured lawns dissolved into a wild, dark wood. The dressing room had three large windows, letting in plenty of light for the spacious closets. Her sitting room was appointed with a fireplace, delicately carved white furniture, and a writing desk complete with parchment, quills, ink, and sand. A huge, oak-carved bed with a million pillows and creamy white bed linens took centre place in Millie's bedroom. She could see the untamed forest from her bedside window.

Major General Drake might be a stranger, but he certainly went to some trouble ensuring a comfortable suite for her. It was more than she expected. More than she deserved after trapping him into a marriage neither of them wanted.

If only he wasn't so damnably honourable. Perhaps she could still convince him to break the engagement. She nodded her head. That was the best path forward. Surely, he could see the wisdom in such a course.

The gossips may have something to say about the major general begging off after ruining Millie, but his reputation would be less damaged than her own. She could happily bear the weight of society's censure if it granted her freedom. She was sure Drake would agree. Millie only needed to convince him.

'I believe I am ready for my meeting, Penny. If you wouldn't mind directing me to Major General Drake's study.'

Penny dipped in a quick curtsy. 'Of course, miss.'

6

Alder House was a maze of corridors. Despite Penny's clear directions, Millie found herself turned around three times before she finally stumbled upon a dark oak door. She could only hope it was the study as by now, she was at least five minutes late. The stern major general was sure to take a dim view of tardiness.

In her haste, she forgot to knock. Striding into the study, she stopped in her tracks. Drake stood facing the window, absently stroking his scar. He held a hand behind his back in a posture reeking of his time in the military.

Bollocking balderdash, the man is beautiful.

The word was all wrong. Far too feminine a term to describe his savage countenance, muscled limbs, thick chest, and shockingly well-formed buttocks. But beautiful is what she thought when she saw him.

He wasn't wearing his coat, and his breeches stretched across a physique, putting Greek gods to shame. Heat washed over Millie. She knew her cheeks would be flaming red thanks to her fair colouring.

The infuriating man chose that moment to turn around.

Brilliant. He's caught me staring at his bottom like some blushing, moon-eyed ninny.

He raised a broken eyebrow at her, his pale eyes missing nothing.

'Miss Millicent.' He took a moment to pull out a pocket watch and squint at the time. 'I wondered if you'd escaped back to London, attempting to jilt me before the wedding guests descend upon us.'

Millie tried for a casual laugh but instead broke into a fit of coughing. Ever so sophisticated. 'Capital plan, Major General Drake. We'll save everyone the trouble of a tedious house party. If I did run pell-mell to London, or the wilds of Scotland, or even further abroad, our doomed nuptials need never occur.'

He took three long steps, eating up the distance between them until he stood so close, his chest almost brushed against her. 'If you try to run, I will follow you, Millicent. And bring you back.' His voice was a deep growl vibrating in the marrow of her bones. A delicious shiver tickled down her spine. 'Hunters love the chase, you know.'

Damnation.

Clearing her throat, Millie willed her body to calm down. 'Lucky for you, I've always preferred to stand and fight instead of fleeing, my lord. I'm not quite as cowardly as you think.'

He leaned infinitesimally closer. Cloves and cheroots tickled Millie's nose as something warm and hungry unfurled in her belly. 'I would never accuse you of being a coward, Millicent. You are far too bold for that. Though it does give one cause to wonder.' For a moment, he lingered.

Her skin, unaccountably sensitive, shivered from the scrape of her corset against excruciatingly budded nipples. If she leaned forward, her lips would press against his.

Scandalous!

Before Millie could come up with a reply, he stepped away, breaking the spell.

'I had Mrs Holland bring us refreshments.'

Millicent racked her brain to recall who Mrs Holland might be. Ah, yes. A plump lady with grey curls and dimpled cheeks. The housekeeper.

'Sit. Eat.' He gestured to a low table that held a tea

tray complete with sandwiches and clever little cakes with orange icing.

Millie had only eaten broth and bread crusts for the last two weeks. Her stomach growled loudly. She slapped a hand against her belly, her blush flaring violently. 'I apologise, my lord. Please excuse me.' Patricia would have been mortified at Millie's lack of decorum.

'Sorry for what? You are hungry. I'd wager you haven't had a good meal in many days.' His voice softened, though his jaw clenched. 'Eat.'

Millie blinked at his rough order. She lowered her voice to mimic his. 'Sit. Eat. I'm not a dog to be commanded, sir.'

He clenched his jaw, the muscles contracting in a mesmerising display. 'Eat, *please*.' His granite voice could crush diamonds.

'I'm sure you are used to soldiers, Major General Drake, who responded well to a firm hand. You'll find women require a gentler approach.'

'I've never had any complaints about my firm hands.' His lips twitched, and something hot and wicked sparked in his eyes. Millie had no hope of forming an adequate response to that. Thankfully, he didn't wait for one. 'I am not a gentle man, Millicent. Something you'll need to accept. But neither am I needlessly cruel. You are hungry. I wish you to be fed. *Please*, sit and eat something before you collapse.'

It wasn't an apology, but he was right. She was famished. And the food looked delicious. She walked over to the table as he tracked her with his pale gaze.

He watched her like a dragon watched a virgin sacrifice. Though Millie was no virgin. A card she was willing to play if Major General Drake didn't agree to her plan. No man wanted a soiled dove, regardless of how honourable he might appear.

His intense gaze unsettled her. Millie would do well to remember the danger an astute man posed. Drake was a private investigator for the prime minister, after all. Lady Philippa had warned her against the intelligence of Prime Minister Russell's men. She couldn't let him guess at her activities with the duchess. Where the prime minister and his men believed in the House of Lords to exact justice, the Queen was less convinced. What would Drake think of his sovereign taking such a vigilante view of justice? Millie would never know because she would never tell him, but it was something to ponder.

Millie walked to a couch and sat carefully, making sure not to lean back against the cushions. Even with bandages, her back burned. Her training hadn't helped in the physical healing process, but she had continued with the demanding exercises because they eased her angry soul. Her training sessions were another secret Drake would never discover. For a woman prone to honesty, Millie would need to guard her thoughts and words carefully.

She poured a dish of tea and selected a sandwich. Fresh watercress, herbed cheese, crunchy cucumber, soft bread. Delicious. Millicent may have moaned.

Major General Drake's eyes dilated. Black pupils almost completely eclipsed his icy irises.

Fascinating.

He took a halting step closer to her.

'Tea, Major General?' Millicent curled her lip in a smile. A hot cup of strong tea. Endless sandwiches. What was sure to be scrumptious tea cakes. Her hopes were buoyed. Her resolve to disentangle herself from this mess reaffirmed. Major General Drake was a man of logic and reason. Millie was confident they would find a path forward.

'No, thank you.' He wrinkled his nose, his scar tissue pulling against healthy flesh.

'Ah. Not a fan of tea. Well noted. You wanted to discuss our situation, but I think perhaps I should start.'

Major General Drake raised a brow. He tugged his trousers up and sat next to her on the couch. His muscled thigh almost brushed against Millie's skirt. Shocking, even with their impending nuptials. She should move away from him. Instead, she arched slightly closer.

'By all means, Millicent.'

It was something about his voice when he spoke her name. Some kind of treacherous magic making her skin hum and her bones vibrate like cello strings. He was wreaking havoc with her ability to focus on anything other than the sensuous lines of his mouth. No man's bottom lip should be so full and luscious. He had pressed that firm flesh against her own mouth, licking her like a lollipop.

Liquid heat pooled between her thighs as she pressed her legs against a hollow ache. What the Devil was wrong with her? A side effect of being starved, perhaps.

She bought herself some time by taking another bite of her sandwich. Her tongue darted out to catch a crumb, and Major General Drake's gaze sharpened like a knife. He leaned ever closer.

She swallowed her bite, clearing her throat. 'I would like to revisit my completely reasonable solution to our problem.'

'Reasonable? Really?' Drake's dry tone was at odds with the dark heat sparking in his gaze.

'When I s-seduced you at my ball...' She hated the

stumble. Her nerves were jangled as his clove and leather scent invaded her mind like a poisonous cloud.

'Are you calling that clumsy attempt at a kiss seduction?' He reached out and brushed his thumb against her lip. 'Perhaps I should show you true seduction.'

Millie's chest froze. Her lungs seized.

'You had a crumb. Just there.' His smirk was self-satisfied at her sharp inhalation. He knew his effect on her, the bastard. Major General Drake was much older, much more experienced, and he was toying with her. While she was becoming a simpering fool, he seemed barely affected.

Pull up your pantaloons and get it together!

Millie straightened her shoulders, shifting away from him and choosing to ignore his last comment. For there was no acceptable response, though her body screamed at her to accept his unspoken invitation. 'I never expected you to offer for me, Major General Drake. Quite the opposite, in fact. I chose you because I knew your aversion to marriage. I had no intentions of trapping you.'

'And yet here I am. A fly caught in your web.'

She snorted. 'Please. I'm hardly a spider, my lord. If anyone is spinning webs, it's my stepmother.' Millicent couldn't stop the involuntary shudder. 'I was merely trying to escape the wedding she had planned. You were caught in her machinations. For that, I apologise. But I also believe the best way out is for you to cry off. That was always my goal. Just think how angry you can make Patricia. It's clear you don't like her. If you don't want to agree to this for my sake, do it to spite her.'

'I don't make decisions based on petty and useless emotions like anger or love.'

Millicent froze with the sandwich halfway to her lips. She'd hardly consider anger or love to be petty. Powerful? Yes. Inconvenient? Most certainly. But petty? Surely not.

Lord Drake's brow drew down in a frown that twisted his scar. 'You wanted to be ruined?'

Millie laughed. 'Such a ridiculous notion. Ruined. Because a woman's only value is her virtue, right, Major General?' Millie enjoyed watching his eyes widen and his mouth open as he attempted to find the correct response. She didn't wait for his fumbling reply. 'Yes. I wanted to be "ruined". It was a clear solution to my predicament. But then you came along with your stupidly honourable proposal and dashed my carefully laid plans to pieces.'

He leaned back, his lips pressing into a hard line.

'Stupidly honourable? That is a serious accusation to make, my lady.'

'It is a serious situation, my lord. Pledging yourself to another for all your earthly days, for what? Reputation? A silly notion at best. And in this case, it's a needless sacrifice on your part. I believe you are offering out of honour, but there is no dishonour in breaking an engagement with a woman determined to ruin herself and finally be free.'

'So, you wish to release me from my promise, paying the price of social suicide to gain personal freedom?'

Millie smiled brightly. She knew he would see reason. 'Exactly! While I appreciate your attempt to save me from my wicked ways, I have no wish for salvation. And by granting me freedom, you also liberate yourself.' There. Done. Disaster averted.

Drake leaned against the couch, his hand flew back to the scar, his forefinger tracing the jagged rip across his cheek. Icy eyes sparked with something she couldn't decipher. 'How magnanimous of you, Miss Millicent.'

'Thank you.' But the warm bubble of satisfaction burst as Major General Drake's lip curled into a cold smile.

Buggering blast.

He wasn't going to make this easy. She knew it.

'You asked me on the night of our engagement why I was offering for you, but we were interrupted before I could answer. I shall do so now. I'm marrying you not because I am an honourable man but rather because I am decidedly dishonourable.'

Millie frowned. 'I don't understand.'

'Allow me to explain. I don't care if you wish to be a single woman or one of ill repute. Your poorly planned escape from Viscount Tread created a situation that works to my benefit. I am in need of a wife. I was contemplating the arduous task of finding one when your fumbling attempt at seduction on the terrace solved my dilemma.'

Millie broke into laughter. 'Surely you jest, sir.'

'Rarely,' Drake replied, his gaze still lingering on her mouth. 'I'm going to ask you several questions, Millicent. I expect you to give me honest answers. Can you do that?'

Arrogant, pompous ass!

His tone begged for a blistering response. Millicent let the anger bloom. 'I can do many things, my lord. Most of them better than you, I'd wager.'

His lips twitched. 'I can only hope.' Like a coin being flipped, his countenance shifted. Any levity fled as his ice-blue eyes hardened. 'Do you find me abhorrent, Millicent?'

Millie huffed out a surprised breath. 'What kind of question is that?'

'The kind that needs an honest answer. Please.' His rough voice hitched.

'I find you...' Millie paused. He asked for honesty. She would give it to him. 'I find you fascinating.'

He froze, his gaze flicking back to her lips. 'Monsters can fascinate people.'

'So can mythical heroes. You are neither. Just a man. Yet still, I find you singularly captivating. That doesn't mean I wish to marry you.'

Drake grunted, his finger once again finding the scar on his cheek. 'My scars, they are far worse than what you see here.' He leaned closer, running his fingers over the slash dividing his face. It was a fearsome wound, but Millicent found it did nothing to detract from Drake's masculine appeal. 'Some women have found them to be... less than desirable.' He broke eye contact for a moment, and Millicent was staggered.

Dear God. He's insecure. This powerful, dangerous, mysterious man is uncertain.

'Some women have the intelligence of wet dough, Major General Drake. I am not one of those women.' It became of paramount importance for Millie to make him understand that she was not rejecting him. Having suffered such injurious behaviour herself at the hands of St George, she would never wish to inflict such wounds upon another person, even one as insufferable as Major General Drake. She was rejecting an asinine offer brought forth by some ridiculously misguided sense of honour. 'Releasing you from this engagement has nothing to do with your appeal and everything to do with my own desire to be free.'

He picked up her hand, placing it against his ruined cheek. The vulnerability in his gaze almost broke her. 'I'll know if you're lying.'

Millie leaned closer. The scent of leather and cloves wrapped around her like a blanket. She was no stranger to desire, but the overwhelming tenderness coalescing with her need was unexpected and alarming. She shivered at the sensation of his warm skin beneath her hand. His stubble scraped over her sensitive fingers, contrasting the smooth scar tissue. Acting on instinct, she turned his head and pressed a kiss to his temple where the injury began. The room was so quiet. Their breaths created the only sound. Slowly, she moved along the scar, marvelling at how it changed beneath her lips, smooth in spots, rigid in others. She followed its course, pressing kisses to his eyebrow, the bridge of his nose, and finally, his cheek.

'We all carry scars, my lord. Yours do nothing to diminish your desirability. Am I lying?' she whispered in his ear.

Drake moved faster than she could countenance. One moment, she was leaning toward him, pressing chaste kisses over his scar. The next, she was lying on the couch, two hundred pounds of hot, hard, hungry man hovering over her. Her back screamed in protest, but she ignored it with brutal focus.

'You are playing with fire, madame,' Drake growled.

Millie thrust her chin up, refusing to back down from the challenge he presented. 'I am not scared of you, Major General Drake.'

'I wish I could say the same.' He spoke the words like a curse, then fell upon her like a savage.

This was no mere kiss. This was an assault on her senses. His firm mouth crushed against hers, his tongue tracing the seam of her lips, demanding entrance. She should pull back, push him away, demand distance. But Millie was never good at doing what she should. Instead, she opened her mouth, granting him access. He stroked and teased until she mimicked his movements, testing the texture of his lips, teeth, and tongue. He nibbled along her jaw, nipping and sucking. She writhed beneath him, needing more. When his fingers tickled along the neckline of her modest day dress, she longed to be free of the constricting material.

Dear God. It's glorious.

Her hurried coupling with St George was nothing compared to this incendiary exploration. She had no intention of marrying the man, but would it be so unforgivably wicked to explore this attraction?

Wicked or not, I don't care. I want him.

Major General Drake was savouring her like some succulent treat, and she needed more. He palmed her breast, squeezing hard enough to flirt with sharp, delicious pleasure.

She moaned as he licked her neck, sucking her skin into his mouth for the most sinfully decadent taste.

A thick thigh pressed between her legs, simultaneously easing and increasing the hollow need growing there.

'Do you burn as hot as I do, Millicent? Do you ache for me here?' His thigh pressed harder. 'Remember, no lying.'

'I never lie... and yes, damn you.' Millie hated being caught on her heels, but in this game of seduction, Drake was far more prepared than she.

Infuriating man.

'I told you I would show you true seduction, and I am a man of my word.' Drake kissed her again, plunging into her depths. His thigh tensed harder than granite against her core. Millie tipped up her hips, demanding rough friction. A small spark of intense pleasure came to life, and she wanted to fan the flame until it consumed them both.

* * *

Drake was in dire trouble. He had lost control of this meeting. And he never lost control. He needed to stop this madness. Immediately. Before he let the burning lust incinerate him.

Yes, definitely. In a moment.

He could kiss Millicent for the rest of his days and die happy. Her mouth was a treasure trove of pleasure. Drake nipped her bottom lip, then sucked it into his mouth as he massaged her breast cursing the yards of material hiding her from him.

Christ!

The woman was built like a siren. Luscious curves all tempting him into her depths to lose his soul forever in the swirling sea of desire. And he would dive into those dark waters without a moment's hesitation.

He had never felt so consumed before, not even with Nora.

Nora.

The thought of his duplicitous ex-fiancée hit as hard as a slap, bringing him back to his senses. He pulled back, watching the haze of lust slowly dissolve from Millicent's dark gaze only to be replaced by confusion. She frowned, a crease forming between her brows. Ridiculously adorable.

Drake found nothing adorable.

'What... why did you... did I do something wrong?' Her husky voice inflamed him.

Drake sat back, taking deep breaths. He stood and turned away so she wouldn't see his raging cockstand.

This was total insanity. Her soft, sweet lips pressing against his scar had broken something loose within him that he wasn't sure he could put back. He valued control above all else, but she was decimating him one kiss at a time. Millicent wanted to release him from his proposal. He should agree to her plan and thank her for saving him from himself.

Nora almost destroyed him, and never did she stoke within him the kind of fire this woman sparked with just a few kisses. Millicent Whittenburg was far more dangerous to his sanity than she knew. He took a deep breath, preparing to accept her offer of freedom.

He could find a different wife. A biddable creature who wouldn't stoke his lust. But those words never emerged.

'This whole situation is wrong. But I am a man of my word, Millicent Whittenburg. I made a promise. I will not break it. We will be married. There is no escape for either of us. You should never have chosen me. You have damned us both.' He was blaming her for his own choice. He knew it. But the need to keep her warred with his desire to maintain control. Blaming her for his weaknesses seemed the best option to grant him absolution for his decisions.

'Stubborn man! Will you persist in this marriage even if I'm not a virgin?' Her words ripped out of her. Drake wagered they cost her more than she thought in a bid to force his hand.

He slowly turned to face his fiancée. Millicent's eyes widened, and her mouth opened in a perfect 'O' at the obvious tenting of his breeches.

Ah, so. Not a virgin, yet still she blushes at the sight of a swollen cock. Interesting.

Drake found he did not care if she was intact or not, though the thought of another man touching her inspired a violent fantasy involving his fist and a yet-to-be-known bastard's face. 'As you so eloquently mentioned, Millicent, some people have the intelligence of wet dough. Thankfully – much like you – I am also not one of them. I find a woman's virtue, and more importantly, her value, has nothing to do with her virginity. It might shock you to know I too am not a virgin, yet my virtue is pristine.'

He allowed himself a small smile as Millicent struggled to stand. Her breath came in heavy gasps. It did wondrous things to the modest neckline of her gown.

'You insufferable, obstinate, arrogant—'

'Careful, dear. Remember, you're speaking of your future husband.'

Instead of replying, she spun on her heel and stormed out of his study. Drake almost laughed out loud when she turned in the wrong direction, only to spin around and march the other way.

Their meeting had not gone to plan, but he hadn't enjoyed himself so much in forever. How alarming.

7

Most of the wedding guests were scheduled to arrive on the morrow. However, Lady Philippa Winterbourne insisted on coming a day early. One did not argue with the Duchess of Dorsett, and for that, Millie was grateful. She would have to wait for Ivy's company, but she welcomed any friendly face, even if that face held the stern expression of a displeased despot.

Millie was meant to be dressing for dinner when Lady Philippa sailed into her room, midnight-blue silk skirts billowing around her like a wave.

'You look positively gaunt. And why are you holding yourself so stiffly? You are injured. What happened? Did you hurt yourself while training?'

Millie was only in her chemise. She quickly turned

to face Philippa, so her mentor couldn't see the bandages. As much as she wanted Philippa's empathy, she wasn't sure unleashing the full force of the duchess' ire on Patricia would be wise. 'I am quite well, Your Grace. Perhaps a trifle tired.'

Philippa walked up to her, ignoring Penny, who stepped hastily back. She grasped Millie's chin in surprisingly gentle fingers and turned her head one way, then the other. Tsking like an enraged hen, she swept her gaze from Millie's feet up to the artfully piled curls on top of her head.

'What has Patricia done?'

Of course, Philippa would guess the truth immediately. Millie bit her trembling lip as tears threatened. 'It's nothing. Really. It didn't even interfere with my training. Or at least, not much.' She would not fall apart in front of her mentor. Philippa would think her a weak fool.

'Turn around so I can assess the damage. If I had known your stepmother was going to hurt you, I would have insisted you cease your training until you were healed. Let me see what she's done.'

Millie realised the futility of resistance. If Philippa wanted to see her back, she would see her back. She dutifully turned around, thankful the worst of her lashes were hidden beneath bandages.

'Malicious little bitch.' Phillipa hissed. 'How dare she whip you like a dog!'

Millie cleared the waver from her voice, refusing to be weak. 'It's not so bad. It will heal. And I was able to train through it. I actually think it was good for me to focus through the pain.'

'Some of these gashes should have been stitched, Millicent. She didn't call for a doctor?'

'She didn't allow anyone to touch me. The second session caused the worst of it, I think.' Millie bit her cheek with ruthless determination. They were just wounds. They would heal. There was no need for messy emotions.

Phillipa's harsh inhale was a strange benediction. To know someone shared her outrage at such injustice was like cool water on her burning skin.

'I have a salve, Your Grace. It will help with the healing. Minimise the scars, I hope.' Penny spoke quietly, her hand clasped in front of a snowy white apron.

Philippa turned to stare at the maid. 'What is your name?'

'Penny, Your Grace.'

Millie had to hand it to her maid. She was a courageous woman to speak so calmly to the duchess.

'Get me that salve, Penny. Now.'

Penny rushed out of Millie's bedroom, returning

quickly with a small pot in her hand. Philippa took the offered pot, removed the lid, and sniffed. 'Camphor and linseed?' She raised a dark-black brow at the maid. Though Millie never asked Philippa's age, her dramatic colouring, smooth skin, and lustrous hair made it impossible to guess if she was in her third, fourth, or even fifth decade. One thing was certain; she was stunning. And bloody intimidating. But Penny stood her ground.

'That and some honey and lard. A few other odds and ends my mother's never shared with me. It works, Your Grace. I swear it.'

Philippa narrowed her gaze. 'Hmm. I'm inclined to believe you. And can you keep secrets as well as you heal wounds?'

Penny nodded. 'I'm loyal to my mistress, Your Grace. Maids with wagging tongues rarely have steady incomes. In my experience.'

'Hmm. Well, in *my* experience, words are cheap. Actions show the true character of a person. You will hear many things that cannot be shared. With anyone. Starting right now, Penny. Can you manage that?'

'I've seen and heard a great many secrets, Your Grace. I know how to bury one so deep, it becomes lost forever.' Penny's hands shook a bit before she clasped them tightly together.

'Interesting turn of phrase.' Philippa tapped her crimson-stained lips with a finger before turning to Millie. 'Keep this one around, Millicent.' She handed the pot back to Penny. 'You'll apply that tonight and every night until the wounds heal.'

'Yes, Your Grace.' Penny ducked her head.

Philippa was usually right about most things. Millie guessed her assessment of Penny was bang on.

'Right. Now that's sorted, we should discuss my meeting with the Queen.' Philippa ignored Penny's gasp, but her gaze did pause on the maid long enough for Penny to turn and find a flannel cloth that needed folding. Philippa's attention returned to Millie. 'But if you need a moment, I understand. Tears are not a weakness, Millicent. Sometimes, they are the only way we have of releasing emotion.'

Millie's throat ached. She swallowed hard. 'No. I am well. Please, continue.' If she let herself cry now, she wasn't sure she would stop.

Philippa didn't speak right away. She watched Millie with her keen eyes missing nothing until finally she nodded. 'As you like. The Queen had some important information to share.'

Millie lifted her arms so Penny could pull the corset over her head and position it around her waist.

'I'll be careful, miss,' Penny murmured as she carefully tightened the torture device, mindful of Millie's wounds. Millie had to give the girl credit. She had recovered quickly from realising the duchess was a confidante of Queen Victoria.

Millie wheezed out a breath. 'Pray tell, what did she say?'

Philippa's sharp gaze speared Millie. 'It would appear our little wedding party will be host to several likely candidates in our investigation. Our prime suspect, and the man we are tasked to focus on, is Lord Franklin St George. A baron, I believe, and someone you are acquainted with, which is immensely helpful.'

Millie's shoulders tightened, but she forced her face to remain impassive. 'I've known him since childhood, Your Grace. But I doubt he'll want to speak with me. We have a... history. Not a pleasant one.'

Philippa rolled her eyes. 'Must I remind you again to desist with the "Your Grace" nonsense? Your name is Millicent. Mine is Philippa. Hers is Penny. Let's not be silly.'

Millie shook her head, her anxiety dissipating in the light of her mentor's obvious disgust with titles. It didn't escape her that Philippa's dim view of social hierarchy was an opinion only the highest of the beau monde could afford to espouse. 'Of course, Philippa. But my statement still stands. If our focus is Lord

Franklin St George, I doubt I will be of much help to you. The man despises me.'

Philippa laughed; a rich melody filling the room. 'There is a thin line between love and hate, Millicent. Don't forget. I was a guest of Lord Bradford's at Everly Manor as well. I saw the way St George stared at you during our fortnight of revelry. He despises you because he cannot have you.'

Millie snorted. 'He already had me, Philippa.' Her gaze flicked over to Penny, but the maid was busy shaking out the folds of Millie's evening gown. A copper silk confection that almost perfectly matched her hair. The neckline would not be so scandalous on another woman, but with Millie's generous curves, she would be lucky to keep her girls contained for the evening. Thinking back to her moment on the couch with Lord Drake, his hand caressing her breast, his mouth claiming her own, she felt suddenly overwarm. With an iron will, she pulled her thoughts back to the conversation. 'Once Franklin plucked my bloom – as it were – his interest dissolved. He longed for a sweeter blossom. One with significantly more to offer in her dowry than myself.'

Philippa nodded. 'Exactly. He abandoned you for a richer prize, but according to the Queen, that well has run dry due in no small part to St George's penchant for gambling badly. Apparently, he has markers all over London. And then there are his mistresses. Three, to my counting. You are the one who got away, Millicent. And while he may have momentarily had your body, he never had you. Let's be clear on that.'

She was right. Millie was infatuated with Franklin as a child, but it was the obsession of a silly girl. He never claimed her heart. Not really. And he never would. She hadn't realised it until Philippa made her point.

'You are very insightful, Philippa. It's highly annoying.'

'I know. But back to the mission. Franklin St George is desperate for blunt, but I also think he needs to prove his appeal. Specifically, by reclaiming the one girl he can't have. You.'

Millie felt a hard ball of dread form in her belly. 'I'm soon to be married, Philippa. I can't possibly spend the week leading up to my wedding seducing another man.'

Philippa moved out of Penny's way as the maid brought the dress to Millie. 'You are soon to be married to a man you have no affection for. A man who holds no flame for you. What harm can come from innocent flirtation? It isn't as though you are actually going to engage in an affair with St George.'

The thought was horrifying. Though she had once believed St George to be the most desirable man she'd ever known, the idea of pressing her lips against Franklin's now made Millie want to gag in revulsion.

Instead, she imagined much firmer lips in a face divided by a ragged scar. She felt the rush of warmth between her thighs.

Absolutely not. The last thing I need to do is dissolve into lust over my ridiculous, pompous ass of a fiancé.

Thinking about what a fool she'd been with Franklin reminded Millie how lust could lead her down a path she had no wish to tread. While she might want to engage in her desire for the major general, the danger of giving herself to him – as she had almost done in the study like a completely besotted fool – would grant him a power he could wield over her without mercy. It was impossible. She had come far too close, but she would redouble her efforts at resisting him and focus her time and attention on what really mattered. Her mission for the Queen. If anything could douse wicked desires, certainly it should be thoughts of Queen Victoria's displeasure at a failed mission.

Millie swallowed before lifting her arms and allowing Penny to pull the dress over her head. The maid settled it around her hips and began the arduous task of fastening a million tiny buttons.

'Or am I mistaken?' The mischievous glint in Philippa's cobalt gaze made Millie pause.

Did the duchess guess at Millie's growing fascination with Major General Drake? Surely not. Though Philippa *had* just proven her skills at reading people. It really was infuriating.

Millie tried to keep her face impassive. 'I'm merely suggesting I try to preserve my decimated reputation by not acting like a trollop. The beau monde already thinks me wanton. Do I now become an unfaithful wife before our vows are even uttered?'

Why was she fighting this? Pretending to have some kind of affection for St George might be the perfect way to get Drake to beg off. She didn't imagine he would tolerate infidelity. But her whole body shuddered in revulsion at the thought. She couldn't. Not with Franklin.

'For a woman with no interest in her future husband, you certainly seem intent on sticking to your vows... Vows you've yet to say, might I add.'

Millie rolled her eyes. 'I don't believe St George has any interest in me, but if he does, I have no wish to throw myself at a man who rejected me the moment I spread my thighs.'

Penny made a strangled sound deep in her throat.

'Sorry, Penny. I am honest to a fault, and St George is a disgusting, despicable, reprehensible bounder. In fact, you should be very careful to avoid finding yourself alone with him. He is not safe, do you understand?'

Penny nodded. 'Yes, miss.'

'Which is exactly why you must entice him to spill his secrets, Millicent. And then we'll deliver justice. I swear it.' Philippa nodded her head. 'If you can think of a better way to get him to talk, then I'm all for it. But there are times we must do terrible things, Millicent. This is the price we pay to hold evildoers accountable for their crimes. Are you up to the task?'

Millie straightened her shoulders as Penny fastened the last few buttons. 'I will not fail you, Philippa. But neither will I become someone I cannot respect.'

Philippa tapped her fingers against her hip. 'Fine. Hannah refused to listen to me as well. I must be cursed to only train disobedient, stubborn women.'

'Women who are just like you,' Millie countered.

Philippa's lips curled at the corners. It wasn't exactly a smile, but Millie counted it as a win. 'Are you ready? Shall we descend for dinner? I can't wait to engage in a stimulating conversation with your stepmother.'

'As much as I would love to see that, I don't think it's worth the effort, Philippa.' The last thing she needed was for Philippa to instigate a war with Patricia. Her stepmother's threat loomed heavy over Millie's head. If Philippa upset Patricia, she knew the horrible woman would make good on spilling her secrets to *The Star*. It was a risk Millie couldn't take and the only reason she'd submitted to Patricia's horrific behaviour. 'Nothing you say will change Patricia. She is a monster who is best left alone.'

'We'll see, Millicent. You've done a wonderful job, Penny. Please extend my compliments to your mother on her salve.' Philippa swept around and walked out the door before either Millie or Penny could respond.

Millie glanced at Penny and shrugged. 'You've won yourself the favour of the Duchess of Dorsett, Penny. No easy feat.'

Penny looked a little flummoxed. 'You better hurry, miss. You wouldn't want to make her wait.'

Millie nodded, gave her new maid a smile, then turned and hurried after Philippa for what was sure to be a disastrous dinner.

* * *

Dinner was a complete disaster. Drake spent the evening torn between wanting to ravish Millicent, strangle Patricia, and uncover whatever secrets Lady Philippa Winterbourne was hiding in her wickedly sharp brain.

Lieutenant General Killian had told Drake his suspicions about Hannah being involved in investigating crimes months ago. It was an idea Drake believed to be preposterous. But then the woman had gone and killed Lord Cavendale with all the skill and confidence of a trained soldier. Drake believed Hannah's protector, Lady Philippa, had something to do with it.

And now the duchess has taken Millicent under her wing.

But it defied reason to think his fiancée might be a part of such violent work. She was a gently bred lady, after all. Yet, it would answer a number of questions building about her confidence, courage, and physical skills.

A lady who rides like the Devil, is bold enough to challenge me, and has the physique of an avenging Valkyrie could very well be capable of a great many things. She bloody-well said as much in my study.

But that only lead him to recall what other things occurred between them in his study. Sinfully delicious things. With so many disturbing thoughts swirling in his mind, it left very little time to appreciate the succulent venison, crisp roasted potatoes, sweet peas, and pheasant pie. Some of his favourites.

Millicent's appetite didn't seem bothered by their meeting. She filled her plate as each course was served. When Patricia sent her stepdaughter a scathing look, pointing at Millicent's plate with her knife, Drake almost launched himself across the table and brained the woman with a gravy boat. But he refrained. Because he was a gentleman, damn it. And the gravy boat would be ruined. A terrible waste.

'You haven't touched your meal, Drake. I recall you always having a robust appetite when we were marching through Afghanistan.' Reynard's twinkling gaze didn't miss much. It was one of the reasons he was such an asset to the prime minister's small band of private investigators. And such a pain in the arse as a friend.

'Too much rich food makes a man fat and lazy, Reynard. You might want to follow my example.' Drake cut a slice of venison and dutifully chewed without tasting the well-seasoned meat.

'I can't help but notice how lovely your betrothed looks tonight.' Reynard glanced down the table at Millicent, ignoring the growl Drake was unable to suppress. 'Are you sure this is to be a marriage of convenience?'

Drake knew what Reynard was asking. Was Millicent available for an interested and discreet suitor?

'It is going to be a marriage where my wife does *not* have an affair with one of my closest friends.'

Reynard raised a thick eyebrow. 'Ah. I see. I thought you had sworn off all women.'

'I have. But even if I don't intend to fall for Millicent's charms, I have no wish to be cuckolded. Especially not by you. Perhaps we should focus more on our investigation and less on my wife-to-be, Reynard. I'd hate to test your aim in a duel.'

Reynard chuckled. 'Stand down, old man. I'm not about to poach a friend's wife. Not without permission.'

'You do *not* have mine.' Drake grabbed a crystal goblet of wine, gulping a swallow and wishing for whiskey.

'I see that. Consider the matter closed.'

'Good.' But Drake hated the possession bubbling under his skin. How had this woman gotten into his blood and made it boil? He was becoming obsessed. It was totally unacceptable. And it would stop. Immediately.

When Drake returned from the war to the news his

fiancée – thinking him dead or close to it – had married his brother, he was devastated. When he realised his brother also hoped Drake had met a bloody end in the desert, he was enraged. Drake was seven years older than his brother. They had never been close, but he didn't imagine his own flesh and blood would long for his untimely demise so the snivelling bastard could inherit.

Like a naïve idiot, Drake thought Nora loved him. When she sent him off to the war, tears streaming down her face, a letter claiming she would wait for his return forever pressed carefully against Drake's heart, he knew he was the luckiest man alive. For the next two years, anything soft in him was burned away except his love for Nora. He committed sins earning him a seat next to the Devil in hell, endured torture cruel enough to break most of their men, and saw his faith in humanity slowly die one innocent victim at a time.

In the Anglo-Afghan war, there were no heroes, only once honourable men drowning in a sea of corruption. Nora was Drake's only hope of innocence, love, loyalty. Her promise to wait for him kept Drake sane in the stinking hole their battalion was forced to share when the Afghan soldiers took them prisoner. During the worst of his torture, he closed his eyes and remembered Nora's lilting voice, her scent of sweet peonies, her soft fingers on his arm, and her warm lips pressed against his own.

But he had been wrong. Nora didn't love him. She loved his title. One brother was just as good as the other to Nora as long as that man held the wealth and power of the Earl of Tetly.

Enraged and intent on confronting her, Drake arrived on his own front doorstep – as his brother had taken over the London townhouse – and demanded an explanation for Nora's actions. When she first saw his ruined face, she nearly fainted. Nora grabbed his brother's arm and hid behind him as if Drake were some kind of hideous monster.

'I don't care about the title. I would never marry a beast like you. No woman would. You'll never produce an heir. We'll inherit everything one day. I'm happy to wait.' She fairly hissed the words at him as if he were the one to blame. As if he were the guilty party in this.

He threw them out of his house that night, though his brother begged him to act like a gentleman and show some mercy. It was only the presence of his commanding officer and best friend, Lieutenant General Killian, who stopped him from committing fratricide on that horrific day.

He swore to never again trust a woman, to never allow his heart to be swayed by a pretty face, and to avoid the treacherous fairer sex at all costs. He also developed a rather dim view of younger brothers.

Jealousy consumed him for months. Food tasted like sand. The sun held no warmth. Life was just something he suffered through a day at a time until the relief of death. He lived in complete darkness. But slowly, with the help of Killian and the missions assigned to him by the prime minister, he found purpose again. His life was muted, lacking the bright colours of his past, but it was also fulfilling to a degree. And quiet. Controlled. Living in the shadows provided him with the peace of solitude. He learned well from his disastrous mistake. Never trifle with the plague of love if one wished to survive.

But now, Millicent threatened his carefully constructed calm. She shone like a beacon in the darkness, and he was terrified to walk into her light. What might be illuminated?

Focusing on the mission and ignoring the charming, stunning, funny, intelligent woman at the end of the table was his only way forward.

Still, something stirred within him. Forgotten desire. An echo of love's glory. A memory of its warmth.

Since when did I let fancy run free, polluting cold, clear reason?

Since meeting Millicent Whittenburg.

They must have a distant marriage. It was the only way he could maintain his sanity. But did that mean he couldn't indulge in his lust before sending her away? His imagination spun at the idea of stripping Millicent naked and licking every one of her freckles. Gorging on her cream and cinnamon skin.

'Franklin St George will be arriving tomorrow with his wife.' Reynard's words destroyed Drake's erotic fantasy, pulling him back to the present.

Drake forced his mind to focus on the mission. 'Yes. We need to watch him carefully. The prime minister believes St George might be working in league with his uncle.'

'Really? The Earl of Scarborough might be involved? He and Lord Chancellor Hargrave are old cronies, are they not? That could be quite the scandal.' Reynard took a healthy portion of pheasant pie and cut into the flaky pastry.

'That is why we are on this job and not Scotland Yard. Who knows how far up the chain this treachery reaches?' Drake speared an unsuspecting pea, imagining it was a very small version of St George's head.

'Generally, I hate wedding ceremonies, and wedding parties are even worse, but I'd put money on yours beating all others, Drake. You should be proud of yourself for turning a celebration of nuptials into the investigation of our careers.' Reynard waggled his eyebrows and smiled around the food in his mouth. Annoyingly, the expression was charming on him when any other person would look disgusting.

'Quite.' Drake raised an eyebrow at Reynard.

He should be excited about the opportunity to determine who was orchestrating this sex-trade ring. Instead, he found his mind – and gaze – wandering to Millicent.

She looked up from her plate and caught him staring. Slowly, she lifted her spoon to her mouth, licking gravy from the silver cutlery like a cat lapping at milk. Or a courtesan licking... something else. Drake's skin tightened as blood rushed to his cock.

Damnation!

She could have easily slid her gaze over to Reynard – as most women would – but instead, she remained locked onto him.

How was he supposed to keep her at arm's length when all he wanted to do was grab her hand, haul her up to his room, and barricade the door against anyone trying to interrupt them? She would be the death of him. And for once, he wasn't opposed.

* * *

The next four days of wedding celebrations would be the death of Millie. She was exhausted. Making her excuses after their meal, she claimed a megrim to avoid the dreaded after-dinner gathering and escaped to her rooms.

While Millie enjoyed socialising, a smaller group – especially their particular combination of guests – could be far more challenging to navigate than a large crush. She hoped Philippa didn't kill her stepmother over sherry. A distinct possibility given the daggers Philippa was throwing Patricia's way during dinner. More importantly, she hoped Patricia held her sharp tongue. She was far more likely to draw blood with it than Philippa might with her myriad of hidden weapons.

Millie called for Penny to come and help her prepare for bed when she first reached her room, but the maid had yet to arrive. She wandered around her bedchambers, her fingers trailing along the papered walls, over the smooth wood of her writing desk, along a dustless windowsill. She hated to admit it, but Major General Drake's country estate was perfectly suited to Millie. The colours of her rooms, the Gothic darkness of the stone edifice, the understated elegance of Drake's furnishings. If she had been given carte blanche to redecorate, she wouldn't change a thing. It was oddly frustrating that a man so horribly matched to her had the perfect house.

She let her fingers slide over the oak door connecting her room with his. It was disconcerting to be so close to Drake's sleeping quarters. With a twist of her wrist and push of her hand, she would be in his bedroom.

I should waltz in there and give the man a heart attack.

The last thing Drake would expect was a brazen invitation from Millie.

He'd probably slam the door in my face and lock it against me.

Which was best. Engaging in her ever-growing desires for Drake would hardly encourage a distant marriage. Millie purposefully turned her back on the dratted door. She toed off her slippers and walked to the fireplace, letting the cheerful flames warm her.

The sound of her door opening and shutting alerted her to Penny's arrival. 'I hope you brought your salve, Penny. I want nothing more than to rid myself of this dress and go to sleep.'

'What a splendid plan.' The rough growl most decidedly did *not* belong to Penny.

Millie spun around to see Major General Drake still in his dinner jacket. He leaned against the door leading to the hall. All the moisture in her mouth dried in an instant, along with every logical thought in her brain.

Bloody hell.

'For a gently bred lady, you certainly have a filthy mouth, Millicent.'

Millie felt her cheeks heat. 'Oh dear. Did I say that out loud?'

'You did.'

It was then she noticed the small pot in his hands. Penny's salve.

'What are you doing here? With that.' She nodded to his hands.

'Penny refused to tell me what ailed you. A loyal creature, that woman. Still, with my masterful skills at discerning truth from lies, I was able to deduce your injured state.'

Millie was at a loss. 'Truly?' A stupid response, but it was all she could think to say.

Drake shrugged, his powerful shoulders shifting under the fine material of his jacket. 'Also, she accidentally dropped the salve when I intercepted her in the hall. I gave her the night off despite her protests. Her willingness to defy orders reminded me quite a bit of you, Millicent.'

Millie's cheeks heated at the insult that felt remarkably closer to a compliment.

'I'm to act as your lady's maid tonight.'

8

Alarm coursed through Millie's body like an electric current. She felt the tingle of anticipation tighten her skin as her stomach clenched and the tips of her breasts budded.

Incredibly inconvenient time to develop such sensitive nipples.

'You can't be serious. This is completely untoward. You cannot mean to—'

'I mean to do many things with you, Millicent. But don't fret. I promise not to consummate our marriage until we are actually married.' He bit his bottom lip and Millie almost melted into a puddle on the rug.

She stepped back, mindful of the fire crackling behind her. The last thing she needed to do was catch her skirt on fire. 'C-consummate the marriage? But surely there is no need.'

Drake stepped closer, his icy gaze burning with a blue flame. 'I admit I thought that too, but then we had that most enlightening discussion in my study and I reconsidered.'

'You reconsidered?' She felt like a rather dull-witted parrot repeating his words.

'Yes. I reconsidered. Do you feel it? The tension pulling between us? The delicious heat?'

In lieu of a response, Millie attempted to breathe normally.

Drake continued, seemingly unconcerned with her difficulties aspirating. 'It occurred to me at dinner the best way to rid oneself of a craving is to indulge in the temptation. Haven't you ever gorged on cake until the very sight of frosting makes you ill?'

The air had certainly thinned since Major General Drake began speaking. Perhaps he was using it all up with his wild suggestions. Just the thought of him gorging on her was the most erotic thing Millie had ever heard. Her earlier determination to deny her lust for him fled right along with her wits.

Sweet baby Beelzebub!

An ache pulsed between her legs as something

warm and liquid melted in her core. 'I don't think people are supposed to gorge on... sexual relations.'

Drake smiled. In the flickering firelight, he was breathtaking. 'Obviously, your experiences did not adequately educate you on the addictive quality of sex. I'd wager you had a sub-par teacher. Trust me, that is not the case now.'

'But you don't even like me.' Millie was sure of it. She had trapped the man into marriage. He couldn't possibly hold any affection for her.

'Sometimes hating someone makes the whole thing that much more incendiary.'

Uhhfff. He hates me.

That hurt more than it should.

She didn't care about Major General Drake, Millie reminded herself. It didn't matter if he hated her or not. In fact, it was better this way.

Maybe she hated him. What about that? He was the one being obstinate and stubborn. This whole mess could be cleared up if he would just break the damn engagement instead of trying to seduce his hated fiancée. The nerve!

Millie narrowed her gaze, letting her anger lend her courage. 'You hate me for trapping you in this marriage. But you could still break the engagement, Drake.'

'Beaufort.'

Millie took a breath. 'Pardon?'

'My name is Beaufort. Beau, if you prefer.'

'Oh, I. Well. Yes. Of course.' She blinked, trying to gather her thoughts. Major General Drake's first name was Beau? It seemed far too friendly a name for the hardened soldier standing in the middle of her room, holding a pot of salve and talking about gorging himself on her to rid his cravings.

Madness!

'That doesn't alter my point, Major... err, Beau.'

His lips softened, and he took another step closer. 'I am not going to break this engagement, Millicent. Cease asking me. You set this into motion the moment you coerced me into joining you on the veranda. And I don't hate you. You must know someone well to hate them. I hardly know you at all. But don't be distressed. I'm sure as we become closer acquainted, our hate will grow, naturally.' His sarcasm was not funny. Millie pressed her lips together to keep them from twitching. 'Now, turn around so I can unbutton your gown.'

Millie sidestepped the fireplace and moved back, increasing the distance between them. 'Absolutely not. If you already sent Penny to bed, surely there is another maid who can help me. Or I shall call for Lady Philippa. I'm sure she wouldn't mind.'

Drake raised a brow. 'You would call the Duchess of Dorsett to your room to assist you in undressing? You are a courageous woman, Millicent. But we have no need to resort to such drastic tactics. I am here.' With each word, he drew closer. Millie found herself backed against a large wardrobe. 'Turn around. I won't hurt you. I promise.'

He was lying, even if he didn't know it. There was no chance his kindness wouldn't hurt her in the end. A cruel, cold, heartless man she could resist. But this honourable, kind, caring version of Major General Drake was impossible to keep at a distance.

But keep him at a distance, I must.

Millie's options were limited. Philippa had taught her some hand-to-hand combat, but she doubted she would be very successful against a trained soldier like Major General Drake. While she was taller than most men and strong enough to hold her own when sparring with Philippa, Drake towered over her, his movements lithe and graceful. The damnable man almost made her feel delicate: a novel experience.

What I need are my knives.

But she had carefully removed them and tucked the deadly leather package under her mattress. Penny might keep her secrets, but there was no need to alarm her maid with Millie's more lethal talents. Even if they were still strapped to her wrists and thighs, she could hardly launch a knife at her betrothed in the middle of her bedroom. Questions would be asked if her fiancé was found dead in her room with multiple blades protruding from his delicious body.

She had only one option available. Follow his orders. For now.

But you will not weasel your way into my heart, Beaufort Drake, no matter how hard you try. I will not sacrifice my freedom on the altar of desire.

He might not hate her yet, but she was quickly growing to despise the damned earl.

* * *

Drake despised the effect Millicent had on him. But still, he desired to increase the burning need sparking in his spine and spinning over the rest of his body. His ever-optimistic cock hardened in anticipation.

He shouldn't be doing this for several reasons.

One: he was seriously questioning his self-control around Millicent.

Two: he'd promised not to consummate the marriage until after they spoke their vows.

Three: he was seriously questioning his self-control around Millicent.

Fucking hell! I already said that. But it bears repeating. She is my every fantasy and nightmare combined.

He was half jesting when he spoke of glutting himself on her, but the idea might hold merit. Maybe he only needed to indulge in his fantasies to realise the reality wasn't nearly as enticing as the idea. But to do that, he would need to keep his raging cock under control. And as he listed... twice... his legendary control was questionable at best when Millicent entered a room.

His single-minded focus on the infuriating woman was becoming a serious problem.

After Nora left him, he lost interest in sexual conquests. For years, he worried that she had broken something in him. Then he saw Millicent playing cards at Lord Bradford's dinner party while on an investigation with Lieutenant General Killian all those months ago, and his body came back to life. He thought it was a fluke and even tried to engage a professional courtesan to slake his suddenly ravenous thirst.

She was a delicate thing: blonde, reminiscent of Nora. But he couldn't drum up a hint of interest from his damnable cock. He tried again with a different woman. This one was tall with hair almost as vibrant as Millicent's, though likely achieved through henna or some other means. Still, she had a sweet smile. Apparently, his penis didn't care about the woman's smile. Zero reaction. It was maddening. And more than a little embarrassing. There was only one possible conclusion. Millicent was using some kind of witchcraft on him.

Or maybe I like her.

Absolutely not. Drake didn't like people. Especially not women. Dark magic was the only reasonable explanation.

When he ran into Penny in the hall and she dropped the salve, a red haze of rage had descended. There was only one reason she would be taking such medicine to her mistress.

He should have left the maid to her business. But something in him demanded he care for Millicent himself. Probably some primordial instinct that should have died with his Viking ancestors long ago. Yet it pervaded, making it impossible for Drake to focus on anything but tending to her.

The idea of caring for Millicent's wounds filled his chest with something warm. Not the heat of lust, but something else. Something *more*. He refused to let emotion terrify him. He had faced down hordes of Afghan soldiers without a hint of fear. Certainly, he could manage a few *feelings*.

Millicent would be his wife in a matter of days. Why shouldn't he offer her comfort? It was a simple task any idiot could complete, and it didn't alter his overall objective to maintain distance.

Drake almost laughed. He could always determine a lie from the truth. Even the lies he told himself. He was playing a dangerous game.

And yet, here I am.

Standing in Millicent's room with salve in his hands and sin thrumming through his blood. Well, there was no point second-guessing his motivations now. Best to crack on with the task at hand. Namely, undressing a beautiful, angry, powerful woman and forcing her to submit to his ministrations.

Unlikely.

He very much doubted he could force Millicent to do anything she didn't want to do. And while the idea of her submission stroked along his senses, sparking awareness in areas best left untouched, he would never expect her to yield to him. He knew the injustice of his personal power being stripped away. Of stronger men forcing his will to their own. He would never do that to another. His body recoiled at the very notion.

But even he could wipe salve on someone's back without ravaging them.

Again, unlikely. Especially when that person is Millicent.

Drake tightened his grip on the pot. He needed to complete this task. He needed to prove to himself that Millicent held no power over him. He could remain indifferent to her supple curves and haunting eyes. He could maintain control. He *would* hold his distance.

Millicent turned, giving him her back. Drake exhaled a breath he hadn't been aware of holding. He put the pot of salve on a nearby table and reached for the first button. His fingers shook as he deftly released the piece of bone from its hole.

Jesus. Get it together! You aren't some green lad.

He squeezed both hands into fists, shaking them out before moving on to the next button.

Slowly, in painfully small increments, Millicent's dress opened for him. When he released the last button, he gently pushed both edges of her gown down. She pulled her arms free of the sleeves, then held the dress to her front.

'For a woman so determined to ruin herself, you're awfully modest.' He rumbled, his breath stirring a loose curl at the back of her neck. She tilted her head, swaying into him for a heartbeat before catching herself and straightening.

'I wasn't trying to ruin myself. I was trying to gain

my freedom. Men fight wars for freedom. They bleed and sacrifice and rage to attain autonomy, and they are honoured for their efforts. Women aren't afforded such noble means to attain independence, but we yearn for it just as fiercely, Major General Drake. I assure you.'

'Beaufort.'

'Fine,' she hissed. Such an angry warrior.

'May I share a story with you?'

She shrugged an elegant shoulder. The closest he'd get to an assent, he wagered.

'In the Anglo-Afghan war, I saw many things. One of the most fearsome was a woman fighting to protect her child. She killed three soldiers with nothing but a sling, several stones, and her bare hands. I've never seen anything more noble.'

Millicent stiffened. 'Some parents will sacrifice everything for their children.'

'And some won't even acknowledge the cruelty of their own spouse.'

'Yes, well...' She fell silent.

'I don't believe women are subservient to men, Millicent. In many ways, I feel they are superior.' *Certainly, in their skills at deception and treachery.* But he wisely kept that thought to himself. Instead, he began unravelling the laces of her corset.

'You are a strangely contradictory man, Beau.'

He decided to take that as a compliment. And her use of his first name thrilled him.

The fire crackled. A clock chimed the half hour. A winter breeze picked up in the alder trees, creating a haunting melody. Millicent sighed in relief when he loosened her corset enough to let her chest expand on a full breath.

'Hold your hands up. I promise I won't peek down your dress.' Drake smiled to himself. She might be an honest creature, but he was comfortable with deception. Every sinew in his body was strung tight. He wanted her more than food, water, or air.

Millicent hesitantly loosened her grip. The material sagged forward, and she started to reach for it.

'Only for a moment, Millicent. I'm not looking. I promise.'

Big, fat liar.

Fine. So, he was looking. It was only breaking one small promise. His soul already belonged to the Devil. A glimpse of Millicent's luscious body was worth whatever extra time he spent burning in the pits of hell. When she slowly lifted her hands up, he leaned forward to pull her corset over her head. And yes. He peeked.

Jesus!

Her breasts were magnificent. Glorious, full globes with strawberry-pink nipples that her nearly sheer chemise couldn't hide from Drake. He only had a glance, but God's teeth! What a worthy sacrifice of his honour.

As soon as the whale-boned contraption cleared her head, Millicent pulled her arms down, wildly grabbing her dress and clasping it against her chest again.

'We have a bit of a conundrum, Millicent.'

'Really?' She spoke in a breathless whisper, simultaneously melting and hardening various parts of him.

'Your chemise. I can't take it off without removing everything else. How attached are you to it?'

'How attached? I don't understand.'

'Do you have others?'

Millicent turned her head, her chin touching her shoulder. She had an arresting profile. Her nose was almost too strong, but her full lips and high cheekbones softened the lines of her face. She was stunning in the firelight. A goddess descended to earth.

'Do I have other chemises? Of course I do. I'm not a pauper, Maj... err... Beau.'

'Perfect.' Drake reached down and pulled a blade from his ankle holster. In one quick flick, he cut the top inch of material, then replaced his knife before grasping both sides and ripping the garment in two to her waist.

Millicent's strangled cry alerted him that his actions may have been a bit aggressive.

'You did say you had others.'

'Yes, but I didn't expect you to rip it completely in half!'

'Only partly in half. The bottom bit is still intact. Would you rather strip naked for me?'

'I'd rather Penny be here,' Millicent bit back.

God, he loved fighting with her. It might be one of his new favourite things. And he didn't have favourite things. Except perhaps whiskey. And a good cheroot. A warm fire on a cold night. But nothing compared to the heat flaring between them as they argued over her ruined underthings. It was marvellous.

'Well, she isn't, and I am.' Drake let his gaze fall upon her bare back. He was torn between arousal and intense anger. Millicent's skin was as pale as porcelain. Freckles covered her like cinnamon constellations, matching his imaginings at dinner with alarming accuracy. But marring the perfection of cream and cinnamon were savage, crimson slashes. The worst were covered in bloodied bandages. He carefully started peeling the linen from her skin, knowing from experience it would pull painfully and newly formed scabs would be ripped away.

Millicent hissed in a breath.

'Fucking bitch!' Drake snarled. Patricia would pay for what she'd done. He wasn't sure how yet, but it would be slow and painful.

'Wh-what did you say?'

'Nothing. I'm just sorry for hurting you.' The words tore from him like the bandages ripped from her back. But it was a necessary evil. He must remove the wrappings to apply the balm. Some of the cuts were angry and red, a sure sign of infection starting. Just the thought of Millicent consumed with fever, wasting away from the damage inflicted by her stepmother, filled Drake with renewed rage.

'You don't need to apologise. You didn't do this. I mean, yes, it hurts, but you're trying to help. Thank you.' Millicent's husky voice wrapped around him like an embrace, giving him the strength he needed to continue. 'I hate to ask another favour, but perhaps you could distract me with a story.'

Drake snorted. 'I don't know any stories.'

'Well, tell me something about you, then. Why are you so opposed to marriage?'

Drake gently pulled another bandage free and

when she hissed in another breath, he started speaking just to drown out the sound of her suffering.

'I wasn't always. There was a time when all I wanted was to marry.'

Drake wasn't sure he could continue. He didn't speak about Nora. When he returned from the war, his brother's marriage had been a juicy scandal. Everyone in the beau monde knew about Drake's rejection which only added bitter insult to Drake's grievous injury. But it also granted him an unexpected gift. He didn't have to explain to anyone what he was experiencing because every peer in the realm knew about the debacle.

'You don't have to continue if it's too painful.' Millicent's words were soft and sweet in the silence, and the irony of her offering him comfort when he was tending to her wounds wasn't lost on Drake.

'I just don't want to bore you with a story I'm sure you already know.' Drake began work on a new bandage. His soft touch contrasting his harsh tone.

Why? Why did she pick at his most tender wound? Even more confounding, why did Drake want to tell her about his hurt? To find some comfort in her empathy? He didn't need the approval of some woman to make him feel better about his past.

'I know what I've been told, but that isn't the truth.

Only three people really know the truth of what happened. You, your brother, and Nora. And yours is the only version I'm interested in hearing.'

Drake snorted. 'My version is biased by my own feelings.'

'Ah, but the beau monde is convinced you have no feelings.'

Drake smiled. He was grateful her back was turned. He didn't need her knowing how easily she teased a vast array of emotions from him. 'Perhaps they are right. Maybe I am just a feelingless monster.' He heaved out a heavy sigh, causing the wisps of Millicent's hair to dance in firelight. For a moment, he watched, fascinated by how many shades of red existed in just a few strands.

'We already established that you are no monster.'

'Men can be the worst monsters of all.' Drake clenched his teeth and pulled free another bandage.

'Some men. Yes. But not you.' Millicent's husky voice broke something in him, and the words began to pour forth without permission or thought.

'I loved Nora. With all my heart.' Once he started, he couldn't stop. 'She wasn't the first woman I fancied myself in love with, but she was the first woman I loved as a man. We dreamed of creating a life together. When I left for that godforsaken war, I carried her with me.' As he spoke, he continued to remove Millicent's bandages. It helped to keep his hands busy. 'I thought she loved me. But when news of my capture reached England, she wasted no time in transferring her affections to my brother. And then, when I returned looking like this...'

Millicent twisted her waist to face him, hissing at the pain it must have caused. 'You are the most beautiful man I've ever seen.' Immediately, her face turned crimson, and she spun back around.

Drake couldn't stop the harsh exhalation of air from his lungs. Not a laugh, but close. 'Beauty is in the eye of the beholder, but even a blind woman would know I'm not beautiful.'

Millicent stiffened her shoulders. 'I just mean to say, I've not met your brother, but I can't imagine him ever being as interesting as you.'

The joy bubbled up in him, cracking open his shields. 'So, I went from beautiful to interesting? That's probably a more accurate description, though still not honest. At any rate, when Nora made it clear she didn't want me, even if I still held the title instead of my brother, it shattered me. I was no longer good enough for her. Or for anyone. After that, I wasn't interested in anything, marriage least of all.'

Until I met you.

Thank God he kept that thought to himself. He renewed his efforts with her bandages, doing his best to be gentle.

'Thank you.' Millicent's words were so soft, he almost missed them.

'For what?'

'For telling me about Nora. She's an idiot, by the way. And wrong.'

Drake shook his head, letting his fingers graze over an unbroken line of creamy skin. 'I suppose there are a few topics on which we actually agree.'

'Yes, but there is also one topic that we decidedly don't agree on. It isn't that you aren't good enough for her; it's that you're far too good.'

Drake's hand paused, and he held his breath.

She is wrong. So wrong.

But he didn't have the heart to tell her. Because it mattered that she found worth in him. He hated how much it mattered.

'At any rate, I don't think Nora deserves any more of our attention,' Millicent continued. 'Tell me something else. What's a funny story about the fierce and formidable Major General Drake?'

Drake sucked in air and bit his lip. She was like balm on his ragged soul. Millicent made talking about his worst moments easy. The least he could do was distract her from her own pain with a silly story. So, he dove deep into his memories and told her about a night out drinking with Killian and the Renquist brothers that ended with Drake waking up in Killian's wine cellar with a broken nose, a massive shiner, no shoes, and no recollection of how he'd gotten there.

By the time Drake removed all the bandages, Millicent was shaking, and sweat trickled from her hairline down her cheek.

'Brave woman. I need to wash your back before I apply the balm. Can you stay standing, or would you rather sit?'

She must be in excruciating pain, but she hadn't even whimpered.

'I'm fine. Your stories helped, though I'm shocked at the behaviour of four such honourable gentlemen.'

'Titles hardly make a man honourable.'

'Another point upon which we agree.'

Drake hurried to a washbasin by the window and poured water into the bowl. A cloth was folded next to it. Taking it up, he lathered the piece of cotton with soap. The lye would sting like the Devil, but there was no getting around it. Keeping wounds clean and well-dressed was the best way to avoid infection.

He returned to Millicent. Before washing her wounds, he placed a hand on her shoulder. She shuddered at his touch as he leaned closer, his lips almost brushing the shell of her ear. 'I will be as gentle as I can. But this will hurt, Millicent. I am so sorry.'

Millicent laughed. A husky melody that tripped over his senses like whiskey. 'Trust me, I've lived through worse.'

In the midst of his burning lust, suspicion flared again. Exactly what had she experienced to be so calm and collected in the face of intense pain? And why was she approaching this terrible event with the stalwart constitution of a seasoned soldier? Did the duchess have anything to do with Millicent's unusual ability to face impending agony with controlled focus?

In a man, such courage would be admirable. In a woman, it inspired distrust. Hardly a flattering truth about Drake's opinion of women in general and his fiancée in particular. He shook his head, trying to clear the swirling thoughts.

'You are a unique creature, Millicent. Such bravery is rarely found in men or women. You face disaster with such determination.' Dear God. He respected her. The startling truth rocked him.

Millicent turned, still holding the dress against her chest. Her eyes were huge in the dim light, her pupils almost taking over the warm chocolate irises. She shifted her hold on the dress to free an arm. Reaching behind his neck, her fingers brushed against the back of his skull. Pulling his head down, she pressed a kiss against his cheek. It was innocent and honest and so fucking arousing, Drake almost dropped his soapy cloth. Lemons and cotton infiltrated his senses.

Pulling away, she held his gaze. 'Thank you.'

And then she turned again, facing the fire, and once more gave him her savaged back.

Holy shit. I'm in trouble.

Drake survived many things. Betrayal. Torture. Imprisonment. But he couldn't survive Millicent Whittenburg. Of that, he was certain.

9

Millie was falling. And whenever one fell, one crashed and usually broke. Of that, she was certain.

To be seen with such clarity was a terrifying thing. Especially when it was so important she remain cloaked in shadows. But Major General Beaufort Drake, hater of women, killer of tyrants, courageous warrior for the prime minister, thought she was brave.

Oh my.

And everything he'd shared about his past with the despicable Nora only made him more desirable. Millie loved a challenge. Finding a soft place in Drake's broken heart would be quite the feat. But was that a space she wanted to inhabit? As Drake carefully applied the balm to her cuts, her heart bled far more intensely than her wounds. How was she supposed to resist the hard, angry, beautiful, broken, scarred, brilliant man?

Because trusting him would give him access to my heart, and he would crush it. Must learn from past mistakes, Millie!

When he placed the washcloth on her back, Millie almost cried out, but she clenched her teeth instead. The lye burned into her wounds as tears stung her eyes.

'Golly, that smarts!' she hissed.

Drake's dark chuckle distracted her from the pain. 'So polite. I've heard far worse from your lips, Millicent. Coarse language doesn't bother me, and I've found it helps in moments like this, oddly enough.'

'Truly?' Millie was willing to try anything to lessen the pain.

'Let her rip, my dear.'

'Well, in that case, bloody fucking hell! That hurts.'

His chuckle turned into a belly laugh that almost had her swooning. She wished she wasn't facing the fire. She wanted to see Drake lost to mirth. It was almost worth the pain. How many people had seen the serious, dour, surly Earl of Tetly actually laugh? Not many, she'd wager.

'Well done. Did it help?'

Actually, it had a bit. 'It didn't make things worse, that's for certain,' Millie admitted.

'Keep going, sweetheart. This next part is going to be rough.'

So, she did, letting loose every foul word she knew and some she invented in the moment, as he used firm strokes to wash her back. He spent considerable time with a few of the cuts, sparing her no mercy as he meticulously scrubbed them out. It took several trips to the basin to rinse out the blood and soap, and Millie was nearly incoherent when he was done.

'I think it might be best for you to lie down before I apply the balm, Millicent. You are shaking. I don't want you to fall if you faint.'

Millie straightened her shoulders, the pull of her skin against the gashes causing her vision to blur. 'Perhaps you are right, Beau. I'll just...' She took a step but stumbled, losing her grip on the dress still clasped to her chest.

Strong arms wrapped around her waist, carefully avoiding the worst of her injuries as he held her tight to his side. She completely lost hold of her dress. It sagged around her waist. Her breasts jostled lewdly as they moved, but Millie no longer cared. She just wanted to lie down and slip into the sweet darkness of sleep.

He helped her to the bed, then uttered a curse. 'I hope you have other dresses as well. I liked this one immensely, but...' A ripping sound alerted her to the fact her betrothed had just cut away the bodice of her dress. After a few tugs, she lay face down on her bed in a half-ruined chemise and nothing else. Patricia would be outraged. The thought of her stepmother sputtering in horror was enough to make her giggle under normal circumstances, but now it came out as a pained gasp.

'I should have called for a doctor. You need morphine. Laudanum. Something for the pain.'

'No. I'm well. I just need you to finish, and then I'll sleep. I'll be much better in the morning. I promise,' she mumbled into the pillow. Already, the blackness beckoned. The only thing tethering her to consciousness was Drake's rough voice and his warm, strong hands.

'Lie still, my love. I'll be as gentle as I can.'

His fingers were steady and sure as they wiped cool balm into her cuts. It hurt. Like the dickens, but not nearly as bad as the soap.

It may have been minutes or hours, but eventually, his hands left her back.

'I'm done. Sleep now. I'll send Penny in the morning to apply more balm and fresh bandages.

You'll have a tray for breakfast and can come down later when you're ready.'

Millie wasn't sure, but she felt the barest brush of soft lips against her shoulder before the door opened and then shut again.

If she wasn't so exhausted, she would have wondered at his words. *My love.* Probably just a meaningless term of endearment. It likely meant nothing. But her lips curled into a smile as she slipped into the embrace of sleep.

* * *

He should never have followed his stupid instincts. Maintaining control of his raging desire was almost impossible when faced with a courageous, vulnerable woman like Millicent. But he wasn't so much a beast he would compromise an injured woman.

Thank God. I maintained control. Like a bloody hero.

Hardly.

He pushed through the door of their connecting room with the memory of Millicent's silky skin beneath his lips fraying every nerve ending in his body.

Stripping bare, Drake poured cold water into the basin on his counter. Sluicing the frigid water over his heated body did nothing to cool his all-consuming arousal. His cock was so hard, a slight breeze would send him over the edge.

He stumbled to the bed like a drunkard, only it was lust, not whiskey flaring through his blood and causing his shaking hands and fumbling coordination.

The cool sheets felt heavenly against his skin, and he flopped on his back, his hand slipping down.

There were no rules against fucking Millicent in his mind. If he couldn't have her body, at least he could imagine all that soft, tantalising flesh pressed against him. And after his sneak peek, he had all the inspiration he needed.

Closing his eyes, he thought of her full breasts, strawberry nipples puckered and aching for his touch. He would press open-mouthed kisses against her skin, circling ever closer to the sensitive buds, then finally, when Millicent was crazed with need, when her husky voice demanded satisfaction, he would cover one nipple with his hot mouth and taste her sweetness. His fingers would pinch and squeeze the other nub as he devoured her. Light licks, hard sucks, bites that blended pleasure and pain. She would scream his name as he plundered.

His hand fisted his cock in hard strokes. Digging his heels into the mattress, Drake savoured the sizzle of desire pulsing at the base of his spine.

He thought of her mouth at dinner, her tongue licking the spoon. It was so easy to imagine her glorious mass of flaming hair falling through his fingers as he guided her head down his body. She would take his pulsing cock in her mouth, her plump lips tightening around him in glorious, wet heat. His hand became her lips as he imagined her pink tongue swirling around his head, licking the sensitive slit where seed spilled from him in arcing jets.

He cried out, lost to his fantasy, as his body reached the precipice and flew higher.

For a blissful moment, he hovered in the ether. Neither man nor spirit. Just sensation. But inevitably, the glory dissipated, and he returned to himself.

The fantasy wasn't enough. Not nearly enough. But as Drake rose to clean himself, he sent a fleeting prayer to a God he no longer believed in that it would grant him control of his unrelenting hunger. For now. That it would allow him to keep the distance he so desperately needed.

Then he remembered the words he'd murmured.

Lie still, my love.

His mind recoiled. Surely not. Lust was bad enough. Love was impossible. Just the thought chased away any lingering need and replaced it with cold determination.

Millicent Whittenburg was many things, but she would not become his destruction. He would fight her with every weapon in his arsenal if he must.

'She is just a means to allow me greater freedom in my investigations. One more mission assigned by the prime minister. I will not fail him. And I will not break my promise.'

Sharing his past with Millicent reminded him of how devastating a woman could be. Love would not lay Drake bare again. Some wounds never healed.

* * *

Light filtered through the drapes, and the scent of toast and tea tickled Millie's nose. She was face down on the bed and started to roll over when streaks of fire lashed her back. Her wounds were not yet healed, but the salve was helping.

'Don't move, miss. Not yet. Let me reapply the balm and wrap your back. Then you can have some nice, coddled eggs, toast, tea, and lemon-currant scones. One of Cook's best recipes.' Penny bustled over from her washbasin with a tray carrying white bandages and the pot of medicine.

Millie lifted her head from the pillow, then let it fall back down, content to let Penny fuss over her for a few more minutes before she needed to put her shields back on, go downstairs, and face her step-mother. Not to mention the hordes of guests arriving today for her wedding.

Penny finished bandaging Millie's back and brought the tray of delicious breakfast treats over to set on her lap.

Four days left. She would be marrying Beau in just four more sunrises. It was impossible not to remember his kind, gentle care last night. But she couldn't let her heart melt as it so desperately wanted to do. Her mission for the Queen must take precedence.

And to accomplish her task, she would need to speak with Franklin St George.

'Ugh,' she muttered, crunching on a slice of toast with butter and preserves.

'Is something not to your liking, miss?' Penny watched her with a sharp gaze.

Millie forced a smile. 'No, it's lovely.'

She refused to think of Franklin St George just yet. Or the daunting task of getting him to divulge his secrets to her while trying to maintain the image of a devoted wife-to-be. Though after last night, that didn't seem quite so difficult to pretend.

Am I pretending?

Her memories of the past evening invaded her

mind once more. She couldn't forget the feather-soft kiss Drake pressed to her shoulder before leaving. Or when he called her 'my love'.

Sweet saints and sinners. The man is impossible. To resist.

But resist him she must. What good would come of being devoted to her husband? A man who would certainly forbid her activities with Lady Philippa if he were ever to guess. A man who was used to issuing commands and watching others scramble to follow them. If she let her affections for him grow, her freedom would decrease in equal measure. Devotion was just another term for beholden, and she would not give up her freedom. Not for a man and his fickle fancies.

She had been devoted to two men in her past. Her father and Franklin St George. Both men had proven the folly of trusting her heart to anyone but herself.

Millie once thought her father's love was forever. He told her when she was just a girl, he would never force her to leave their family home. She could stay with him as a spinster for as long as she wished in a house full of books and cats and vases of freshly cut hyacinths sweetening the air. They would chase butterflies in the flower garden, lie out on the grass making magical kingdoms out of the clouds, and stay up well past her bedtime to watch the stars twinkle into wakefulness in a black, velvet sky. She was his sweet pea, and he was her pea-brained papa... two peas in a pod. Until she dallied with St George. Not long after, he met Patricia. Those two events changed everything.

Her loving father became distracted, distant, and disapproving of the child he once deferred to in all things. It broke her heart. Shattered her soul. Poisoned her faith in constancy.

Franklin St George had been equally fickle. He came to her like a prince in some children's tale. If his chin was a little weaker than Sir Galahad, or his shoulders were padded instead of carved from granite, who was she to criticise? She was tall and plump and stronger than Franklin, even as a child. Clearly, she had her own flaws, but Franklin never pointed them out to her. Or at least, not often and always with the aim to correct her behaviour. Love painted over his imperfections like snow covered the fields and turned everything into a sparkling fairyland.

The fateful afternoon when Franklin St George asked her to join him in a picnic at the ancient folly between their two estates, Millie was thrilled. He didn't have to coerce her to lift her skirts. She wanted Franklin to be the one who took her virtue. After all, he already had her heart. And he promised her forever. Whispered it frantically in her ear as he thrust once, twice, a third time before shuddering and letting his weight fall upon her. The pain was a small price to pay for her lover's unending devotion.

The next day, Franklin St George arrived at her estate. Not to take her on another outing as her silly heart wished, but instead to confront her father about her actions. Forever must mean something very different to men. Millie stupidly thought it meant always.

If her father's love was so easily lost, and Franklin's was just a lie, how could a man like Major General Drake ever hope to convince her of faithfulness?

No. It was far better she stay the course. She wasn't going to convince Drake to break the engagement, but at least she could keep her heart safe and secure in the depths of her chest. Where it belonged. Where it couldn't be shattered like crystal glass or a girl's hopes or dreams of castles in the sky.

Creatures can't survive without a heart, so I won't be giving mine away. Never again.

Penny helped Millie don a sprigged muslin day dress with tiny, green leaves embroidered into the skirts. It was a simple pattern, but the cut set off her figure, and the neckline was just low enough to let the girls peek out while still remaining modest. Drake seemed rather impressed with her breasts. Well, let him look his fill. He'd certainly seen far more than that the previous night.

Just thinking about his hands on her bare back was enough to make her shiver. She ruthlessly shut down that avenue of thought while Penny piled her red curls high on her head in an artfully messy bun. Spirals spilled down her neck, tickling her skin.

She pinched her cheeks a few times, bit her lips, then rubbed beeswax on her eyelids and mouth, popping her lips together once more for good luck.

'Right, well. This is as good as it gets, Penny. Thank you. You've done a marvellous job of my hair.'

Penny's cheeks grew pink as she ducked her head. 'It's no bother, miss. You have such beautiful hair. I can't imagine it ever looking bad.'

Millie laughed. 'Well, lucky you didn't know me as a girl. It was a frizzy, tangled mess back then. Thank goodness Cocoa Glycerine keeps it contained. Right. I believe I'm ready to face the fray.' Smiling at Penny, she rose and swept past the maid to her door.

Millie carefully descended the curved staircase leading from the family wing to the Alder House's entrance. Beeswax, roses, and lemons scented the air.

Just as she was about to seek out a maid to discover where Major General Drake and the other guests were, the young lad she had met when she arrived came skidding into the entryway.

'Oh. Hullo. I didn't fink any toffs were 'round. The major general says everyone was getting a tour of the grounds.' He stuck something into his pocket and gave her a charming smile despite the smudge of dirt on his cheek.

'Master Bright, am I right?'

''Oos askin'?'

Millie hid her smile. 'I am. I'm soon to be the mistress of this house, young man. It's important I know who I can trust with important tasks.'

'Cor blimey, miss. If you're lookin' for a bloke whose can get things, deliver things, or keep things under me cap' – he doffed an imaginary cap and gave her a jaunty wink – 'then I'm yer man. Even the major general trusts me, and he don't trust no one.'

'Doesn't trust anyone,' Millie corrected gently.

'That's wot I said, innit? Don't tell me you're one of them barmy toffs 'oos always going on about the proper ways to say things. I says things 'ow I sees them and that's good 'nuff for me.'

'A wise mantra to live by, Master Bright.'

'I don't know nuffink 'bout no man trays, nor no mont rahs neither, but I knows quick feet'll get you out of trouble, and a quick tongue can get you into it. That's what me mum says, and she's never wrong.'

'She sounds very wise.'

Master Bright blinked his large eyes, tilting his chin up as if to take her measure. 'Too right, she is.'

Clipped steps echoed down the hall. Before Master Bright could make a quick exit, Patricia swept into the entryway. She wore a pink, frilled monstrosity. Her corset was laced so tightly, she could barely take a full breath without her breasts spilling out.

'You!' she screeched at the boy.

Instinctively, Millie stepped in front of him, blocking him from Patricia's view. Master Bright clung to Millie's skirts, his little hands shaking. She didn't need to glance down to know her dress now carried twin handprints from Master Bright. Well, she was bound to stain the thing herself before the end of the day. The dangers of wearing white could not be overstated.

'What on earth are you yelling about?' Millie put her hand behind her and grasped the lad's shoulder, squeezing softly to reassure him.

'What am I yelling about? That little thief stole my necklace. The emerald one your father gave me for my birthday. Step aside, Millicent. I will have my necklace back and demand Major General Drake whip this boy for his crimes before dismissing him immediately. The little guttersnipe can't even speak without betraying his low birth. It's a wonder he isn't covered in vermin.'

'Oi! I take my baths every month.' Master Bright poked his head out from the side of Millie's skirts before quickly ducking back into his hiding spot of sprigged muslin.

Millie scrunched her nose for a moment. Yes, her dress would most definitely need to be laundered. Patricia's high-pitched scream forced her to refocus. 'Why on earth do you think he stole your emerald necklace, Patricia? Surely, he wasn't in your rooms.'

'How dare you question me?' Patricia walked to Millie and raised her right hand to strike. As it flew through the air, Millie pushed Master Bright back and leaned out of Patricia's range. With her left hand, she caught Patricia's wrist. Following her stepmother's momentum, she wrenched Patricia's wrist across her body, pulling her stepmother off balance. Letting go, Patricia stumbled, landing in a tangled heap on the floor.

Philippa had taught Millie this move, though she could have altered it to keep control of Patricia's arm. With the woman's wrist captured and enough pressure put on her elbow, she could easily break Patricia's arm if she wanted. Instead, she opted to push her away.

The stupid woman would never know how lucky she was to be released.

Millie could feel the wounds in her back stretch painfully as wetness seeped through the bandages. She refused to show any weakness to Patricia. No longer did she live under this vile woman's roof.

'Cor blimey, miss. You're a right corker, you are!' Master Bright had stepped away from her in the scuffle and watched them from a safe distance.

'You little bitch!' Patricia hissed as her dress ballooned around her like a lily pad of silks with her the toad at its centre. 'Dare you forget how tenuous your future is, Millicent? With a simple note to the right people, I could destroy you and your precious friend.' Her green eyes blazed with an unholy fire even as tears filled them from the embarrassment of her fall.

Millie knew backing down would only give her stepmother more power, but the idea of Lady Philippa's name being maligned so cruelly, her safety brought into question, was unimaginable. Better for Patricia to think she'd won this little skirmish than to fan the flame of her ire.

'I must have slipped. Terribly sorry, Patricia. Let me help you.' She reached to grasp Patricia's arm, but the woman slapped her hands away. She struggled to stand on her own, transitioning from croaking toad to flapping chicken. No doubt her cinched corset didn't make the job easier.

'Lying little whore,' Patricia hissed at Millie once she'd regained her feet.

Millie forced her hands to remain loose when she could so easily imagine the satisfaction of thrusting the heel of her palm into Patricia's nose, breaking the pointy little beak. 'Insult me if you must, but I would remember, this isn't your house. These aren't your servants, nor will the earl take kindly to you accusing his people of thievery. I'd search your rooms more carefully before risking offence to our host.' She was careful to keep her body between Patricia and the young lad. Patricia might not care about dragging her stepdaughter's reputation through the mud, but neither would she appreciate being thrown out of Drake's home in front of all the wedding guests. And Millie was sure Drake wouldn't hesitate to do just that with the smallest provocation. Appealing to the woman's vanity was the best way to control her.

Patricia's hand caught on a tear in her skirts. She stifled a frustrated scream. Angry tears ran down her face, creating red, splotchy streaks in the rice powder she used to keep her complexion pale and smooth. 'Look what you've done! You've ruined my dress, you ungrateful, insufferable, fat trollop! You'll pay for this, you stupid, ugly—'

The deep sound of a throat being cleared effectively silenced Patricia. Her red-rimmed eyes widened as she looked behind Millie.

Drat.

Millie didn't need any guesses to know who stood behind her. She could feel his heat as the scent of cloves and leather surrounded her. Hopefully, he hadn't seen her attack on Patricia. He was the last person who needed to discern her fighting skills.

Philippa will kill me if she finds out.

Millie turned around to see Drake looking fit and fine in a dark-charcoal jacket, grey waistcoat, and black breeches. His hessian boots gleamed in the cold sun streaming through the window.

Oh my.

'Have a care when you speak of my betrothed, Lady Whittenburg. It looks as though you might want to return to your rooms and do something about...' Drake waved his hand around his face. 'All that. Your face seems to be melting. And your skirt...' He let his voice fade.

Patricia pressed her lips together, her body vibrating with fury. 'You'll be lucky if she doesn't cuckold you before the end of the week.'

'Enough, madame!' Drake roared loud enough to make Millie's bones quake and Patricia squeak like a frightened mouse. 'Leave us,' Drake thundered.

Patricia pulled back her thin shoulders. Gathering her ruined skirts, she gave Millie a hateful glare before turning to walk up the staircase, turning left toward the guest wing.

'You picked yourself a right grand lady, guvnor.' Master Bright walked over to Drake and nodded sagely. He turned to Millie. 'If you ever need anyfink, you come find me. I'm your man, miss.'

'You can call me Millie.' She smiled at the boy though her heart was beating triple-time after the confrontation with Patricia and Drake's furious response.

'Right you are, Miss Millie. And you can call me Billy. Caw, do you 'ear that? Millie and Billy. Like a right fairy rhyme. We're friends now, Millie. An' I protect me friends.'

'So do I, Billy. By the by, if you *did* happen to find an emerald necklace lying about, you could certainly give it to Penny. I'm sure she'd return it to its rightful place.'

Billy's lopsided grin revealed a gap in his two front teeth. 'That's some good advice, Miss Millie. If I 'appens to find any missing necklaces, I'll make sure to do just that.' He winked at her before turning to push open the front door, whistling a bawdy tune as he strutted on his merry way.

'My goodness. What an interesting young man.' Millie's gaze flicked to Drake and she tried for an innocent smile.

Drake raised his broken eyebrow in an expression she was coming to recognise. 'That is one way to describe him.'

'I wonder exactly where you found him. I only mean, he doesn't seem to be your average country lad.' Perhaps she could divert his attention away from her interaction with Patricia by focusing on his unique choice in servants.

'Nothing about Billy is average.' Drake tugged at his cravat – an oddly endearing gesture reminiscent of Master Bright himself. 'Billy may be young, but he's experienced far more tragedy in his life than most people. When I met him, he'd just lost his sister.'

Millie raised her brow and forced her tongue to stay still despite the questions bursting forth. Exactly what circumstances had led to his sister's death? And was Drake involved in investigating them? Buttons to sweet buns said Philippa would know about it. Millie would make sure to quiz her mentor at the earliest opportunity.

'That's terrible.'

'Yes. It was. And instead of letting such unfair cruelty twist him, Billy was determined to find justice for his sister. He showed more virtue in adversity than most of the blue-blooded buffoons in the entire beau monde.'

Millie's heart stretched painfully imagining what kind of trouble Billy had experienced. 'I'm glad you took him in, then.'

Drake shrugged. 'It was hardly an act of charity. I expect Billy to earn his keep.' He clenched his jaw, and for a moment, Millie thought the conversation was over. Instead, his icy gaze fell upon her, holding her in his thrall. 'That isn't the truth of it, though. Billy deserved a better chance than what life gave him, and by no effort of my own, I was in a position to help.'

'So, you offered him a post in your house? Just like that?' Hardly in character for a man of Drake's cold reputation.

In lieu of an answer, he shrugged, his gaze astutely avoiding hers.

Millie was certain few people had the courage or opportunity to tease the oh-so-serious Earl of Tetly. She was determined to take full advantage of this serendipitous moment. 'Who would have guessed Major General Drake was prone to such flights of fancy? Can you imagine if the beau monde caught wind? Your reputation would be in tatters. The earl with a heart of gold. Ah, but fear not, my lord. Your secret is safe with me.'

Drake's gaze swept back to her. His eyes narrowed. 'Are secrets something you often keep, Millicent?'

Damnable man!

Millie had stepped right into that. 'Only for such a sensitive soul as yourself, my lord.'

'I think you are imagining things. First a heart, now a soul? You don't know me at all.' Drake leaned closer, and Millie prepared herself for his next volley of questions. But instead of pressing his advantage, he did something completely unexpected. His eyes softened and his mouth quirked into a self-deprecating hint of a smile. 'Sometimes, an impulsive decision made on instinct alone has the power to irrevocably alter one's course. Not just mine, or Billy's, or yours, but everyone's. Like a ripple in a lake.'

Oh my.

The angry dragon was hiding a soft underbelly full of both heart and soul despite his protestations. How interesting. And inconvenient, as Millie found herself desperately wishing to capture both. And what on earth would she do with Drake's heart, let alone his soul?

Don't be a silly ninny! You don't want any part of him.

Except his rough hands, his warm lips, his hard thighs.
Botheration!

Millie forced her thoughts back to the boy and ignored the sudden ache between her own thighs. 'Well, no matter the reason for your choice, he certainly holds you in high regard.' Millie wished her voice wasn't quite so breathless.

'I never said the lad was bright.'

Millie couldn't stop the chuckle. 'I'd wager he's far cleverer than most of the pompous stuffed shirts in the House of Lords. And he trusts you.'

Drake snorted. 'He trusts a full belly and a warm bed. And you aren't distracting me with this discussion, no matter how hard you try. Exactly where did you learn that move you performed on your stepmother just now?' His gravelled voice created a buzz in her belly as blood rushed through her veins like warm honey.

Damnation!

So, her efforts to divert him had failed. Fine. She would feign ignorance. 'I'm not sure I know what you mean.'

'Really?' He took a step closer. 'You are a terrible liar, Millicent.'

Millie's wide smile dimmed. 'I know. It's always

been a problem.' She glanced out the window, desperate for another topic of conversation.

Before Drake could undoubtedly revisit his question, the sound of carriage wheels on the drive signalled a new arrival.

Thank God! Saved by wedding guests.

'Oh, look! More guests. Shall we go out and greet them?' Millie had never been happier to play hostess.

Drake's gaze could have cut her dress to ribbons. 'Fate would seem to have granted you a reprieve.' He held out his arm. 'But this conversation isn't over, Millicent.'

A shiver of dread – or was that desire? – swept through her.

'Shall we?' Drake tipped his stupidly attractive head in her direction, a parody of the perfect gentleman.

10

Drake couldn't keep his eyes off Millicent as he helped her into a sage-green woollen coat and offered her his arm to walk outside. She looked magnificent in her white dress, even with the addition of dirt smudges, thanks to Master Bright.

But it was more than her dress that attracted him. Despite his growing suspicions about her, Millicent had somehow found her way into the fractures of his shattered heart. Instead of letting Drake squeeze the damn thing back together, she was blowing it wide open. A rather alarming thought as it was impossible for a man to live with a splintered heart. He would have pondered this longer, but the carriage arriving distracted him.

The crest decorating the door of the beautifully outfitted Landau boldly declared his brother's coat of arms. Rage washed through Drake like a rogue wave.

'Bastard!' he hissed.

'Pardon?' Millicent turned, her coffee gaze widening at what she saw.

Drake couldn't blame her. He probably looked like some kind of crazed monster. Clenching his teeth and tugging her along, he narrowed his gaze as the ostentatious carriage pulled to a stop. 'It's my brother. And his wife.'

'Really? I can't wait to meet them.' Drake turned to see if she was mocking him but there was no hint of humour in the curves of her expressive face. Her eyes were focused on the carriage. 'I have a few things I'd love to say to Nora.' She looked like a fierce avenging Valkyrie, ready to do battle. In his defence. His lips twitched despite his determination to remain enraged.

'Don't waste your time with her. As you said last night, she isn't worth it.' Drake could just imagine Millicent confronting the pale, delicate Nora. His former fiancée was no match for Millicent, and the last thing he needed was scandal to distract him from his mission. He never should have shared the entire sordid, embarrassing, heart-wrenching affair to Millicent. He still wasn't sure why he had. Not that it mattered. Millicent would have to be deaf, dumb, and blind not to notice the tension between the two brothers, and she was none of those things. Far from it, in fact.

Drake found Millicent frustratingly astute, unnervingly intelligent, and wickedly sensitive to all manner of stimulation. After watching her attack her bitch of a stepmother, he was beginning to realise she was far more than he ever expected.

His earlier suspicions about Millicent's connection to Lady Philippa reawakened. If Killian's bride, Hannah, was actually an investigator working under Lady Philippa's direction, it wasn't much of a jump to imagine Millicent following in her friend's footsteps. Her fighting skills certainly weren't the product of dancing lessons. And it would help explain her courage the night before. If that were the case, he needed to find out exactly who she and Philippa were working for and, more importantly, if Millicent was working against him. As if their impending marriage needed any more complications.

While he desperately wanted to focus his attention on his current fiancée, first, he needed to deal with his ex-fiancée. Nora was here. At his estate. For his wedding.

Bloody fantastic.

'I shall endeavour not to claw her eyes out, but I make no promises.'

'Your decorum is admirable,' Drake teased. Which made no sense. Drake never teased.

Millicent actually growled. It was surprisingly erotic.

The footman leapt down from his perch, opened the door, and set the step with a flourish.

'Pompous, arrogant ass,' Drake hissed.

'Yes, she is.' Millicent kept her gaze on the carriage.

Despite the fact his little shit of a brother – wearing a canary-yellow waistcoat, pea-green breeches, and a fur outer coat – was descending from the carriage, despite the fact the woman who ruined his heart was about to emerge from the aforementioned carriage, and despite the fact he was about to jump headlong into the parson's noose with a woman who may or may not be secretly working against him, a bubble of joy burst somewhere in the vicinity of his belly at the sight of Millicent waging war in his defence. It made his heart flutter.

I am a soldier. The private investigator to Prime Minister Russell. Killer of men. Destroyer of evil. I was tortured for over a year and never once uttered a cry. My heart does not flutter.

It fluttered again.

Bollocks!

He turned his full attention to Millicent. 'Lowering yourself to her level helps no one, regardless of how much I would enjoy watching you castigate her. And don't think these new guests will distract me from our previous, unfinished conversation, my lady.' He didn't miss the flare of colour on her cheeks or how her breasts pressed against the sprigged muslin peeking out from her coat as she took a deep breath. There it was. That damn fluttering again. Perhaps he needed to see his doctor. Mayhap, this was a warning sign of impending apoplexy.

Drake tore his gaze away from Millicent to watch his brother help Nora from the carriage. He hadn't seen them in almost five years. Half a decade had changed his brother. He was thicker in the waist and thinner in the hair. His cheeks were red from broken capillaries, and Drake wondered how often his brother sank a little too deeply into his cups.

As Nora emerged from the carriage, he felt Millicent stiffen next to him. While the years had left their mark on his brother, Nora looked much unchanged. Her figure remained slender, and her blonde hair still shone in the afternoon sunlight. She had been blessed with the cream and rose complexion so highly regarded in the beau monde. There was a time Drake could imagine the exact shade of her eyelashes. He could tell you the number of freckles on Nora's shoulder. He marched into the horrors of the Afghan desert with Nora's face shining like a beacon, giving him courage and faith when the world around him disintegrated into chaos. He thought his heart would never cease aching when she left him. But now, looking at her bluebell eyes, seeing her pink lips pursed in a perfect cupid's bow, watching her gaze flit over Millicent to land firmly on him, he felt... nothing. Not a damn thing.

It was glorious.

'Brother!' Godric Drake, Baron de Vane, strode forward, his baroness floating along beside him in a gown matching her blue eyes and a white, fur-lined coat contrasting her black heart. 'May we offer you our most heartfelt solicitations on this most wonderful event!' His brother reached out a hand in greeting. Drake did not move. After an awkward pause, his brother dropped his hand.

'Come, Beaufort.' Nora's voice was soft and far too high. Drake realised he preferred a lower, huskier tone. She let go of her husband's arm, walked up to Drake, and put a gloved hand on his arm. 'We are family and have missed you. I was thrilled to receive your invitation.'

Millicent growled again. The damnable flutter was back.

Nora's sweet scent of peonies clashed with Millicent's much more appealing citrus and sun-warmed cotton. But while seeing Nora in the flesh did not reignite his former feelings, it did remind Drake of all the reasons distance was key with his new bride. Allowing himself to become vulnerable would only end in destruction.

Drake moved away from both women. Nora's eyes widened. Her mouth crimped at the corners. She didn't miss his rejection of her. Neither did Millicent. Her dark eyes flashed with an emotion he couldn't interpret.

Stepping back, Nora took her husband's arm once more, though her gaze never left Drake's face.

'Lord and Lady de Vane, allow me to introduce my bride-to-be, Miss Millicent Whittenburg.' Drake held his hand out to Millicent, though now he was too far away to touch her. His fingers itched and his heart kicked hard in his chest. Drake ignored the stupid organ. 'Her stepmother organised this entire week. Including the guest list.'

Godric threw his head back and laughed, his jowls quivering with mirth. 'Lord and Lady de Vane. Beaufort, please. We need not be so formal. As Nora said, we are family.'

Drake clenched his jaw. There was a time he would have happily planted his fist into his brother's face and derived immense pleasure from hearing his nose crack like a walnut. But now he lacked the energy to fuel his ire. It all seemed so patently petty.

'It is a pleasure to meet you, Lord and Lady de Vane.' Millicent's husky voice vibrated with unspoken hostility. When Godric stepped forward, taking Millicent's hand in his and pressing a kiss to her gloved knuckles, Drake's jealousy spiked, inconveniently distracting him from remaining aloof. He took a jolting step forward, reclaiming Millicent's hand from his brother and tucking it in the crook of his elbow.

Jesus! I am the world's biggest fool.

'I'm sure you would like to refresh yourselves before meeting the rest of our guests.' Millicent emphasised 'our', making her own subtle statement. She and Drake were a unit, and based on the glare she sent to Nora, she wanted the woman to be very clear on that point.

Drake forced his twitching lips to remain in a firm line. He refused to be charmed by his future wife.

Their fraught conversation was interrupted by another carriage crunching down the alder-lined drive.

'Bugger,' Millicent whispered.

Drake turned to his betrothed and watched her face pale as she narrowed her gaze on the approaching carriage.

Nora gasped at Millicent's coarse language, her hand fluttering over her chest like a moth hovering over a flame.

Godric's cheeks reddened in splotchy crimson patches. 'I say!'

Millicent looked at each of them, straightening her shoulders. 'Err, I meant there is a bug on her, just there.' Millicent leaned forward and swatted at a non-existent insect on Nora's white coat. 'The words ran together in my alarm. Heavens, I wouldn't want something nasty to sting you, Lady de Vane. You might swell in unsightly bumps or develop a fever if you aren't careful.' But quickly, her gaze returned to the approaching carriage.

'It appears we have another guest to welcome. Lord Franklin St George, if I'm not mistaken.' Drake watched Millicent carefully as he spoke the name.

St George was a prime suspect in Drake's investigation. Was that why Millicent reacted so strongly to his arrival? Did she also know of his potential crimes? If she was engaged in her own investigation, was St George her focus as well?

Or did her reaction stem from something else? He knew his fiancée had a history with St George, but exactly what that history entailed was unclear. Drake didn't gamble, but he would place money on the odds that Franklin St George was the bastard who compromised his wife-to-be.

A slow-burning rage filled him like hot tar. If St George was the man who treated her innocence so callously, his mistreatment of Millie was reason enough to kill the bastard, let alone whatever connections he might have to the sex-trafficking ring.

'I've played cards with him at White's before. Capital fellow. How do you know him?' Godric asked.

'He's an old friend of Millicent's, isn't he, my love?' He shouldn't have used the term of endearment. It came out without thought. But he was too shallow not to enjoy Nora's sharp inhalation or Millicent's gaze completely refocusing from the carriage to Drake's face. With two words, he had accomplished several goals.

Millicent's lips parted. Whether her reaction was caused by 'my love' or referencing St George as an old friend, he could not tell.

'I wouldn't call him a friend, darling. More of a family acquaintance.' Millicent drew out the syllables in 'darling', and Drake once more fought the urge to smile. She was sparring with him, even in the use of pet names. What an unexpected moment to find joy.

Fluttering. In his chest.

Definitely something to tell his doctor.

'Shall we welcome him? And then we can all return to the house together.' Nora smiled brightly. 'Millicent, you must tell me how your maid was able to dress your hair so... casually. I wish I could be that brave in my fashion choices.'

Even Drake, with his limited knowledge of female warfare, knew a gauntlet had been thrown. Nora was waging her own battle, and terms of endearment were not her weapon of choice.

Millicent lifted a brow several shades darker than her fiery hair. 'Don't feel bad, Nora. Not everyone is as courageous as I am. For example, I would never let fear of competition ever stop me from claiming what I want.' Millicent turned to Drake and gave him a dazzling smile. Whether her implied declaration of desire was real or simply a reflection of her competitive nature, the flutter in his heart turned into an alarming thunder. 'Ah, here comes Lord St George.' Millicent let go of Drake and stepped away from Nora and Godric. 'Coming, darling?' She was making it clear. Drake had a choice. He could stay with his brother and sister-in-law, or he could follow her.

Billy was right. She is a corker.

Despite his determination to maintain distance from the woman destroying any hopes of maintaining control, he had no intention of choosing his despised family over his desirable bride.

Drake took two long strides to reclaim his position by her side, recapturing her hand and tucking it in the crook of his arm.

'Lead on, my lady.'

This was proving to be a most interesting wedding party.

* * *

Millie found Drake's reaction to Nora interesting in the extreme. But she had no time to think on the deeper meaning of his choice to join her instead of remaining with his first love. She thought she had successfully cleared the biggest hurdle of her day when Drake joined her side, but she was wrong.

At least I'm used to being wrong.

One thing was certain. She did not like Elnora Drake. Clearly, the petite, beautiful, awful woman was rethinking her choice of spouse. And who wouldn't when comparing Drake and Godric?

Nitwit of a woman.

Nora must have been devastated when Drake survived his imprisonment, and she lost her chance at his title.

Nitwit and a ninny.

Even if Drake had no title and Godric was the bloody King of England, Millie would rather spend her days with an impoverished, dangerous, decidedly devilish man than the bowl of pudding parading around in hideous pants and a canary-yellow waistcoat.

Before she could congratulate herself on being a far smarter woman than Drake's first love, *her* first love rolled up and ruined everything. Per usual.

Franklin St George, Baron de Borogue, strode forward after stepping out of his carriage, leaving his poor wife to descend alone. Thankfully, the footman assisted her.

Millie tried to imagine Franklin St George drugging a young woman and then nailing her into a coffin to be shipped across the Channel and sold into sex slavery in France. Not a difficult image to conjure, actually. Her stomach rolled, nausea blooming.

'Major General Drake! Wonderful to see you again. Victoria and I were thrilled to receive an invitation from one of my oldest family friends.'

Lord Franklin St George always had a weak chin. It

was something Millie noticed even at the height of her fascination with him. Now, years later, his chin had not improved. He did have lovely, clear grey eyes, but the glint of malice in them ruined the colour completely.

Franklin glanced behind him at his wife. 'Do hurry up, dear. I'm sure Major General Drake has more important things to do than wait for you to shake out your skirts.'

Victoria was a small, plump woman with strawberry-blonde hair. She wasn't so much shaking out her skirts as trying to disentangle the lace from where it caught on the carriage step.

'May I assist you, madame?' Drake strode over, his black Hessians chewing up the distance easily. He bent over to pull Victoria's skirt free, and Millie fought the urge to ogle his well-shaped bottom.

Stay focused!

Victoria fluttered her hand over her chest as Drake offered his arm to escort her to her husband. She had large eyes usually focused on her feet, a slight lisp, and her complexion was prone to splotch when she was embarrassed. As it was doing now. She sent her husband a wide-eyed glance as if seeking his approval to take Drake's arm.

Dear Lord. She has no backbone at all. I'm sure Franklin walks all over her. Or worse.

Millie knew Victoria from their first season together. Millie and her best friend Ivy Cavendale both preferred to decorate the walls rather than parade on the dance floor. They struck up a friendship with Victoria, sensing she was of a similar ilk until the debacle with Franklin St George. Once he made his rejection of Millie clear and set his cap for Victoria, Millie hadn't felt quite so friendly toward the girl. Which was stupid. She doubted Victoria had any choice in the marriage. And it certainly wasn't Victoria's fault Franklin abandoned Millie as soon as he dipped his wick and collected his money.

All the rumours pointed to Victoria's father being quite the dictator. Then Franklin had stepped in. Millie presumed he picked up where Victoria's father left off. The poor woman stopped attending events and was only seen at the largest balls, clinging to her husband's arm despite his obvious attempts to ignore her.

What did I ever see in this man? And why on earth did I care so much about his opinion of me? Perhaps I'm just as big of a ninny nitwit as Nora.

Nora and Godric joined them then. Nora stood far too close to Drake and kept sending him looks that Drake completely missed. Or ignored.

Perhaps not.

Introductions were made. Millie endured Franklin

grasping her fingers and pressing a kiss against her knuckles. She would need to thank Penny for insisting she wore gloves. And the quiet growl of Drake behind her, the way he placed his hand on the small of her back, deftly moving her away from Franklin, was quite lovely.

The group of six returned to the house where they were saved from awkward small talk as the rest of the guests returned from their tour of the grounds.

Philippa, looking regal in a deep-plum day dress trimmed with black lace, swept over to Millie. 'Your betrothed has an excellent greenhouse. During our tour of the estate, I found the exact hue of roses I wish to plant in the gardens at Belgrave Square. Let me show you.' She didn't even glance at the other guests before walking out of the drawing room where everyone had gathered.

'Ahh, the perks of being a duchess.' Drake leaned close and whispered in Millie's ear. Shivers tickled down her spine as cloves and leather once more invaded her senses. 'Best follow her. I only wish I could join you.' Then, as if he realised his actions, he pulled back, his shoulders stiffening.

Millie couldn't stop the smile curling her lips, but it froze when she saw Nora manoeuvring for a closer position to Drake. The sneaky woman was batting her lashes at him, no doubt flashing an invitation with her bluer-than-a-bluebell eyes. And why shouldn't she? Millie's marriage was one of convenience, not affection. Of course other women would show interest in Drake. It was really none of Millie's concern and one more reason why she couldn't allow Drake's moments of charm to woo her. It would only end in heart ache.

She resigned herself to the fact she couldn't escape her marriage, but to continue her training with Philippa, she would need to establish a distant union. While she had no interest in pursuing a paramour, she was certain Drake would continue to find his pleasures in whatever way he currently found them. But the jealous rage filling her chest and making it impossible to breathe made her realise a distant marriage may not be to her liking.

Millie was in another pickle.

'I would like to speak with you privately about an important matter, perhaps later this evening?' Millie placed a hand on Drake's arm, partly to reassure herself with his solid mass and partly to stake her claim. She glanced at Nora and narrowed her eyes, widening her lips in a vicious smile.

Back off, or you shall see how accurate I can be at throwing a knife.

Her hidden blades pressed against her skin, and

she resisted the urge to tuck her fingers in the slit of her skirt and finger the knife on her thigh. It would be worth it just to wipe that smug expression from Nora's face.

Drake shifted so his wide back blocked Nora from her view. 'As would I. There are questions still burning in my mind, madame. Questions that demand answers. Though, I must admit, I'm all aquiver with curiosity as to what you wish to discuss.' His sarcasm was softened by the warmth in his pale eyes.

Bugger. Speaking with Drake privately means I shall have to be very careful to evade his questions.

She would start the conversation first. Perhaps after she spoke her piece, he would forget all about her behaviour with Patricia.

'Shall we meet before dinner? While everyone is getting ready?'

'I'll come to your rooms. I am beginning to enjoy playing your lady's maid.' His broken eyebrow rose as his lips twitched.

'Scandalous, sir.'

'I certainly hope so.'

Millie pinched his arm softly and turned before she convinced herself not to follow the duchess at all. Indeed, sparring with Drake was becoming one of her most favourite things.

11

Millie hurried out to the greenhouse and took a moment to marvel at the structure. Made from wood and glass, its domed roof was magnificent and shone like a jewel in the wintry gardens. Opening the door, she immediately discarded her coat in the warmer, humid air. Wandering down the gravelled path, she found Philippa standing next to a tri-coloured rose bush. The blooms had petals beginning with sunny yellow at the heart of the rose, then shifting to pink, and finally red. Striking and fragrant. She could understand why Philippa would want the same roses in her garden.

'I wondered if you got lost.' Philippa didn't look up at Millie as she stroked a petal. 'This greenhouse is a marvel. I will speak with the major general about who designed this so I can erect one at Belgrave Square. Until then, perhaps his groundskeeper will give me a cutting of this in the spring. Divine, aren't they?'

Millie slowed her pace as she approached Philippa. Before she could reply, Philippa spun, a dagger in her hand. She threw it at Millie, who turned sideways and smacked the weapon out of the air. Deftly releasing the blade on her wrist, she noted how the heft weighed pleasantly in her palm. One flick and it would hurtle through the air, aimed for Philippa's heart.

Philippa's perfectly arched brows rose. 'Well done. Just because we can't train as we normally would is no excuse to let your skills slip. We must stay alert, Millicent.'

Millie tried to calm her heart from the surprise attack. 'A warning would have been nice.'

'You won't get a warning from Franklin St George. Though I am glad your wounds aren't hindering you.'

'I told you, it helped to have the pain. Allowed me to sharpen my focus.'

'And how are you progressing with Major General Drake? Have you spoken with him about the parameters of your marriage?'

Millie hesitated. 'I'm not sure exactly. I mean, I'm wondering if... would it be so terrible if he knew about us? Mayhap he would approve, and I could train with you while still living with Beau.'

Philippa snorted, her blue eyes flashing. 'I'd never guess you for a fool, Millicent. No man would allow his wife to engage in the kind of dangerous activities we must perform for the Queen. Especially not a man like *Beau*.' Her lips pressed together as if his name tasted sour on her tongue.

Millie shook her head. It was a crazy idea. She was being foolish, allowing her attraction for Drake to sweep her away. Stupid to think about a close marriage when he was sure to forbid her behaviour if he knew. 'You're right. Of course you are. We are going to speak tonight. I will impress upon him my desire for distance. I'm sure he wants the same.' But she couldn't forget the possession in his gaze when Franklin St George pressed a kiss against her gloved hand. Or the ache he inspired between her thighs every time his hand touched the small of her back. But it didn't matter. Desire must be sacrificed for freedom.

'We cannot afford to lose focus, Millicent. We are dealing with dangerous men who won't hesitate to remove any impediment to their plans. Do not let your concentration be broken by something as ridiculous as a well-made man.'

Sage advice. 'Of course. Yes. I am completely focused on this mission. I swear it.'

Philippa nodded, her hand stilling. 'I mentioned your progress to the Queen. She is impressed with your natural skills, as am I. This is a wonderful opportunity for you, Millicent. Don't waste it.'

Millie nodded. 'Of course.' But her heart beat in rebellion. She had never been good at following orders. Even those delivered by someone who had her best interests at heart.

'Watch St George. Get close. See if he reveals any secrets. But remember, if we must engage the enemy, I will take care of him.' Philippa's jaw hardened, and her eyes flashed like steel in the sunlight. For a moment, Millie almost felt sorry for St George. Almost.

'I won't let you down, Philippa.'

'I know. You are fearless. You remind me of someone I once knew.' Turning back to the rose, Philippa leaned down and inhaled deeply. 'Roses were her favourite, you know.'

Millie quirked a brow. Philippa never spoke about her personal life. 'Whose favourite?'

'Someone very dear to me from long ago.'

Desperate for Philippa to share more, Millie chose her words carefully. 'Where is she now?'

Philippa was silent for several breaths. She turned

her head, so the petals brushed against her cheek. 'Gone. Forever.' Her low voice broke, the only indication of her emotions, but enough to make Millie's heart ache for her mentor.

'I'm so sorry.'

'As am I.' Philippa straightened, clearing any emotion from her face. 'We should return to the group. The investigation is afoot, Millicent. Stay alert. Keep those knives on you. Don't die. Understand?'

It was hardly a declaration of affection, but Millie felt the warmth of Philippa's friendship all the same. 'I will. I will. And I won't.'

'Good. Now, let's see if we can use Franklin St George's false sense of security against him. One thing is certain. He'll never suspect you. That is a powerful advantage. One Major General Drake cannot attain.' Philippa winked at Millie, then lifted her skirts, leading the way back down the path to exit the greenhouse.

Just thinking about engaging Franklin St George in anything outside of a bout of fisticuffs left Millie cold as she redonned her coat. But this was why Philippa needed her. Millie's history with St George – and his belief she was a trifle he could seduce or ignore at will – did give her a certain advantage.

Exhaling a long breath, she squared her shoulders

and renewed her determination to use her past with St George to aid their mission as they made their way through the frozen gardens to the house.

Philippa was prepared to cause him bodily harm. Surely, Millie could endure a few hours of false pleasantries while engaging the horrid man in conversation and hoping he let something slip. Something more helpful than his blatantly wandering gaze as it roved over her breasts when she re-entered the drawing room.

Her stomach rolled like a ship at sea, threatening to heave up her late breakfast. She put her hand to her mouth and realised she still wore her gloves.

'Drat! I need to return these to my room. I shan't be long.' Millie left Philippa at the foot of the stairs and ran up to her room to deposit her gloves and coat, promising to re-join the party in a trice.

'Stiff upper lip, Millicent. Think of the Queen. It's only a few hours, after all,' she whispered to herself as she climbed the stairs. But when she pushed open the door to her bedroom, something felt wrong. Someone had been there. She had left a brush on her vanity that was now under the chair. The covers of her bed were rumpled, and one of the nightstand drawers was left ajar.

Millie's skin pricked with alarm. She looked

around her room, terrified the intruder might still be hiding somewhere. After checking under the bed, behind the drapes, in her dressing room and study, the mysterious snooper was either gone or able to contort himself into the smallest of hiding places.

'What in the Devil?' She opened her drawers, but nothing seemed amiss, though it was clear her writing pen had been moved, her papers were shuffled, and one of her favourite books had a small tear on the cover.

Millie shook her head, walked out of her room, and firmly shut the door. 'Strange,' she muttered to herself before descending to the main floor. She was still puzzling about her room when she crashed into Franklin St George. He caught her, but as she stepped back, Franklin refused to loosen his grip around her waist.

'I'm so sorry, Franklin. I didn't see you there. I must have been wool-gathering.' She tried to step away again, but instead of releasing her, he pulled her closer. She could smell his aftershave, a pungent blend of patchouli and pine. Crinkling her nose, she tried to breathe through her mouth. 'What are you—'

Franklin swooped in and pressed his wet lips against hers before Millie could squirm away. The shock gave her a kick of adrenaline, and she shoved against his chest, twisting her head to break their kiss.

'What the blazes?' she hissed, wiping her mouth with her hand.

'Don't try to deny it, Millicent.' Franklin's eyes were crazed, his colour high. 'I knew from the moment I arrived.'

Millie's brow drew down. 'Knew what?'

'You still want me.' Franklin smiled triumphantly. His chin almost completely dissolved into his neck as he nodded at her. 'Who would blame you when facing a lifetime looking at Drake's hideous face? I can see how your body reacts to my presence. Stop resisting. Even married women can have dalliances if they remain discreet.' He tilted his chin and looked down his nose at her. 'You're wild for me.'

Millie would have laughed if not for the horror of the situation. 'The only wild thing here is your imagination.' She wished she could reach for her blades. But then he was leaning closer, his wet lips pursed.

Enough of this!

Franklin's hand was wrapped around Millie's waist. She grasped his thumb and twisted hard. His mouth – only moments ago intent on crashing into hers – twisted painfully and a high-pitched cry emitted from his lips.

Millie increased the pressure on his thumb, forcing him to release his grip on her. Letting go of his hand, she shoved hard against his chest, and he stumbled back a step, his eyes wide with shock.

'Let me be very clear with you, Franklin. I am not interested in any dalliances. I would rather kiss one of the slugs in the garden than ever subject myself to your affections.'

Franklin recovered faster than she would have thought. A sick excitement flashed in his grey eyes. 'You've got more fight in you than last time. I like that, Millie.'

'It's Millicent,' she bit out between clenched teeth. 'And I don't think you'll like my brand of fight, Franklin. I'm not the young, naïve girl you once knew.' Millie ruthlessly shoved down her fear and focused on the rage. She *hated* that he had used her pet name as if he had a right.

'You don't need to pretend, *Millie*.' The bastard put undue emphasis on her name. 'Not around me. Some things never change. Your obsession with me from childhood was always flattering. I know I hurt you when I rejected your wanton advances, but I find myself drawn to you now.'

Millie did laugh, then. 'My obsession with you died rather quickly when you took my virtue and abandoned me like a whore. Trust me, Franklin, Major General Drake may have scars, but I find him to be the most desirable man I've ever seen. He surpasses you in all ways. Touch me again, and you will regret your decision.'

Hmm. Maybe pretending a friendship with Franklin wasn't going to work. She was a terrible liar, after all.

Franklin took a step forward.

Millie lifted her hand and slapped him hard, his head whipping to the side.

Franklin lifted a shaking hand to his cheek. His gaze narrowed. 'Filthy little bitch.'

It was the second time she'd been called a bitch in one day. She didn't love it. But she did enjoy seeing Franklin's eyes fill with fear. He was a bully at the heart of things. And bullies didn't want a fair fight.

'I won't speak of this to Major General Drake. But if it happens again, he will be notified. How are your skills at duelling, Franklin? As I recall, you were always a terrible shot and even more dismal with swords. Beaufort is a skilled marksman, and his sword work is masterful. Trust me.'

Fear transitioned to anger, his mouth pressing tightly together. 'This conversation isn't over, Millicent. I had you once. I mean to have you again.'

Millie swallowed the bile rising in her throat. 'You never had me, Franklin. I chose you. Unwisely, as it were. And I will never choose you again.' She turned and quickly walked into the drawing room, her neck prickling. She was sure his gaze burned into her as she walked away.

Wonderful! Franklin will certainly trust me with his secrets now.

Millie sought out Drake. His gaze fell upon her, then looked behind her to see Franklin entering the room. Two parentheses formed on either side of his mouth. She couldn't read his mind, but it didn't take all her sleuthing skills to determine he'd jumped to the wrong conclusion.

Men. Are. The. Worst. Even decent ones.

Millie took a deep breath and prepared herself for what was sure to be a dismal afternoon.

* * *

Drake paced in his room. It had been a dismal afternoon. His dinner jacket was stiff at the elbows, his white cravat tied too damned tight. The evening promised to be even worse than his day thus far. There was still an hour before dinner, but already he was dreading the meal with so much unwanted company.

His limp was worse than usual. He'd not taken time to massage his leg with the linseed oil prescribed by his doctor. It eased some of the tension and helped to keep the scars from seizing, but he had no patience for it tonight.

Patricia had been so thrilled to welcome Godric and Nora into Drake's goddamned house. And when Franklin St George peeled himself away from staring at Millicent, he had spent the remainder of the afternoon at Patricia's side like a little lapdog. The stupid woman had practically purred with satisfaction. She had used the guest list to ensure Drake and Millicent would both be miserable. And she had succeeded. He was livid.

But his anger had only increased as he watched Millicent avoiding Franklin. Something had occurred between them. Something ugly, knowing Franklin. Every time the bastard's eyes had wandered below Millicent's chin, Drake's hands clenched into fists, and a haze of red descended. Being tortured at the hands of hardened soldiers in the suffocating heat of Afghanistan had been a lark compared to an afternoon watching Franklin looking at Drake's woman as though she were a treat he'd like to consume.

But she isn't my woman.

Millicent yearned for independence. Freedom. She

didn't want a husband, even if her physical desire for him was obvious. Even if she didn't want such liberation, he was determined to have a distant marriage where his control wouldn't be sabotaged by his lust.

Millicent would never truly belong to him. The only reason she'd trapped Drake into this wedding fiasco was because she thought he'd beg off.

But I can't. One taste of her on that damned veranda made me an addict.

And now, after suffering through the longest afternoon in his memory, he could hear her in her bedroom, only one sodding door away, moving about. Every sinew in his body tightened at the thought. He wanted her. More fiercely than he'd wanted anything. It was madness. This need hovering between pleasure and pain. How was a man supposed to think logically when all Drake imagined was the taste of her skin against his mouth?

The bloody fucking flutter in his chest was back.

Two incredibly unpleasant thoughts had taken root in Drake's mind over the course of the afternoon, choking out everything else like ivy. First, Drake's earlier suspicion about Franklin divesting Millicent of her virtue was gaining traction in his mind, which brought on the second and far more troubling question. What if she still wanted St George? It defied logic, but if

Franklin had been Millicent's first love, her feelings about him would be powerful and difficult to dismiss. A tryst would explain why the two of them came into the room together and were acting so awkward.

But Millicent wants me as much as I want her.

At least physically. He knew by the way her eyes warmed when he approached. How she teased him when everyone else ran and hid from his nasty temper. How her body melted against him when he held her. How she moaned when he nuzzled her delicate throat.

And she *loathed* Franklin St George. She'd not said as much, but she didn't have to use words to convey her feelings. She had stiffened her spine when his coach approached Alder House. Throughout the afternoon, any time St George came close to Millicent, her whole body leaned away from him. Though Drake well knew, sometimes a person avoided what they wanted most. It begged the question, what exactly had transpired between them before they re-joined the group that afternoon?

Patricia had warned Drake that Millicent would cuckold him before the week was out, but nothing that vile woman said rang true. So, what was his devious wife-to-be playing at? And was it a coincidence she was speaking privately with the very man Drake had been tasked to investigate?

There was only one way to find out. With a determined growl, he marched to the door and flung it open.

'Bloody hell! Drake! You scared me half to death.' Millicent had been sitting on a padded stool in front of her vanity, but at his abrupt entrance, she jumped up, her hands disappearing into her emerald skirts. She looked magnificent in a scoop-necked dress. Drake wanted to lock the door and devour her. Instead, he focused on his suspicions.

'What occurred between you and Franklin St George this afternoon?' Not exactly subtle, but Drake wasn't some sonnet-spouting idiot. His gentleness from the night before was an anomaly. Best she get used to his rough ways.

Millicent raised her brows, her full lips parting in a prolonged breath. 'I ran into him after returning to my room to deposit my gloves and coat.'

'That doesn't exactly answer my question, does it? It's the second question I've asked today that you've evaded.' Drake slowly walked closer, stalking her like some limping beast. He knew his behaviour was unforgivable, but he didn't care.

Millicent's luscious mouth curved in a smile as she looked away. 'You're right. A novel experience, I'd wager.'

He wouldn't rise to the bait. Instead, he prowled closer.

She huffed out a breath. 'I was hoping you wouldn't notice.'

Drake's cock hardened, and his heart thrashed in his chest. 'I notice everything when it comes to you, Millicent. Even when I wish I didn't.'

Millicent's skin darkened into a shade of red he was beginning to crave. 'As my future husband, you deserve to know some things about my past. Franklin is the man who...' She fumbled.

'He was your lover?' Drake spat the accusation at her like a poisoned dart. 'Hardly a mere "family acquaintance", darling.' Perverse pleasure in using her own words against her twisted his lips into a painful smile. He hated the anger boiling in his blood, burning away his control. What did he care who she'd been with in her past? Or who she would be with in her future? That is what a distant marriage entailed. Both partners were free to take discreet lovers, and yet the very idea filled him with fury.

Millicent paused, a soft, husky laugh escaping. 'Neither of our descriptions are true. He was not just a family acquaintance, yet calling him my lover implies there was some level of love involved, and there wasn't. Certainly not for Franklin. But, yes. He was the man who took my virtue. Though in fairness to him, I offered it up freely. And while I fancied myself in love, it was really only girlish infatuation.'

'Yet, despite this lack of love, he wishes to renew a physical relationship with you?' Drake was going to kill Franklin St George. He cared not if the man was guilty of any crime other than propositioning Drake's almost wife.

Millicent's beautiful eyes widened and her blush spread, painting across her ample breasts. Breasts Drake dearly wanted to bury his head in, forgetting everything except her scent and softness. 'How did you know?'

The harsh sound he emitted couldn't be called a laugh. 'He's a man. And you are far more desirable than you think.'

Millicent bit her bottom lip. Drake suppressed a groan as her white teeth buried themselves into plump, red skin.

'I don't think I'm... That's really not the point.'

'What did you say to his proposition?' Drake held his breath and pretended her answer didn't have the power to shatter him. He shouldn't have allowed his useless heart to defy him.

She took a halting step closer. 'I told him if he ever

dared approach me again about the subject, he would be duelling with you at dawn.'

Drake's relieved exhale left no doubt as to his fears.

'Did you think I might accept his offer?'

He couldn't answer. Instead, he stood silent, blinking hard and wishing the earth would open up and swallow him whole. Of course he thought she would choose her unbroken first love over the stern, angry, scarred man Drake had become. To expose such vulnerability in front of her was excruciating.

'Well, that doesn't say much for your opinion of me, does it?' Millicent huffed out an exasperated breath. The woman could speak volumes with no words at all. 'Neither of us have much trust, it would seem.'

He was close enough to smell citrus and cotton. One more step, and she would be within arm's length. 'No. We don't. Explain something to me, Millicent. What exactly is your connection with the Duchess of Dorsett?'

Her gaze flitted away from him.

Ah. So. She isn't going to be honest.

'What does she have to do with Franklin St George?'

'Exactly.' Drake watched her closely, but she kept her face carefully blank. 'What does she have to do with Franklin St George? And is she asking you to help her?'

He closed the distance between them. Lifting his hand, he brushed the tips of his fingers down her cheek. She was so goddamn soft. Like warm silk. He watched in fascination as her pupils dilated, leaving only a ring of chocolate around the edges. 'You're keeping secrets from me, Millicent.'

'And what about you? Are you being honest with me?'

Drake clenched his jaw.

'Precisely. As I said, neither of us have much trust.'

Before she could say more, he stopped her mouth with his own. This was easy. This was honest. This connection between them, pulsing with tension and need was so much simpler than conversation. So much better than ugly questions and even uglier answers.

Plunging his tongue into her depths, he caught her around the waist, pressing her lush curves against the hardened planes of his body. When she melted, he wanted to roar in triumph.

I am not giving her anything but physical pleasure. I'm still in control of what matters. My heart. My loyalty. Myself.

So, how was he any better than St George? Only offering physical pleasure. No more. He pushed the question aside, unwilling to destroy this moment with useless introspection.

He tangled his tongue with hers. His bold temptress scraped her teeth over his bottom lip and bit hard enough to make him growl.

His hands wandered down her back, cupping her generous arse and squeezing hard. She was firm and fit where most women were soft and delicate. Just what made her so athletic was a question for later. Now, he gave in to his wild need. Pulling away from their kiss, he nibbled along her jaw, down her throat, until he buried his nose in the fragrant patch of skin between her clavicles.

'Did you ever feel desire like this for him?' It was a cruel question, but Drake wasn't feeling kind. He was nothing like St George and he wanted Millicent to admit it. What they shared together, what she felt for Drake was more. He was better than that snivelling, vile excuse for a man.

'No. Never.' Millicent's harsh whisper only heightened his need.

'You won't feel this for anyone else. I promise you. We may not have much trust, but I'm asking you to pledge to me your faithfulness. I will not share you, Millicent. Not with anyone.' Distant marriage be damned. At least in this. At least for now. He spoke around heated kisses as his fingers traced along the neckline of her gown.

Millicent scraped her nails against his scalp, scratching hard enough to spike his lust a notch higher. She pulled him away from her with a strength that shouldn't surprise him. 'And what about you, my lord? I am not a woman who tolerates inequity. My fidelity is only yours if you promise me the same. I don't like to share either, Drake.'

God, she was magnificent. Strands of her hair had come loose from his fingers tunnelling into the silky depths. Her lips were swollen from his kisses, her eyes heavy-lidded. How could he possibly want another woman when he could have her?

'You have my promise, Millicent. However long this lasts between us, my body is yours completely. Will you give me the same promise?' This wasn't how their conversation was meant to progress. Drake had planned on questioning her, determining what her game was with Franklin St George, then outlining exactly how their marriage would proceed. But she had derailed him. Something she did with alarming regularity. And now, instead of demanding her faithfulness, he was asking for it. Like a love-sick swain.

But this isn't love. It's lust. Only desire. And I can control that.

'I swear it, Beau. My body is yours alone for as long as this lasts.'

I want more.

What more could he possibly want? He pushed the question aside and leaned down to press kisses against the swell of her generous breasts. Reaching into her neckline, he scooped a delicious globe out, her strawberry nipple puckering for his mouth.

He fell upon her like a starving man upon a feast. Biting, nipping, sucking. So much better than his dream. He freed her other breast, her dress pushing them up and out like some pagan offering.

'Beau!' Her strangled cry unravelled him.

Lavishing her right breast with his mouth, his fingers mirrored his efforts with the left.

'Are you wet for me, sweetheart?' Soft words so unfamiliar to Drake, but they poured out of him whenever she was near.

'I don't... This never happened before.' Millicent's nails were like crescent indentations of fire on his neck as she held him closer.

Pulling free of her, he tugged her over to a chaise, laying her out like some decadent feast. Her breasts – gloriously free from their constraints – were blatantly naked while the rest of her remained clothed. It was erotic and so fucking sensual. His cock jerked. He could rub himself to completion just looking at her. But she had given him a better idea.

'Lift your skirts for me, Millicent.'

Millicent's eyes flew wide, brave even in this. Her hands reached for the emerald silk. She pulled up her skirts, uncovering delicate ankles and shapely calves covered in sheer stockings and held in place with garters. But Millicent revealed even more than her seductive body. A blade was tied to her left ankle. Another to her right thigh. A third to her right ankle.

Drake fingered the leather strap around her thigh. 'My, my.'

Millicent froze, her beautiful eyes filled with alarm. She tried to pull her skirt down as she realised too late her mistake. Drake was quicker, encircling her wrist with his much stronger hand, halting her progress.

'It's just for protection. A young lady can't be too careful.' The words rushed out as Millicent looked over his left shoulder.

A courageous woman might carry a small muff pistol for protection, but throwing blades like the ones strapped to Millicent's delicious body required a level of skill no young miss of the beau monde would ever master without significant training. She was lying. But Drake didn't give a good goddamn in that moment. There were more important things to focus on just now.

Drake had never been aroused by weapons before. But seeing the pewter glint of steel against Millicent's pale, gorgeous leg sent a new rush of blood to his already straining cock. Too lost to his desires to ask her questions, he determined there would be time for interrogations later. Much later.

'Spread your legs for me, Millicent.'

She must have been so relieved he wasn't questioning her, she didn't hesitate to follow his command. She thrust her chin into the air and boldly spread her legs.

Dear God. I know what heaven looks like.

Her pale thighs widened to expose copper curls and pink lips dripping with need.

Drake sank to his knees.

'What are you doing?' Millicent's courage seemed to have failed her. She closed her thighs tightly, her eyes widening in alarm.

It would seem Franklin St George never shared this pleasure with Millicent.

Idiot!

Oh, the things Drake would show her. Putting a large, calloused palm on either knee, Drake slowly pushed her legs apart again. He kept his gaze on Millicent's face, watching the war of desire and fear play out in devastating detail. 'I know we share little faith between us. But trust me in this. Please.' He wouldn't force her. But he hoped with every fibre of his being she agreed.

Blinking, Millicent swallowed hard and then nodded. It was all the assent he needed.

Drake pressed a kiss against her right knee, then her left. Her skin smelled of lemons. He trailed more kisses up her thighs, switching from one side to the other. He nipped and licked a pathway to heaven, carefully avoiding the wicked blades. Slowly, her legs eased further apart, making room for his wide shoulders. He settled himself at her apex, lifting one leg over his shoulder, then the other.

'Beau, what are you doing? This can't be right.'

'Let me show you how right it can be.' He caught her gaze in his own. 'Yield to me, Millicent. Just in this. Just for now.'

She bit her lip and his cock wanted to explode. He groaned, willing his body to behave.

'Okay.'

Thank the Devil!

'And, if you'd like to call me Millie, er, that is what my friends call me. Given our current situation...' Her voice trailed off as she swallowed loudly.

Inexplicably, the flutter in his heart was back as something warm and liquid filled his chest. 'Relax, Millie. I have you.'

Leaning closer, he didn't break eye contact. He pressed his nose into the crinkling curls hiding her secrets from him and inhaled. Her earthy scent almost drove him over the edge.

'Beau!' She tightened her thighs around his head, but he wasn't stopping now.

'Touch your breasts, Millie. Pretend your hand is mine.'

He licked her slit, revelling in the salty tang of Millie, glancing up to see her strong fingers pinch, caress, and stroke her beautiful nipples. It was the most gorgeous sight he'd ever seen.

She cried out in shock, so he delved deeper, finding the cluster of nerves that held her pleasure captive. He sucked and nuzzled, kissed, and nibbled, scraped gently with his teeth before slipping a finger into her tight channel.

Millie writhed, her cries creating a map to her climax. He followed her dips and hollows, his finger creating a rhythm that opened her further. He pushed a second finger into her depths, marvelling at how tight she felt against him as she flexed her thighs on either side of his head. He crooked his finger, finding a special, secret place that caused Millie's body to seize. Her cries stopped, and she held her breath. He knew she was close. So close.

Licking in rhythm to his fingers, he drove her higher, harder, faster. When he sucked her nub between his lips and crooked his finger in tandem, she screamed out his name as her body clamped around him, her legs gripping tight, her entire being vibrating like a cello string.

It was glorious.

Until the door burst open, and a very angry scream had him scrambling from beneath Millie's skirts.

A pale, thin woman in a gown the colour of storm clouds rushed into the room.

'Unhand my friend, you bastard!' The delicate woman looked around and grabbed a hairbrush left on the side table near the door. She brandished the thing like a battle axe. 'Step away from Millie or I shall pummel you, sir!' The woman strode forward like an avenging angel.

Drake pulled Millie's skirts down as she frantically attempted to shove her breasts back into her bodice.

'Ivy!' Millie's husky voice was equal parts surprised, joyful, and chagrined. 'One moment.' She continued to right herself as Drake stood. 'Oh, my Lord, I've missed you.' Millie pushed up from the chaise, then nearly collapsed again. Drake steadied her, hoping to God Ivy didn't notice his granite cock pressing against the cotton of his pants, straining for release.

Millie ran to her friend, wrapped her arms around the thin woman, and hugged her so tight, Drake worried his betrothed might break her friend in half.

Ivy kept her gaze focused on Drake even as she hugged Millie back.

Ivy Cavendale. Best friend to Millie. Daughter of Lord Cavendale. Sister of Alfred Cavendale. Unfortunately for Ivy, both men tried to kill Drake's closest – some might say only – friend, Lieutenant General Robert Killian.

The house party Drake and Killian had attended at Lord Bradford's country estate several months prior ended in three deaths. Alfred Cavendale died at the hands of his father. Lord Cavendale died at the hands of Hannah Simmons. And Killian's state as a confirmed bachelor also died at the hands of Hannah Simmons. At the time, Drake thought his best friend was a complete idiot. Only moronic imbeciles were stupid enough to fall in love.

He shifted in his jacket as the cursed flutter worked double-time in his chest while his cock reluctantly receded.

Please! Lust and love are not the same. I survived the nightmare of love once. I won't risk that hellfire again.

His heart pounded painfully against his ribs, flagrantly disregarding his thoughts, but he ignored the stupid organ.

'Miss Cavendale. What a pleasure to see you again so unexpectedly.' He let sarcasm coat every syllable as he raised his eyebrow at her, straightening to his full six foot four inches. Hopefully, his tone would quell her lethal intent. But the delicate woman didn't even flinch.

What is wrong with these ladies?

First Hannah Simmons, then Millie. Now, this slip of a woman who looked like a strong breeze could blow her away. Yet here she stood, facing off against him with murder in her eyes and only a damned hairbrush as a weapon. Didn't they know he was an intimidating, powerful, dangerous man? Someone with whom you did not trifle?

Ivy stepped out of Millie's embrace, strode up to

Drake, put both hands on his chest, and shoved him. Hard.

No. She doesn't know. She's trifling. Drake heaved out a sigh.

'You stay away from my friend, you blackguard! How dare you take advantage of her in the safety of her own rooms?' The woman was furious. Ivory skin blotched with crimson shades of rage. Her blue eyes, almost as pale as his, flashed with fury.

Millie came up behind her friend, putting a hand on her shoulder and turning her around. 'Ivy, I'm fine. He wasn't taking advantage. That is to say, er... I was quite enjoying the ravagement, though I don't think that's a word.'

Ivy froze, her eyes going wide. He watched the rage drain out of her like a hot air balloon deflating. 'Oh. I see. Well. How... unfortunate. For me, I mean.' She flapped her hand between Millie and Drake. 'I'm sure it was quite fortunate for the two of you. I fear I've overstepped.' For some bewildering reason, his rogue heart squeezed painfully at her obvious embarrassment. It wasn't enough that Millie crawled into the cracks and crevices of his heart; now some woman he neither knew well nor cared about was making him feel things. Bad things. She was Millie's closest friend, but why on earth would it matter to him if she was upset?

Because it matters to Millie.

First fluttering, then pounding, now this. Angina. That's what this is. Angina pectoris.

'Of course not!' Millie rubbed her hand down Ivy's arm in a reassuring gesture.

'You were trying to protect your friend. Quite bravely, Miss Ivy. I don't know many men with enough courage to challenge me with a hairbrush.' Drake clamped his jaw shut. What was he doing now? Reassuring a woman who interrupted him just as he was about to let his poor cock have a desperately needed moment of release? He'd taken leave of his senses. It was the only logical answer.

Ivy's face crumpled. As the first tear emerged, Drake began to panic. He never panicked. He faced hordes of marauders, torture, starvation, freezing cold, and sweltering heat. Not once did he panic. But one tear and he was ready to beat a hasty retreat.

'Perhaps you should return to your room, Drake. Ivy's had a long journey and we haven't seen each other in weeks.' Millie wrapped her arm around Ivy's shoulder, shielding her friend with her body.

'Yes. That is good. I shall just...' Drake backed away, feeling equal parts shame and relief for wanting to escape. 'I will see you downstairs. Later.' He turned and made haste for their connecting door.

Dear God. Women are far more terrifying than any Afghan warriors.

It wasn't until he reached the safety of his room, he realised he'd completely forgotten to question Millie about the blades. Or Philippa. Or St George.

'Fucking hell.'

12

Ivy crumpled into a wingback chair sitting next to the cheerfully crackling fire in Millie's bedchamber. She covered her face with her hands. 'Oh, Lord. I'm so sorry, Millie. When I came in and saw him under your skirts... I mean, what on earth was he even...' Her voice trailed off.

Millie's face heated. 'He was, that is, it was quite... I can't really...'

Ivy waved her hand in front of her face. 'No. Don't tell me. I don't really wish to know.'

Millie knelt on the floor at her friend's feet, leaning against Ivy's legs. She grasped Ivy's hands and pulled them away from her face, holding them in her own. Her dress would be crushed and likely wrinkle, but she didn't care. 'Ivy, you were only trying to protect me. There's nothing to be embarrassed about. If anyone should be embarrassed, it's me. And honestly, I think Lord Drake was impressed with your courage and loyalty.'

Ivy's lip trembled. 'I think something is wrong with me, Millie. I think I'm broken in some horrible way.' Tears tracked down her face.

Alarm tightened Millie's throat. Her stomach clenched. 'Broken? What do you mean? It's okay to tell me, Ivy. I won't say a word. It shall stay just between us, here in this room.'

Millie had long wondered about Ivy and Lord Cavendale. Ivy's father always seemed kind. But there was something beneath his smile, the way his gaze would sometimes linger, the glint of something hungry setting her on edge.

'When father died, I was so relieved.' A sob wrenched free from Ivy. She pressed one hand against her mouth as Millie squeezed the other. For a time, they sat like that. Ivy quaking with emotion, Millie stalwart and steady by her side even as her body still echoed from the mystifying glory Drake had created with his teeth, tongue, and lips. Not to mention his clever fingers.

'It's okay, Ivy. You don't need to say any more. Your

father was a bastard. A sick, cruel horror of a man. I'm glad he's dead as well. I only wish I could have done it myself.' Rage immolated the lingering pleasure pulsing through Millie's veins. She wrapped Ivy in her strong arms. 'I'm so sorry, Ivy. So very sorry.' For what, she still wasn't sure. But it didn't matter. Not all hurts needed to be shared in order to give and receive comfort.

Ivy shuddered again. 'I can't imagine doing what you were just... I don't *want* to, Millie. I'd rather die.'

'Then you'll never have to. I promise.' Inspiration struck Millie. 'I will speak to Lady Philippa. With Hannah gone, I'm sure she'd open her house to you. Her view on marriage is just as dim as yours. She'd never expect you to tie yourself to a man.'

Ivy took another shaky breath. 'That is far too much to ask of anyone not obligated by bloodlines. No. My aunt has kindly taken me in. I'm quite comfortable there. She is aware of my desire to stay single, and we are looking into positions as a governess.'

Millie pulled back. She had no idea Ivy's situation was so dire. 'Ivy, is that what you want?'

Ivy laughed, a dry, coughing sound. 'Do you want to be marrying the Earl of Tetly?'

Millie's mouth opened, but she had no answer. Did she want to marry Drake? A week ago, she would have vehemently said no. But now... things were much more complex.

Ivy mistook her silence. 'Exactly. Sometimes, we do things because we must. But will I hate being a governess? No. I don't think so. It will grant me independence, and I shall be free of ever having to marry. But there is one thing I wanted to ask.'

Millie blinked. 'Of course. Anything.'

'While I don't expect an offer of lodging, I wanted to know if Lady Philippa would work with me... before I take a position.'

Millie had told Ivy of her time with Philippa. The duchess swore Millie to secrecy, but Ivy was her best friend. Best friends didn't keep secrets. And Millie didn't feel like she had betrayed Philippa. Ivy was an extension of herself. Telling Ivy about her training with Philippa was the same as writing in a journal or talking to herself in the privacy of her own room.

'I'm sure she would... Are you wanting to join the investigation?'

'Dear Lord, no. I couldn't possibly be so daring as you or Hannah. No, I just want to know I can protect myself. If I am to live in a stranger's house with a family I don't know, I want reassurance I can keep myself safe.' She tangled her fingers together, focusing on them instead of looking at Millie.

A governess was vulnerable to the whims of her employer's wishes. While never discussed openly, it was no secret these women were easily taken advantage of, much like female servants. It was a silent plague only afflicting the women in society. Therefore, the atrocities were accepted by men as unfortunate but minor issues best left in the shadows. Accountability for such crimes would put far too many of their brethren at risk. Better to leave things as they were and let the women endure. Boys would be boys, after all, and what were men but grown boys?

Another wave of anger washed through Millie. 'Of course she will help. I'll speak to her about it, and she can organise something with you before you leave. But Ivy, you aren't broken. He didn't break you.'

Ivy shrugged, wiping her cheek with a shaking hand. 'Can we speak of other things? Please?'

Millie wanted to say more, but it was clear Ivy had shared as much as she could. Instead, she nodded and stood, shaking out her skirts. 'Of course. You'll never guess who Patricia invited to this mess of a wedding.'

They spent the next three-quarters of an hour catching up on all the happenings at Alder House. When Millie and Ivy descended to dinner, Ivy's eyes were clear, her shoulders back, her face serene. But Millie ached for her friend's hidden pain and vowed to redouble her efforts in discovering Franklin's plans. She couldn't save Ivy from her past, but she could prevent such crimes from happening to other young women just as innocent and just as worthy of protection. Because even if Franklin was only a grown boy, he was committing the crimes of a man, and she would hold him accountable.

* * *

Patricia must have arranged the seating for dinner. Millie was placed next to Victoria. On her other side was Lord Bradford, an old family friend with the most extravagant moustache Millie had ever seen. She wondered how the man managed the soup course without dripping like a walrus. Glancing down the table at her betrothed, she narrowed her gaze. Nora was seated to his left and kept leaning over to whisper things to him. Her dress was cut so low, Drake would get quite the view if he chose to look down. Which he did not. Indeed, he spent most of the dinner staring at Millie.

Something vital had shifted in Millie since her moment on the chaise with Drake. She felt awake. Aware of a whole world most women never even glimpsed. She couldn't forget their heated promise. His body belonged to her alone, as hers belonged to him. But what if she wanted more than just his body?

I've always been a greedy thing.

Delicious trails of heat skated along her skin, pooling low in her belly and sparking like stars in a midnight sky. She had never imagined a man could do something so wicked and delicious with his mouth.

'Miss Millicent, have you had a chance to explore the shops in Bedford?' Victoria batted her large eyes and lifted her fork to her mouth, only to put it back down again without taking a bite of her turbot.

'I haven't, and please, call me Millie. Have you?'

'Franklin treated me on our way here. He knows my love of Bedfordshire lace. It's most exquisite but so dear, I never thought he would allow me to purchase any.' Victoria's cheeks grew pink with pleasure. 'He's usually quite strict with my pin money.'

'Is he?' Millie glanced over to Franklin. He was sitting next to her stepmother, but when he caught her gaze, he lowered his hand beneath the table. She didn't have to guess what he was rubbing. She forced her face to remain impassive and turned quickly back to Victoria as a wave of nausea rolled through her belly.

Disgusting man. He probably spends all of Victoria's

pin money on whores who can't refuse his hideous advances.

'Franklin's concern with frugality is commendable, but he must have wanted to spoil me this week because we came a full three days early just so I could shop. He sent me off with a footman and my maid every day to wander the town. It was glorious.'

'He didn't join you? What on earth did Lord St George do for three days in Bedford?' Millie couldn't imagine Franklin being so generous with his wife without some ulterior motive.

He probably drank the days away and found a house of ill repute.

'He had business to attend to with a local merchant.'

Local merchant sounds a lot like local mistress. Didn't Philippa say he had three?

Victoria continued, blissfully ignorant of Millie's dark thoughts. 'That's the way with husbands, isn't it? Always disappearing to do important things while we sit around and embroider cushions or paint plates.' Victoria's smile dimmed. 'Still, I shouldn't complain. I was able to buy a lovely yard of lace. I can't imagine what I'll do with it. I'm sure to ruin something so fine.'

Millie frowned. 'I'm sure you'll make something

absolutely divine. You deserve some finery in your life, Victoria.'

A jelly tart had more backbone than poor Victoria. Millie could only imagine how Franklin would run circles around her. The man was probably shagging his way through town while his wife praised him for allowing her to buy a yard of lace.

Millie sent a silent prayer to the deities for saving her from such a fate. Her gaze slipped back to Drake. He was watching her, his icy eyes hot with intention.

Holy hollyhocks.

Her core tingled. She forced her attention back to Victoria. The woman blinked her wide eyes furiously. 'I know there are whispers in the beau monde about Franklin. Unsavoury gossip about him straying, but all men do, don't they? It's part of married life, letting them sow their wild oats while we keep the home fires burning.' Maybe Victoria wasn't as ignorant as Millie thought. 'I'm sure it will be the same for you.' Victoria pushed her turbot around, covering the fish with cream sauce but still not eating anything. Perhaps she didn't enjoy fish, which was a shame. Turbot in dill cream sauce was Millie's favourite.

She would have savoured another bite, but just the idea of Drake sowing any wild oats had her reaching for the blade strapped to her thigh. A blade Drake now knew about. She was so foolish for letting him see her secret. Philippa would be furious. And what on earth would she say to Drake if he questioned her further? She would need to think of some convincing lie and quick. He was the prime minister's investigator, after all. He certainly wouldn't let himself be distracted from discovering her secrets for too long.

Which should terrify me. Not fill me with a sense of relief. I might trust him with my body, but only a fool would trust a man like Drake with her secrets.

But a dangerous question tickled her mind. *What if?* What if she could trust him? What if their relationship was based on honesty and respect instead of utility and deception?

She looked again at Nora, whose hand was inching closer to Drake's on the table. A red haze descended as she forgot all about perilous questions with impossible answers.

She'll touch his hand over my dead body. Or better yet, over hers.

The blade at her wrist pressed into the delicate skin. It would be so easy to release one and let it fly.

Mustn't fillet Nora during dinner. Perhaps later, during a nice game of whist.

Drake pulled his hand away to reach for his cup as he pivoted to speak with Reynard Renquist, who sat on his right. His broad back created an impenetrable wall, blocking Nora completely.

Millie's heart beat out of turn as warmth crept from her chest to her cheeks. He was ignoring the beautiful woman who once held his heart in her bony little hands. And taking every opportunity to scorch Millie with incendiary looks so full of lust, she felt like the most desirable woman at the table. Which never happened.

She pulled her attention back to Victoria, wanting to encourage the woman. 'I think Franklin has no idea what he's missing if any of the gossip is true. If he isn't willing to please you, then perhaps you should think on ways to please yourself.'

Victoria's eyes widened further and her mouth fell open. 'Miss Millicent, what on earth do you mean?'

Millie knew exactly what she meant but explaining the finer points of self-pleasure to Victoria St George during the fish course seemed unwise. 'Oh, you know, things like your lace or taking long walks in the park. Needlepoint, if that thrills you.' She smiled at Victoria and nudged her with her shoulder. 'You have a household staff to keep the fires burning. Instead, why don't you explore some of your interests?'

Victoria stared at her fork. 'I do quite enjoy poetry. Franklin says it's nothing but a bunch of drivel from' –

she glanced around and lowered her voice – 'Molly men. But I find it quite invigorating, though I'd never admit as much to him.'

Nodding her head, Millie patted Victoria on her hand. 'I quite agree. Poetry stirs the heart and feeds the soul. The next time Lord St George is conducting his "business", I'd take your pin money to Hatchards and buy yourself some Lord Byron or, if you're feeling daring, Elizabeth Barrett Browning.'

Victoria speared a pea and popped it into her mouth. Her chin lifted as she swallowed. 'Excellent suggestion, Miss Millicent. I think I just might.' She covered her mouth and giggled like a mischievous schoolgirl.

Oh dear. Not exactly a femme fatale, but the poor woman deserves some joy and excitement in her life, and poetry is a wonderful place to start.

Millie raised a cup of wine to her lips and sipped. Drake was looking at her again, his eyes heavy-lidded as he watched her swallow. She darted her tongue out to catch a drop of wine on her bottom lip and marvelled at how tightly Drake gripped his fork. The warmth in her chest migrated lower as delicious tingles erupted along her skin.

Sinfully sensuous man!

She wasn't sure her nervous system could handle

playing cat and mouse with her scarred, grumpy, delightfully skilled fiancé, but she was game to try.

* * *

'I've made some enquiries in Bedford. The proprietor of the Ram's Head informed me a private room was booked earlier this week for domestic interviews.' Reynard spoke quietly to Drake as the fish course was removed and Cook's famous roast beef was brought to them. He pulled Drake's attention away from watching Millie's delectable lips.

She was killing Drake in small degrees as she darted her pink tongue out to catch a ruby drop of wine. And she knew it, the saucy woman. Drake closed his eyes tight for a moment, willing his cock to behave and his attention to stay focused on Reynard.

'Did he say who booked the room?'

Reynard laughed, his golden hair catching the flickering candlelight. 'Yes. Apparently, a John Smith of London was asked to conduct interviews for his employer. And before you ask, the proprietor couldn't give me a description of any use. "Average-looking bloke", and that's a direct quote.'

Drake shook his head. 'He didn't happen to mention anything about a weak chin, did he?'

'No. And I asked. According to the man, "one chin's the same as any other".'

'Wonderful. Shall we inform the prime minister we've cracked the case?'

Reynard sipped his wine. 'Perhaps not.'

Drake shared a look of commiseration with Reynard before his eyes tripped down the table. St George sat next to Patricia. Franklin leaned closer, whispering something to the horrid woman whose canary-yellow evening dress nearly blinded Drake. She had some kind of feathers in her hair fluttering every time she tilted her head back to laugh. The awful tinkling sound made Drake cringe.

'Well, regardless of the faulty intel, it's bloody good to have you here. We'll catch him. St George is sure to trip up. We just need to keep our wits about us.' Drake cut into his excellently seasoned beef, his knife slicing through the meat like butter.

'Perhaps I should spend some time with St George. Win his trust. See if he's stupid enough to reveal anything.'

Drake raised a brow at his old friend. 'Not a bad plan. You are a far more skilled actor than I. Five minutes alone with St George and I would be forced to kill one of us just to end the conversation.'

Reynard laughed, the strong column of his neck

contracting. 'Leave St George to me. I'm certain your delightful bride-to-be would appreciate more of your time and attention. This is your wedding party, after all.'

Drake shifted in his dinner jacket, his cravat nearly strangling him. 'You know this is not a marriage of affection but rather one of necessity.' Though his actions on the couch belied his words. He shut down the traitorous memories. 'I gave up all hope of romance long ago when a particular woman reminded me that love is nothing more than a dream.' He refused to look at Nora.

'Abandoned dreams have the most power to haunt us.' Reynard's easy smile hardened a bit. 'If life gives you a second chance to chase your dream, maybe catch it this time? Only a fool would pass up the opportunity. I've never known you to be a fool, Drake.'

Drake stilled. When he stopped believing in love, he also lost his fear. The two were strangely intertwined. The death of one caused the other's demise. But Reynard's words rebirthed fear in Drake once more.

He swallowed hard, the beef turning suddenly dry in his mouth. 'What if the dream becomes a nightmare? And chasing it destroys me?' His voice was harsh, his heart beating painfully.

Reynard didn't answer right away. He took a sip of wine and leaned back in his chair, looking at Drake for a long moment. 'You've survived your share of nightmares, Drake. We all have. And in doing so, it's easy to believe that's all we have left. The horror, the loss, the ache. But life moves forward, and dreams still visit us in the darkest hours of night. Are you brave enough to try again? Knowing you might fail and fail spectacularly? Is the risk worth the possible reward?'

It was a great question. Drake hated Reynard for asking it. Because he didn't have a fucking clue.

His gaze flicked to Millie. She was smiling at Victoria, but she glanced over to him as she had been doing all night. They were drawn to each other like iron to a magnet.

She held the answer to Reynard's question. It was the only thing Drake knew with certainty. And he would find out for himself if she was his dream or one more nightmare. Tonight.

* * *

Drake savoured a puff of his cheroot, then sipped from a glass of Scotland's finest whiskey. The gentlemen were enjoying their time before they re-joined the women in the drawing room for an evening of cards and conversation.

I'd rather pull my teeth out with tweezers.

Drake rarely had guests at his country estate. Alder House was his retreat, and he resented the crowd of people invading his billiard room. He watched Reynard stroll over to Franklin and strike up a conversation. Reynard glanced back at Drake, a quick wink betraying his intent.

A hot poker to my balls. Far more appealing than talking to that snivelling swine.

He wasn't sure he could control his temper around a man so unworthy of Millie's time or affections. The very idea of Franklin touching his betrothed filled Drake with a fury that caused him to pause and reflect.

Reflection is for poets and priests. I am neither of those.

And yet, he sat brooding like a love-sick fop. It troubled him. How much he *cared*. His ridiculous heart, an organ that never bothered him in the past, suddenly couldn't keep a rhythm. This infernal consideration extended beyond Millie, encompassing matters of importance to her. Like Ivy Cavendale. Since when did he get embarrassed for women he barely knew and had little interest in getting to know?

Since Millie.

Damnation. He was even starting to notice the

food Millie favoured so he could speak with the cook about ensuring their placement on the menu. It was ridiculous.

Of all the women to suddenly pique his interest, he chose the one lady impossible to contain or control. Which was highly unfortunate. For Drake, control was paramount. If he couldn't control her, he couldn't protect her. He couldn't ensure she stayed with him. He couldn't keep her.

Because she isn't some goddamned pet to be trained or property to own.

But that didn't stop him from wanting to lock her away, safe and secure. The complete opposite of what Millie wanted. Freedom. What human being didn't yearn for autonomy? But free will meant she had choices. And one of those choices could be to leave. Allowing her freedom would be trusting her to stay, and as Millie said, they didn't have much trust between them.

But what we do have between us is incendiary.

He took another deep drag of his cheroot and let the fragrant smoke fog his vision. Not that it mattered. He couldn't see anything clearly now. Not when he closed his eyes and filled his mind with blazing-red hair, warm coffee eyes, and soft curves so abundant, he could drown in her body.

Maybe it was just lust. He hadn't been with a woman in too long to remember. Perhaps his body had gone into overdrive, and he merely needed to slake his voracious thirst to regain a sense of inner calm. He certainly enjoyed his time between her thighs. In those moments, all the frustration, fear, and fury had disappeared.

Yes, what a brilliant excuse to invade Millie's room. A bid for spiritual enlightenment. Hardly! I promised I wouldn't compromise her, but if I visit her tonight, I'll not be a man of my word. Although it wouldn't be the first promise I broke. Of all the sins I've committed, this is one I'd happily burn for.

What kind of honourable gentleman broke a promise to his intended? Drake, apparently. He was disgusted with himself, Millie, love, and all the fates who brought him to this place. He wished Killian were here. The man would be crowing in victory over Drake's obsession, but at least he might offer some sage advice. Millie's heated looks over dinner stirred more than just Drake's cock. She was like an infection he couldn't purge.

And she wants me to break my promise as much as I want to break it. It's hardly dishonourable to rescind a stupid vow neither of us wants to uphold.

His cock twitched hopefully at the thought.

Wonderful. The last thing I need is any input from you.

And now he was talking to his erection.

Fabulous.

So, his brilliant plan of seduction was to knock on Millie's door and see if she would allow him entrance. And if she did, he'd hope like hell one night with Millie purged this burning need from his blood so he could focus on more important things. Like trapping a killer.

No wonder we're no closer to finding evidence against Franklin. I can't even bloody well speak to the man without losing my temper. Because of Millie.

But it wasn't fair to heap that blame on her. It was because of how Drake *felt* about Millie.

I don't have feelings.

The drum of his heartbeat begged to differ.

Lord Bradford ambled over, a fat cigar between his fingers. He stroked his moustache and bumped his shoulder against Drake's.

'Finally decided to leap over the sword, eh?' Bradford's deep laughter echoed throughout the room.

'More of a push than a leap,' Drake mumbled. But that was a lie, and he knew it. He was choosing this marriage. He wanted it. Which was insane.

'I've been with my dear Ethel over five and twenty years.' Bradford's eyes grew hazy, though it could have just been the bluish-grey smoke from his cigar. 'I wouldn't give her up for all the whiskey in the world, and that's saying something. You've picked a good one there, Drake. She'll see you right.'

Drake tried to shake his sour mood. 'Have you any words of wisdom for me, Bradford?'

Bradford smiled, clearly tickled to be asked his opinion. 'Always fight naked, eh? Even when you lose, you win.' He broke into another bout of laughter that ended in a coughing fit. Taking a deep puff of his cigar, he tipped his head back, blowing a stream of smoke toward the ceiling. 'Trust, my boy. That's the key to a good marriage.'

Great. Drake was doomed. He gulped another sip of whiskey as Bradford carried on, oblivious to Drake's despondency.

'Trust, honesty, and never underestimating your wife. Women have a habit of being right more than men would like. Something I learned the hard way, but it's a lesson that's saved my bacon more than once. When my Ethel tells me to listen, I do. Never once re-gretted it.' He slapped Drake on the arm. 'You'll do just fine, my boy. You've a good head on your shoulders and a strong heart in that barrel of a chest.'

'It seems to be off kilter of late.' Even now, it thumped painfully.

'That just means you chose the right woman. Or she chose you. I think it's time we joined the ladies, eh? Stop them from gossiping about all our shortcomings. Course, my Ethel wouldn't have much to say there. She loves me, though I've no idea why.' Bradford stroked his moustache and waggled his thick eyebrows at Drake.

Drake guessed Ethel's affection wasn't based on the man's eccentric facial hair. He joined Bradford in leading the men to the drawing room, feeling mildly better than he had prior to his discussion with Bradford.

Trust.

Honesty.

Listen to her.

Fight naked.

He could certainly follow one piece of the offered advice.

13

The Earl of Tetly's drawing room offered a feast for the eyes. Millie wasn't sure who Drake consulted on the decoration of this room, but the dusty-blue walls contrasted beautifully with dark wood furnishings. An Aubusson rug graced the parquet floor, and pastoral paintings decorated the walls. She tried to focus on those details instead of her stepmother.

'I've always said my daughter was lucky to have such an indulgent father. And if I hadn't put forth such efforts on her behalf, we'd never be having a wedding.' Patricia's shrill laughter grated over Millie's frayed nerves.

'I must admit, I was surprised to see an invitation

from Beaufort for a wedding.' Nora ducked her head in false modesty. 'Certainly, there was a time when he was intent to wed, but I thought he'd given up such ideas.'

How dare you use his name as if you had a right.

Millie swallowed hard, forcing her breathing to remain calm. Nora was diabolical and found her perfect match in Patricia. Those two women joining forces did not bode well for Millie.

Nora's dress was a rose velvet, highlighting her creamy complexion and pink lips. The neckline dipped daringly, exposing small, pert, perfect little breasts.

Ugly ropes of jealousy wrapped around Millie's ribs, tightening with every word from Nora.

'I often wonder how different things would be if he'd never gone to war.' Nora's bluebell eyes filled with tears, and Millie fought the urge not to slap the silly woman.

'I imagine he would have grown to regret his choices and resent anyone who stopped him from following his heart. I'm sure he'd tell you going to the war made him into the brave, honourable, dedicated man he is today.' Millie glared at Nora.

Nora's delicate features hardened. Her tears magically dissolved in the heat of her ire. 'I'd wager his heart remained here. With the one he proposed marriage to out of love, not duty.'

Ouch. Well played, Nora.

'Few women have the ability to really capture a man's heart.' Patricia jumped in, forcing Millie to swallow her bitter response. 'Take Lord Whittenburg, for example. He's besotted with me. Denies me nothing. I'm the only woman who holds his affections.' Patricia stretched her lips into a vicious smile as she glared at Millie.

Grand. They're joining forces against me. Fine. I'll take them both out.

'I find men who are so beholden to their wives never had much backbone to begin with, so bending them to your will isn't much of a feat.' Philippa drew alongside Millie. She looked resplendent in a gown of deep purple. Her fan thwacked against her thigh to punctuate her words. 'Far better to have mutual respect. Even if it means more friction. I admire how Major General Drake has left behind the silly infatuation of his youth to embark on a journey with someone better suited. Millicent is certainly his equal in intelligence and moral fibre. Something I wouldn't say of his first choice.'

Millie could have cheered in triumph. Not only had Philippa delivered a wicked blow to both Patricia and Nora, but the duchess' dim view of men in general made her support of Drake even more meaningful.

Nora's cheeks darkened, and her eyes darted around the room, refusing to meet Philippa's frank stare. 'I'm sure I wouldn't know, Your Grace.'

Patricia took a different tack, glaring at the duchess. 'After so long being without a man, perhaps you've forgotten how they can be both strong and pliant.'

Philippa tapped her finger against her lip in false consideration. 'As I said before, it's a good thing you are mildly attractive, for your intellect certainly leaves one wanting more. I forget nothing, Lady Whittenburg. You might want to think on that.' Philippa turned and walked away, perusing the paintings on a far wall.

'Dreadful woman! If she wasn't so closely tied to the Queen, I would cut her direct,' Patricia fumed. 'Oh, there's Lady Bradford. I'd best speak with her about tomorrow's activities.' She left in a flurry of blinding-yellow silk.

Nora sipped her sherry, leaning closer to Millie. 'He'll never care for you the way he does me.' Nora's sweet smile hardened into something almost feral. 'No matter what your duchess says. I am his one true love.'

Harsh laughter burned Millie's throat. 'You are

nothing to him. He may have loved you once, but you threw it away for the hope of a title. You are his past. I am Beau's future.'

'Only because you trapped him into this sham of a marriage. What man would ever want a fat, lumbering giant of a woman?' Before Millie could reply, Nora looked beyond her to where the men were re-joining their party. She walked away from Millie toward Drake and his brother. 'Darling, I was just telling Miss Whittenburg about the time you and Beaufort almost came to fisticuffs over who would row me around the lake in your little boat when we were children. Do you recall?'

Millie refused to chase after the woman, but everything in her wanted to drag her back by her perfectly silky hair and show her what fisticuffs really looked like.

Damnation, I've become a violent creature.

Franklin St George walked into the room with Reynard behind him. He bypassed his wife, whose eyes lit up until he breezed by and joined Millie near the fireplace. Why Victoria still cared about the man was beyond her. The cheerful crackle and warmth of the flames no longer felt soothing to Millie in his cold presence.

'What a wonderful party you've gathered.' Franklin's gaze strayed to her breasts before slowly returning to her face.

'Hardly my doing, sir. Patricia is responsible for the guest list. Had I been given the task, we would have far fewer past acquaintances present.'

'Patricia is a delightful hostess. We had quite an enlightening discussion over dinner. She seems devoted to your happiness. Willing to do almost anything to ensure your safety.'

Millie almost laughed, but the sharpness of his words set her on edge. He was making a play. She just wasn't sure what his goal was yet. 'I'm not sure I know what you mean.'

Franklin inclined his head to Lady Winterbourne. Philippa held a glass of whiskey despite the shocked looks of many ladies in the room. She was conversing with Lord Bradford and eyeing his moustache with a perfectly arched brow of censure.

Franklin moved, blocking Millie from the other guests' view. He stepped forward, forcing her to back up until she hit the papered wall. She winced as the wainscoting pressed into one of her bandages.

'Your sweet mother was quite scandalised to realise her daughter was engaged in an illegal and sinful relationship with another woman. I must say, Millie, it makes more sense now that you would reject my initial advances this afternoon. But never fear. I can be just as adventurous as you. There's no reason we couldn't include another member in our little game.' He reached out and grasped her hand. Pulling it up to his lips, he pressed an open-mouth kiss on her knuckles, leaving a trail of spit between her fingers. Millie shuddered in revulsion. 'Don't worry, darling. Your secret is safe with me. As long as you're willing to repay my favour.'

Damn Patricia and her loose tongue!

Of course her vicious stepmother would share her suspicions with St George, giving the disgusting man more ammunition in his war to claim Millie.

She ripped her hand out of his grasp, wiping it on her skirts. 'Please maintain your distance, sir. My stepmother's imagination is almost as wild as her taste in dresses.'

'Truth rarely influences society's judgement. Perhaps your mother is mistaken, but it matters not a whit once the beau monde gets wind of such a salacious story. Whatever you do, I wouldn't upset your sweet mother.' His fine grey eyes flashed in the firelight, the darkness in their depths turning Millie cold despite the heat from the flames. 'Nor should you refuse me.'

She narrowed her gaze and contemplated the ramifications of punching him in his trachea. 'Are you threatening me, sir?'

Franklin shrugged, the action causing his chin to disappear. 'I'm merely giving you some good advice, Millie.'

'Your threats are as empty as your soul, Franklin. You don't scare me. I'm no longer the trusting young woman you took advantage of so long ago.'

St George twitched his lips in a cold smile. 'I don't recall you objecting when I threw up your skirts and fucked you like a cheap harlot on the grass.' Again, he focused on her breasts, his wet tongue swiping over thin lips.

Millie almost gagged. She let this man kiss her. Touch her. Defile her. All because of a silly misconception they were in love. What a fool she'd been. But no more. She wouldn't let this little toad of a man intimidate or threaten her.

I hope he is guilty. Philippa need not bother with him. I'll happily take care of Franklin St George.

Time to bluff and see what Franklin revealed. 'You may plan on spreading lies about me amongst the peerage, but I have something far more dangerous to give them about you, Franklin. The truth. And while your fruitless falsehoods might cause a stir, my information will put your head in a noose.'

Franklin's gaze sharpened, and his pathetic jaw flexed. 'What exactly do you mean?'

'Try to intimidate me again, and you'll find out. Major General Drake is coming this way, Franklin. I think you'd better scuttle. You're quite good at that, aren't you? Slipping away when things get messy?'

Franklin gripped her arm, squeezing tight. 'You've no idea how messy things can get, Millicent.' His breath wreaked of stale wine and something rotten. Probably his soul.

'Ah, there you are, darling.' Millie pushed Franklin out of her way to join Drake's side. 'We were just discussing the wedding.'

Drake's impenetrable stare shifted from Millie to Franklin, then back again. He pulled her closer, his hand resting on her waist. A scandalous show of affection from a man who claimed there was no such emotion between them. More likely, he was making his claim of ownership. It didn't really matter. Millie leaned into his warm, solid body. The band around her chest eased.

'Really?' His judgemental brow was up again, along with his temper based on the flush painting his high cheekbones. He pinned Franklin with a violent glare.

Franklin's pinched lips betrayed his own anger. 'I promised Lord Renquist a game of faro. Best not disappoint the good man.' He nodded curtly at Drake. 'Major General.' Then cast his gaze once more on Millie. 'I'm so enjoying our chance to become reacquainted, *Millie*. So much has changed since we were children.'

She desperately wanted to hit him in that moment. And St George knew it.

'You will call her Miss Whittenburg, or Lady Drake if you wish, as that is the name she shall be taking in a few short days. Chances are fleeting, St George. For example, the chance of you ever being invited here again is completely gone.' Drake's gravelled voice brooked no argument. Millie felt his grip tighten on her hip.

'Yes, well.' Franklin nodded again, then turned to find Lord Renquist.

'Thank you,' Millie murmured, but when her eyes met Drake's, his glacial stare held none of the earlier heat.

'I don't care if you have a history with that man. I don't care if he is a family friend. You will stay away from him. Do you understand me?'

While Millie had no desire to spend time with

Franklin, she also wasn't thrilled to be commanded like a child. 'I don't take orders, Drake. Not from anyone.' Except Philippa, who received them from the Queen. And no one disregarded the Queen.

'You'll take them from me.' He pulled her even closer.

'Franklin is a brute, a coward, a bully, and an arse. I have no wish to spend any more time with him than absolutely necessary. But you are acting much the same, Major General Drake. Perhaps I should stay away from both of you.'

She spun out of his grip. Ivy was sitting at one of the whist tables with Victoria and Lady Bradford. 'Ivy, shall I be your partner?' she called out as she walked away from her future husband, not sparing him another glance for the remainder of the evening.

Major General Drake controls many things, but he shall never control me.

Even if her heart ached from the loss of his company.

* * *

Millie slept terribly. She spent most of the night listening for the click of her connecting door opening.

It never did. Which was good. She didn't want a midnight visit from the high-handed earl, even if her whole body felt strung tight enough to snap. If he'd come into her room, she would have sent Major General Drake back to his bed with boxed ears and a blistered hide. She certainly wouldn't have allowed him access to her person. Nor would she have allowed him to work his magic on her with his mouth, tantalise her with his tongue, thrill her with his questing fingers.

Liar.

Millie thumped her pillow and all but leapt out of bed when Penny arrived. She had called upon her maid to help her dress early and Penny was still blinking the sleep from her eyes when she arrived in Millie's room. She felt terrible for rousing her maid so early, but if she spent one more moment in her room imagining what the man on the other side of the door was doing, she would go mad.

Penny helped her dress in Millie's favourite riding habit with split skirts. It had been ages since she'd been on a long ride. Patricia didn't allow her to ride in London, believing her insistence upon riding astride to be far too scandalous for the lords and ladies trotting along Rotton Row or taking their phaetons or gigs to the south side of Hyde Park to see and be seen. Only when they retired to the country was Millie allowed to ride as she wished.

Well, I'm in the country now and no longer under Patricia's command.

Nor was she beholden to Drake's opinions on how or when she should ride. Yet. While she longed for freedom, there were no guarantees she would be granted an independent life once married. Drake had been correct about one thing the previous night. Chances were fleeting. If this was her one window of opportunity, she intended to savour it with the wind blowing through her hair and a powerful beast between her legs.

I can think of another powerful beast I wouldn't mind riding.

Scandalous! Apparently, she could be angry with the man and still want to ravage him. Millie shut down such lascivious thoughts. They hadn't helped her in the middle of the night, and she wasn't going to waste any more time fantasising about the Earl of Tetly's head buried between her thighs.

She strode out to the stables well before the rest of the house was even awake. If there were no stable boys around, she could saddle one of Drake's fine animals herself.

'Millie! Wot are you doin' out 'ere so early? Toffs

ain't out and about till well past noon.' Billy Bright greeted her with a cheerful grin, smudging the dust on his cheek in a hasty swipe.

'Hello Billy, what a lovely surprise. I didn't know you worked in the stables.' Millie was delighted to find her little friend with a curry brush in one hand and a hoof pick poking out of his pocket.

'I'm trying a bit o' this and bit o' that 'til I find summink wot suits me. Major General Drake tol' me to do jus' that. 'E wants me to find a livings I like and one I'm good at.' Billy leaned close and whispered loudly, 'Course, it ain't easy, as I'm right good at so many things.' He winked.

Millie covered her smile and tried to keep her voice serious. 'Quite a burden to bear, Master Bright. And what do you think about working in the stables?'

Billy puffed out his chest. 'I right like brushing the 'orses and feeding 'em too. Mucking out stalls ain't so grand, but old Jonesy, the stablemaster, says we gotta take good care o' the horses as they can't do it themselves, and no one wants to live in shit, does they?'

She couldn't stop the laughter bubbling up her throat. 'No, Billy. I dare say they don't. Well, do you have time to help me saddle up that sweet little mare over there?'

Billy's gaze followed where Millicent pointed.

'Medusa? She's a right Devil she is. Faster'n most o' the others, even if she is a girl, but don't much like to mind 'er riders. Major General Drake's the only one 'oo can ride 'er wifout gettin' thrown.' He shook his head, biting his lip as his brows drew down in concern. 'I don' fink she's a good choice for you, Millie. Himself'd 'ave me 'ide if anyfink 'appened to you.'

Millie wasn't so sure, but she appreciated Billy's concern. 'Don't you worry, Billy. I don't mind a head-strong lady. In fact, I bet we have quite a lot in common.'

Billy didn't look convinced, but he helped Millie brush down the horse, clean out her hooves, and saddle her. Medusa only tried to nip Billy once, but Millie put a quick stop to that with a stern command and firm grip on Medusa's halter.

When she mounted the mare, Medusa stomped her hoof impatiently, pawing at the gravel drive. Millie ran her hand down the horse's powerful neck.

'You just need a nice long run to get out some of those nerves, hey girl?' she murmured soothingly.

'You sure you'll be all right, Millie?' Billy took a step back as Medusa pawed at the ground again, shifting anxiously as Millie kept her hands low, grip-ping with her thighs to ensure a steady seat. She would bet Medusa had a sensitive mouth and a strong will, never a good combination if the rider wasn't skilled at guiding her mount without pulling hard on the bit.

'I'm quite sure, Billy. I shall see you in a few hours.' She tightened her legs and loosened the reins, giving Medusa her head and whooping as the horse leapt forward.

Billy was right. She was swift, strong, and bloody magnificent. Millie felt the thrill of flying through the air as the wind ripped through her loose chignon, pulling her hair free. She and Medusa were two wild creatures joined in will and temperament, tearing across the paddocks surrounding Alder House and heading for adventure.

Millie knew Medusa needed a long run to wear her out before she turned her toward the forest. She had been desperate to explore, but until the horse calmed, riding through such unpredictable terrain was too dangerous.

When they finally hit the tree line, she and Medusa had reached an understanding. The horse followed her direction, reading Millie's leg pressure like a dream. The woods were thick and dark, colder without the winter sun to warm her back. But Millie felt she'd entered an ancient, magical woodland. They followed a deer trail deeper into the overgrown thicket, crashing through brambles and ferns. The scent of pine, black earth, and damp leaves comforted Millie.

Crossing a shallow brook, Millie wished she'd worn an extra layer. Snow was certainly coming soon. She couldn't wait to explore these same paths in the heat of summer, perhaps take a sneaky dip in the babbling waters.

Glancing through the trees, there was a small clearing where an old hunting shack stood snug and neat. Smoke rose from a stone chimney. Millie wondered if Drake allowed the villagers to use it during the summer, though it seemed strange for someone to be living there now. Hunting season was well over, as most of the animals were hunkering down for winter. She urged her mount forward to investigate, but before she could get closer to the clearing, the crashing sound of another rider had Millie swinging her horse around.

Drake!

Her heart beat harder as a male rider picked through the forest toward her.

'Miss Millicent! What the Devil are you doing out here alone?'

Not Drake.

She ignored the disappointment filling her.

'Lord Renquist. I could ask the same of you.' She smiled at the charming man. While she hadn't spent much time with him, in every interaction, he'd proven to be kind and respectful. More than she could say for most men of her acquaintance.

Renquist returned her smile. His dimples flashed as his eyes, a golden colour quite striking in his tanned face, lit with humour. 'I was running an errand for our mutual friend.'

Millie exaggerated her frown. 'I'm not sure who you're speaking of, sir.'

Renquist threw his head back and laughed, the strong column of his neck moving with the pleasant rumble. 'Come, shall I ride with you back to Alder House? I'm sure your stepmother has something scintillating planned for her guests. We wouldn't want to miss a moment.'

Rolling her eyes, Millie groaned. 'She is awful. I would apologise, but there's nothing I can do to stop her. She's quite the tyrant and destined to become even more so without my presence hindering her.'

'I don't envy you having had to live with her. I'm sure your situation with Drake will be a vast improvement.'

Millie fell behind Renquist as the trail narrowed,

making it impossible to continue their conversation until they emerged from the forest.

'I'm not sure I agree with your earlier assessment. But you know Drake far better than me. Perhaps you can share some tips to encourage a happy union.' Millie was only half jesting.

Renquist didn't answer right away. A slight frown turned the corners of his mouth down. He really was a dashing young man, yet Millie felt no stirring within her as she did anytime Drake was near.

'The war was hard on all of us, but especially a man like Drake.' Something dark flashed in his eyes but then was gone. 'When he returned to find his fiancée had married his brother' – Reynard shrugged – 'no one would take the news well. But it was harder for Drake. He's never had an easy time trusting others. He doesn't speak about his childhood, but I don't think things were pleasant. I know his mother was rumoured to have affairs. His father was a stern, distant figure. And you've met his brother. Two siblings could not be more different.'

Millie couldn't stop her snort of laughter. 'Godric's hardly equal to his brother. A fact his wife is well aware of. Drake told me about Nora. I must say, I'll not be sad to see them both leave.'

Renquist raised a brow. 'He told you? That's... surprising.' He grew silent. For a time, there was only the squeak of leather, the jangle of metal against the reins, and the wind blowing across the open fields.

'I suppose I shouldn't expect a close union then.' Millie finally broke Renquist's reverie. The idea should please her, but instead, she felt an aching loneliness. She needed a distant marriage to continue her work with Philippa, but she was begrudgingly beginning to realise she didn't want to keep Beaufort at arm's length. She liked the man, as infuriating as he was and as complicated as that made her situation.

Incredibly inconvenient, and all Drake's fault.

Renquist turned to her, his amber eyes sharp. The grey sky behind him promised rain soon. Perhaps even sleet or snow. 'Don't give up hope, Miss Millicent. Drake has never met his equal in a woman. Until now, I think.'

'What a thought, Lieutenant Renquist. Equality between a man and woman. It's almost sacrilegious.'

Reynard didn't try to hide his smile. 'But still true. Sometimes, you are battling, which is fearsome, as either could win or both could lose. Sometimes, you are flirting. Don't try to deny it. Your attraction for one another is impossible to ignore. Imagine if you were working together instead of against each other. The beau monde wouldn't know what to do with the pair of you.'

Millie swallowed, taking a moment to consider his thoughts. 'It's a lovely idea, but in reality, it would never work.' There was always a disparity of power in marriage. Usually, it tipped in favour of the man, but in some cases, like her father and Patricia, the woman wielded the control. Neither option resulted in a happy union. But the idea of shared autonomy, equality in partnership, or a perfect balance of power was fantasy. Only a ninny would believe in such dreams. And Millie was no ninny.

'Well, if you want my advice – and I doubt you do but I'll tell you anyway – never back down, Miss Millicent. Meet him on the battlefield, knowing you are his equal and acknowledging that he is yours. If soul mates are really two halves of one whole, then neither can be more powerful. Don't you think?'

'I think you have a poet's soul, Lord Renquist.'

The man's cheeks darkened, and he rolled his shoulders as though his coat was too tight. 'My soul is steeped in darkness, Miss Millicent. Don't go digging too deeply into that quagmire. You may never escape.'

Millie wished she could say something to comfort him, but her mind went blank.

'Come, let us have a race home.' Renquist broke

the suddenly serious moment, his eyes sparkling in the sunlight as if he had no care in the world but to beat Millie back to Alder House. He spurred his mount on, and Millie urged Medusa to catch him. It was a wild race, but Millie beat Lord Renquist by a nose. They returned to the house together, Millie having much to think on as she excused herself to change for the afternoon's activities.

14

Of all the insufferable, despicable, horrific, painful tortures Drake could devise, parlour games might be at the top of his list. Therefore, it made perfect sense Patricia had planned an afternoon of such diversions to combat the bad weather.

I need to make the best of it. With all of us crammed in here, it's prime time to observe St George and see who he talks to. I only have three days left.

Millie was proving quite the distraction to his mission. He needed to crack on with the case or risk displeasing the prime minister. Even if it meant participating in ridiculous games. Drake would prefer standing in the sleet and rain, stripped to his skin, forced to suffer the freezing temperatures than endure an afternoon of charades, blind man's buff, and pass the slipper. Yet here he was in his cosy front parlour, standing in the centre of a ring of idiots, trying to determine who held a slipper behind their back, all in the hopes of capturing a killer.

Millie kept her gaze focused on Drake's earlobe instead of his eyes. Dead giveaway.

'Miss Millicent, I believe you have the slipper.' Drake raised his scarred eyebrow at the beautiful redhead.

She pulled both hands from behind her back, holding her palms out for all to see. Empty.

Ivy pulled her hands out, a pink slipper held in her left. 'It was me. I had the slipper.'

'Ugh. I'm sick of this game.' Nora rolled her eyes. 'Let's play something new. I know! Forfeit. And because I came up with it, I shall be the judge.'

Patricia clapped her hands, blonde ringlets bouncing with enthusiasm. 'Capital plan!'

St George stood close to Patricia. If only she were his partner in crime. Drake would happily haul them both in front of the House of Lords to receive their punishments. Not that a secret brotherhood would allow any woman into their circle, even one as diabolical as Patricia.

'I shall get a bowl to deposit our items.' St George winked at Patricia, who giggled like a brainless moron.

'Nora, you wait out in the hall.' Patricia pointed to the door, and Nora quickly spun around and made her exit.

The duchess had declared parlour games to be asinine. Instead, she was sipping whiskey and watching the others, her red lips crimped in mild disgust.

'Forfeit is a dangerous game unless you truly trust the players.' Philippa arched a black eyebrow. 'One might lose something of great importance if they aren't willing to complete the task assigned.'

'Of course, we trust one another.' Godric's waistcoat for the afternoon was a robin-egg blue. His pants were wool and dyed a glaring lime. Drake felt slightly ill looking at him. 'Most of us are family or close enough. I hardly imagine we'd pilfer items from each other.'

Philippa stared at Godric until the man's face turned an alarming shade of crimson, clashing terribly with his waistcoat and pants.

'In my experience, family is the most dangerous.' Philippa's voice carried throughout the silent room.

Patricia's tinkling laughter broke the spell. 'Don't be ridiculous! The most danger we face is Millicent stepping on someone's toes with her large feet.'

Drake glared at Millie's stepmother.

Patricia – oblivious to the threat she faced – held up a gorgeously inlaid box of dark wood decorated with jade that St George had found. 'Quick, everyone put something in the box before Nora returns.'

Patricia, Ivy, Godric, St George, and Renquist fumbled for small personal items to place into the box.

Millie stepped closer to Drake, speaking low enough that no one else heard her. 'Thank you, Beau, but there's no need to fight with Patricia. Her words are harmless.' She bit her lip. She was lying about something, but exactly what mystified Drake. How could Patricia's words possibly harm Millie? Unless Patricia knew something about his betrothed. Something Millie refused to tell him.

Like working with Philippa on some dangerous investigation.

It pained Drake to think Patricia knew more than him on any subject. But worse was the idea that she might hold a threat over Millie.

'Her words might find her on the wrong end of my pistol if she isn't careful. I owe her for every lash on your back.' He wanted to reach out and touch her arm, reassure himself she was well, and near, and his.

But she isn't mine. Nor am I hers. And that is a good thing.

'Trust me, she isn't worth a murder conviction.' Millie reached up and took an earring from her left ear. The intimacy of the movement had Drake aching in unusual places. His heart for one, as he imagined her completing such a simple task while preparing to join him in his bed. Which was where he wanted her. Not just to strip her naked and lick every delicious inch of her cream and cinnamon skin, but to hold her against him, to cradle her strong body with his, to press his nose into her hair and inhale her into him as if he could capture a fragment of her soul and keep it safe inside.

His heart didn't flutter any more. It fractured. Every time she was near. And in the cracks and crevices, something terrifying leaked out.

It is just affection. Lust.

He *liked* her. And that was the trouble. Because he also respected her, desired her, bloody-well admired the woman.

Fuck. I'm in trouble.

'What will you put in the box, Major General Drake? A button, perhaps? Lint from your pocket?' The teasing glint in her eyes caused his chest to tighten. God, she was breathtaking when she teased him.

Drake searched his pockets, but he didn't even

have a farthing. He was loathe to tear a button from his coat, so instead, he twisted off the signet ring that once belonged to his father.

Millie's eyes grew wide. 'Surely not, my lord. It's far too valuable.'

'My brother said family would never steal from each other. Let's put his theory to the test.'

He watched as Millie's body grew rigid. She patted down her skirt, fingered the gold chain around her neck, then worried at an opal ring on her middle finger. It was beautifully set in gold. 'Perhaps you could borrow something of mine instead.' She twisted the opal ring off. 'Here. Take this.'

Drake shook his head. 'I couldn't possibly. It looks far too important.'

'Not any more than your signet ring. It was a gift from my father when I was but five and ten. Please, take it. A keepsake from your fiancée. Surely, you won't deny me the pleasure of giving you a gift.'

I can't seem to deny you anything.

Which was a huge problem. He needed to keep his distance from her, but it was becoming more and more impossible.

'Pleasure is the one thing I'd never deny you, Millie.' He couldn't stop the gravel in his voice or the thickening of his cock as he imagined all the ways he could repay her for such a sweet gift.

Lust. That is all. Once we get our fill of each other, the need will fade.

He still hadn't forgiven himself for making the previous evening such an unmitigated disaster. After his brutish behaviour, he thought it best to give Millie some space despite urgent protests from certain appendages.

'Truly, you are a wicked man.' She lowered her gaze as her cheeks heated. He loved making her blush. And he was relieved she seemed to have forgiven him for his harsh words the night before. Perhaps he could put his theory to the test tonight. Indulging in his need for Millie, letting her do the same, surely that was the best way to purge himself of this incessant hunger.

'Ah, Nora is back. Who has the box?' Patricia's green gaze swept across the room, landing on Drake and Millie.

Drake took the ring from Millie's hand, savouring the sensation of his fingers brushing over hers. He dropped it in the box and shook the items around before walking over to Nora and handing the box to her. She licked her lips and smiled, her eyes offering an invitation he would never accept.

'Right, let's begin. I'll guess which object belongs to

each of you. If I'm right, you owe me whatever forfeit I choose. If I'm wrong, you get your item back. Ready?' Nora's gaze never left Drake, but he spun on his heel and reclaimed his place next to Millie.

Leaning closer to his betrothed, inhaling the scent of citrus and cotton, he whispered in her ear, 'I see your game. She's unlikely to guess that ring belongs to me. You devious woman.'

Millie's warm eyes sparkled at him in the waning light. 'Didn't you claim all women are devious, my lord? I'm just hoping to live up to your expectations.'

Drake swallowed. He told Millie that, the night she lured him out to the veranda. How wrong he'd been about her! He wished they were alone, so that he could apologise to her for his cold behaviour on that night, and his far too heated behaviour last night. But Nora moved into the centre of the room and pulled out the first item. The game had begun.

Nora surprised him with her clever judging. She was able to guess almost every item. Patricia's was a garish peacock feather covered in goldleaf to match her over-the-top golden gown. Renquist gave a half-smoked cigar, Godric a guinea, St George a poker chip, and Ivy a broach. Unfortunately for Drake, the opal ring was the last item in the box. It was clear he was the owner of the ring.

'Beaufort, I don't recall you being so fond of women's jewellery in the past. This is your ring, is it not?' Nora raised both brows at him, holding the ring out in her palm.

Drake tried not to be charmed by the possessive growl Millie made as Nora approached them.

'You are correct. It is mine. Given to me by a very special woman.' Drake turned to Millie and winked. Instead of noticing his playful gesture, Millie's narrowed gaze remained focused on Nora. Like a sharp-shooter sizing up a target.

Good Lord, she is fearsome.

The flutter was back, and with it, a liquid warmth spreading from his chest to the rest of his body. Even his toes tingled with this strange new feeling.

'What is my forfeit?' Drake returned his gaze to Nora, whose lips spread in a smile reminiscent of a cat who caught the mouse.

Damnation. This is not going to end well.

'A kiss, Beaufort. For old time's sake.'

Patricia's tinkling giggle almost drowned out Godric's blustering exclamation.

'Nora, that's a bit beyond the pale, wouldn't you say?' Godric broke from the circle to approach his wife.

'Darling, please. It's just a game.' Nora patted her

husband on the cheek, leaning forward to give him a peck where her hand had just rested. 'Unless you don't trust me?'

'Of course I trust you, it's just—'

'Wonderful.' She turned back to Beaufort. 'So, what is it to be, Beaufort? A little kiss to return your precious ring, or shall you forfeit such a heartfelt memento to me?' Nora's eyes flashed with something nearly feral. It was a bold play, bordering on scandalous. No matter what Drake chose, he lost.

'I'd like to offer another solution.' Millie stepped forward, placing herself between Drake and Nora.

Blast and bugger. She's going to challenge Nora to a duel. Can women even issue such a challenge?

It didn't matter. Drake might not know his fiancée well, but he knew she wouldn't give a fig about the beau monde's rules on who was and was not allowed to demand a duel.

Nora smiled at Millie, a vicious expression nearly as deadly as the daggers Millie threw at Nora with her sharp gaze.

'How valiant of you to sweep in and save your betrothed's honour. I'm all ears.'

Millie tipped her chin at the far wall where a leather dart board hung. It was something Drake kept from the war. A game the soldiers loved to play and one pleasant memory he still retained from such a horrific time in his life.

'A game of darts between us. If I win, Beau keeps the ring. If you win, you get your kiss, *and* you keep the ring. What say you?'

An almost visible thread of tension stretched between Nora and Millie. Everyone in the room fell silent. Drake glanced at Reynard and saw his gaze bouncing between both women, a faint smile on his lips. Of course he would find this amusing. He didn't have to deal with the outcome of Millie losing and then attacking Nora, as Drake was certain she would, or Nora losing and throwing the ring into the fire, as she no doubt might try.

'I accept.' Nora's wide grin ratcheted up Drake's apprehension. She shouldn't look so pleased. Something was amiss. 'Whoever hits their dart closest to the centre?'

'Lovely. Best of three?' Millie's husky voice was rigid as she rolled her shoulders.

'Of course.' Nora blinked slowly before sauntering to the dart board.

'I say. How exciting to see two such lovely ladies pitted against each other in a game of skill.' St George licked his lips, and Drake restrained himself from issuing his own invitation to duel.

Millie followed Nora to the dart board, and the rest of the party formed a half circle around them, except for Godric. He stalked over to the sideboard and poured himself a large glass of brandy. Not his first of the afternoon.

'You first, Nora. I insist.' Millie handed Nora three darts. They were a gift from Killian to Drake and beautifully hewn, with nickel barrels and steel tips.

Nora took the darts, winking at Millie before she turned to stand in front of the board. She gave a few test flicks of her wrist.

Damn. She knows what she's about.

Drake was familiar with sizing up an opponent from their stance and hold on the dart. Surprisingly, Nora looked like an expert. This did not bode well.

Holding her arm at a ninety-degree angle, Nora pulled her forearm back and let the dart fly. It spiralled through the air, landing in the middle right quadrant. A good shot. She looked over her shoulder at Millie. 'Oh, did I forget to tell you? I love darts. I play at home all the time. Godric bought me my own board for a birthday gift last year, didn't you, darling?'

Godric took a healthy sip of brandy, refusing to answer his wife. But his face was flushed, and his lips pressed together in a white line as he swallowed.

Nora threw her other two darts in quick succession. One landed in the lower right quadrant, not quite as accurate. But the third was just left of centre. Almost a bull's eye.

Fuck.

Drake would need to find an excuse to avoid kissing Nora at all costs while still reclaiming Millie's ring. Short of screaming fire and grabbing the ring from Nora while he ran for the door, he was completely flummoxed.

'Your turn.' Nora sauntered past Millie, whose face had paled slightly.

Drake would have cut off his damaged leg if it would protect his fiancée from embarrassment. But he was helpless to save her from what was sure to be a devastating loss.

Millie stood in the same spot Nora vacated. She rolled her shoulders, testing the weight of the dart in her hand. But instead of gripping the dart between her thumb and forefinger in the middle of the shaft, she held the base of the dart just before the flight. Her position was also wrong. She didn't hold her arm at a ninety-degree angle but instead let it rest against her thigh.

Patricia's bell-like laughter filled the room. 'The silly girl isn't even holding it right,' she crowed.

'Of course not. When has Millie ever played a

game of darts?' St George smiled at Millie like an indulgent father.

Drake was torn between glaring at Patricia and plotting St George's imminent demise. He noticed Philippa at the edge of the room. She was watching Millie, a small smile curling her lips.

What the Devil is going on here?

Thwack!

Drake turned his head sharply back to the dart board. Millie's dart still quivered from the force of her throw. It was buried dead centre in the board. The crowd gasped.

Millie took the next dart and, in a movement so fast, he could barely track her, she flicked her arm out like someone brandishing a whip. The dart flew like a bullet. Drake watched it slam into the leather, almost knocking her first dart from its place in the bull's eye. The third dart hit the only one Nora threw close to the centre, knocking it free from the leather. Both darts landed with a clatter on the wooden floor.

In the complete silence following her display, Millie's skirts rustled like wind through autumn leaves as she walked to Nora, standing so close the smaller woman had to crane her neck to meet Millie's gaze.

'Major General Drake's ring, please.' She held out her hand; her tone brooked no argument.

Nora fumbled the box, almost dropping it to the floor before she grasped the ring and shoved it at Millie.

'That isn't how you throw a dart, you know,' Nora hissed.

'Well, it certainly isn't how *you* throw a dart.' Millie looked meaningfully at the board before turning on her heel and striding across the room to Drake.

'Your ring, darling,' she drawled, dropping the opal into his palm. Drake's playfulness evaporated after he saw her throw the first dart. His suspicions were turning into accusations.

He narrowed his gaze at her, but before he could ask any questions, she turned away, gliding across the floor to stand next to Philippa.

Something was very wrong.

Drake had never seen a person throw darts in that manner, but he had seen soldiers who threw knives. Knives that looked a lot like the ones Millie had strapped to her luscious body. Which begged the question: who trained his betrothed to throw her daggers with the accuracy of an assassin? And why?

His gaze lingered on Millie as she leaned close to Philippa and whispered something into the duchess' ear.

One thing was certain. His blushing bride was dangerous. And he was determined to discover the truth behind her lies.

* * *

'For a woman with secrets to keep, that was rather bold, don't you think?' Philippa kept her eyes on the rest of the guests as Millie leaned against the wall near her mentor.

'Some lessons can only be taught with a firm hand. A lesson I learned from my dear stepmother.' But truth be told, Millie knew her actions had been reckless. Especially after what she'd revealed to Drake on the chaise. It didn't stop the warm flush of satisfaction from washing over her skin.

'Your fiancé is sure to have questions.' Philippa's thumb rubbed circles against her index finger. She was not pleased.

He would have even more questions than Philippa could possibly imagine. But perhaps that was why Millie had been so bold.

Or maybe it was her earlier conversation with Renquist. 'I've been thinking on that.' Millie's belly filled with fireflies, flapping their little wings a million beats a second.

'Have you?' Philippa's arched brow spoke volumes.

She had. As much as she tried to discount Renquist's words about shared power between herself and Drake, they had filled her with an insidious hope for the impossible. One she couldn't easily dispel.

'What if I tell him? About me? About the missions I hope to take on for Queen Victoria?' It was a wild plan, but Millie was a wild woman. 'What if he and I approach this marriage as equal partners instead of distant acquaintances joined by a mutual goal instead of just a marriage contract?'

For a small eternity, Philippa remained absolutely still. 'What if revealing your secrets only gives him more power over you? Power to take away everything?'

Fear warred with Millie's reckless hopes. Philippa was painting a far more realistic picture of marriage than Renquist. But at this point, Millie might have already travelled too far down the path of revelation to turn back.

She opened her mouth but had no answer.

'In my limited experience with men, trusting them with anything – especially the truth – ends in disaster. For the woman.' Philippa turned her head, spearing Millie with her cobalt gaze. Fine lines fanned out from the corners of Philippa's eyes, marring the perfection of her skin. Sometimes, Millie forgot Philippa was flesh and blood. A woman carving out her fortune in a man's world. Not nearly as impenetrable as she wanted the beau monde to believe. It was a startling thought.

'Can you promise me he'll support you? Can you look me in the eye right now and say with 100 per cent certainty that he won't take your information and use it to control you? To contain you? To lash you to him with bonds you won't dare be able to break?' Philippa's low voice struck like a blade.

Millie couldn't. But neither could she abandon the idea of a true partnership with her husband-to-be. 'I...' She couldn't hold Philippa's gaze.

Damnation. What if I've made a terrible mistake revealing so much to him?

'Exactly. I won't tell you what to do. Hannah taught me well how little power I wield over a woman in love, but—'

'I'm not in love with him.'

Philippa tipped her head back and laughed.

'I'm not,' Millie hissed as panic filled her.

Desire is not love. Need is not love.

What of affection? Admiration? Respect?

She closed her eyes and shook her head, refusing to let fancy fly away with her good sense. Liking Drake was one thing. Loving him would put her in far too vulnerable a position.

'Fine, you don't love him... yet. But you are close to the fall, and once you step over that precipice, there is no turning back. There is one thing I know with certainty: a woman in love is a very foolish creature indeed.'

Anger bubbled up in Millie as Philippa's words struck far too close to the mark. 'I am not foolish. And what could you possibly know of love? You held no such affection for the duke.'

Philippa gripped Millie's wrist in a vice. 'I know more of love than you could ever imagine. I know how it can devastate you. How it can hollow you out until you are nothing but a shell. How it can steal your will to live. How it can amputate the very best parts of yourself until they are just a memory. Don't speak to me about what I do or do not know of love.' Tears filled Philippa's eyes before she pressed her lips together in a grim line.

Dear God.

Millie had never seen Philippa show emotion, let alone the raw pain pouring from every pore like poison from a lanced wound.

'I shouldn't have said that. I'm sorry. But I am not a fool, Philippa.'

Philippa took a deep breath, blinked the tears away, and loosened her grip on Millie. 'We are all fools, Millicent. I was the biggest fool of all. Because I believed in the glory of love. The promises it whispered of hope, and joy, and forever. But those promises are lies. I only wish to save you from a similar fate. You will do as you please, but I warn you. Don't trust Major General Drake with your secrets. He's not worth the price of your heart.' She walked away from Millie to join Lady Bradford on the sofa, donning her composure as one might put on their armour before battle.

Shit.

Whoever Philippa had loved must have hurt her terribly. Millie couldn't begin to imagine how someone as strong and powerful as the Duchess of Dorsett could be brought so low, but her wounds were still wide open and bleeding underneath the fortress she created.

But love doesn't have to destroy. It can protect. It can heal.

Despite her best efforts, the hope blooming in her chest refused to be doused by logic and reason.

Philippa was right. Millie was a fool.

She was falling for Drake. But did he feel the same? And more importantly, did he care about her enough to trust her?

More to the point, am I foolish enough to trust him?

Her gaze flitted over the crowd, catching Drake's

heavy-lidded stare. Flames of need licked over her skin, wrapping around her thighs, her neck, her breasts. 'Dear Lord,' she muttered. The man enraptured her like opium seduced its addict. 'Fortune favours the bold, but does it also favour the fool?'

She was going to find out.

15

Millie sat patiently at her vanity as Penny carefully dabbed her back with the thick, cool goop.

'You're healing well, miss. You might have scars, but there's no more infection. A few more days with the salve, and I think you'll be well on your way. I don't think we need the bandages any more.'

'You're very good at this, Penny.' Millie smiled at Penny's reflection in the mirror.

Penny just ducked her head, her eyes staying focused on Millie's back. The woman had secrets, it was plain to see, but getting her to trust Millie enough to share her story would be quite the task. Hopefully, in time, she would allow Millie into her world.

'There you are, miss. All done. If you don't mind, I

promised I'd cover for one of the other maids tonight. She's assigned to Lady Bradford.'

'Of course, Penny. Is anything amiss?'

Penny shook her head, biting her lip. 'It's quite awful, miss. The staff are all buzzing about it. Her sister's gone missing. Just a young lass, only ten and five. She was hoping to go into service like her sister, but no one knows where she's gone. Her sister is terrified she ran away with some boy. She's asked for time to be with her family and aid in the search.'

Suspicion spiked, fuelling Millie's adrenaline. 'That's awful. Of course, you must go. If you need anything from me...'

'No, miss, though that's terribly kind. I'll take my leave and see you in the morning.' Penny gave an abbreviated curtsey and quickly left.

Millie pulled up her nightgown, threading each arm through the delicate lace sleeves. It was one of her favourites. The silk was a soft sage, and the lace had been dyed to match. The bodice was mostly lace, revealing as much as it hid with the silk creating a diaphanous skirt. She'd bought it years ago and never imagined she might wear it in front of a man.

Her mind worried over Penny's information. St George had been in Bedford for three days while his wife shopped. Was it possible he could be responsible for the young girl's absence? It seemed a long shot, but still, it was something worth speaking to Philippa about – if Philippa was still speaking with Millie after tonight.

She was going to confess her dealings to Drake. Her stunt with the darts was already a declaration, but it was time to tell him the whole truth. She would keep Philippa out of it, but it was the only way forward. One thing was as clear as the frigid night air: Millie did not want a distant marriage if there was even a chance of true partnership with her husband. She might be a fool, she might fall and shatter, but she would know for certain if Drake was worthy of her trust.

Her gaze returned to the glass. Even she had to admit, this night gown flattered her. Once Millie was old enough to visit the modiste without her father, she decided wearing sinfully decadent underthings was a pleasure every woman deserved. She spent a fair portion of her pin money on daring chemises, scandalous night-rails, and shocking corsets, knowing the only person who would ever see them was Millie herself and perhaps her maid. But she wore them because she could. They made her feel beautiful. It was her little secret pleasure.

Had she thought about Drake when she chose her eveningwear tonight?

Perhaps.

Was she thinking of him now as her skin heated and her pupils dilated?

Highly probable.

Did she desperately hope her physical appeal would help win over his trust and fill him with such passionate desire, he didn't mind a whit if she went on secret missions for the Queen?

Undoubtably.

There was no point in dawdling. Her decision was made. Now, she just had to complete the plan she'd already put into action.

Taking a moment, Millie pinched her cheeks, pressed her lips together hard, adjusted her breasts, and nodded.

'It's high time I propositioned an earl.' A million dusty moths took flight in her belly. She pressed her hand just below her clavicle and felt her pounding heart. This was no time for nerves. 'One, two, three, go,' she whispered, standing and quickly padding to the connecting door, her bare feet sinking into the thick Aubusson rug. Lifting her hand, she paused, exhaled, and knocked before she lost her nerve.

'The hens are out of the chicken coop now. No putting them back,' she whispered as her nipples tightened into hard buds, chafing against the lace.

Before she could think of all the reasons she should turn around and leap under her covers, the door swung open.

Drake stood before her in breeches but no shirt. Despite all they had done together, it was the first time she'd seen him so undone. Millie's mouth went dry, and her eyes widened. She may have gasped.

His chest was an eloquent story of beauty and pain. Drake was a large man, but not one ounce of fat graced his muscular body. His chiselled pectoral muscles led down to a stomach divided into eight rectangles of hardened flesh. Scars covered his skin, some like slashes from a blade, others resembled melted wax re-shaped into odd formations, and still more were perfect circles, as though a burning cigar or cheroot had been extinguished on his body. The pain he must have endured shocked Millie. She took a half step closer, her hand reaching out to offer what comfort she could.

'Don't.' Drake's voice was cold as steel. His jaw flexed, and his icy stare froze her in place.

'I just—'

'I don't want your pity, Millicent.'

She shook her head, her loose hair brushing against her shoulder blades and sticking to the salve. 'I'm not offering pity.'

Drake's hard stare heated, sparks leaping across the space between them and igniting her desire. His eyes made a leisurely journey over her body, pausing on her breasts and making her nipples tighten to even more painfully sensitive peaks. He growled when his smouldering stare stalled again at the apex of her thighs. The silk was so fine, it was almost translucent. He would see the shadow of her copper hair. Millie shivered as she imagined what he must be thinking.

'What are you offering?' His rough voice deepened.

Millie let her eyes take their own journey down his chest to where blond hair, slightly darker than the spikes on his head, started below his belly button and disappeared into his low-slung pants. Two ropes of muscles beginning at each hip bone created a V, drawing her eyes to the obvious bulge pressing against the placket of his breeches. As she watched, the bulge grew harder, more defined.

Millie struggled to swallow. 'I'm offering myself. In exchange for you.'

Drake's lip twitched at the corner. 'A trade? My body for yours? Even with all my scars? Doesn't seem a fair exchange, Millicent.'

'I prefer when you call me Millie. And, I don't mind your scars.' Millie licked her lips. She wanted to touch his chest, to test the textures of soft skin

stretched over hard muscle. To kiss the violent sou-
venirs he carried and try to absorb the echoes of pain
still embedded within him.

'You haven't seen all of them.'

'Then show me.' She needed to speak with him
about their relationship. Share her truth and see if he
held it close or crushed it, but right now, this seemed
more important. If he didn't honour her revelation, she
still wanted the memory of this moment with him. No
matter how much it hurt if everything went to hell.

Millie was stepping into a new self. Instinctively,
she understood joining their bodies into one would be
a cataclysmic event rebirthing her into an entirely different creature. And she wanted that rebirth, even if
her time with Drake was limited to this one night.

He stepped back, sweeping his arm out in a gesture
of welcome. 'Come in, Millie.'

A thrill of victory at both his use of her pet name,
and his invitation pushed Millie through the threshold
and into Drake's domain. She forced her gaze away
from him to take in his room. His walls were papered a
dark colour, blue or maybe brown; it was difficult to
see in the firelight. A massive, mahogany bed domi-
nated the centre of the room. Thank God she was tall,
or she would need a ladder to reach the mattress. Just
the idea of climbing onto his bed shot her heart rate

into a new stratosphere. She pushed the thought aside. One incendiary fantasy at a time. She needed to keep her focus on this moment, or the evening would over-whelm her.

There were two wingback chairs sitting in front of his fireplace, and a solid dresser sat against the far wall. Leather, cloves, and smoke permeated the room. She inhaled deeply. Spinning to face him, Millie ig-nored the bed at her back.

She didn't reissue her command but instead crossed her arms beneath her breasts, lace straining against her sensitive skin. She raised her brows and tipped her chin at his pants.

'I promised I wouldn't compromise you until we wed.'

'And while I love that you're a man of your word, I'm asking you to break that promise tonight.'

'There are things we must discuss first. Not the least being your skill with darts. A suspicious man might wonder how a young lady of your breeding be-came so adept at a soldier's pastime. I can't imagine your stepmother approving of such diversions.'

'Patricia spends a lot of time looking for the bottom of her wine bottle. It allows me a certain amount of freedom to pursue my own fancies, and darts is a harmless game, is it not? Certainly less dangerous than archery, which is a skill many women are encouraged to pursue.' Millie couldn't stop her triumphant smile. It was a masterful evasion, and she didn't even have to lie. Darts was a harmless game. And archery was encouraged for upstanding young ladies. Never mind that she hadn't *played* a game of darts or *shot* an arrow.

Drake's lips twitched, but he wasn't taking the bait. 'Archery might be all the rage for young ladies, but throwing knives of the quality you keep strapped to your person are reserved for activities far more nefarious than garden games.'

Damn his intelligent hide.

Maybe Millie could distract him with more truth. Just not the truth he was seeking. 'I don't have any weapons strapped on tonight. It's just me under this gown.'

Drake's gaze took a noticeable detour from her eyes to breasts, then lower. He ran his hand over his head, his bicep flexing in an arousing display of power. 'How can any man keep his wits about him with you standing there, in that?'

Millie wanted to purr like a cat. Her gamble with the nightgown was paying off. 'I don't want your wits tonight, Beau. I want you.'

'Are you sure? If we start this, I will want all of you.

Now. Are you ready?' His gravelled voice stroked over her senses, and she arched toward him.

'I'm starting this because *I* want all of *you*. Tonight. Are *you* ready, Drake?' Her voice only shook a little as nerves skittered through her veins like a million fireflies.

'I thought I asked you to call me Beau. Tit for tat, Millie.' His mouth twitched again. A small curl tipped up the left side of his sinful lips, creating crinkles at the corner of each eye.

She'd made the man smile. *Miraculous.*

Drake took a step closer to her. 'Bold and brave, my lady. Rare characteristics to find.'

'In a woman?' She narrowed her gaze. His disparaging view against her sex was legendary.

'In anyone.' He shrugged then turned to lower the lamplight, whether for her benefit or his, she couldn't be sure. Even in the dim lighting Millie could discern the lines and angles of his back. It was just as fascinating as his chest. Millie had no idea a man's back could display so much carved definition. But scars covered him there as well. He had been whipped. Far more brutally and more often than Millie. Her heart squeezed as she imagined the horrors he must have suffered. Still, she schooled her expression to show no softness. Drake made it clear he wasn't ready for her empathy. Not yet. So, she would be patient.

He turned back to face her, his hands hovering at the waistline of his breeches. 'I don't speak about the war. After tonight, I won't again. But you should know, my leg is shocking. I've no wish to disgust you. I can keep my breeches on for now, remove them later, or not at all.'

A hazy memory of Franklin fumbling with the fall of his pants before thrusting into her resurfaced. She was well aware the act they were about to share could be accomplished with minimal disrobing. But she didn't want that. Not tonight. Not with Drake. She wanted the intimacy of total nudity. She wanted to feel all his hot, hard skin pressed against her soft curves. And she couldn't give a damn that his body was just as broken as it was beautiful.

'I'm hardly a delicate miss, my lord. Nothing about you is disgusting. I want to see you. All of you.'

Drake's hand trembled as his fingers brushed the button holding his waistband tight.

He was nervous. No doubt because the last woman he cared for betrayed him by marrying his brother. Rage washed through Millie, and she was glad she'd decimated Nora in darts, even if it put her at risk. Nora's perfidy had done as much damage to the strong, fearless, proud man before her as the Afghanistan soldiers. Despite all his strength, the danger dripping from him, the carefully controlled power he wielded in his body's vigour and skill, he feared her rejection.

Silly man, I could never reject you.

How could she reject the man she lo—

No. It isn't that.

But the vice that tightened around her chest every time she lied squeezed painfully. Ruthlessly, she ignored it.

'Show me all of you, Beau.'

* * *

The flutters in Drake's chest intensified to shudders at her refusal to be disgusted by him.

Heart, don't you dare fail me now. Cease your ridiculous fluttering and beat like a normal organ. I will not die before bedding Millicent.

Drake had been arguing with himself for almost an hour about exactly how he would confront Millie. His suspicious mind couldn't ignore the signs. She was far more than just a beautiful woman longing for freedom. Her skill with the darts, the knives she kept hidden on her body in the most delicious places, the way she confronted Patricia when the pernicious woman was hellbent on attacking poor Billy. Even her interactions with St George hinted at strength, courage, and determination not often found in young ladies of the peerage. She might not be lying to him, but she also wasn't being completely honest. She was hiding something. But what if her secrets were more than he could accept? More than he could bear?

One thing was certain. He couldn't let her be harmed. A world without Millie wasn't one he could endure.

When he had heard the knock, Drake was sure he must be hallucinating. But then he'd opened the door, and there she was. The object of his fantasies, standing in the flickering firelight, her nightgown utterly destroying any hope Drake had of composure or control. Every tactic he had planned to use to discover her secrets fled his mind as blood filled his cock.

Her damn nightgown should be illegal.

It was a far better tool at scattering his wits than any torture device he'd experienced. Fine lace hid nothing from sight. Drake could see Millie's strawberry nipples peeking out from the material. God, he wanted to taste them again, test their texture with his tongue, nibble and bite them until she writhed, begging for release.

In a crushing moment of clarity, he knew his heart

was forever lost. To her. A woman he could neither control nor contain. She would destroy him. One day, she would realise he wasn't worthy of her, and she would leave. Any hope for a future would cease to exist for Drake. It was a terrifying prospect. To let love back into his life, knowing the damage such vulnerability might invite. But it was also too late. Love was there, whether he wanted it or not.

Fuck. I love her.

He loved the chaotic, charismatic, courageous woman standing before him, demanding he undress so she could fill her gaze with his broken body. It was terrifying.

Thank God Drake was so brave.

He clenched his shaking hand into a fist, willing the tremor to cease.

'If you change your mind...' He wanted to give her an out. Drake couldn't endure watching her melting chocolate eyes harden in disgust as he revealed the worst damage wrought upon his body.

'I won't.' Her husky voice was like whiskey to his soul. Intoxicating.

Drake unbuttoned his breeches, pushing them down and stepping free while he watched her face for any signs of revulsion. His hard and pulsing cock twitched with demand. Though his lame leg was partly hidden in shadows, even the firelight couldn't disguise the warped muscle and ruined skin. There was no hair on a large portion of his upper thigh where scar tissue took over. The Afghan soldiers had started with hot pokers, moved onto blades, and finished by pouring boiling tar over his leg. He was lucky he didn't lose his limb completely, though he'd certainly lost huge chunks from damage and infection. When he returned to England, Killian insisted he see the best physicians, paying for some of the treatments himself, but after so much time, little could be done. Drake's only option was to accept his new limitations and move forward. Even if it was with a painful limp.

He watched Millie for any clues about her thoughts. Her eyes widened, and her mouth opened on a silent inhalation. But she wasn't focused on his leg. She was staring at his erection. His cock grew impossibly harder as Millie took a step closer.

'You're so large.' She reached out her hand but paused.

He might die if she didn't touch him. Now.

'Please, touch me.' Major General Drake Beaufort never begged. But he would get on his knees and plead if it meant her fingers wrapped around his aching cock. 'I mean, if you'd like.'

Just the thought of her soft hand curling around his length caused a bead of liquid to form.

Millie bit her lip, her gaze never leaving his cock. She took another tentative step forward. Her hand was pale in the dim light. She shone like a fairy as she reached for him.

Drake bit his cheek until he tasted the metallic tang of blood. He would not lose control. Not in front of Millie. He would stand still and let her learn him, even if he died from frustrated desire.

She glanced up, her pupils huge. 'Are you sure?'

He'd never been more sure. Not trusting himself to speak, he gave a shaky nod.

She wrapped her hand around him and squeezed.

'Jesus!' he hissed.

When she would have pulled back, he caught her wrist.

'Don't. It feels so good.' He gentled his grip without letting her go.

'Did I hurt you?' Millie was so close, he could bend down and press his mouth against hers. But then he wouldn't be able to take things slow. It was important he gave her time. As paramount as control was to Drake, he was loathe to take hers away.

'No.'

She smiled and crinkled her nose. 'A man of few

words this evening. I never saw Franklin's, er... Well, it all happened in such a rush. I can't imagine his was nearly so... prodigious. But even then, there was pain. I'm not sure how...'

Drake already hated Franklin St George. Now, he promised to end the arrogant prick. 'The first time for a woman is often painful. Especially if your partner is an arse who doesn't take his time. I'm not an arse. And tonight, we have nothing but time. Trust me.'

She blinked, opening her mouth as though she might say something, but instead, she licked her lips and puffed out a sigh. 'Trust isn't an easy thing.'

'It's not,' he agreed.

'But I trusted you before, and it was...' Her heavy lids closed for a moment as a flush crept up her chest and covered her cheeks.

Goddammit, she is a wonder.

Millie opened her dark eyes, a world of secrets unravelling. 'It was magical.'

'This will be even better. I swear it.' He tensed his stomach, loving how her gaze caught the movement of his ridged muscles hardening.

Nodding a silent assent, Millie tightened her grip again. She dragged her fisted hand toward the root until her knuckles brushed his hair.

'Fuuuuck.' He might die tonight, but what a glorious way to perish.

He couldn't help himself from leaning down and pressing his lips against her soft cheek. She leaned into him, her hand growing bolder as she stroked back to his tip. Her thumb circled his flared head, rubbing the moisture gathered there.

'Dammit, woman. You'll end this before we've even begun,' he growled in her ear before taking the lobe between his teeth and nibbling.

'We wouldn't want that,' she murmured, letting go of his very disappointed cock and gently pushing him back. She tilted her head, her gaze shifting from his proudly straining erection to the ruined thigh he wished were invisible. She ran soft fingers over the desecrated skin. 'Does this hurt?'

Drake couldn't look at her face, so instead he watched her hand run down his thigh and then back up again. The skin was numb in areas, but he could feel the gentle pressure of her fingers. His throat tightened. 'Yes. But not because you're touching me. It always hurts. Sometimes more, sometimes less.'

She ran her hand up his thigh, along his hip bone, her thumb tracing the line of muscle leading from his hip to his stomach muscles. She bumped along each ridge and hollow, over his ribs to his shoulder, where she gripped him tight, pulling him closer. Before Drake could react, she enfolded him in her embrace.

16

Drake was surrounded by lemon and cotton, warmth and soft curves, strong arms holding him tight, silky hair tickling his cheek.

What is happening to me?

They were supposed to be fucking, but instead, she was hugging him. It was too much. He was prepared for lust, friction, heat. But his heart wasn't ready for comfort. Sanctuary. Kindness.

He froze. His lungs stopped working. His heart halted. His mind stalled. She rubbed one hand down his back, tripping over the uneven scar tissue.

'I'm so sorry, Beau. For what they did to you. For the pain you suffered. If I could take it away, I would.'

Her soft words wound around his heart as securely as her arms wrapped around his body.

Drake tried to swallow, but a rock was lodged in his throat. His whole body began to shake.

What is happening to me?

He was losing his carefully cultivated control. He was drowning.

'It's okay. You're safe with me. I'm not going anywhere.'

Soft lips pressed against his cheek, and he was lost. He wrapped his arms around her strong, sweet body and held onto her like a desperate man clinging to his last hope.

That's what she is. My last hope. My only hope.

'I've got you, Beau.'

They stayed that way for minutes, or millennia, as he shook like a leaf in the winter wind. When his body stilled, and he could breathe again, Millie loosened her grip and leaned back to look at him. His face was wet.

Goddamned tears.

He couldn't remember the last time he cried. But she wiped them away, taking with her some of his shame. 'Is there anything that helps the pain?'

My leg, or everything else?

Focusing on the leg seemed safest.

'I massage it. With linseed oil. It helps to stop the scars from becoming tight. Eases the muscles a bit.'

Millie nodded. 'Get the oil and lie on the bed.'

Drake's brow drew down in confusion. 'Now? Why?'

'Because, you silly man. You're hurting. I want to ease some of your pain. I'm going to rub your leg for you.'

Drake was never at a loss for words. He always knew exactly what to say, even if it wasn't something people wanted to hear. But she flummoxed him. He was speechless.

He was standing naked in front of her, a raging cockstand making it difficult to think, and yet she wanted to hold off being ravished in order to rub medicinal oil on his massacred leg.

She's mad. I'm going to wed an insane woman.

'Go on. The sooner we deal with your leg, the sooner we can move on to rubbing other things.' She winked at him.

What kind of alternate world have I stumbled into?

Not only did Millie show no signs of revulsion at his brutalised body, she did so while making sexy puns and eyeing his cock like it was a vanilla ice she wanted to lick. It made no sense.

Seriously, what is happening to me?

He shook his head, trying to clear his foggy thoughts.

'Unless you want me to go searching through your drawers myself?' Millie raised her brows, putting both hands on her hips.

Jesus, her breasts are amazing.

And the sooner he got the oil, the sooner he could touch them.

Decision made.

Drake turned and limped to his dresser.

'I must say, it's almost as much fun to watch you leave as it is to see you coming.' Millie gave him a wicked smile when he turned back to determine if she was mocking him. 'You might not be an arse, but you certainly have a beautiful one, Major General Drake.'

Drake retrieved the oil and turned back. 'You are a wicked woman, Millicent Whittenburg.'

'So I've been told,' Millie said.

'Wicked redheads are my weakness, Miss Whittenburg. One in particular.'

She smiled as he walked over to the bed and pulled back the covers. He patted the mattress in invitation, and Millie hiked her skirts to climb up from the opposite side.

Once Drake was settled on his back, she shuffled over to him, hindered by her long nightdress.

Drake pressed his back against the pillows, trying to relax. But watching her breasts sway as she crawled across the feather mattress made his erection jerk.

Her gaze flew to his lap.

'It looks like he wants to be next.' She addressed his penis. 'You're going to have to wait your turn, sir.'

A bubble of mirth burst from Drake's chest in a rusty laugh. 'I've never had a lady talk to my cock before.'

Millie's cheeks darkened with a blush. 'Obviously, none of them knew what they were doing.' She tipped up her chin in a stubborn expression he was growing to love and held her hand out expectantly.

'Obviously,' he agreed, handing over the oil.

Without another word, she pulled open the stopper, poured oil into her hand, resealed the bottle, and rubbed her hands together. He waited for her to hesitate before touching his leg, but she was bold, even in this.

She put both hands on his thigh, rubbing the linseed oil into his skin before she started to knead the tight muscles.

God, that's good.

Drake groaned, and Millie paused.

'Too hard?'

'No. Perfect.'

She nodded again and kept rubbing. Her hair fell around her shoulders in fiery waves. Drake reached over and toyed with the ends, his hand moving to her shoulder, finding the dip of her spine, and following the bumps down. He stroked her back as she stroked his thigh. It was a strange amalgamation of peaceful arousal until her fingers brushed the side of his cock.

His body tensed.

'Is that better?' she asked, her eyes heavy-lidded, her voice rough with need. She licked her bottom lip.

Drake's hand tightened around her side, pulling her on top of him. She let out a surprised squeak. He cupped her cheek with his rough palms, letting his fingers glide over smooth skin until he buried them in her thick hair. Pulling her closer, their lips almost touched.

'Better,' he rasped before leaning forward and claiming her mouth.

* * *

Sweet saints and sinners!

Sparring with Drake had been her favourite thing. Now, it was kissing him. He was the very Devil with his tongue, licking, laving, inviting her to tangle with him as he bit her bottom lip hard enough to spark pleasure in her core.

Kissing Franklin had never been like this, but Millie was a quick study. She took a page from Drake's book, sucking his tongue, then kissing along his jaw and sinking her teeth into his neck.

He growled.

She moaned.

His hands tightened on her hips, pulling her against the thick ridge of his cock.

'Christ's teeth,' she hissed.

'I had no idea you were religious.' He rumbled against her temple before grabbing her head and turning her face toward him. He plunged into her depths, licking and nibbling her lips, tangling his tongue with hers, and Millie's brain scattered into a thousand sparks.

She writhed against him. Her core ached as wet warmth flooded her. The same thing happened on the chaise, but never once with Franklin. Her body was weeping for Drake, readying for him.

'You are so fucking wet for me.'

Of course he noticed.

The man noticed everything. Her body's reaction

to his hardened flesh only seemed to increase Drake's passion.

'This never happened with... er... I mean... I didn't know I was supposed to until you kissed me... there.' She spoke around soft kisses pressed to his cheek, his neck, his temple, but her hips kept grinding against him. A sweet pleasure, so sharp she wanted to sob, pulsed between her thighs. Rubbing her core against his granite ridge with focused intent, a tiny fragment of nerves burst with new sparks, each one more intense. The pleasure pulsed outward in concentric circles until every part of her felt the echoes of desire. Thanks to Drake, she knew what was coming, and she wanted it with an intensity that consumed her.

'Your body is getting ready for me. The slicker you are, the easier it will be, love. Remember, I'm not an arse. I don't want you to feel anything but pleasure. Just let go.'

Millie pulled back, her fingers brushing over his full bottom lip. 'Your mouth is sinful. The first time I saw you, I couldn't stop staring at this lip. I thought, how could such a serious man have such a lewd mouth?'

Drake smiled. Not a twitch of his lips. Not the left corner curling in a smirk. A full-blown smile. Millie almost swooned. 'Did you enjoy learning exactly how lewd this mouth can be?'

'Yes.' She spoke without thought.

'Would you like another lesson?'

'I thought perhaps this time, I could...' If he could bring her such pleasure with his mouth, certainly she could do the same.

His icy gaze sharpened. 'You want to suck me?'

Millie wasn't sure exactly what she wanted except to gift him with the same pleasure he'd shown her. 'You'll have to tell me what to do.' She slithered down his body, making space for herself between his legs. Up close, his erection seemed even larger. Ropey veins pulsed beneath his skin. The head of his cock flared a bit as a bead of milk formed at the slit. She leaned forward and licked it, tasting salt.

'Fuck me, woman.'

'That is the idea,' she murmured against his hard flesh.

Drake's hand was in her hair, squeezing, and she knew he wanted to guide her mouth to where he pulsed with need, but he waited.

'Are you sure? You don't have to.' His voice was harsh with contained desire, but she wanted to see him fly apart.

Millie glanced at him, his jaw clenched, his arms

straining with cords of muscle so beautifully defined in the candlelight. 'I want to.'

He asked if she wanted to suck him, so that is what she would do. Taking the head in her mouth, she widened her lips to wrap around him and sucked him deep.

Dear Lord. How does one breathe while doing this?

Panic threatened, but Drake's hand guided her, pulling her back a bit.

'Easy, Millie. Just like that, suck me as deep as you can.'

Applying herself to the task, she found a rhythm. She could only take part of him into her mouth, so she used her hand to grip his root, stroking in tandem. The taste and texture of him fascinated her. Swirling her tongue around his head, another spurt of salty tang coated her mouth. Oddly, the entire affair created a twin ache within her core. She squeezed her thighs together, trying to ease it, but it only increased. When his hand drifted from her head down to grasp a tight nipple and pinch, Millie nearly lost her rhythm. She moaned, the vibrations causing Drake's whole body to tighten.

'Jesus, Millie. You'll finish this before we've begun.' Drake grabbed her shoulders, pulling her off and dragging her up his granite torso.

'Are you... I mean to say, I thought you would...' She wasn't exactly sure what she thought he would do, but certainly, she expected something similar to the cataclysmic crisis she experienced.

'I don't want to spend in your mouth, Millie. Not tonight.'

Her brows drew together as disappointment took hold. 'Oh. Did I do something wrong?'

Drake repositioned her on his lap, her legs straddling him. His face was tight with strain. 'You were perfect. Better than my dreams. But I want this to last, and if you kept that up, I wouldn't be able to wait.'

Millie tried to puzzle out what he wasn't saying. 'So, once a man... spends... he can't do it again?'

Drake's laughter was more like a wheeze. 'Not for a bit. But a woman can climax many times. It's one more way you are superior to us.' He pressed up with his hips, and she felt the hard length of his cock rubbing through her wet folds.

'Oh,' she gasped. The slide of his hot, hard flesh against her sensitive bud was glorious.

'Did you like that?'

Millie bit her lip. 'Yes.'

He pressed up again, and she cried out as the blunt head of his cock created silky friction with the cluster of nerves encompassing her world.

He gripped her hips, guiding her as he ground against her wet core once more.

'Are you ready for me, Millie?'

'Yes. Please.'

He lifted her hips up and positioned himself at her entrance.

His gaze captured her, swirling with too many emotions to define. 'Now?'

She bit her lip and nodded.

He pulled her hips down, his cock sliding through her wet channel, stretching her, filling her. It was too much. It wasn't enough. It was everything.

When he was fully seated in her, he paused, letting her body adjust to his width and length.

Millie took several deep breaths as her internal muscles slowly melted, making space for his invasion. She twitched her hips, the movement eliciting new sparks of pleasure.

'That's it. Ride me, Millie.' He pulled her back up his cock until the head almost came out, then slid his hands up her ribs to hold her breasts. It was clear the next move was hers to make.

She'd never been more grateful for her skills as a horsewoman. This was something she knew how to do. She sank back down, taking him deeper until he hit a sharp and wondrous point within her.

Millie hissed out a curse and pulled up before slamming back down, harder. Drake kneaded her breasts, his clever fingers rolling her nipples into twin points of sensation that only magnified the pleasure pulsing in her core.

'Yes. Take your pleasure, Millie.' Drake's growl of encouragement was like breath on fire, increasing the inferno.

She tightened her thighs around Drake's narrow hips and revelled in his throaty cry. Perhaps she couldn't bring him to completion with her mouth, but she would ride them both into glory.

He caught her rhythm, jolting up with his hips each time she sank harder. She braced her hands on his chest and rode him higher, faster, deeper until, on a cry, they both flew off the edge together.

* * *

Millie stretched, caught in the hazy in-between world of sleep and waking. She reached for the solid, hard warmth of Drake and he snaked an arm around her waist, pulling her back into his chest and surrounding her with his powerful body.

'I could stay here forever,' she murmured, her voice rough from the passionate screams he'd inspired.

'I'm amenable to your suggestion.' His rumble vibrated through her chest.

She couldn't lie to herself any longer. She loved Major General Beaufort Drake. She loved him, and she wanted to create a life with him. Together. As equal partners.

Millie needed to tell him. She couldn't share her body with this man and not also give him her heart, her mind, her secrets. Surely, after such a raw moment of truth between them, he would understand.

'I need to tell you something, Beau.'

His body hardened around her. He didn't say anything, just squeezed his arm tighter around her waist. She took it as a sign of encouragement.

'There's a reason I was so good at darts yesterday afternoon.'

Drake ran his nose up her neck, nuzzling the sensitive skin under her ear. 'I thought I'd have to employ sophisticated tactics of wit and interrogation before you revealed your secrets.'

Millie turned in his arms so she could see his face. 'No. Just your trust, Beau. That's what I'm asking for. I need you to trust me. Because I'm going to trust you right now. And we both know, that isn't easy.' She felt her heart thumping against her chest as if it wanted to escape. But she needed to tell him everything. Now.

He wouldn't dare betray her. Not after what they'd shared.

'Tell me.' His icy-blue eyes flashed in a beam of early-morning sunlight.

'I have been training as an investigator. For the Queen. And this wedding is part of my mission. Well, the wedding guests, really.' She could feel her cheeks heating. She was talking too fast, but if she didn't get it out quickly, her secrets might stay stuck in her throat forever.

Drake stayed quiet. His eyes were unfathomable arctic pools as he waited for her to continue.

Millie fiddled with the sheet, folding it back and forth through her fingers, then flattening it again. 'I know you work for the prime minister. And I'm guessing we're after the same man. I want us to work together, Beau. Not just on this mission. But always, with everything. I want this marriage to be real, and close, and strong. So, we need to be partners. Equals. Fighting on the same side, for the same cause.'

There. She said it. All of it. Her heart felt lighter as she took a liberating breath.

Drake released her, sitting up and pulling the sheets with him to cover his lap. He clenched his jaw. 'You're investigating Franklin St George?' His deep voice gave nothing away. But Millie had come too far to back down now.

'Yes. I am.'

'And you know the crimes he's committed?'

'Kidnapping innocent girls and selling them into the flesh markets in France? Yes.' Millie sat with him, pulling the sheet to cover herself, feeling more vulnerable than she had with her thighs spread and Drake impaling her.

'You know how dangerous this man is, that he works for a secret society?'

'The Devil's Sons. Yes. I know. And I want to work with you to take them down. Of course, I know you plan on bringing these vile men to the House of Lords. The prime minister still believes they'll receive justice, but once you speak with Philippa, she'll explain. Exacting justice upon these bastards ourselves is the only way to ensure no more girls are taken.' Millie held her breath. He had to agree. Even if it took time to convince him, she knew he wanted justice just as badly as she did. And she trusted him. He would make the right choice. He must.

* * *

Drake needed to make a choice. The hardest of his life. He had just spent the last few hours in the arms of the only woman he ever wanted. The truth of his love for Millie crashed through his soul like an anvil, re-shaping his priorities, his understanding of life's meaning, his reason for breathing. And now, she had finally revealed her secret.

Killian was fucking right all along.

Once he knows, he'll be impossible to live with.

Drake heaved an internal sigh. Millie secretly worked for the Queen, just like her friend – and Killian's now wife – Hannah.

But Millie trusted him. Revealed everything without him even asking. She wanted to be united with Drake in their bodies and in their mission. It all sounded perfect.

And Drake was going to ruin it. He must.

She was too precious. Her life too valuable to risk at the hands of evil bastards like Franklin St George. Even imagining her standing next to him while he fought the twisted men responsible for this evil filled him with an emotion long-dead. Fear. A warrior full of fear quickly became a dead man. Dead men couldn't protect the ones they loved. The whole idea of them investigating crimes together was an impossible fairy tale. Now he just needed to explain that to Millie.

Of course, she would be angry. At first. But she was an intelligent woman. She would see reason. She must.

'Millie, I swore never to love another woman the way I loved Nora.' He reached out and traced his finger down her smooth cheek, tangling his hand in her hair as it draped over her shoulder. 'You've proven me right.'

Shock parted her lips on a sharp inhalation. She tried to pull away, but he shifted his hand to her shoulder, holding her steady.

'I don't understand.' Tears filled her rich brown eyes.

'I will never love you the way I loved Nora. Because my love for Nora was like a shadow. An echo ringing hollow and cold. What I feel for you is...' He swallowed, looking out the window at the rising sun in a winter sky, desperate for inspiration to quantify the infinite in syllables and sounds. A fool's task. But still, he had to try. 'What I feel for you is forever. It's my breath. My beating heart. It eclipses every other emotion. If I have a soul, you are the essence that fills it.'

Tears rolled down her cheek, but her eyes crinkled at the corners in a smile so precious, Drake's fluttering heart almost flew away.

'You must know, Beau, it's the same for me. It's why

I told you everything. Because you are everything to me.'

This next bit was going to be hard. 'And it's why I can never allow you to continue your work for the Queen.'

She blinked several times before shifting away from him on the bed. Her soft expression hardened like his lake in December. 'You won't *allow* me?'

Stay calm. Don't push her.

Of course, she needed time to accept his words. He would give her as much time as she needed. 'Millie, you must understand. As your husband, it's my job to decide how best to keep you safe. I love your bold ways, your wild spirit, but in this, you need to see reason.'

Millie clenched her teeth. 'You aren't my husband yet. And you want me to see reason? Because what I'm suggesting isn't reasonable?'

'It's reasonable for you to expect that we are equals in all other things, but you must see how impossible it is for you to fight alongside me.'

'I must understand that I'm unreasonable. I must see that our equality is impossible. Is that what you're trying so desperately to explain to me? All the things I must agree to when I also agree to marry you?'

Drake put his hands out. 'Calm down, please.'

'Calm down? Now you're telling me I need to calm down?' Her husky voice rose a decibel.

Shit. That was unwise.

All of Drake's alarm systems went off. He had faced many threats, innumerable dangers, and his body was telling him this situation was lethal. He needed to get out. Run. But he wasn't going to leave until she understood. 'Millie, you are strong and brave, but you are still just a woman. You cannot possibly fight a man with the same speed, strength, and skill of a trained warrior.'

Millie's burst of laughter was sharp and hard. Much like her gaze. 'I'm *just* a woman.' Every time she parroted one of his phrases back to him, he wanted to wince. 'I recall you telling me about *just* a woman who killed several soldiers with nothing but a slingshot and her hands. One would presume she fought with superior speed, strength, and skill than the trained warriors she defeated. Perhaps they also told her to calm down right before she flung a rock at their heads.'

Fuck. I am deep in the shits now.

When his soldiers started to panic in the war, often they just needed a strong hand to lead them in the right direction. Perhaps that tactic would be more successful.

He used his firm, no-arguments, major-general

voice. 'I can understand your frustration, Millie. But in this decision, I will not bend.'

Drake expected anger. He expected her to yell. Cry. Perhaps slap at him. He expected the fire of her rage.

He didn't expect ice.

It hardened around her mouth, turned her limbs rigid, tightened her hands into fists.

No. This is not better. This is much worse. I'll explain the danger. If she knows I'm just trying to keep her safe, she'll understand.

'Millie, these men will kill you without a thought. What kind of husband would I be if I let you walk into that danger?'

'The kind who *trusts* his wife to be capable, skilled, resilient, his *equal*.'

Drake took a deep breath, willing his temper to recede. 'I will not lose you,' he growled.

'You are losing me right now, Drake. Don't you see that?'

She was killing him. Didn't she understand he was doing this *because* of how desperately he loved her? Because the thought of a fucking weasel like Franklin St George touching her, let alone hurting her, drove him to the brink of madness. If he lost Millie, he lost everything.

She shook her head, her fiery hair cascading

around her shoulders like a waterfall of lava. 'Philippa was right.' She swept the blanket aside, exposing her gorgeous breasts, soft belly, and strong thighs.

His thoughts scattered like leaves in a gale.

She scooted to the edge of the bed, flinging her legs over the side and sliding to the floor. Her muscles flexed and shifted in the most fascinating display of athleticism. Drake's cock twitched optimistically.

Not likely.

'Good day, my lord.' Millie bent over to grab her nightgown where it had fallen, and Drake's brain seized at the sight. He was too trapped by his stupid lust to move fast enough.

Millie walked across the floor, her red curls brushing over the dimples at the tops of her buttocks. Drake struggled to untangle his legs from the sheets, but by the time he freed himself, her door shut. It was impossible to ignore the loud click of her lock sliding home.

'Fuck. That could have gone better.'

Drake ran his hand over his spikey hair and blew out a long breath.

What was he supposed to do? Agree to willingly put the most precious thing in his life in lethal danger? Impossible.

She asked me to trust her. But how can I trust fate to keep her safe?

He shook his head. No. She needed some time and space to think this through, and then she would come around to his decision. It was the only way to ensure she stayed here. With him. Safe. Alive. Protected.

Trapped.

His stomach rolled, and Drake sat heavily on the bed.

Dear God. Had he made a terrible mistake?

Have I lost her anyway?

His fluttering heart gave a painful thump.

17

Drake couldn't return to sleep after Millie left. Though it was unfashionably early, he dressed without disturbing his valet and walked into the breakfast room to find Reynard walking out.

'Rough night?' Reynard's famous smile tempted Drake to punch him. Right in the teeth.

'You're up early.' Drake refused to take Reynard's bait.

'Haven't you heard? There's word that one of the maid's sisters has gone missing. A local girl. The family is organising a search party. I thought it might be wise to join them. I'm heading that way now. I would extend you an invitation, but I think perhaps some food and coffee first, hey?'

Drake scowled. 'What do you mean?'

Reynard sucked air through his teeth. 'I mean, you look like shit. Take a moment. Get your thoughts together. Eat something. These search parties always take an age to organise. You won't miss anything by being an hour late.'

Damn it! He's right. I'm letting my stupid heart mess with my head.

He needed to refocus on the investigation. The sooner he put this case to bed, the sooner he could convince Millie that he wasn't some kind of monster trying to take away her freedom.

Except that's exactly what I'm trying to do.

Reynard slapped him on the back. 'Cheer up, old man. You're two days away from wedded bliss. And we're going to catch a break on this case. I know it. Finish your breakfast. I'll see you in the village square.' He stood, tugging down his coat and winking at Drake. 'Maybe you can fill me in on whatever stick is rammed up your arse when you get there.'

'The only stick up my arse is you,' he muttered as Reynard strolled out, passing the duchess as she entered.

Did no one sleep past nine in the bloody morning?

Filling his plate with eggs, haddock, and mushrooms, Drake paused to slather preserves on a thick slice of toast. He didn't want to eat any of it, but there was no need to alert the duchess to his state of deep unrest. Slumping in a chair, Drake poured coffee from a carafe, took a long swallow, and scalded his tongue.

'Shit,' Drake growled.

Lady Winterbourne walked past the food, and before he could stand and pull out her chair, she did so herself. Sitting next to him, the striking, terrifying, powerful woman pulled a cup and saucer closer. She filled the painted porcelain teacup with coffee.

She drank the brew black. No sugar. No cream.

'Good morning, Your Grace. I hope you slept well.' He hated small talk, but when one sat with a friend of the Queen, one put forth their best manners.

'I did.' Philippa glanced at him, raising a perfectly sculpted black brow. 'You did not.' This close, Drake could see where her smooth skin was marred by fine wrinkles around her eyes and mouth. Instead of diminishing her fierce beauty, it highlighted the striking combination of cobalt irises framed by thick, black lashes and crimson lips contrasting against white teeth. He couldn't imagine a man strong enough to match the Duchess of Dorsett.

'You don't miss much, Lady Winterbourne.'

'No. I don't.' She sipped her coffee. Her black hair was pulled into an intricate coiffure of braids and curls. Streaks of silver threading through it created a dramatic effect, like lightning in a midnight sky. 'She told you everything, didn't she?'

Drake's fork froze halfway to his mouth. A chunk of haddock splatted back to his plate. 'Pardon?'

What the actual hell?

'I don't repeat myself, Major General Drake.'

'I'm not sure I understand.'

Philippa snorted, an oddly endearing sound coming from such a dignified woman. 'You have many faults, sir. Lack of intelligence is not one of them. Millicent told you about her work with the Queen. Judging by your pale face and delicate appetite this morning, I'd say you mucked things up quite thoroughly.'

Drake gave up trying to eat. The food tasted like ash, and it was an impossible task at any rate when his mouth kept dropping open from shock. He followed her lead and sipped his own coffee. 'I did not muck things up, thank you very much.' He was tired of being bested by every woman in his goddamned house.

'You did. And you know you did. You just don't like that I'm pointing it out. But hiding your mistakes won't fix anything. What did you tell her? That you wouldn't allow her to continue her work?'

Impossible woman! How does she know so much?

'Did you speak with Millie?' It was the only possible answer.

'I spoke with *Millie* last night. *Before* she spoke to you.' He didn't miss her emphasis on his use of Millie's pet name. He was going to be her husband in a few short days. He damn well had the right to use such a familiar nomenclature. It didn't stop the blush from heating his cheeks and fuelling his frustration. He was a war-hardened soldier, for Christ's sake. He *did not* blush. His cheeks got hotter.

The duchess ignored his obvious discomfort, or – more accurately – revelled in it as she continued talking. 'She told me she was going to trust you. That is all I needed to hear to predict the outcome.'

Anger, mortification, and shame swirled in his belly with the little bit of food he'd choked down. 'Predict exactly what, madame?'

Philippa's lips widened in an expression too sharp to be called a smile. 'You are a man who values control above all else. And Millicent is a wild typhoon you're desperately trying to contain. She will destroy you if you don't let her go. And you will decimate her if you hold on.'

'I would never hurt her.' He fisted his hand and pounded it on the table to punctuate his words.

Philippa's hand dipped into what must be a pocket.

Highly unusual. But then, so was the duchess. Drake wondered exactly what she kept hidden in her midnight-blue skirts. Whatever it was, he'd bet it was lethal.

'I wouldn't recommend you raise your voice to me again, Major General Drake.'

Drake clenched his teeth and counted to ten. He did not apologise. Because he did not make mistakes.

Until last night. And this morning.

'I am sorry, Your Grace. I know Millie is important to you. She is even more so to me. As her future husband, it's my duty to protect her. And my honour to keep her safe.'

Philippa's low laugh filled the room. 'Protect her. Keep her safe. Do you know what I hear when you say those words? Control her. Contain her. Take away her choices because she couldn't possibly be intelligent enough to make her own decisions.'

Fucking hell.

The truth of her words hit deeper than a bullet to his chest.

'So, you would just have me let her go?' Even the thought of it stole his breath.

'If you want any chance of earning her trust, proving your faith in her? Yes.'

Philippa was crushing him into dust. But she wasn't done yet.

'I rarely impart my wisdom on men. Most are too stupid and too full of their own ignorance to appreciate it. But I will take a risk with you, Major General Drake. Don't make me regret this.'

Drake forced himself to straighten his shoulders, hating that he was desperate to hear whatever advice the duchess was willing to impart. He nodded – as if she needed his permission to do anything.

Philippa rubbed her thumb and forefinger in rhythmic circles, then leaned forward. 'Love, real love, the kind that binds two souls together, amalgamating them in a crucible of trust and commitment, that rare and wondrous miracle of true love doesn't take choice away under the guise of protection. It doesn't strip someone of power with the pretence of safety.'

He shook his head, instinctively rejecting her words. 'I'm not trying to take away her freedom.'

But he was. The truth of it broke over him like a vicious wave. By exerting his power over her in an effort to keep Millie safe, he was doing exactly as Philippa said. Decimating the woman he loved. The horror of it shattered him. His heart fractured. He pressed the heel of his hand against his chest.

'You see it now, don't you Major General? How your edicts erase any chance of equality for her?'

As shattering as it was to admit, the duchess was right. Issuing any order and expecting it to be followed inherently assumed a hierarchy of power that put Drake above Millie. 'Dear God. I've ruined everything, haven't I?'

'You will. If you don't trust her, Major General Drake. If you don't give her the one thing she should never have to ask you for. Freedom.'

'I must find her. I must speak with her.'

Philippa tipped her chin at the window. 'She went out for a ride this morning. About half an hour before I came down.'

Drake sprang from the chair, almost tipping the heavy thing in his haste to find Millie.

'Lovely chat, Major General Drake,' Philippa called to him as he raced out the door.

* * *

Millie was far too angry to climb into her bed after she stalked out of Drake's room.

'Stupid, idiotic, thick-skulled, moronic bastard,' she hissed to the quiet room. Anger filled her limbs with buzzing energy.

Philippa had been right.

'Of course she's right. She's always bloody right.'

That revelation did nothing to ease the burning ache in Millie's chest.

'Fucking numbskull!' She kicked the bed and howled in pain as her toe cracked against the wooden post.

Wonderful. Now my toe and *my heart are broken.*

Storming into her dressing room, Millie threw petticoats, chemises, dresses, and jackets about until she found her favourite riding habit. A gorgeous tartan wool of forest green and deep brown. It buttoned at the front, allowing Millie to dress without needing to call for Penny. She shoved her stockinged feet into well-used riding boots and braided her hair. It would be cold so early in the morning, but Millie cared not.

'It would serve him right if I froze to death. Hard to protect an icicle, Major General Blockhead!'

She fought her way into her thickest riding jacket and stomped out of her dressing room to dig through her armoire for a pair of wool-lined gloves. Without pausing to glance in the mirror, Millie swept out of her room, down the grand staircase, and out the front door. What she needed was a fast, hard ride on a beast who knew something about loyalty. Trust. Freedom.

'Who needs a husband when I can have a horse?'

Millie declared to the windblown alders and pewter skies.

Pushing open the stable doors, she almost ran right into Master Bright.

'Cor, Millie! You right near took me 'ead off!'

'Billy! I'm so sorry. What are you doing about so early this morning?'

Billy was carrying a heavy saddle in his skinny arms. He almost tipped over as he sidestepped a bale of hay left in the centre of the barn.

'Didn't you 'ear? Theys arranged a search party. For Lucy.'

Millie followed him down the line of stables until he stopped in front of Medusa's half door.

'Billy, you aren't thinking of riding Medusa, are you? Do you even ride?'

Billy ducked his head, the back of his neck turning crimson. 'I've ridden before.'

'When?' Millie put her hand on her hip. She would cut all her hair off if Billy had ridden anything bigger than a pony.

'Wot's it matter to you anyways?' He hunched his narrow shoulders. 'I need the fastest 'orse so's I can find 'er. Before they move 'er. I knows summink none of those others do.' His voice quavered, and Millie wished she could pull him in for a hug. It would do both of them a world of good. The new missing girl must remind him of his sister. How much weight this small boy carried.

Wait a tick. Before they move her?

'Billy, what do you mean "before they move her"?' Millie took the saddle from him. There was no way she could allow him to ride Medusa alone. It would be akin to letting him jump off a cliff while hoping he sprouted wings.

'Will you come wif me? I couldn't tell the rest of 'em. Loud bunch of half-wits. They'd just muck things up and ruin the rescue. But not you, Millie. We're alike, the two of us. Major General Drake is a nice bloke, but 'e doesn't fink we can 'andle this. 'E finks we'll just get 'urt. But we won't. We're tuffer than any of those toffs with their guns and swords. An 'eaps smarter too. You an' me togefer, we can save 'er.' Billy nodded but ruined the confident gesture by biting his lip and tugging at his hair.

Millie didn't think. She jumped into action. 'Of course I will. Tell me what you know while I saddle Medusa. She's very fast, Billy. You're going to have to hold on tight.'

'I won't let go of you, Millie. I swear.'

* * *

Ten minutes later, they were racing across the fields toward the forest, heading for the hunting lodge Millie saw the day before. Billy clung to Millie's back like a determined little spider monkey, refusing to budge even when Medusa leapt over a fallen log.

Billy believed the girl was being kept in the cabin. He liked to sneak away every once in a while. When things became a bit too 'stuffy'. Running wild in the country was nothing like living on the streets of Bethnal Green where he grew up, but it gave him a sense of freedom when 'the walls got tight'.

He had run across the same cabin as Millie, but before he could go in, two men had come out. He was too far to see them clearly in the shadowed woods, but the instincts honed on the streets of Bethnal Green had kicked in, and Billy had found himself a snug hiding spot under the bush. The men were arguing about a package. One wanted to move it right away, but the other thought it best to wait. In the end, one of them had left while the other stayed. Billy thought the whole conversation was odd, but he could hardly go poking about the cabin knowing one of the men was still in there. It wasn't until later he realised what that package could be. Lucy. The missing girl.

'I knew I should have investigated that cabin yesterday,' Millie muttered as the wind ripped through her hair and Medusa shifted left to avoid a large boulder.

Billy let out a yelp and tightened his grip around her waist.

Millie needed to keep her focus on the deer trail they were following instead of punishing herself for the past. The terrain was tricky. The last thing she or Billy needed was to be thrown or for Medusa to be injured.

They would find this girl. They had to. If only Franklin didn't get spooked by the search party being organised. Billy explained that his haste was partly motivated from fear of the men trying to move the girl before he and Millie reached the cabin.

Imagining the shock on Drake's stupid, handsome, infuriating face as she brought poor Lucy back – safe and sound – was a moment Millie prepared to savour.

She slowed Medusa as they entered the tree line.

'The trail is rough, Billy. Keep a tight hold,' she warned, not wanting the boy to loosen his grip just because they'd slowed from a gallop to a careful walk. The uneven terrain could be just as treacherous as their blistering pace in the fields.

Twenty painstaking minutes later, Millie reined Medusa to a stop. They were still a fair distance from the cabin, but if Franklin was there, she didn't want the sound of Medusa to alert him.

'We go on foot from here, Billy.'

They tied Medusa to a tree and picked their way through the thick bracken as quickly and quietly as possible. She had to hand it to Billy. He was swift and silent on his feet. He knew the trail much better than Millie and took the lead.

After ten minutes of scrambling, Billy crouched down low and waved her closer.

'Just there,' he whispered, pointing through the ferns at the clearing.

The cabin looked much as it had the day before, though no smoke came from the chimney.

Shit! What if he's already taken her?

The very idea of poor Lucy being spirited away to a life of horror across the Channel was untenable. Millie swallowed her nerves and created a plan.

'There's no use barging in before we know the situation.' She spoke in hushed tones to Billy as the wind rustled the leaves around them. Haste would only create mistakes. If Lucy was gone, it wouldn't matter how long they took to assess the situation, and if she was there, caution was even more paramount. 'Let's circle around. I can go right, you left. We'll meet at the back. If you see signs of anyone or see a horse, stay where you are, and I'll find you. Same for me. Yes?'

'Right you are, Millie. Careful.' His wide eyes blinked like an owl, and Millie's heart expanded in her chest.

What a precious lad.

'You too, Billy.' She nodded to him, and they both headed quietly and carefully in opposite directions.

The forest had patches of thick gorse bushes, muddy streams, and hidden rocks, all determined to thwart Millie. She was grateful her split skirts were narrow, but they still got caught on every branch, thornbush, and dead fern. Her hair was pulled from its braid, her arms and cheeks scratched by the angry forest, some deep enough to bleed, but none of it mattered if they could save Lucy. Millie reached into the slit Penny had sewn into her skirt, allowing her access to the blade strapped on her thigh. She was immensely grateful for Philippa's gift.

Philippa!

In her haste, Millie hadn't even thought about alerting Philippa to her plans. The duchess would not be pleased.

Well, she can join the list of people I love who are angry with me.

Millie heard the distinctive nicker of a horse.

Damnation!

It came from her right. Turning away from the cabin, she held her breath and moved at the speed of a snail. A hoof stomped and the distinctive sigh of an equine guided her gaze deeper into the trees. A copper swish of hair swiped in her peripheral. She dropped to the ground and waited. Nothing except the crunch of a horse sneaking a mid-forest snack from a low-hanging oak branch.

So, someone had the same idea as Millie and Billy. But were they here to help, or was it Franklin?

Franklin's here. Trying to get Lucy and move her.

She didn't know how she knew, but she knew.

As quietly and swiftly as she could, she made her way to the meeting point with Billy.

Billy was almost completely hidden behind a huge oak trunk. She joined him and hunkered down as the cold air seeped through her wool coat.

'I didn't see anyfink. You?' Billy kept his gaze on the back of the cabin.

'There's a horse, just there.' She tipped her head in the direction of the mare. 'Someone's in there with Lucy. We must be quick and careful.'

'I'll go in.' Billy started to move, but she grabbed his wrist.

'No. If it's Franklin, he wouldn't hesitate to kill you, but I don't think he'd kill me.'

''E would, Millie. I've seen 'im watch you this week. 'E's got the very Devil in 'is eyes.'

Even more reason for her to keep Billy out of the cabin.

'Look, you are much faster than me, Billy. If I get caught, you run like the dickens back to Medusa. Ride her to Alder House and get Drake.'

Billy's eyes grew huge. 'I can't ride 'er wiffout you. You said it yerself. I would've fallen a million times if you weren't wif me.'

He was right, but she didn't have time to come up with a different plan. 'You can, Billy. You'll do grand. And that's only if you need to.'

'No, Millie. Let me go. I'm right strong. I can take that toff St wotever-'is-name. 'E's likely as weak as 'is chin. 'An iffen I get in trouble, you ride like a dream. You'll get 'elp and save me.'

Tears sprang to Millie's eyes at his absolute confidence in her ability to save him. But this was no time for silly emotions. She blinked her eyes and shook her head. 'You don't even have a weapon, Billy. I'm sure Franklin has at least one pistol, and a sword. I won't send you in there unarmed.'

'Neither do you,' Billy hissed, his bottom lip popping out in a pout that betrayed his youth.

Millie pulled up the sleeve of her coat, revealing the blade strapped to her wrist.

'Cor blimey! Where'd you get that?'

'There's not time, Billy. Stay here. Watch. If you hear me scream or see Franklin come out of that cabin, run for Medusa. You promise?'

Billy swallowed, blinked his huge eyes twice, and bit his lip. Finally, he nodded. 'Awright. But you be careful, Millie. The major general will kill me if anyfink 'appens to you.'

She patted him on his shoulder and carefully made her way to the back of the cabin. A glassless window was the only opening. She crouched low beneath it, holding her breath and listening.

A feminine whimper gave Millie hope. At least Lucy was still alive.

If ears had muscles, hers would be straining to hear any other sounds. The scuff of a boot on the floor, the rumble of a masculine voice, a cough or sigh. Anything indicating Lucy wasn't alone. Millie waited for what felt like an eternity but must have only been minutes. She could see Billy's head poking out from his hiding place, his worried eyes wide.

Time to go.

Trusting her instincts, Millie continued around the house, opting to use the front door instead of trying to scramble in the window. If someone was watching them, they'd know either way.

She slowly opened the door and Lucy's whimpers turned into frightened, muffled screams until she saw Millie in the dim light of the cabin.

It smelled awful in the small space. Sweat, refuse, mould, and stale air. Poor Lucy was lying on her side, her hands tied behind her back, her ankles also wrapped in rough rope. Her clothes were dirty, her hair an oily matt of tangles. Tears created streaks of pale skin in an otherwise filthy face. It was hard to tell what the girl looked like beneath the dirt and ragged clothes.

The hunting shack only had one room. It was clear no one else was in the space waiting to pounce on Millie.

Bugger.

That meant whoever owned the horse was slinking around the forest.

Billy!

She needed to hurry. Save Lucy, find Billy before Franklin did, get the hell out of there.

Easy peasy, feeling queasy.

It wasn't how the rhyme was supposed to go, but

nonetheless.

Millie wasted no time, rushing over to Lucy and releasing a blade to cut through the ropes around the girl's wrists and ankles.

As soon as Lucy's hands were free, the girl ripped the gag from her mouth.

'Thank you, thank you!' she sobbed, helping Millie remove the ropes from her ankles. 'We must hurry. He'll be back. He heard something and left...'

'Damn,' Millie muttered, her fears for Billy mounting.

She helped Lucy to her feet, but the girl was too weak and almost fell. Millie caught her and didn't hear the door creaking open.

A bullet slammed into the wall next to Millie's head, wood splinters flying everywhere.

Without thought, Millie let go of Lucy and dropped to one knee, letting the blade in her hand fly.

The masked man at the door grunted, his pistol clattering to the ground.

Another loud report sounded outside. Someone was shooting from the forest at the front door, though Millie didn't know if they were aiming for her or the masked Devil.

The man didn't wait to find out. He let out a frustrated bellow and ran straight for Millie. She wrapped her arms around Lucy, protecting the girl with her body from whatever onslaught the bastard planned. But he bypassed them, leaping out the window and landing behind the shack.

He was running for his horse. The slimy weasel was trying to escape. But Millie couldn't leave Lucy with an unknown shooter, and she still needed to find Billy to ensure the boy was safe before she chased after the masked monster.

'Fuck!' She stood, helping Lucy up again.

'Y-you don't speak like a lady.' Lucy's voice was rough, likely from screaming and lack of water.

'No. She doesn't,' a deep voice growled.

Drake!

She kept her arm around Lucy as she turned to the front door. Drake's great coat swirled around him. His broken brow rose in assessment. His hair, so light it was almost silver, glinted in a spear of sunlight. And his full lips, far too luscious for such a hard face, pressed together in a firm line.

The man is bloody beautiful.

He was sure to be livid, but Millie didn't care. He was there. She wasn't alone.

Straightening her shoulders, she tightened her grip on Lucy. 'He's wounded. I winged him with my blade. But we must find Billy before we go after the bastard.'

Drake's mouth curled into a smile, transforming him from a hardened warrior into something even more stunning – the man she loved. 'I found Billy. He has a nasty bump on his head, but otherwise, he's well. Or will be after Mrs Hammond fusses over him for a few days.'

Relief almost felled her. But she held onto her composure with an iron grip. If she ever hoped to prove she and Drake could be partners, becoming a watering pot in her moment of triumph would not help.

'Right. Well, then. We must pursue the masked man. He definitely wasn't St George.'

At the sound of Franklin's name, Lucy broke into panicked tears. 'St George. He's the one I met with... He, he interviewed me. For a maid's position. Told me I got the job. Gave me tea. But everything went black. I, I woke up here.' She was speaking too fast, her broken sobs making it almost impossible to decipher her words.

Millie *knew* St George was part of this. But, of course, the weak-chinned dolt couldn't work alone. He had neither the intelligence nor the confidence. So, who was the masked man? It was imperative they discovered his identity. He would be the brains of the operation.

Millie squeezed the girl. 'It's okay, Lucy. You're safe. I won't let him hurt you. I swear it.'

'We,' Drake said.

Millie swung her gaze back to him, struggling to follow his single-word sentence in the madness of the last few moments. 'Pardon?'

'*We* won't let him hurt her. You did say you wanted to work together, Millie. Or have you changed your mind?'

Major General Beaufort Drake would be her undoing. Despite her best efforts, tears filled her eyes. She couldn't form words.

Drake's Hessians clomped over the rotten planks, he wrapped her in his warm embrace, catching Lucy in the hug as well. Millie breathed in leather and cloves and the feeling of hope.

18

Drake could have held Millie in his arms forever. Knowing she was safe after nearly losing his mind imagining every possible worst-case scenario while racing across fields and forest to find her had taken years off his life. But he would happily trade a decade to the grim reaper if it meant Millie was safe.

While he shared her urgency to chase after the masked man, there was little chance they would catch him after such a head start. Given Lucy's state and Billy's injuries, it would be impossible to leave them while Drake and Millie pursued a ghost. It seemed prudent to get back to Alder House, secure St George, fill in Philippa and Reynard, then come up with a plan.

'Why is Reynard not with you?' Millie asked as she

sat behind Lucy, holding the girl steady as she guided Medusa around an outcropping of rocks. With her skills as a horsewoman on full display, Drake was having trouble keeping his focus.

Billy listed left in front of Drake. He grabbed the boy with one hand while keeping his reins in the other. Billy had taken a hard smack to the back of his head, and while he insisted he was fine, worry gnawed at Drake's heart. He wouldn't rest easy until a doctor had seen both Billy and Lucy and declared them fit.

'He went to help Lucy's family search for her. I was going to join him when Philippa informed me of your early-morning ride.'

'You spoke to Philippa?'

'Yes. She is annoyingly astute.'

'Agreed. What exactly did she say to have you galloping after me?'

'She pointed out a truth I've been avoiding. I would very much like to tell you everything, but now is not the right time. Can you wait? Until we are home and alone?' He ached to pour out his heart, but not on horseback with a traumatised girl and an injured boy between them.

Millie narrowed her eyes, watching him as they rode side by side. 'I can wait.'

It wasn't a declaration of love, but neither was it a

dismissal. She gave him more than he deserved and less than he wanted. Cause to hope, but not reason to celebrate. Yet.

'How did you find me? We had a healthy head start on you.' Millie speared him with her sharp gaze.

The flutter in his heart returned with a few skips and a painful thump.

'I learned how to track in the military.'

Her brow rose, a trick she must have learned from Philippa.

'And Billy told the stable master his plan.' He shrugged. 'So, that helped.'

'Ah.' Millie's dry response had his lips twitching.

God, he loved sparring with her. He only hoped he hadn't lost his chance to continue their battles for the next five or six decades.

When they reached Alder House, Drake led Millie to the kitchen entrance. He had no wish to alert St George of their arrival.

Cook took in the bedraggled foursome with a raised brow.

'Please, get Mrs Hammond and Penny.' Drake's tone was gruff, but he applauded the woman for her presence of mind. She blinked twice, turned, and gave a sharp command to a young woman up to her elbows in chicken feathers. The girl wiped her hands on her apron and rushed out of the kitchen.

While they waited, Cook put a kettle on to boil.

'Tea's what's needed,' she said stoutly.

Lucy was given a steaming cup of strong, black tea, while Billy's was more milk and sugar than anything else.

Mrs Hammond bustled into the kitchen, her starched apron white as a dove, salt-and-pepper hair swept into a perfect bun, and grey eyes taking in every detail. Penny was right behind her.

'Master Bright!' Mrs Hammond clucked over him, her steady hands feeling his head for injuries. 'Ice, Margaret. Now.' She glanced at Cook, who nodded and quickly left the kitchen, taking a steep staircase into the darkness of the cellar.

Millie turned to Penny. 'Please help Lucy to one of the guest rooms. You can have the lads bring up a bath and warm water. She'll need help bathing, and then have Cook send up a tray. Eggs, toast, porridge, I think.'

Penny nodded. 'I'll find a fresh nightgown she can wear.' She turned to Lucy. 'Don't worry, little miss. We'll tuck you into bed snug as a bug until the doctor arrives.'

Millie smiled, her eyes crinkling at the corners. 'Thank you, Penny. You're a dear.'

Drake's heart thumped painfully. God, she was beautiful. And calm in the chaos. And confident in her care of Lucy. And fearsome against her enemies.

She's a goddamn wonder.

Penny helped Lucy from where she sat at the table, put her arm around the girl, and helped her out of the kitchen.

'We should find Philippa. She can help us with St George. We might not be able to wait for Reynard to return.' Millie chewed on her lip, distracting Drake. He wished desperately this mess was over so he could retreat with her into the safety of his room, strip her naked, hold her in his arms, and forget everything except her soft skin, her tart mouth, her lemon and cotton scent.

But first, they must apprehend a killer. Or, at the very least, a kidnapper.

'Mrs Hammond, will you have the duchess meet us here, please.' Millie's husky voice was calm and soothing. It was easy to imagine her leading armies with her confident command and cool composure. She would have made a fierce lieutenant general.

Mrs Hammond squeezed Billy's shoulder before

nodding at Millie. 'At once, my lady. Of course.' She turned and took the servants' stairs to the right of the kitchen table.

Drake sent a boy to the village to inform Lucy's family she had been found and was safe at Alder House. They were welcome to come immediately and be with her until the doctor allowed her to be moved. Another lad rode like the Devil to collect the doctor. A third was told to find Reynard Renquist and have him return to the house post haste.

Cook arrived with ice.

'Perhaps we should pour another dish of tea for the duchess,' Millie murmured, taking the ice from Cook to hold it against Billy's head.

'The Duchess of Dorsett? In my kitchen?' For a moment, Cook looked ready to faint. 'I can't have a duchess down here amongst the chicken feathers and pig intestines.'

Millie put a staying hand on Cook's thick forearm. 'Have no fear. She's seen much worse in the ballrooms of the beau monde, I'd wager. This kitchen is clean, well-organised, and a credit to your skills. Chicken feathers and pig guts are all part of the charm.'

Cook ducked her head, and Drake couldn't stop his smile.

Millie turned to him with a fiery brow raised. 'What?'

'Billy was right about you. You're a corker, Millicent Whittenburg.'

Her cheeks darkened. Drake lifted his hand to feel the heat of her blush against his fingertips.

'Please don't tell me I was summoned to the kitchen to watch you two acting like idiots.' Philippa entered the room, her sharp glare catching Drake like a barb.

'Philippa.' Millie turned away from him and quickly updated the duchess.

'You went after the girl alone?' Philippa's black brow arched like a scorpion's tail, readying to strike.

'I didn't have time to find you, Philippa.'

'You trained her well, Your Grace. She saved the girl and wounded the masked blighter with her blades. You would have been proud.' Drake jumped to her defence.

Millie looked over her shoulder at him, her full lips parting in surprise.

Yes. I see you. I know how brilliant you are. I just hope I'm not too late.

'I *am* proud, but that's hardly the point.' Philippa glared at Drake.

'Don't you trust her to make her own decisions?'

God, it felt good to throw Philippa's wisdom back in her face. Even if the duchess reached into her pocket and murdered him with whatever weapon she hid amongst the silk and lace.

'Smug men are highly annoying and tend to end up with a bullet in their chest. I'd try to remember that, Major General Drake.' Philippa returned her gaze to Millie. 'We must apprehend St George immediately. Before he catches wind of this and attempts escape.'

'I've an idea.' Millie glanced at Drake, the worry in her eyes alerting him that he wasn't going to like her plan.

Either I trust her, or this doesn't work.

'Tell us.' He nodded.

* * *

She should never have told them her silly idea. Now, not only must she speak with St George. She needed to pretend a seduction.

I might be ill.

But it would work. She knew it.

For Queen and country, I suppose.

St George still hadn't come down for breakfast despite the hour approaching noon. His valet informed them he stayed up late playing cards with some of the men and fell a little too deeply into his cups. Millie asked the valet to deliver a note to Franklin while he helped the bastard get dressed.

The servant gave her a quick nod, showing little loyalty to his employer. She could hardly blame the man. Her guess was Franklin treated his servants as poorly as his wife.

Millie waited for St George in the gardens. Philippa secreted herself behind a holly bush while Drake found a helpfully wide-trunked oak. They weren't close enough to where she sat on a stone bench to reach Millie if Franklin became violent, but Philippa was an excellent shot, and Drake promised he could cover the distance in a moment if she needed him.

Do I need him?

She didn't have an answer. Reynard's words came back to her. She was Drake's equal.

But can we become partners?

Another question with no easy answer. And one that depended on him as much as Millie. Could they trust each other so fully?

She shook her head. She didn't have time for such musings when St George still needed to be contained and a masked man needed to be found.

She refocused on the garden path, waiting for Franklin to arrive.

Hopefully, her note would work. She indicated she could no longer fight her attraction to St George. With her wedding looming – less than two days away – she wanted to indulge in her passions before her monster of a fiancé became her husband.

It appealed to the man's vanity while also giving him what he wanted.

Millie.

Just the idea was enough to make her toss up her accounts in the dormant rose bushes. But when she saw Franklin emerge from the house, she forced her lips into an eager smile.

St George strutted down the gravel drive like a peacock preening. He approached her, blocking her view of the oak.

'I knew you couldn't resist me forever, Millicent. But the question is, do I still want you after having to wait so long?' He lifted his failure of a chin so he could look down his nose at her.

Millie stood, knowing her height always intimidated St George. She was taller than him, even when he wore lifts in his shoes. His gaze locked onto her breasts.

Lovely. I'm going to enjoy this next bit.

Millie rested her hand near the slit in her skirts. She spoke before he had a chance to make any advances.

'I know about the girl, Franklin. If you tell me who you're working with, I won't tell anyone about your part in this.' It was a lie, but one she hoped he would buy.

Franklin's grey eyes widened. 'What are you talking about? What girl? You said in your note you wanted to discuss a liaison. Is this girl an addition you want to make to our little twosome?'

She rolled her eyes, not even trying to hide her disgust. 'No, you idiot. I lied. Please pay attention. I want to know who your brethren are in the Devil's Sons. Who are the men organising this horrific trade of women, Franklin? Tell me now, and I'll do what I can to keep your name out of it.' For a woman who abhorred lying, Millie was pouring them out rather easily when it came to duping Franklin.

'So you don't want to have an affair?' Comprehension dawned in painfully slow degrees. He grabbed her wrist in a harsh grip. 'You stupid, little bitch!' He hissed, pulling her close enough to smell the stale gin on his breath. 'You don't know anything! You can't prove *anything*.'

'I found Lucy.'

His grip tightened, and his sad little chin began to quiver.

I have you now, you bastard.

'She is safe. And she identified you as her kidnapper. It's over for you. Unless you tell me who you're working with. It's the only way out for you, Franklin.'

Watching his face pale as his eyes widened filled Millie with pride at a job well done.

'It's not possible. You're just a silly, useless woman. How could you possibly—'

'I'm much more than that. I'm the woman who is going to ruin you far more thoroughly than you ever ruined me.'

He pulled back his hand in a move Millie had seen a thousand times from her stepmother. He was going to try to slap her.

He wouldn't succeed.

As his hand flew, she knocked it aside with her left hand, then slammed her right fist into his throat.

Franklin's face turned an alarming shade of purple. He clawed his throat with both hands, gasping loudly as he fell to his knees. She grabbed his head in her hands, slamming her knee into his nose. It exploded in a spray of crimson all over her dress.

'Even my stepmother hits harder than you, Franklin.' She spoke to his prostrate form as he writhed on the ground.

'Miss Millicent!' Reynard came running around the hedge, skidding on the pebbles as he reached her.

Franklin rolled onto his side, one hand cupping his nose while the other was pressed to his throat. High-pitched gurgles made the blood still pouring from his broken nose bubble in a most distracting way.

Philippa emerged from the holly bush as Drake sauntered over from the oak tree.

'Nicely done, Millicent. Shame about your dress.' Philippa eyed the crimson stain on Millie's split skirts.

She looked down. Her favourite riding habit was a mess. 'Yes. Next time, I'll make sure to avoid breaking a nose if at all possible.'

'Are you well?' Drake's icy eyes melted in the sunlight with an emotion Millie was too fearful to name.

Does he truly love me? Is that what this is?

Because words were one thing, but actions were quite another, and far more telling of a person's true feelings.

'What the actual hell is going on?' Reynard looked at each of them, his voice rising. 'I got word to return post haste, I left the search for the missing girl, saw Miss Millicent being accosted by Franklin St George. Meanwhile, you two were hiding in the shadows. Why did neither of you try to help? And when did you learn to fight like that, Miss Millicent? And why confront St George now? Will someone please explain?' Reynard looked ready to explode.

'I wouldn't mind hearing this tale.'

Millie followed the sound of a vaguely familiar voice. She looked beyond Reynard to see a tall, dark, handsome man strolling along the walk with a petite woman at his side.

'Hannah!' She squealed and ran past a shocked Reynard to almost bowl her friend over in a massive hug.

Hannah and Killian were back! And standing in Drake's garden. It was unbelievable.

'Millie! We couldn't possibly miss your wedding.' Hannah's strong arms tightened around Millie before releasing her. 'When Robert received word, we cancelled the rest of our trip and took the next steamship to London!' Hannah Simmons, former ward to Philippa, now Lady Killian, Duchess of Covington, was a sight for sore eyes.

'Does Ivy know you're here?' Millie kept Hannah's hand in her own, tugging her closer to where Philippa still watched over a whimpering St George.

Hannah's eyes crinkled as she smiled. She looked happy and healthy. Marriage agreed with her fierce friend. 'Not yet. The housekeeper told us you were in the gardens, so we came straight out. I see you've been busy.'

'Hannah. You've arrived.' Philippa nodded at her ward, but the twitch in her lips and slight tremor in her hand betrayed her emotions.

Hannah walked up to Philippa, wrapped her arms around the woman, and pressed a kiss to her smooth cheek.

Millie tried not to stare as she watched Philippa's porcelain skin turn pink.

Dear Lord. The Duchess of Dorsett is blushing. May wonders never cease.

Philippa awkwardly patted Hannah on the back for a moment before pushing her away. 'Yes. Well. No time for histrionics.'

Hannah smiled at Philippa. 'No, we wouldn't want to be labelled emotional females, would we?' She poked St George with her toe. 'Your work, Philippa?'

Philippa shook her head. 'Millicent. She's come a long way in a short time. You would be proud.'

Millie's chest expanded as she tried to contain her joy. First, she took down St George singlehandedly, then Drake was giving her those smouldering looks full of *something*, now Hannah was here, and Philippa was complimenting her skills at warfare. If she wasn't trying to dismantle a ring of flesh traders while determining if her future held marriage or a career or both, it would be a fine day.

Drake and Reynard were still huddled around Killian, slapping backs and shaking hands as men were wont to do.

Philippa nodded at the gentlemen. 'We have much to do and little time in which to accomplish it. Gather the men. They might be useful. A rare event indeed.'

Philippa directed the men to secure Franklin in a wine cellar beneath the kitchen while Philippa and Millie filled Hannah in on everything she had missed.

When Drake, Killian, and Reynard returned, the entire group gathered on the lawn.

'We need to interrogate Franklin. Once he's able to talk again, that is.' Millie looked at Drake. 'How is he?'

'Better than he will be after the House of Lords sentences him to hang.'

'If he lives long enough to hang,' Philippa added dryly, her arched brow combating his broken one. 'The Queen has little faith in the House of Lords. If he is going to die anyway, she would prefer the sentence be fulfilled quickly without risk of a corrupt pardon.'

'Vigilante justice is hardly worthy of a civilised nation.' Killian crossed his arms.

Hannah put her hands on her hips, narrowing her

gaze. 'And corrupt lords are hardly up to the task of determining a fair judgement. I thought we already discussed this, darling.' Never before had an endearment held such venom.

'Discussing and agreeing are not the same thing.' Killian's eyes flashed at his wife. Millie wondered if she should throw a bucket of cold water on them. Clearly, arguing was a form of foreplay with Killian and Hannah.

'If we are to be partners in this, we need to work on the same side. The right side. Queen Victoria's side.' Millie thrust out her chin. No point in beating around the bush. Either the men were with them, or they would work alone.

'You would so quickly dismiss a justice system that has worked for centuries?' Drake clenched his jaw.

'The House of Lords has only tried one peer this century when we all know how guilty these men are of crimes ranging from theft to rape to murder. Yet the "honourable" lords refuse to hold their brethren accountable. Does that sound like justice to you?' Millie faced Drake, refusing to be distracted by his bottom lip, or his icy gaze, or his wickedly erotic brow as it rose in judgement.

'Perhaps we should all return to the house.' Reynard stepped between the men and women who had created two distinct lines of battle on the manicured lawn. 'Luncheon is being prepared. After the beating he took from Miss Millicent, St George can hardly answer any of our questions today. Why don't we leave him to stew in the cellar, enjoy the rest of the day, and determine our next steps tomorrow morning after we've all had time to calm down and think?'

'Allow me to illuminate the dangers of telling well-armed women to calm down and think, Lord Renquist,' Philippa spoke quietly.

All three women slipped their hands into their pockets simultaneously.

'What on earth is going on out here? Did someone organise lawn games without informing the rest of us?' Patricia's shrill voice announced her arrival moments before her glaringly fuchsia day dress came into view.

Millie never thought she'd see the day when Patricia actually defused a tense situation.

Apparently, it is today.

Both ladies and gentlemen took a few steps back, dissolving their lines of warfare.

'Wonderful. My stepmother has brought the entire house of guests with her.' Millie forced a smile and turned to the group picking their way over the frosty ground.

Drake stepped closer to her. 'I would still like to speak with you privately. Please.'

Millie glanced at him, struck again by the heady contrast of his handsome features and violent scars. 'Tonight. I shall send Penny to bed early.' Her body warmed and her core melted even as her mind despaired. How could they possibly find a way forward when they fought for justice on opposite sides of a silent war?

19

Drake felt the moment called for whiskey rather than lawn games. He convinced the guests to return to the house, to enjoy their luncheon before the men indulged in cigars and billiards while the women organised a rousing game of whist. As the weather was beginning to turn, the entire party agreed to such a capital plan. All very civilised. And boring as hell. Perfect for Drake, Killian, and Reynard to slink away and reconvene in his study.

'Who is speaking to Lady St George?' Drake poured three fingers for each of them.

Reynard took his glass from Drake with his left hand and sipped. 'I'm having his valet give her a note. St George was called into town for business. She is to stay here until the wedding. He will return as soon as he is able or meet her back in London once the wedding party ends. It buys us a few days.'

'I feel sorry for her. This will be a great shock.' Killian settled himself on Drake's leather couch, warming his whiskey in his large hand.

'Or a great relief.' Drake took the wing-backed chair. He tried not to think of what he and Millie had done in this room only a few days prior. He tried not to think of her at all with so much left unsaid between them, but it was impossible. 'What are we going to do with these women? I don't believe they are completely wrong. And they have the blessing of Queen Victoria, who is our sovereign.'

'But they do not have the blessing of the prime minister, who is our direct commander,' Killian pointed out.

'Do you think Russell knows the Queen is working against him?' Reynard joined Killian on the opposite side of the couch.

'Perhaps. One doesn't confront the Queen, even if you are the prime minister. It is a fine kettle of fish we find ourselves in, gentlemen.' Killian sipped his whiskey. 'I haven't even congratulated you on the wedding yet. Major General Beaufort Drake falls prey to his worst enemy. A woman.' Killian's eyes sparkled with mischief.

'Ah. Here it comes. I knew you didn't come here to support me. You just wanted to rub this in my face.' Drake clenched his jaw.

'At least you found a woman who is your equal, Drake. Her knife-throwing skills will come in handy when you need to rid yourself of pesky mothers-in-law.' Reynard laughed.

'I recall being told on many occasions – by you in fact – that hell would freeze before you married. I hope you're wearing woollen smalls, Drake. It looks like you might lose your bollocks to frostbite.'

'You are a bastard, Killian,' Drake growled.

Killian's smile was bright enough to blind him. 'It's good to be back with friends.'

* * *

Millie, Ivy, and Hannah sat in a close huddle while Philippa, Lady Bradford, Patricia, and Victoria played whist.

'Millie, are you really going to marry Drake? I can hardly believe it. The man despises women. And you were dead set against marrying. Do you need help escaping? I'm sure Philippa, Ivy, and I can arrange something.' Hannah looked to Ivy, who nodded.

'I don't know.' She wished they were alone in her room without Patricia's sharp glance raking over her every few minutes. 'I love him.' Saying the words aloud shook something loose in her core. 'I love him, but is that enough? I won't compromise my goals. If he wants me, he'll have to accept my need to work with Philippa, to continue our mission. Killian has done that with you, right?' Millie was desperate for some kind of reassurance. She looked at Hannah hopefully.

'He accepts me, but I think it's still a struggle. Men don't want to admit they aren't needed to keep us safe. Because safety is a lie in this job. None of us will ever have that security. So, if we don't need them to keep us safe, they worry we might not need them at all.' Hannah squeezed Millie's hand. 'The truth is, I don't need Killian to survive, but I want him. And having him in my life allows me to thrive in ways I wouldn't without him. The question is, do you feel the same about Drake? Do you want him? Does he help you thrive?'

Ivy shook her head. 'I won't depend on anyone for my happiness but myself.'

Hannah nodded. 'And that's wonderful for you, Ivy. Some souls are meant to remain single and free.

Others are only free when they find their partner. The question is, which one are you, Millie?'

Millie shook her head. 'I've no idea. Can we focus on something a little less complicated? Like how we're going to get St George to reveal his accomplice. The masked man I wounded is still out there somewhere. Watching. Waiting. I can feel it.' She rubbed the goosebumps breaking out on her arm. 'That is one problem we can solve.'

'I think you have the best chance of getting him to talk, Millie.' Ivy nodded, her fair hair catching the dying sunlight through the window and shining like gossamer strands. 'He knows you. You have a history together. There must be something you can leverage.'

His pride.

'Franklin cares about his reputation more than anything else. If I can convince him betraying his brethren will save his skin, I think he'll tell me. But it won't work unless we're alone. He would never take such a risk with anyone else watching.' Millie bit her lip, trying to imagine how she could weasel the truth out of a weasel.

Ivy tapped her fingers on her skirt. 'I agree. He always wants to look superior. Lead him down that path.'

'Yes. Tell him he's better than the other Devil's

Sons. Far more worthy of pardon. Appeal to his vanity. You can do this, Millie. In actuality, you may be the only one,' Hannah agreed.

Millie nodded, feeling the truth of their words in her bones. 'I'll go before dinner. Will you make my excuses if I'm late? Whatever happens, keep the men at the table.'

'Consider it done.' Hannah smiled.

'We have this, Millie. I promise.' Ivy's pale-blue eyes flashed with purpose.

* * *

Millie dressed carefully for dinner. She wore an evening gown of decadent chocolate velvet, almost perfectly matching her eyes. Gold thread wove through the material in intricate patterns, catching the light and glittering. Her hair blazed in contrast to the rich colour of her gown. The neckline was low enough to raise a few brows. If she were to capture St George in a silken web, it couldn't hurt to maximise her assets. They were hers, after all.

She used the servants' stairs to make her way down to the kitchen and found the staircase leading to the wine cellar where St George was imprisoned.

Fear sharpened her nerves.

I can do this. I'm just asking a few questions. And he's tied up. What harm can Franklin do to me?

Slowly, she descended.

The room was dank and almost pitch black. A small candle burned in the far corner, but it took Millie's eyes a few moments to adjust. When they did, she gasped, pressing her hand against her lips to stop the scream.

Franklin St George hung from a rope tied around a ceiling brace.

He was very dead.

Millie rushed to him, but there was nothing she could do.

Despite his atrocious actions, his horrific behaviour toward her, and the crimes he had committed, grief filled her.

Franklin was her childhood friend. Her teenage infatuation. Her first love, regardless of how unworthy he may have been. She wanted to hate him. Not mourn his death.

But now he was gone, and sorrow was an unwelcome surprise.

The scrape of a boot alerted her. She wasn't alone.

Emotion took a step back for survival.

She loosened the blade at her wrist, holding it in her palm as she turned to face a murderer.

'Miss Millicent. What are you doing down here?' Reynard Renquist's famous smile flashed in the dark as he blocked the stairs.

'Reynard. I could ask you the same.'

He raised a gun. In his left hand.

Because I already wounded his right.

Because Renquist is the masked man.

Renquist was working with Franklin.

Renquist is the murderer.

Each truth crashed over her like wild waves, stealing her breath.

'Drop the blade, Miss Millicent. I didn't mind killing St George, but I'd hate to shoot you. It won't stop me, though. I have very few choices left, you see.' The pistol was pointed directly at her heart. If she let her blade fly now, she ran the risk of a bullet to her chest.

He lifted his right hand. 'Ah-ah. I don't think I need another demonstration of your throwing skills. Drop the blade. Now.'

Shit!

'And before you do something rash, know I'm just as good a shot with my left hand as I am with my right. Your major general insisted all his men could hit a target at one hundred paces with either hand. Awfully dedicated soldier, Drake. I owe him my life on more than one occasion, although I doubt it was worth his effort. I'll only say this once more. Drop it. Now.'

Millie bit her lip.

Renquist cocked his gun.

With a frustrated growl, she let the blade drop. She had four others. This wasn't over yet.

'I must admit, your aim is better than I expected, especially for a lady. Made it damned difficult to hoist that idiot up with only my left hand. Still, I managed. Couldn't have him blabbing about the Devil's Sons, could I?'

'You work for the Devil's Sons? Renquist, why?'

He laughed, though it was not a joyful sound. 'Sometimes, we do things because we must. In the war, I committed untold sins under the banner of patriotism. Now, I do it for my own security. I don't know why atrocities in war create heroes, but the same actions done for personal gain make men monsters.' His lips twisted in a grimace. Millie worried he might actually start to cry. She was torn between pity and rage.

Rage won.

'How could you betray Drake? Killian? The prime minister?' Millie needed to stall, but she also wanted to know. Drake, Killian, and Renquist had gone through hell together. They were brothers in arms. It made no sense.

'I told you.' Renquist took a step closer to her, his golden eyes hardening. 'Don't dig into my depths. There is nothing good there. The war took everything from me. As a second son, I don't have a title to fall back on. Nothing Drake or Killian can do about that. I'll be damned if I go to my friends for charity. And Prime Minister Russell's wages won't hold off my debtors. But the Devil's Sons have powerful leaders. Leaders who reward their faithful. I've always been a good foot soldier. They value my skills. And what else can I do? I'm useless outside of charming silly ladies in a ballroom and killing silly men in a war.'

Millie shook her head. 'You're better than this, Reynard. I know it.'

His bark of laughter created a cold shiver of fear down her spine. 'You know nothing.' His lips trembled as he shook his head. 'I was right when I called you Drake's equal. You are equally matched in the misguided belief that people hold honour higher than personal gain.'

'Personal gain at the price of your soul?' Maybe appealing to his eternal damnation would make an impression.

'My soul was damned the day I put on that bloody uniform.' A single tear tracked down his face. He swiped it away. 'My father wanted me to enlist, so I did.

He died before I came home. Didn't even get to tell me how proud he was of his soldier son. And what did all that sacrifice bring me besides one unending nightmare of untold horrors?'

Pity made a second play at Millie's heart. The man was so broken. So lost. It didn't excuse his actions, but it did make her ache for him. 'So, what now? You killed St George because he knew your role in this. Am I next? Would you sink so low as to kill a defenceless woman?' Hardly true, but she needed to keep him talking until a window of opportunity presented itself to overpower him, or escape.

Reynard's eyes widened, and he shook his head. 'I told you. I don't *want* to hurt you, Miss Millicent. I didn't want to hurt any of those poor girls. Wanting something and doing it are very different things. But I have a solution.' He smiled, and it was like watching someone put on a mask. His face creased into familiar, charming lines, but his eyes were wild. 'Thanks to your little sleuthing mission, I am now in need of a new girl to deliver to the Devils. You're older than we like, but you're also a lady of quality. I bet we could still get a pretty profit. And then I don't have to kill you. See? Everyone wins.'

Reynard's version of everyone winning was very different from her own. She had another blade strapped to her left wrist, one on each thigh, and a last strapped to her left ankle. If she could just get him to lower his bloody pistol, she could try to disarm him.

'And you think I'll go quietly?'

He shrugged, the pistol shifting with his movements, but still aimed at her torso. 'It's the only way, Miss Millicent. Unless you force me to shoot you, and as I said, I really don't want to do that.'

Anger washed through her, taking the fear and pity away and replacing it with cold purpose. 'You use your circumstances as an excuse, but in truth, you are just being weak, Reynard. There is a better path, but you turn away because this is easier. You doom helpless women to a life worse than death, all so you can afford your excesses.'

There was a dip in the floor behind Reynard. If she could get him to back up just a step, he would hit it, perhaps lose his balance, and give her the moment she needed.

Reynard broke into sobs, but his pistol never faltered. 'Yes. I do. And I feel so much shame about it.' He sniffed, wiping his face again and shaking his head. He cleared his throat, his emotional outburst spent. The man was vacillating so quickly between intense rage, hopelessness, and odd optimism, Millie couldn't keep up. Perhaps the war had broken more than his honour.

Perhaps it had stolen his sanity. 'And I have suffered too, Miss Millicent. Never doubt that. Perhaps it is selfish, but in the end, I would rather live in comfort. I deserve that after sacrificing so much.'

Fucking arse of a toad!

Wounding him wouldn't be enough. He was committed to his path. Nothing she said or did would sway him. If she aimed for his left hand, he'd likely rush her. In hand-to-hand combat, she stood little chance against a man his size who knew how to grapple. And he would. Drake would have been sure his men were all well taught in physical combat.

But could she actually take his life? Wounding a man and killing one were very different things. She would only get one chance.

* * *

Drake hated being dressed like a doll. He refused the services of a valet for that reason. Instead, he stood in front of the mirror, tying a simple knot in his cravat and glaring at the stubble on his cheeks. He could shave before dinner; there was time. Still an hour yet before he needed to suffer through a tedious meal.

He hated to admit it, but knowing Killian cut his honeymoon short just to stand with Drake as he faced his biggest fear – marriage – warmed him in an area near his heart. It was good to have friends like Reynard and Killian.

A snag caught in his mind as he reflected on their afternoon together in Drake's study.

Reynard wasn't left-handed. Drake had forced him to practise shooting with that hand because his right was his dominant. But when he had reached for his whiskey, he used his left hand. In fact, as Drake recalled the details of their time together, he used his left hand exclusively.

Odd.

And the comment he made about Millie. What did he say?

Her knife-throwing skills... How would he know Millie threw knives?

Unless she'd thrown one at him.

While he was masked.

In the hunting shack.

'Fuck!'

It all became so stupidly obvious. Reynard Renquist, fellow soldier, compatriot, and friend, was the masked killer.

Drake ran for the door.

* * *

Millie took a tentative step forward, hoping Renquist would step back. Instead, he tightened his grip on the pistol, his hand shaking slightly.

'Stay back.'

She put both hands out. 'Reynard, surely, we can work this out. I know the war wasn't easy for any of you. You're right. You deserve peace after so much conflict. Can't we come to an agreement?'

'You don't understand!' he screamed, his hand shaking so badly, Millie feared he might accidentally fire. 'It's too late for me. I'm one of the monsters now. Unredeemable. Father would be so proud.' He laughed, a chilling, high-pitched sound. The features once making him so handsome, twisted in pained rage.

And then he stepped back.

His heel hit the dip.

He bobbled.

This was her chance.

Millie released the blade on her wrist, feeling its heft in her palm.

Renquist fell to his knees. The pistol dropped to his side and he covered his face. Tears and snot streamed down his cheeks. His heart-wrenching sobs stayed her hand.

'Dear God. Renquist.' Pity once more took centre

stage. She hunkered down next to him, her free hand patting his shoulder while she still clasped the blade in her left. 'We'll figure something out.' She wished her words were true.

'It's too late for me. Too fucking late.' Reynard's words were muffled, his hands covering his face.

The stairs creaked, shattering the moment.

Reynard dropped his hands, his gaze moving from the stairs to Millie.

Before she could react, he grabbed her with his strong left arm while scrabbling for the pistol with his right. He cried out in pain from his wound, but it didn't stop him pulling her up as he stood and twisted her around. His left arm banded around her chest like a vice while his injured right hand pressed the muzzle of the gun to her ribs.

Drake stepped into the cellar.

'Let her go, Reynard.'

'No! She's coming with me. I'll kill her, Drake. If you don't let me pass, I'll fucking kill her right now. My hand might be too damaged to aim, but I can still pull a trigger.'

Drake's wild gaze flitted to Millie. He had a gun in his hand, but he put it down on the floor, kicking it out of the way. 'Don't! Please don't. Let her go and I won't raise a hand against you. You can walk out of here a free man. I swear it!'

'Like you swore victory would be ours in the war? Your promises are as empty as my pockets, Drake.' Reynard was screaming again. Millie cringed away from the force of his words.

She needed to think. She couldn't let Reynard escape. Nor would she put Drake in danger. Levelling her gaze on Drake, a strange calm descended. Everything slowed, like a raindrop creeping down the windowpane.

Widen your stance.

Centre your weight.

Concentrate on your breath.

In a fast, smooth movement, she bent at the waist, thrusting her back into his pelvis, creating space between them before ramming her head back, slamming it into his nose. Stars flashed in her vision, but she bit down hard on her cheek, forcing herself to focus. The blade pressed into her palm. His grip loosened, and Millie spun, lifting her left hand in an arc that swept across Reynard's windpipe.

A warm spray of blood covered her face as Reynard fell.

Dear God. I killed him.

20

Drake heard an ungodly roar. He lunged for Millie as Reynard fell. Grasping her shoulders, he turned her to face him.

Her face was deathly pale, contrasting against the slash of crimson across her left temple, over her nose, and down her right cheek. It was a gruesome parody of his own scar.

Millie began to shake violently. She looked at Drake, her beautifully dark eyes huge and full of horror, before she doubled over, retching the contents of her stomach all over his shoes.

He rubbed her back, pulled her hair away from her face, and whispered nonsense words to her.

'I killed him,' Millie gasped as the sobs took over.

Drake picked her up in his arms, cradling her like a child. 'Yes, my love. You had no choice.'

'I need to get out of here. Please. Get me out of here.' She buried her head into his chest, smearing blood over his white cravat. He didn't give a damn. She was safe. Alive. In his arms.

* * *

Drake carefully carried Millie up the stairs. He took the servants' corridor to the family wing and strode down the hall, shaking his head at a shocked Killian and Hannah as they emerged from their rooms.

'Make our excuses. We won't be attending dinner. And there is a mess in the cellar.' Drake didn't wait for Killian to acknowledge his words. He didn't ask his friend to handle it. Because he knew Killian and Hannah would manage the task. The only thing he cared about was Millie.

He couldn't wait for a bath to be prepared. Instead, Drake carefully placed Millie in a chair by the fire. He poured water into a bowl on his dresser, soaping a washcloth. When he approached her, Millie's gaze came into focus. She grabbed the cloth and began scrubbing her face. Jolting to her feet, she staggered over to the bowl. She rinsed the cloth, water sloshing over the rim and onto the table. She scrubbed at her face again, rubbing her skin raw.

Drake walked over to her, resting one hand on her shoulder and the other gently gripping her wrist, pulling the cloth out of her fingers.

'Let me.' He rinsed the cloth and gently dabbed her already clean face. As tears rolled down her cheek, he wiped them away.

For a time, they didn't speak.

'I killed him,' she whispered, her eyes red-rimmed and haunted.

'Yes.'

'It was horrible.'

'Yes.'

'Am I a monster?' Her bottom lip trembled.

Drake leaned forward, pressing a soft kiss to her mouth. 'No. You stopped a monster. And it's never easy, Millie.'

Dropping the cloth into the bowl, he took both her hands, walked her back to the chair, sat down, and pulled her into his lap. She curled into him like a small child seeking sanctuary.

He ran his hands down her hair in long, firm strokes, and they said nothing for a while.

'Beau, will you come to bed with me?' Her husky voice wrapped him in velvet fingers.

'Yes.'

Millie clambered off his lap and he helped her undress. Pulling back the covers, she climbed into bed, watching as he removed his jacket, vest, shirt, and trousers. He crawled in next to her, and she burrowed into his arms. Silken, warm, naked, she pressed against him as she wrapped her arms around his ribs and tightened her embrace.

He breathed in her scent as she nuzzled closer. Despite his best intentions to comfort, his cock thickened as her warm breath puffed against his chest.

'I don't expect us to... That is, just because I desire you doesn't mean we need do any more than this.' He cleared his throat and pressed a kiss against her hair.

Millie loosened her hold around him. Tipping up her chin to face him, she kissed the side of his mouth, then the scar on his cheek, and finally his lips. He let her take her time, exploring his mouth with her tongue, sucking on his bottom lip.

She pulled back, and her gaze unravelled him. 'I want more. I need it.' She stroked her thumb over his lip. 'I don't want to think about any of it. I just want to forget everything except this.'

Drake's body tightened like a cello string being tuned. He rolled her on her back, grabbed both of her wrists, and pinned them over her head. Her breasts thrust out, strawberry nipples budded and crying for attention. Drake sucked one into his mouth, scraping his teeth over the puckered skin until Millie writhed beneath him.

He understood her need. To forget everything in the raw, visceral act of fucking. But he didn't want to fuck her. He wanted to comfort her. Love her. Reassure her that she was whole, and healthy, and capable of creating something beautiful even after experiencing such horror.

Willing his cock to contain itself, he slowed his movements. Stroking down her body, his hands delighted in every soft curve, every strong line, each bump of her ribs, the texture of hair covering her mons, the slick heat as he dipped a finger into her core and circled the bud of flesh holding her pleasure.

'Beau,' she moaned.

Instead of plunging another finger into her depths, he pulled back, kissing her with complete focus. He nibbled her bottom lip before sucking it into his mouth. Balancing the tightrope of pleasure and pain, he bit down then peppered soft kisses over her cheeks, along her jaw, nuzzling her neck, biting the fragrant skin, and sucking. He could drown in Millie. Spin this moment into eternity. Stay lost in her until they both ceased to exist.

* * *

Millie needed more. She wanted the wild abandon, the desperate plunge into madness, the all-consuming blaze of need. He was dismantling her with excruciating care, but she didn't want to be treated like a delicate thing which might shatter. Because she was so close to doing just that.

'Harder,' she commanded, wrapping her legs around him, pulling him tight to her and rubbing against his arousal with blatant demand. She needed to be torn apart by their passion so she could emerge a new creature.

'You want this rough?' His brows drew down, his icy gaze searing her with intense focus.

'I don't want you to hold back. Give me all of you. Everything.' The ache of grief, relief, joy, and despair coalesced into a wave of emotion, washing away any reservations. She only wanted him. Her mind to be consumed with their moments together. Her whole self to be saturated with what they created. No room left for thought or memory or regret.

Knocking her thighs wider apart with his own, he made space for his body and plunged. He gripped her wrists again, pulling her arms over her head. She was

pinned beneath him with no ability to give. Only receive what he poured into her.

He feasted on her breasts, biting, nipping, sucking,
while he thrust again with his pelvis. Filling her to the
point of burning pleasure, Drake gave no quarter.
Slamming harder, the slap of his skin against hers created an erotic rhythm. He bit hard on her nipple.
Millie cried out, lost to sensation and needing to fly
higher. She twisted her hips until he hit her. Just there.
A bright burst of incandescent joy filled her body.

'Again!' she cried out, greedy in her quest for absolution.

He let go of her wrists, grabbing her hips and
pulling her pelvis higher as he plunged deeper. Faster.
Over and over until she was nothing but sensation,
spilling over the edges of reality, spinning into the
ether, a cataclysmic shower of sparks.

* * *

Dawn fought with the lingering darkness as the room
shifted from shadows to light. Drake buried his nose in
Millie's wild tangle of curls and breathed deeply. He
sought courage in her familiar scent.

'Millie, are you awake?'

She stretched against him, her back pressing into

his chest, her luscious bottom rubbing against his suddenly interested cock.

But this wasn't the time for seduction. This was the time for honesty. For total truth. Fear tasted metallic on his tongue.

'I'm not sure,' she murmured, then laughed. She turned her head and pulled him close, kissing him, her tongue testing the seam of his mouth.

It would be so easy to slip back into her body. Forget the words he needed to say, stay in this moment, and push reality into the far distance.

But it would come back. It always did. And the longer he postponed, the harder this would become.

'I need to speak with you.' Drake did what he most loathed to do. He pulled away from Millie. Getting out of bed, he found his trousers and her chemise.

She sat up, eyes widening in alarm. When he handed her the delicate cotton, her hand shook. 'What's happening? What do you need to say that requires us to dress?'

Quickly shoving his legs into his pants, he pulled them up and buttoned the waist before climbing back onto the bed. Sitting at the foot, he faced Millie.

She struggled to pull the chemise over her head, tugging her hair from the loose neck in an effortlessly arousing movement and letting it fall around her shoulders.

Drake wanted to imprint this moment into his memory forever. Millie's mouth swollen from his kisses. Her hair a wild and fiery halo from their love-making. Her eyes still heavy-lidded, even though now they also filled with alarm. This was their beginning. Or their end. Either way, it would define the rest of his days.

'Beau, please say something. You're scaring me.'

He wanted to touch her. Reassure her with his body. But he knew his control was far too tenuous.

'I'm releasing you from our engagement.'

Millie leaned back against the headrest, her mouth hardening. 'What? Why? Is this because of what happened last night?'

Shit. That was badly done.

'No. Please don't think that. I don't mean I no longer wish to marry you.' He rushed to explain. 'All I want is to be with you. Now and forever.'

Millie's eyes – the exact shade of freshly brewed coffee – narrowed. 'You wish to be with me forever, so you are breaking our engagement? Remind me why men are considered more logical than women.'

Drake's lips twitched, but this was no time for levity. 'When we first spoke of this engagement, in your father's study after that kiss, you told me you didn't want to marry me. You released me from any obligation to marry you.'

'I remember.' If a woman's tone could cut, Drake would be bleeding all over the sheets.

'But no one ever gave you the same choice. Not me. Not your father. Certainly not your horror of a stepmother.'

Millie scrunched her nose. 'I'd rather not talk about Patricia when we're in bed together. Or any time, actually.'

'Good point. But so is mine. You deserve the right to choose. Not because you're trying to escape a dirty old man. Not because you are trapped with a scarred earl and seeking freedom. Not because society is forcing you to follow rules of decorum.'

Drake was momentarily distracted by the elegant column of Millie's throat contracting as she swallowed.

'You are releasing me from this engagement so I can make my own choice about marrying you?'

Drake's courage almost abandoned him. What if she left? What if he lost everything?

If she is free and happy and does not want me, then I will accept a solitary life.

'Yes. I release you from this. I will tell your parents you broke the engagement. That I was not worthy of you. If you don't wish to marry, Philippa will offer her home to you as long as you need it. You deserve freedom. If I give you nothing else, I hope to give you that.'

Millie crossed her hands under her breasts. 'Do you still wish to marry me? Not because of your honour. Not because of our obvious attraction for each other. Not because I tricked you into compromising me. But because you want to be my partner in this madness.'

Drake never knew hope could hurt, but tears stung his eyes as he clenched his hands into fists and willed himself to stay in control. 'More than anything. Yes.'

'I wish to continue working with Philippa. Even after yesterday, maybe because of it. What happened, what I did was awful and terrifying and the most difficult moment of my life, but stopping Renquist saved you. It saved me. It saved countless other innocents. Will you be my partner in that as well?'

Drake exhaled. 'I believe we are two sides of one coin, Millie. Your work with Philippa is just that. Yours. I may not agree with all your views, but I also won't stop you from pursuing your goals.'

'What if our goals conflict?'

'Then we'll compromise.'

Millie twisted her hair into a knot that immediately unravelled. 'Compromise requires trust, Beau.

This whole endeavour demands total trust. That isn't our strength.'

'I'm trusting you right now. To make the choice that is best for you. And if you choose me, you'll be trusting me. I know a woman loses all autonomy to her husband. If you marry me, you'll be trusting me to give that control back to you.'

'You, a man who values control above all other things.'

'A man who used to value control because it gave me comfort. Now, I just want you. Because you bring me comfort. And sanity. And endless frustrations as well, I'm sure, but I wouldn't want it any other way. I will never try to control you or your choices. I may offer my opinions, even when you don't ask for them. I won't shy away from disagreements, and I won't back down from conflict. I expect the same of you. But if we join our lives together, we do so as equals. Always.'

'Our wedding is tomorrow, Drake. You would just let me leave? Knowing how the beau monde would ridicule you? How Nora and Patricia and all those hideous gossips would tear us both apart?'

'I don't care about them. I care about you. I want you to be happy, Millie. With or without me. And I have enough pride left to desire a union where my wife actually wants me. Where she hasn't been forced or coerced or trapped into a lifelong commitment.'

And if I can't have you as my wife, I don't want another.

* * *

Millie shook her head. Pressing her hands against her eyes, she exhaled a shaky breath. It was all too much. He was offering her everything she wanted if she could just trust him to be true to his word. It was the biggest risk of her life.

'I love you, Beau. I didn't want to love you, but it happened anyway. It was like an unexpected gift to fall in love with the man I had to marry. But now, you're telling me I don't have to marry you. I never expected to be able to choose.'

When she didn't have a choice, it was easy to make peace with the situation. But now, he was changing everything. This wasn't an event happening to her. It was something she could influence. She was being given the greatest gift of all. Freedom to choose. And with her choice came ownership of the consequences. What if she chose Beau and they both regretted it?

'I love you too, Millie. It's because I love you, I won't

force this upon you. Even if it means losing all control.' He huffed out a dry laugh. 'I never had control of you to begin with, and I don't want it now, or ever.' He picked up her hand, pressing a kiss to her palm. 'But I would like to share this life with you forever.'

There were still so many unknowns. And there always would be surprises, compromises, give and take. With two people as stubborn as Drake and Millie, the course of true love was bound to have a fair number of bumps, twists, and turns. But she wanted to travel that road with him.

'If the choice is mine, Major General Beaufort Drake, Earl of Tetly, then I choose you. Now and forever.' She leaned forward, pressing a kiss to his delicious mouth. 'And my only regret is knowing Patricia will get her Yuletide marriage after all.'

* * *

Millie stood in front of the looking glass, her riot of flaming curls piled into an artful cascade, drawing attention to her elegant neck and sharp cheekbones. Her wedding dress was a confection of creamy silk, nearly matching her skin and showing off her curves to devastating effect.

She pinched her cheeks and pressed her lips together.

'I don't think Drake will manage to wait long enough for you to walk down the aisle. I'd wager my favourite dagger on him sprinting past the pews, sweeping you into his arms, and dragging you right back here.' Hannah came next to Millie, sliding an arm around her waist. A waist cinched so tight, Millie wasn't sure she could take a full breath.

'You look like an angel.' Ivy came on the other side, tilting her head to the left as she watched Millie's reflection.

Millie scrunched her nose. 'Careful, I'm not sure the angels will stand for such blasphemy.'

'Who wants an angel when devils are so much more fun?' Hannah winked and nudged Millie with her hip.

Philippa strode into the room. Her silk and lace gown was a shade lighter than blackcurrant. 'You look well, Millicent. Ready to sacrifice yourself on the altar of societal stupidity.'

Millie gave Hannah and Ivy a long look before turning. 'Thank you, Philippa. You look ready to attend a funeral.'

'Exactly.' Philippa thwacked her jewel-encrusted fan against her leg. 'I do wish you ladies would stop succumbing to Cupid and his ridiculous arrows.' She turned to Ivy. 'Perhaps I have some hope with you, Miss Cavendale.'

Ivy's cheeks flushed pink, and she ducked her head. 'I'm in no danger of falling in love, Lady Winterbourne. I can assure you of that. But while I appreciate you being willing to work with me, I could never accomplish the missions you, Hannah, and Millie complete. I just want to learn how to keep myself safe, Your Grace.'

Philippa's sharp blue eyes lingered on Ivy. 'And so you shall, Miss Cavendale.'

'Miss Millicent, I have your veil.' Penny came in, a gauzy length flowing behind her like a cape. There was a crown of white roses attached to the top.

'Penny, it's gorgeous!'

Philippa swung around to raise a brow at Penny. 'Always ready with what's needed. A wonderful trait to have in so many situations.'

Penny returned Philippa's steady gaze. 'Thank you, Your Grace.' She turned to Millie. 'Come and sit, miss.'

Millie sat at her vanity and Penny fitted the crown on her head, fluffing the veil.

The moment was perfect. Until Patricia arrived.

She sailed into the room in a turquoise gown with peacock feathers sewn into the skirt. A few of the gaudy feathers fluttered around her perfectly curled ringlets.

'Dear God.' Philippa thwacked her fan again. 'How many poor birds were massacred for that monstrosity of a dress?'

Patricia narrowed her green gaze at Philippa. 'I would like to speak with my daughter.' She turned her glare on Ivy, then Hannah, then Penny. 'Alone.'

Ivy walked over to Millie, her hand resting on Millie's shoulder. Hannah put one hand on her hip, the other slipped into her pocket. Penny stayed perfectly still.

'Fine. Stay if you like. But I imagine Your Grace will wish you'd left when I reveal her most horrifying secret.' Patricia hissed Philippa's title like it were a curse before pursing her lips in a sour pucker.

Millie stood and turned to face her stepmother. 'Don't, Patricia. I beg you. Stop this madness now.'

Patricia's tinkling laughter cut through the air like a thousand pieces of shattered glass. 'Don't what? Share your secret with your closest friends? Surely such an intimate group of women already know your sins, Millicent.'

Philippa tapped a finger against her blood-red lips. 'You seem a woman intimately acquainted with sin, madame. Hold us in suspense no longer. Share your secret. But I warn you, those who threaten me do so at great personal risk.'

Patricia blinked quickly and swallowed hard. A bead of sweat trickled down her perfectly powdered cheek. 'Not even the Duchess of Dorsett can survive the scandal my words will unleash. The beau monde will tear you to shreds when the *Star of Venus* reveals you to be a sapphist! Don't play innocent with me, Lady Winterbourne. I know your proclivities. Your sinful choice to fornicate with other women – including my stepdaughter – will ensure your destruction.' Patricia's wild gaze flew around the room. 'What do you think now of your precious duchess?'

Hannah burst into laughter. 'My opinion of Philippa hasn't changed. However, I now believe you are stark raving mad, madame.'

'I won't be the one sentenced to an asylum. Trust me on that. The House of Lords won't stand for such deviant behaviour from one of their own.' Patricia pointed her bony finger at Philippa. 'If you want my lips to remain sealed, you'll pay. Large sums. To me.' She turned to Millie. 'As will you, dear daughter, unless you want your husband's name to be dragged through the mud. Imagine what they'll say about the Earl of Tetly being cuckolded by a woman. A duchess, no less. I doubt Queen Victoria will maintain a friendship with such a wicked wanton.' Patricia wheeled back to Philippa. 'You'll lose everything. Everything!' she screamed.

Philippa took three long strides toward Patricia. She slapped her hard. Patricia's head snapped to the side. Before Patricia could react, Philippa grabbed the back of her hair, pulling Patricia's face close enough for Philippa to whisper in her ear.

Millie watched in fascination as Patricia's eyes widened, her mouth dropped open, and her pale face went almost completely white save for the red mark of Philippa's hand. Tears filled Patricia's green eyes as she gasped.

'You wouldn't.'

Philippa pulled away. She stretched her blood-red lips in a vicious smile. 'Oh, my dear. I most certainly will. And I'll savour every single moment.'

Patricia stumbled backward, tripping on her skirts. She would have landed on her skinny bottom had Penny not swooped in and caught her, righting the woman. 'I think... I'll just... I'm suddenly feeling very ill.' She turned and ran out of the room, her peacock feathers fluttering around her in wild disarray.

'What on earth did you say?' Millie was almost too frightened to ask.

'Did I ever mention my dear friend, Charlotte Barrows? She's always had a way with words, dear Lottie. Probably what makes her so good at her job.'

'What job is that?' Hannah's lips curled into a smile before she even heard the answer.

'Oh, she's the head writer for the *Star of Venus*.' Philippa brushed a stray hair back into place.

Ivy burst into laughter. 'Your Grace! A most shocking acquaintance for a duchess, wouldn't you say?'

Philippa raised her brow. 'I would say a duchess is allowed a great many shocking things. Remember, ladies, threatening a predator never ends well for the prey. A lesson we should all heed.' Philippa walked over to Millie. She put her hands on either shoulder and pulled Millie close, pressing a quick kiss to her cheek. 'I don't think your stepmother will be attending the wedding, Millicent. Consider it my wedding gift to you.'

* * *

Major General Beaufort Drake had faced hordes of fierce warriors determined to cut him down. He'd endured years of torture. He had met Queen Victoria *three* times. Never had he felt more nervous in his life than he did standing in the small chapel in the centre square of Bedford's township. The pews were full of faces he didn't recognise, save for the first two rows. There was a good chance he would toss up his accounts all over his shiny shoes.

Killian leaned closer. 'Steady on, man. Wouldn't want you swooning at your own wedding. I left the smelling salts in my other jacket.'

'Fuck off,' Drake growled.

'Millicent is a lucky woman to marry such a poet.' Killian snickered.

Drake would have displayed the range of his poetic prowess if all the air hadn't suddenly been sucked from the room.

Millie stood at the entrance of the church. Snow fell behind her in a wonderland of white.

Drake's fluttering heart stopped completely.

She smiled at him, and it raced back to life, the jolt almost painful.

She glided down the aisle, a proud Valkyrie come to claim his soul. But it was too late. She already had it.

When she reached his side, he gripped her hands with cold fingers. 'I had a sudden and terrible fear you changed your mind.'

Millie's eyes warmed like melting chocolate. 'Never. We're in this together, Beau.'

'Partners.' He lifted her hand and pressed a kiss against her knuckles.

Reaching her hand to cup his face, she traced her thumb over his bottom lip. 'For better or worse.'

'For now, and forever.' Drake pulled her close, pressing a kiss to her mouth despite the indignant huff of the vicar behind him.

Millie pulled back. 'Scandalous, sir. Compromising me in front of all these people.'

'Ah, but didn't you say it's just a kiss? Certainly not worth sacrificing your life over.'

'That depends entirely on the kiss.'

'God, I love you.'

'Well, that seals it. Because I love you too. You'll have to marry me now.' Millie's rich gaze caught the light, turning from chocolate to whiskey.

'Your wish is my command.' He took her right hand in his left, and they turned to face their future. Together.

ACKNOWLEDGEMENTS

I want to thank my team at Boldwood, including my endlessly encouraging editor, Megan Haslam; my wickedly talented Sales and Marketing Director, Nia Beynon; my media-savvy-in-ways-I-shall-never-be Marketing Executive, Niamh Wallace; my ever helpful Production Executive, Ben Wilson; my always patient copy-editor who must correct all of my Americanisms, Emily Reader; and all of the staff working so hard behind the scenes to make this story shine. I also want to thank my agent, Katie Reed, for championing my work, my family (Mom, Dad, Brennon, Ray, Charlene, Charla, Bryant, Elizabeth, Emily, Shaun, and Colton) for supporting me in this time-consuming passion, my beautiful girls – Makielah and Meguire – for being the bad-ass women who inspire me (and make all of their friends read my books regardless of their opinions on historical romance), and the amazing group of female friends who create my inner circle, rally around me, always show support, never judge me, celebrate my successes and encourage me through the challenges. You ladies are my tribe. Finally, my husband, who makes every difficulty an adventure, every success a celebration, and every moment together a memory worth savouring.

ABOUT THE AUTHOR

Darcy McGuire is a high school counsellor who grew up in the wilds of New Zealand but happily settled in the Pacific Northwest. In between dodging territorial geese, gathering duck eggs, taking the dog for long walks, Darcy loves writing about fierce female protagonists who may dodge daggers and bullets but never seem to escape Cupid's Arrow.

Sign up to Darcy McGuire's mailing list for news, competitions and updates on future books.

Follow Darcy on social media here:

ALSO BY DARCY MCGUIRE

The Queen's Deadly Damsels

The Secret Life of a Lady

A Lady's Lesson in Scandal

You're cordially invited to

The Scandal Sheet

The home of swoon-worthy historical romance from the Regency to the Victorian era!

Warning: may contain spice 🌶️

Sign up to the newsletter

https://bit.ly/thescandalsheet

Boldwood

Boldwood Books is an award-winning fiction publishing company seeking out the best stories from around the world.

Find out more at www.boldwoodbooks.com

Join our reader community for brilliant books, competitions and offers!

Follow us
@BoldwoodBooks
@TheBoldBookClub

Sign up to our weekly deals newsletter

https://bit.ly/BoldwoodBNewsletter

www.ingramcontent.com/pod-product-compliance
Lightning Source LLC
Chambersburg PA
CBHW010658100726
47900CB00010B/2708